Times by the Thames

An Indian Cruise

Times by the Thames

An Indian Cruise

Vijay Dutt

Konark Publishers Pvt. Ltd.

KONARK PUBLISHERS PVT LTD
206, First Floor, Peacock Lane,
Shahpur Jat, NEW DELHI - 110 049 (INDIA)
Ph.: (011) 41055065, 65254972
e-mail: konarkpublishers@hotmail.com

Distributor in UK:
India First plc.
622, Western Avenue, London W3 0TF

Typeset and designed by Rahul Sharma

Printed at ASK Advertising Aids Pvt Ltd, New Delhi-110020

To the One I Love

Foreword

Vikas Swarup
Author of Q&A (The Slumdog Millionaire)

I once asked a newspaper editor on the qualities he looked for in a good journalist. He reflected on it and said that a good journalist is one who combines workaday values such as excellent drafting skills and a willingness to put in long hours, with professional virtues such as trustworthiness, reliability and the skill to persuade people to talk about their experiences. "But the quality I value the most," he added, "is the ability to recognise a good story."

It is this almost preternatural acumen to recognise and follow a good story that sets apart veteran journalist Vijay Dutt. During his three decades long career he has broken many stories, but his interest has not been limited simply to 'hard news'. He has also focussed on the social, economic and cultural milieu in which news gets incubated. This is clearly reflected in the broad and eclectic canvas of this book, based on the time he spent in the United Kingdom as the representative of the *Hindustan Times*.

The historical encounter between India and Britain, in which an age old civilization met the dominant Empire of the day, impacted both countries, and the process of cross fertilization is continuing even today. Chicken tikka masala has become the national dish of Britain and India is on course to become the largest English speaking country in the world.

Vijay was fortunate to be posted to London for fifteen long years. His stay spanned the end of one century and the beginning of another, and was peppered with landmark events. He was witness to the beginning and the end of the Blair era, the death of Diana and the birth of the 'war on terror'. Fortuitously, this period also coincided with the re-emergence of India as a global powerhouse and it is interesting to see how this played out in the UK. Vijay documents the rediscovery of India by the British media; how the perception of India as 'a backward nation wrapped in the snake-charmers and rope trick times' morphed into that of 'a country moving fast towards becoming an economic superpower.' He saw at close quarters the birth of the

'Friends of India' groups in the three major political parties in Britain, and the end of India-baiting in the British parliament. Even more significantly, he chronicles the rise of the 1.6 million strong community of Indian origin in Britain; how through sheer ability, grit and hard work, Indians were able to break barriers of prejudice, racism and intolerance to come to be seen as irreplaceable contributors to Britain's economy.

Vijay has always considered himself to be a gourmet and it is not surprising that he has devoted an entire chapter to the saga of the 9,500 curry houses in Britain. It is fascinating to learn how Indian cuisine became part of British dining habit, though even Vijay is unable to discover the actual provenance of CTM – chicken tikka masala!

"I never really felt I was in a foreign land," writes Vijay of his time in England. That is because he became a part of London, and began reporting like an insider. But whether he was attending Baisakhi in Southall or a Labour Friends of India function in Brighton, his journalistic instincts never left his side. Every conversation that he had, whether with Martin, a humble cab driver, or Alan Campbell Johnson, the powerful Press Adviser of Lord Mountbatten when he was Viceroy, led him to some new insight and this book is a distillate of all that he found significant and worthwhile in a decade and a half of reporting from London. Everything that you need to know about the changing face of Britain and of the Indians there, from the excess and success of Bollywood which has made London an extension of Mumbai, to the difference between Hampstead Indians and Southall ones, from 'Bus Foot' disease to 'chequebook journalism', you will find within these pages.

Vijay, with his characteristic modesty, describes this book as 'a kaleidoscope of impressions' of his time in London, but it is much more than that. It is an enlightening look at diverse topics that forces the reader to think more seriously about issues such as the racist effect of immigration controls, the phenomenon of forced marriages and honour killings in South Asian families, the changing attitudes towards NRIs, and the enduring values that make Britain the mother of democracy despite the continuing allure of monarchy. Written in an easy, free flowing style, it reads like a chat with an old friend.

Joseph Pulitzer once outlined the task of journalists working for him: "Put it before them briefly so they will read it, clearly so they will appreciate it, picturesquely so they will remember it and, above all, accurately so they will be guided by its light."

Vijay has clearly followed the famous publisher's advice in producing this lively, educative and entertaining account of an important period of Indo-British history.

I commend it to you.

Acknowledgement

As I finished writing the book, my first attempt to be a writer, I realised, in the course of completing it, I had come to owe gratitude to a large number of friends and well-wishers for their invaluable help. I have been a journalist for three decades but never knew that writing a book was much more complex than sending off reports, analyses or interviews, howsoever newsworthy they might be.

Apart from getting inputs in tracing back the grim life of early settlers who came in trickles hoping for better future in Britain, the story of the slow but steady transition of Indians from slums to millionaires row, their assimilation and acceptance in all walks of life, getting pictures from London while sitting in New Delhi seemed more problematic. The reflections on politics, racism and the media involved sensitivities. Here, too, I needed help and briefing, and I got it in ample measure.

Of course I must first thank the Hindustan Times which trusted me enough to keep me in London for over 15 years—possibly the longest time spent by a foreign journalist there. I could become almost a part of the life, fast-paced, challenging and kaleidoscopic. The close interaction with the establishment, the media, the city executives, corporate heads and with my own Indian community gave me priceless and rare insight into all facets of life to be able to string together this book.

I must thank my friend Krishan Bhatia who provided precious information about the immigrants, their fight against discrimination and humiliation. He completed their story that laid the foundation for the Indian community to achieve the stature of most successful and flourishing of all ethnic groups, a story that began with late Balwant Kapoor, a freedom fighter and a friend.

I owe much to Lord Meghnad Desai who, whenever I sought his help, was always ready with his candid analyses and comments. I could not contact my other friend Peter Oborne but his book *The Triumph of the Political Class,* which he gave me was like a pathfinder. I thank him. Mohammad Sarwar, publisher-editor of the Nation, UK, provided me some marvelous pictures without which several chapters would have looked drab. I can never thank them enough.

Lord Bhiku Parekh, too, was always there in London to help me with information, and was forthcoming whenever I contacted him to clear some points. Thank you!

I owe thanks to Rohit Khattar, his London Man Friday Anshuman Saxena, Namita Punjabi and her husband Ranjit Mathrani for their guidance about food and restaurants in London that enabled me write about the hold of curry over the English. I must also thank journalist friend Nabanita Sircar, Vikas Pota of Saffron Chase, Vaishali Malhotra of Eros International and Mrs Kamla Singhvi, all of whom were real help. I owe special gratitude to Ms Sircar for her efforts in braving freezing temperatures to shoot pictures for me in London and egging me on to complete this book! And so did another long-time friend Vijay Dhar, who once threatened me that he would cut me off as a friend if I did not foray into book writing.

Special thanks are also due to Raj Loomba who encouraged me to diversify into writing books when I was on a sort of crossroad not knowing what to do after returning from London. Then there is my publisher K.P.R. Nair who I feared more as a friend than as my publisher, for he always adopted a very warm friendly tone whenever he complained about some laxity or the other. While thanking the editor Anna Chandy, I owe an apology to her for my utter ignorance about writing for a book. She must have endured a lot while editing. Thank you, Anna!

Last but not the least I owe a great deal to my wife, Leshma. For years she cut my London reports and pasted them, every Sunday, in hardbound register. The over 12 volumes became my reference material which was of immense help to me in writting the book. I owe her big thanks also for leaving me alone while I wrote the book. Thank you.

Contents

1

London Odyssey: The Beginning

> "*Why, Sir, you find no man at all intellectual, who is willing to leave London. No, Sir, when a man is tired of London, he is tired of life; for there is in London all that life can afford.*"
>
> —*Samuel Johnson*

Dr. Johnson's words swirled in my mind as I waited to board the flight to Heathrow. I was excited at my posting as the *Hindustan Times* representative based in London but there was trepidation too. I had been there several times and once as a guest of the Government and seen many places in England. But, that was like a packaged tour. A visit to Windsor Castle, to Shakespeare's home or seeing the 'Mousetrap', Agatha Christie's murder mystery—the longest running since 1952— was a great experience, especially pleasant because it was courtesy Her Majesty's Government. But all that was unlikely to help me to understand the country, its politics or its people.

A journalist in his home ground has the backing of his paper, useful contacts and more crucially knows the background of most newsworthy individuals and happenings. But in a foreign posting such obvious advantages are just not there. It takes time to develop worthwhile sources, yet one has to get down as quickly as possible to start sending dispatches. News does not allow luxury of acclimatization. I realized as the Boeing 747 started its descent at Heathrow that it would be a different ball game altogether.

The hard reality of the unknown that lay ahead hit me with the AI-101 flight's Captain's announcement, 'We have landed at London Heathrow. The local time is 3.35 pm. It's a bright, sunny day and the outside temperature is 18 °C.'

It was summer of 1994 and I did not know then that I was to 'live' in London for over 15 years; the years which were so full of 'news' that now in retrospect I realize I had hardly any time to relax or socialize. But the 'Great Expectations' I had from the London posting were fortuitously largely fulfilled.

Once I started to 'hunt' for contacts and news I went to the usual sources, the Press Minister in the Indian High Commission, Rajiv Dogra and High Commissioner L.M. Singhvi himself, whom I knew from before, some Indian-origin MPs, and 'the' much familiar Lord Swraj Paul, media persons, some columnists like Sir Simon Jenkins, who I had met in Delhi. Suddenly I felt that the world had opened up, just as Boswell noted, 'By seeing London, I have seen as much of life as the world can shew'.

Gradually, the city grew on me, sources became familiar and friendly and within a short period I felt at home away from home. So much so that when I left London I felt nostalgic. I loved the city, and as it happens in all love affairs, there were disenchantments, disappointments, uncomfortable moments, but my feelings for it never faded. How right was Dr Johnson when he wrote '*for there is in London all that life can afford*'.

They were indeed the most wonderful years, both professionally and personally. But I never ever thought of putting together whatever I experienced, saw, heard and learnt and write a book. This is why I never kept any notes nor collected pictures. But, on my return to Delhi Tarun Basu, an old colleague who I discovered had become head of a multi-million worth news agency, suggested at a casual meeting at India International Centre in New Delhi that I should write a book on my years in Europe. 'Living as long as you did, you must write all that you learnt from close quarters all about politics, media and Diaspora. You have the advantage of writing on politics here (India), people, society and of course you have been part of the media.'

I mulled over what Tarun said. I liked the idea and just started writing whatever came to my mind. The result is a collection of impressions of a sort of a traveller, of an Indian's passage to England. I went there with trepidation but ended up with a sense of equanimity—of having experienced two contrasting worlds of people, politics, ethos and values. And I have chronicled them here, encompassing not only the Indian Diaspora—1.6 million and growing—their family life, attitudes, achievements, acceptance in the society and their lingering Indianness, but the politics and life in Britain generally as seen by an outsider who became an insider as years rolled by.

The book reflects on politics and politicians, good, bad and ugly facets of the multi-ethnic, multi-cultural society, an amalgam of the English and the ethnic values, and of course the media which seems to have an awesome influence and operates without any shackles. I quote Baron Macaulay, 'The gallery in which the reporters sit has become a fourth estate of the realm'. It indeed has. The British media also has unlimited resources to rip off the lid over best kept secrets. Some of them I have recorded.

The long and close association with the Indian families—Tony Blair christened Indians British Indians in 1995, much before he entered Downing Street—most of them to my utter surprise quintessentially Indian, was personally enlightening. I could see the British Indian in a new light. They are so different from what we feel about them in India. Even the younger generation seems to have its psychological roots in India.

I have brought out interactions with many of them —Peers, MPs, Mayors, GPs, business magnets, students and the academicians—some extraordinarily brilliant and well-regarded. Many have defended India and its causes stoutly without expecting a thank you. Instances are in a surfeit.

The changes in the perception of India among the second and third generations as the country's economic sinews developed and its prominence rose in the west is incorporated and hopefully it will make for interesting reading.

> The NRIs are so different from what we feel about them in India. Even the younger generation seems to have its psychological roots in India.

I was amazed to see the difference between the Southall Indians and the Hampstead ones. The former essentially stick to the culture back home, especially when it comes to marriage, the latter have imbibed more English ways but maintain close links with India.

The assimilation of two cultures, Indian and western is also remarkable. Bhangra remains authentic Punjabi, but the Indian cuisine has been suitably 'diluted' for the English palate, except the 'non-Indian' chicken tandoori masala curry, about the origin of which there are interesting stories which I have related. The Indian food is so much part of the British cuisine that readymade dishes are stocked by even the upmarket Harrods, Selfridges, the biggest chain, Tesco and the English's own Marks & Spencer. Some of the Indian restaurants have become institutions. I believe that more than Bollywood, it is the Indian food that has spread its 'Raj' and 'caged' the British.

The westernization is, indeed, more discernible in Indian bands and singers that have mushroomed blending the western and Indian pop. But Hindi pop is Hinglish. True, Bollywood has helped. Most programmes at Asian functions include 'entertainment by Bollywood artists'. But generally these artists have possibly never seen Mumbai and are indigenous.

I went to one of the dinners by Air India way back in the nineties hoping to see some stars who I thought must have been flown from Mumbai to perform. Instead I found a local troupe doing Indian-film style dances to popular Hindi film songs. I realized that quite often Bollywood artists in the country meant groups from Southall or Birmingham, albeit enthusiastic performers. It was always a treat to see them in colourful lahengas and cholis cavorting Bollywood style. Anupam Kher's film acting academy in Ealing, London will surely churn out more 'local' Bollywood stars.

But, with more films being shot in England and premieres of Indian films having become a norm, Indian stars are frequently there. And the well-heeled enterprising hosts do get hold of them for their functions, even if it is limited to a 'Guest' appearance. I saw Kajol anointed one of the brand ambassadors for empowerment of women by Cherie Blair. Then Preity Zinta was very much present at the Diwali Charity dinner at Guildhall by Raj Loomba. I am sure more than Cherie Blair, David Miliband the young Foreign Secretary, was thrilled to meet her.

The organizers of the 2010 Commonwealth Games in Delhi might not like it but I feel— some Indian media persons agreed with me— that

Prince Charles at Bharatiya Vidya Bhavan:
Cultural assimilation

M.F.Husain: enthusiastic supporter of charity events

Gurinder Chadha with Shabana Azmi, star in It's a wonderful Afterlife: amalgamating two cultures

Malkiat Singh and his troupe, based in Birmingham, contributed 'vigorously' in clinching the Games for India. In their jazzy Punjabi attire they performed Bhangra at its most colourful and vigorous at the end of the presentation by the team, led by Suresh Kalmadi, competing for staging the Games in India, at the Marlborough House, the Commonwealth Secretariat on Pall Mall. I could see faces of the judges light up. They swung and tapped, the ambience turned electric. Its beat had won the day for the country.

I have dwelt on the celebration of religious events and festivals, like Diwali. At home, families stick to rituals when praying to Lakshmi, the Goddess of wealth, and try please her by following all Vedic rituals. But big parties to mark the festival, where invitees include eminent people from Britain as well as all over the world, show that festivities have gone 'English'. These celebrations and campaigning by Indian-origin MPs and Peers, and many NRIs have led to annual celebration of Diwali and Dussehra in Parliament and Whitehall. How it came about is revealing of the growing influence of Indians in society and politics.

These two festivals are now known across the country. It may not be far when Diwali becomes a 'national' festival. Thousands of Indians have signed petition for it. The lighting of diya (lamp), a ritual to mark Diwali, for the first time at Downing Street by Prime Minister Gordon Brown was seen by many Indians as a step forward for persuading the Government to declare it as a national festival, like Christmas.

Another interesting aspect of the 'British' hue on the festivals is that they are seldom celebrated on the actual date according to the Hindu calendar. Once I sent a report of Diwali dinner hosted by Bharatiya Vidya Bhavan to my paper only to be pointed out by the desk that the Diwali was a month ago. I had to explain that public celebrations of festivals in England were scheduled according to the dates convenient to the chief guest, who generally happened to be some important public figure. Their presence helps in greater donation for charity.

> "I am sorry that I never tried to find out if after the Toast to the Queen was with a raised glassful of wine was it to the President of India brimming with orange juice."

I have tried to describe such events that are unique in their own way and blend the black tie culture with invocations in Sanskrit and Toast to the President of India and the Queen. I am sorry that I never tried to find out if after the Toast to the Queen was with a raised glassful of wine was it to the President of India brimming with orange juice.

It is remarkable that all such festive dinners have been turned into charity events when funds are raised for good causes. If scotch flows—and it does whenever Indians, even those who have lived there for decades assemble-- so does the largesse for philanthropic purposes. Indeed funds raised by individuals for education of the children of poor widows and street children, and for the welfare and development of areas their families lived before emigrating reflects the desire of such Indians to share their success with the people their ancestors had lived with. I have devoted one chapter on how lives in India have been helped by some of these individuals. There are now Trusts which raise funds for causes in India and are doing remarkable work in the country.

A few other facets of life—settling of marriages for instance—need special mention. We all know that Southall is known as Little India but not many know of 'swyamvars' held for finding spouses. Extended families gather with their eligible, dressed to kill. These are a big draw and are prospering despite speed dating and the marriage bureaus. One however is not sure how many end in the mandaps. At least the well-known journalist and a desirable bachelor, Sanjay Suri, has remained bride-less despite attending a couple of them. But they surely got him enthused to write the book *Brideless in Wembley*.

Other chapters cover monarchy, democracy British style, the attitude towards prime minister, members of parliament and their very public visibility and unbridled censorious attitude of the media towards them. I feel the comparison with the democracy in India is of significance and of interest to readers both in India and Britain.

Initially it felt odd to see prime ministers and cabinet members without 'lal bati' syndrome or surrounded by black cats. But one lives and learns. Where else would an opposition leader like David Cameron himself telephone and say "I am David. Ask your questions". His call had come on my mobile while I was going from Liverpool to Blackburn, driven by my good friend Dr Shiv Pande, to meet Jack Straw. When I said I needed about 15 minutes, he shot back, 'Seven. I have a young family and I am on holiday, one child of mine is on my shoulders.' And thus was the interview conducted.

Some Peers and MPs of Indian origin have been mentioned as well for their contributions to the community and in keeping the flag flying for India. But I thought that the "regaining" of friends among British politicians by weaning them away from the anti-India and pro-plebiscite in Kashmir lobbies by High Commissioner Lalit Mansingh merited a chapter. He with support on the ground by Minister of Coordination K.M.Singh laid the foundation for the close political and economic ties which benefited both the countries. It is largely due to some of them that no mention is now made about referendum in Kashmir, or of alleged human rights violations. The pro-Pak lobbies which in the nineties made the Kashmir issue part of domestic politics have become extinct.

I also had the opportunity to watch international diplomacy at first hand — G-7s, G-8s and G-20s, EU Summits, several tripartite meetings and the growing importance of India at such forums. I have covered elections of three German Chancellors, travelling to rural constituencies, watching campaigning by the likes of Helmut Kohl; there were some uncanny similarities with the campaigning in India. The most edifying was meeting some adventurous Indians in Paris, albeit few in number, who have set up websites on their own initiative to make the French aware of the Indian culture and values.

I have also dwelt on the travails of the early immigrants and the scourge of racism. It includes the special and indeed unique contribution of individuals, from the early emigrants to the present generation that helped counter race-related violence by skinheads, the disappointment at the loss of the Raj, along with the Government's sincere efforts to ostracize racial hatred from the society for the last few years.

Being a media person, my interest in the British journalism was natural. I have narrated in some detail the working style of journalists, the newspapers there-- comparing them with the Indian newspapers, the editorial contents, difference of style and focus between the broadsheet journalism and the tabloids, whose unbridled obsession to peep into boudoirs and unearth zealously guarded secrets of 'celebs' and politicians is awesome. They are in many ways quite different from the India media.

During my stay, as the twentieth century faded and the twenty-first dawned Britain underwent kaleidoscopic changes in all aspects—social, political and economic. The terror strikes and the continuing threat of more terror carnage changed the life of all of us. Suspicion blended with nervousness about who is the terrorist and when and where another bomb would explode. In fact it changed the character of the country, its much hailed freedom of speech,

The Diaspora, since the nineties, got more opportunities to show its merits and capability to contribute to the development of the country of their adoption, and they seized it.

tolerance et al were affected. Political correctness entered the political lexicon further restricting freedom of expression. It stifled the media, the government and even common people. I have discussed this at length.

But there were some nice developments too. Many Indians, especially the highly educated and talented younger generations have taken the centre stage, become in many ways British, indeed British Indian, as Tony Blair conceptualized. The word has a mystique about it and needs a bit of clarification, which I have done.

The Diaspora, since the nineties, got more opportunities to show its merits and capability to contribute to the development of the country of their adoption, and they seized it. They have done exceedingly well and their contributions have been noted. This is reflected in the increasing numbers of Peers, knighthoods and other top honours awarded to and the inclusion of greater number of Indians in councils, local bodies and welfare boards.

I have endeavoured in the book to mention a few such Indians in Britain. I can say without fear of contradiction that many have helped stabilize and develop Britain socially, politically and economically and done India proud.

A slight variation to what Wilhelm II, the German Kaiser, said would describe well the satisfaction of the Indian Diaspora in Britain— 'We have fought for our place in the Isle and won it'.

My own assimilation that enabled me to understand the multicultural Britain and talk about it in detail in the book can be summed up by what I once wrote for the *New Statesman*. It had asked me to describe London in 250 words. "It was perhaps the lingering memory of Monopoly. I always seemed to land on Park Lane with two hotels and had to pay thousands of pounds in rent to my fellow players. So when I was actually driving on Park Lane, I felt

London is the best city to live in when you're away from home. It believes in live and let live.

a tingling of nostalgia. The soap-box orators on Sundays were new to me but they were like the coffee house regulars back home who spend hours fretting about issues of no concern to them.

"London is the best city to live in when you're far away from home. It believes in live and let live...But I sometime wonder where all the English have gone. I seldom see them in Oxford Street or Knightsbridge. But when one does meet them, they are as familiar or formal as a Bombayite is to a Delhite", I concluded. Sir Nicholas Fenn, the then British High Commissioner in India, later told me he had cut that article and kept it in his records, because the linkage with Monopoly was 'interesting' and he 'could not agree more' with what I wrote.

I hope readers both in India and Britain will find this book informative and a bit thought-provoking. It will interest many in India because quite a few may correlate instantly with persons, events and places mentioned. I feel the book has turned out to be an English curry with an Indian recipe!

2

New World, New Ways

Side by side keep pressing, victory will come

—*Gen. William T. Sherman*

Lessons from A London Taxi Driver

The omens were good, I mentally made a note of it as I walked out of the immigration hall. The Indian lady at the immigration desk had looked up to verify that my face was similar to the photograph in the passport and stamped it within moments. Realising from the visa that I had come on a posting, she said, 'Welcome to London, you will like it here. I came here 20 years ago, and have never regretted it'. I still remember how prophetic she was.

Outside the Terminal 3 building looking for a taxi, I 'encountered' the typical English weather, the drizzle and soft, fresh breeze. The saying in India is that a bit of rain at the start of any new venture is auspicious. I subscribed to the belief soon after I got into a black cab at the Taxi Rank. 'New to London?' he asked me as we drove towards Central London. 'No,' I said 'but this time I have come on a posting. I am a journalist'. This is when he passed on his paper, the *Daily Mail.* The paper had splashed in bold an interview of Prince Charles with Jonathan Dimbleby in which he admitted his liaison with Camilla Parker-Bowles and his unfaithfulness to his wife Diana.

During an hour and a half drive to my in-transit apartment in West Kensington near Cromwell Hospital, the cab driver, I think he said his name was Martin, seemingly an avowed monarchist, gave me invaluable insight into monarchy, British politics, media, how well Indians had done, pubs and, of course, the 'good Indian restaurants'. Wisdom comes from strange sources. And Martin, God bless his soul, literally prepared the ground for me to launch my understanding of many aspects of politics, monarchy, status of Indians, all of which helped me in news-gathering.

He was so disturbed at Charles's 'indiscretion' that he could not help voicing his disgust. 'The Queen, and God give her a long life, is unfortunate to have a wayward bunch of family members.' Berating Charles for not keeping his marital vows, he fumed that Charles 'justifies his adultery by saying he already saw his marriage as being over. What balderdash'. Martin was obviously a devoted Diana fan (I discovered later that millions like him were her fans) and minced no words in blaming Charles for the 'Royal mess'. I learnt a lot about the background of Diana and Charles's affair with Camilla Parker- Bowles.

He had much to say in sympathy for Princess Diana—just a beautiful young person betrayed for an elderly married woman, not a patch on Diana. It was much later when I came across two comments about London's Black Cab drivers that I realized that Martin was definitely god sent.

'London taxi drivers are not the flotsam and jetsam spat out by a teeming metropolis; they're ambassadors for the city. They know that if London is to maintain its status as the capital of the world — the New York of the 21st century, in fact — our cabs need to be the best in the world', Toby Young wrote in *London Today.* The other observation was equally pertinent.

'I base almost my entire view of the world on conversations I have had with cab drivers: perhaps the most interesting, diverse and informed people on the planet,' said James Delingpole in the *Telegraph.*

Recalling what Martin said about Diana, I tried to find out more about her. I soon discovered that she was the most 'magnificent' and remunerative obsession of the British media; any news (read gossip) about her boosted circulation. Royal correspondents seemed to follow her 24x7. This practice of papers having correspondents for literally sleuthing on the Royals was a new thing for me. We have in India political or business or science correspondents but we do not have a 24x7 correspondent exclusively for the president or the prime minister or even for other important personalities like Sonia Gandhi. In fact royal correspondent Richard Kay was said to be a close confidant of Diana, who often used to meet him covertly and pour out her heart.

It was not long before I realized that Kay was indeed more of a close friend than just a journalist for the Princess. Sir David Frost introducing him on his BBC 'Breakfast with Frost' programme had said, 'And we're delighted to have with us the *Daily Mail* journalist Richard Kay, who was one of the few journalists who was trusted by Princess Diana'.

She was, as we all know, not left in peace even after her death. A section of the media continued to squeeze as much as it could from Diana stories, 'exclusives and exposures', for years after her tragic death in Paris. It stopped only after public pressure that reports were distressful to her two sons William and Harry. In any case news relating to the two young princes became more saleable.

I cannot recall how many dispatches I sent about her, but it was quite frequent because my Editor had said there was immense interest in her in India. The result was that when I was on home leave in Delhi, a gentleman at the Coffee Lounge in India International Centre remarked, 'Are you Diana's correspondent? How close are you to her?' I could only smile.

The only time I saw Diana from close quarters was at Harrods. She was accompanied by a lady and they were looking at shoes. Then they moved towards the elevator. I debated whether I should go and request for an interview. As I moved closer to her she gave, in her typical style, a slanted look with her eyes half closed and a glimmer of a smile. Unfortunately by then the lift came and she was gone. The moment was lost and I still regret not being quick enough to at least say hello. She certainly had an allure and charm about her. But I could not disappoint the gentleman in the Coffee Lounge by giving these details and admitting that I never did get an opportunity to meet her.

Political Updates

I did not know then that black-cab drivers were not only the most knowledgeable, but also quite well-to-do with investments in side businesses, widely travelled, had opinion about everything and everybody, and many, according to the grapevine, belonged to a network of informers feeding the Met Police of anything suspicious or untoward. I recall meeting a cab owner and driver and his wife once crossing the Channel by boat while coming from Antwerp to London. We sat at the Captain's Table and started chatting. He was drinking wine with abandon while his wife was content sipping orange juice. He told me they went on a two-month trip to Europe in their private car and were now returning with the car's boot full of French cheese which they would serve at their pub. 'I drove on the continent most of the time so could not drink. Now my wife would drive me from Ramsgate to London so I am drinking."

Over a three-hour conversation I learnt they owned not only a pub but two small flats as well. They were a very nice couple, as knowledgeable as Martin. They kindly offered to drive me to London.

I realized that they were the best source for opinion on anything and everything and understood how admirable and useful Martin's political briefing was. I must also admire them for being one of the most honest cab drivers in the world. I was never taken anywhere except by the shortest routes and their meters were never manipulated. It was such a welcome change from my experience in Delhi.

I learnt from Martin that the Conservatives under John Major, then prime minister, were getting increasingly unpopular. 'Major is a nice man but some others around him are rotten eggs. They don't seem to keep out of scandals and are busy plotting to throw out Major rather than do any positive work for public good.' He took names of one or two rebels but then I had no idea about them.

I was half listening to him, being more interested in looking out, trying to spot familiar buildings. But what perked me up were his comments on the Labour Party. A few months earlier I had come to London as a part of the media party accompanying the then Indian Prime Minister P.V. Narasimha Rao and met John Smith, the party leader and Jack Cunnigham, in the shadow cabinet.

Smith, a charismatic leader, died shortly after. But according to Martin, Labour was modernizing and shaping up well. 'John Smith was a very promising leader but he died suddenly. Labour however seems to be moving up. That young chap, Tony Blair, has succeeded him and he is shaping up well. Watch out for him.' His other advice was to ignore Lord Tebbit's call to throw out all immigrants before rivers of blood flowed. 'The ethnic communities, especially Indians, are by and large hard-working and peaceful. You are unlikely to encounter any racial prejudice.'

He proved right. I never felt racially discriminated except once. I had turned my car into Highfield Road in Golders Green when a police car, making a U-turn from the Golders Green Road, came towards me and signalled to stop. One police officer got down and came to me. He asked me about my identity, and not the driving licence. I gave him my passport and after looking at it he went back to his car and his colleague drove away. They said nothing to me. I still wonder why they made a sudden u-turn and investigated me. Maybe, they suspected me to be an illegal immigrant.

The incident was forgotten quickly, although it rankles me no end as the reason still remains a mystery. They were neither traffic police nor were they in a patrol car. They were possibly going to the police station which was nearby. They could not have taken me for a terrorist, 9/11 was far away. But other than this isolated incident, I never had a problem. I was never stopped and searched even during the 7/7 red alert, although I used to hear a lot about stop and search of non-White drivers.

In fact, I admire the London police. I never saw any officer in uniform smoking or drinking. And those patrolling on foot in shopping areas were not only polite but very helpful. When I told this to Sir Paul Stevenson, Metropolitan Police Commissioner whom I met at the British High Commissioner Sir Richard Stagg's dinner at his residence in New Delhi, Sir Paul said, 'Any time you see the contrary please call me immediately. But thank you for the appreciation.'

The other thing is that all of the police officers are trim and fit. No bulging bellies or pan-chewing and betel spitting ones that we are used to here in India. No haftas (protection-money) are collected. I have never heard nor seen any driver paying a traffic police officer a bribe. And funnily enough they address everyone as 'Sir', even when investigating a person.

Racial Prejudices

Over the years I did hear from many Indian friends instances of racial insults and, also reported a few obnoxious incidents in my paper. But admittedly such cases are rare and more confined to inner cities. The Government, police and even local authorities have made sincere efforts to curb the menace. I think some unemployed, loutish elements in smaller less cosmopolitan cities get provoked seeing an Asian with a white woman or driving a nice car.

> "In fact I admire the London police. I never saw any officer in uniform smoking or drinking. And those patrolling on foot in shopping areas were not only polite but very helpful..."

There was this incident when a 32- year-old Indian scriptwriter, Sunil Modi, based in north London, had to fight for his life when his car was ambushed and he was dragged out and repeatedly kicked by four white youth near Merseyside, as far as I can recollect. Modi later said he was driving with his fiancée through suburbs of Liverpool when he was hit in the face by a man carrying a beer can and then pulled out of his car. He heard one of the attackers shout 'Spike him, put the Paki's head on the spike'. The viciousness of the attack alarmed the Merseyside Police so much that they called a Press conference. Ironically, Modi was writing a script on race-related issues.

> "While taking me to Savoy Bar for the 'best Dry Martini in England' Peter Oborne, then with the Evening Standard, with a broad grin asked me to precede him. When I asked why he said that Indian imbibers were favoured by the bartenders there. "You people tip well."

In another drive called 'napkin operation' by a county police force, plainclothes policemen and women visited restaurants owned by Chinese and Indians. Customers from ethnic minority communities were briefed to pick up and wipe their mouths with their napkins if there was any hint of racial insult. I was told that a couple of arrests were made during the operation.

A few months later, after the cops stopped me, there was a pleasanter experience. While taking me to Savoy Bar for the 'best Dry Martini in England' Peter Oborne, then with the *Evening Standard*, with a broad grin asked me to precede him. When I asked why he said that Indian imbibers were favoured by the bartenders there. 'You people tip well.' The Dry Martini was superb but the price had a rather sobering effect. I did not have to fork out a hefty tip to keep up the popularity of us Indians at the Savoy Bar. Peter paid for our drinks.

Meeting the Indian Community

I was given a summary about the Indian community by Martin which I later realized was quite perceptive. He had been to India on vacation and seen the Taj, which he thought was the eighth wonder of the world.I was happy to know that Indians in Britain were by and large well-educated, peaceful and hard working, this was Martin's view too. He had mentioned Swraj Paul in great detail. 'He hosted Indira Gandhi when she came here. He has donated a million pound to the London Zoo in memory of his young daughter who died here. He has an office on Baker Street not very far from Sherlock Holmes's place.' He added that Paul often took black cabs. Seemingly, it was a major plus point for Swraj Paul—he was not a Peer then.

Coincidentally, I knew him much before I shifted to London. My first meeting with him was 38,000 ft over the Atlantic while flying from London to New York way back in 1983. I had written critical articles against his attempt (*in Probe* magazine of which I was then the editor) to take over Bharat Ram's DCM and H.P. Nanda's Escort. Other senior commentators too vehemently opposed his move. Swraj Paul responded with a scathing attack on most commentators, but I was spared.

During the flight, just a few months after the publication of those articles, the steward came to me and said that Mr Paul would like to meet me. I went over to him a bit diffidently. But I was welcomed with a smile and offered coffee. I asked, half-jokingly, 'Aren't you upset? You called a couple of much senior journalists sluts of the media.' I still recall his loaded reply. 'No I am not upset with you because I know you wrote in full faith believing what was shown to you.' We both understood what he meant.

Among the other Indians whom I had met earlier included Joginder Sanger, then GSA Air India, through Salman Khurshid. His office in Poland Street just off Oxford Street was a popular rendezvous for several Indians many of whom would come for getting seats on flights to India. On my visits to his office I met Ajit Prasad, a chartered accountant with a roaring practice, who later became a good friend.

I had also met Ranjit Sethia at his office. While in India I had written about his brother Raj Sethia, who was then serving a sentence in India on some alleged fraud charges. To my welcome surprise he did not complain. Instead he took me to Sethia House and showed me around. A huge replica of a ship owned by them encased in glass was the *piece de resistance.* I interviewed him later wherein he was quite outspoken about the trial and my article.

I discovered that many Indians were invited to Sanger's office, even some unknown to Sanger, by a staffer of his, who was a 'compulsory inviter for just a cup of tea'. I too was once almost dragged by him to have a cup of tea at the office. Sanger told me he brought people even from as far as Marble Arch. Quite a hospitable man he was!

Culture of Hospitality

Most Indians have retained the culture of hospitality as exists back home despite the western lifestyle creeping in. I was amazed at the number of social-dos and functions hosted by the community at the slightest pretext. It was nice to find that parties by Indians were not just a cheese and wine, and bread and biscuit affair. They lay an assortment of preparations—Indian cuisine tailored to suit the western palate. Unlike western hosts who do not insist after asking once 'will you have some more', most Indians in Britain have stuck to the old custom of asking repeatedly.

These parties were the best conduits for me initially to get acquainted with a lot of Indians and simultaneously collect background material for news reports and features. I was, I believe, quite often invited not just because I was a journalist, but also because I lived alone, and many Indian families took pity on me. I have memories of delicious food by warm, welcoming hosts and hostesses.

Arun Bhatnagar, then Minister Commerce in the Indian High Commission, and his wife Kalpana invited me over for meals regularly. Their cook was extremely good and equally enthusiastic in serving large portions. Their invitation was always most welcome because they lived in Maida Vale which was hardly 15 minutes drive from where I lived. Likewise Rajiv Dogra, Minister, Press and Information in the Commission, and his wife Meenu were equally great hosts. Meenuji never tired of providing me delicious shami kebabs. Being a Lucknow- man I liked these the most. Authentic Bihari food was always available for me at K.M. Singh's, then Minister, Community Relations. His wife Jayashree, a Bihari, having come to know that my mother was from Bihar too, invariably served me pooris and aloo ki bhujiya, poorbi style. Another couple, Sushil Kumar, who was Director, Tea Board there, and his wife Sadhavi too were extremely hospitable. I did not have a car in the early days of my posting. But Kumar would always drop me back, even after late dinners.

I am glad the tradition they set was continued by some of their successors, like P.C. Haldar, Asif Ibrahim, whose wife Zeba served delicious Luckhnavi food, and Tilak Deveshwar. Monica Mohata came much later as Director, Nehru Centre, but the aroma of the Rajasthani dishes she served still linger.

The first to call me at home for dinner was Ashok Tandon, then the Press Trust of India chief in London. Not only did I enjoy the Indian delicacies served, but I also met a number of interesting guests at his place. Everyone was keen to fill me in with all sorts of information, all very useful. But the gentleman who offered to drop me back to my place was much amused when he learnt I could not direct him to my house even without having had any wine. I was very new to the city and all streets seemed the same to me, especially at night.

The Core Group

I was slowly able to meet almost all the Indians who formed the core group of NRIs and developed respect for their contribution to the economy, and the influence they wielded — the Hindujas, L.N. Mittal, Lord Bagri, the Loombas, Nat Purie, the Sethias, the Noons, the Nirulas, Lord Bhiku Parekh, Lord Meghnad Desai, Lord Bhattacharya, Maneck Dalal, Lord Hamid and several Patels to name a few. Many others rose to prominence as years rolled by. The list is too long, signifying how well Indians have distinguished themselves in various fields.

The Indian High Commissioner Dr LM Singhvi was also proactive and there were many get-togethers at India House with community members. I remember meeting Gopi Hinduja for the first time at a function in the Gandhi Hall. He knew about my posting and was very charming and gave me useful information on various subjects. I realized later that Gopibhai, as one called him, was always abreast of anything and everything, whether in England or India.

News about India was 'hot' with the older and the second generation in Southall. On Tuesdays, when latest Indian newspapers were put on sale in a couple of shops on Broadway in Southall, there would be a rush and most copies would be sold by late afternoon. At Delhi Chaat House started by Brijendra Gupta in 1947, discussions over political news from India over dosas, papdis, samosas topped up with innumerable cups of tea could some time get as hot as the curry specially prepared by Mrs Gupta for favoured customers. Now, of course, computers have changed the news reading habits and the Chaat House closed down. But there are still around 30 curry houses in Southall.

The first Independence Day celebrations I participated in London showed how well the Indian ambience was created at such formal receptions. Many came in national dress and talked nostalgically of their early years in the country. Even some British invitees seemed to know a lot about India and eagerly joined in reminiscences. Dr Singhvi was particular about inviting a large number of Indians and British MPs and Peers to the reception. In Southall, sweets were distributed and tricolour was flown.

Talking of Southall, by the time I returned to India, it had become so different from what I saw in the early nineties. Most noticeable was the change of attitude about India amongst the young. The nonchalant and dismissive attitude of the younger elements in early nineties riled me. I did comment on their uninformed opinion of the country in one of my weekly diaries, at a heavy cost to my acceptance amongst the young in Southall. But, as ties with Britain grew and the west was awed by the growth of the Indian economy, their attitudes started to change.

The Southall youth's concept of India and Indians started to change completely with the arrival of the IT revolution and of a new generation of Indians. The Indian cousins were no longer looked down upon as backward desis, nor was the country regarded as obscurantist. Their visits to the country further ensured that they would be as Indian as their grandparents, but with the added advantage of being equally British. Southall is now the real Little India, just an extension of the mother country.

After 26/11 Virendra Sharma, MP for Southall, organized a special meet in the Members Committee Room in the House of Commons to discuss possible relief for victims and to mutually agreed measures to stave off any adverse fall-out on the community relations in the UK. It was a very well attended meet, with Peers, MPs, and community leaders attending it. The Indians in Southall and nearby areas also initiated a drive to collect funds for Mumbai attack victims.

It is amazing how much the Indians there remain interested in politics in India. I could understand their desire to know about economic policies after liberalisation and Bollywood because of its glamour and music, but most seemed to know the latest political news. I remember when there was only Zee News, Mr Mahendra Kaul would silence all his guests to listen to the 15-minute news from India.

Interaction with Indians

I was keen to start contacts with some prominent Indians, whose acquaintance I realized was imperative for understanding the community's integration in the society and their acceptance there and their interest, if any, in India. I was also keen to know how much the English mixed with the community. I was eager too to visit a few Indian restaurants about which I read regularly in food magazines and dailies. Martin too mentioned one restaurant in Bayswater, another off Baker Street and Bombay Brasserie, 'its briyani was a favourite of Charles and Diana when they were still love birds'.

But on a 'journalist from India' salary I hesitated, not knowing how deep a dent would one dinner make in my wallet. The problem was soon solved. I was invited by Mahendra Kaul, the first Asian to be awarded OBE, and his wife Rajni, who co-owned the then popular Indian restaurant Viceroy, on Glentworth Street just off Baker Street. Vijay Dhar had telephoned them about me and they were good enough to invite me. The food was excellent, better than many top restaurants in Delhi. Later I came to know them well. Of course, I kept going there so very often.

I found that my chairman Dr K.K. Birla liked the food there. I happened to be there twice when he came for dinner. I jokingly told Mr Kaul that I would stop coming to the restaurant because if my Chairman saw me there again, he would think I don't work and just enjoy eating out. Well, he was above all this and I still revere his warmth towards me. In fact, the staff there just loved 'Birlaji's' visits. 'He treats us so well and gives us tips that cross £100,' the manager Godffrey told me.

Kaul introduced tandoori food in London and opened one of the first Indian restaurants Gaylords International in Mayfair, which is now Chor Bizarre, one of the top eating joints in London, run by Rohit Khattar. Kaul also helped immigrants from India to understand the basics for integrating in the English society through his programme on BBC. It was indeed diaspora's favourite programme, 'Apna Hi Ghar Samjhiye' (Make yourself at home), which ran for 14 years.

"Kaul also helped immigrants from India to understand the basics for integrating in the English society through his programme on BBC. It was indeed Diaspora's favourite programme, 'Apna Hi Ghar Samjhiye'(Make yourself at home), which ran for 14 years."

Southall: Truly little India

London Black cab drivers: knowledgeable, honest and diverse

Princess Diana: media obsession

BBC celebrated the 40th anniversary of 'Apna Hi Ghar Samjhiye' programme which was anchored by Kaul from 1966. One of his advices given was to avoid using too much hair oil. When Indians stayed in a B and B or a hotel, the pillows used to get stained. It made the hoteliers reluctant to give them rooms.

Like Kaul, many Indians in the early years did try to help the community adjust in an alien society. The stories I heard told of hard work and determination to succeed and be accepted. That was much before I was posted in London. I found a well-regarded, highly successful and adjusted community.

Most Indian families took special interest in acquainting their young to Indian culture and ways. Baroness Shreela Flather, great granddaughter of Sir Ganga Ram, who had gone to Britain to study law and later married Gary Denis Flather, told me that she always wore saris—all of them exquisite— in the House of Lords as an Indian identity. She used to take her two sons when they were small to weddings in her relatives in India and made them sleep on the floor in one room with their cousins to get them understand the Indian ways.

It is thus not surprising that 'British' Indians have benefited from being part of two cultures. I once met the son of the late Tarsem Singh Purewal who established the Punjabi weekly *Des Pardes* around 1985, in his Southall office. A student of University of London, he told me that whenever he went to the college in kurta and pyjama his friends teased him for coming in sleeping suit. He said he told them that he wore what was Indian and also wore suits for he was English as well. 'I have the benefit of two cultures.' It was so true.

Nobody should be surprised that with the advantage of integrating in culture and values of two societies, Indians there, just two per cent of the population, have come to occupy influential positions in politics, business and the society. There are now 20 Peers and baronesses and six MPs and over a hundred councillors. In every year's Honours List, many Indian-origin persons are listed for services to the community and commendable work in utility and welfare bodies and educational institutions. No Indian feels out of place in Britain. And I cannot visualize Britain sans Indians.

Meeting the British Media

My initial round of meetings with some known India-centric commentators in the mainstream media—Ian Jack of the *Granta*, Ray Whittaker of the *Independent* and Trevor Fishlock—were also very useful and gave me a valuable insight into the thinking about India while learning about British politics and the sectarian conflict in Northern Ireland. I was keen to understand the issue because of the assumed similarity to the Kashmir dispute. I was fortunate to be able to go to Belfast before the first ceasefire and experience the dread that enveloped Belfast. Death seemed to lurk everywhere.

I stayed at a hotel owned by Lord Daljit Rana, who had not become a Peer then, but was the richest Indian in the province. The Northern Ireland Secretariat was very helpful and provided me with a guide and a car. I was taken round the Loyalists and Republican areas, which were all clearly demarcated. It seemed so unreal, everything was demarcated—schools, hospitals, bars and clubs. Catholics and Protestants seemed to have separate lives, and lived in different worlds.

I met a Professor of Political Science at the Queen's University over dinner to understand the factors behind the sectarian conflict. I wanted to understand how similar the problem was to that in Kashmir. For an hour, he recounted to me the sixes Rusi Surti had hit when he came to play in a friendly match. Obviously the Professor was an ardent cricket fan. But the briefing by him, after his admiration for Surti ended, about the sectarian divide and the beginning of the bloody feud was invaluable.

It was past midnight when we left the restaurant. I could not spot a taxi and was too frightened to walk to the hotel which though was not too far. I could see tough, hefty heavily armed officers patrolling wearing bullet-proof jackets. Armoured vehicles also could be seen in the shadows. I decided to be candid about my fears and told the Professor. He was quite understanding and volunteered to walk with me to the hotel. 'We live in the midst of death. Its shadow is everywhere. I will reach you to your hotel. It's almost on my way.'

Just a week after I returned from Belfast, the IRA declared its first ceasefire. I got the news late evening on television, in a hotel in Hamburg. There was no laptop, and the hotel computer was unavailable at that hour. I faxed the report about the ceasefire typed on an ancient typewriter which the hotel supplied. The thrill of reporting from outside India had begun.

I must admit that most senior journalists and columnists were extremely helpful. Sir Simon Jenkins, whom I had met once in India, invited me home and over a glass of wine gave me some very useful advice. Peter Oborne told me that I would find it invigorating 'fishing' for real news but at the same time I would never be starved of newsworthy happenings. 'So much happens here. It's both a challenge and a pleasure. You will learn of the world, sitting here,' he summed up. He was so right. The world seems to zero in on London.

The World in London

I spotted a lone, silent Tibetan protester keeping vigil that started 20 years ago in 1989 – since the imposition of martial law in Lhasa. This was the longest running vigil in the West-- opposite the Embassy of China on Portland Place. It summed up for me in a nutshell why sans the glitz of the Raj and sway of the Empire, every grievance in the world is orchestrated in London.

Be it Cypriots, camping and waving placards in front of the Turkish Embassy, anti-war demonstrators marching from Hyde Park to Parliament, Tamils demonstrating in Whitehall, the Islamists marching along Baker Street shouting death to infidels, Khalistanis ritually gathering near IndiaHouse every year or JKLF members creating commotion outside Pakistan High Commission, they all seem to believe that their protestations in London would echo around the globe. And hope their problems will be resolved.

One of the Cypriot protesters told me that since they were mentioned in the papers and questions put in the House of Commons, 'we have received support from various organisations and individuals.' Enthused, they were trying to meet party leaders, especially Blair, to get a resolution passed in the House of Commons.

Over the years I realized that the English reporters were quite cooperative. They were always willing to share information about India or Pakistan and exchange notes. Oona Blackman, then with *Daily Mirror*—as far as I can recall—had reported that Benazir Bhutto purchased a 'hideaway' – a £2.5 million mansion--in Surrey. I called her and asked for more details which she gave easily. We exchanged more information on the purchase. It was later said that Bhutto did not know about the deal and it was reportedly bought by her husband.

> "... most senior journalists and columnists were extremely helpful. Sir Simon Jenkins, whom I had met once in India, invited me home and over a glass of wine gave me some very useful advice. Peter Oborne told me, I would find it invigorating "fishing" for real news but at the same time I would never be starved of newsworthy happenings."

Oborne likewise briefed me on British politics. I sought his advice frequently and he later invited me for a few cricket matches that he arranged and also to Ascot. I could thank him only through lunches and dinners at Indian restaurants. He simply loved Indian cuisine, as did most other English journalists. I left London satisfied that I had gained many friends in the British media.

Early Days

Once settled in the 'news' groove, I decided to gather as much as possible on the upcoming Blair. The dailies also helped me get an inkling of the sleaze that blighted the Tories. Ironically, a few scarred ones seemed to hit the jackpot, after being disgraced. One MP was alleged to have indulged in a three-in-the-bed romp; another was said to have accepted several brown envelopes, each allegedly containing thousand pounds from the Harrods owner Mohammed Al Fayed for putting questions in the House of Commons.

This MP lost at the polls but overnight became a TV star and was most sought after speaker at various meets and events. He along with his wife has reportedly raked in more money after the scandal than he could on an MP's salary — even if he, like many other parliamentarians, could manipulate his expense account.

In contrast,the write-ups on Blair were almost adulatory. He seemed to be a knight crusader come to cleanse the Tory mess. There seemed to be a nationwide interest in him. My first dispatch, initially written by hand and then taken to a typing centre and finally faxed to my paper was, thus, on Blair. I am glad that what I wrote about him in my first dispatch came true three years later. " Mr Blair is not only threatening Mr Major's tenancy of 10 Downing Street but also depriving him of reasons to justify another term for the Tories."

Oborne was proved right that London was the most exciting venue for any journalist. Being new, I rushed around to gather as much information

> "Over the years I realized that the English reporters were quite cooperative. They were always willing to share information about India or Pakistan and exchange notes.

> "Kier Hardy, one of the founders of the Labour Party in the 19th nineteenth Century, was born on August 15 and was such a staunch supporter of India, in those days of the Empire, that he was called Member of Parliament for India."

as possible. In the first month I travelled to Northern Ireland and then to Germany to report on the forthcoming election for the post of German Chancellor. Back in London, my hands were full reporting on Diana, her upswings and downswings with the tabloids, revelations of lurid details of Charles-Camilla liaison. The travails of the 'nice guy' John Major and the struggle by Blair to reinvent Labour, evolve the New Labour and bring it to the right of the centre to make it electable kept one busy with the typewriter (later computer!).

The exposure to a different level of reporting and trying to keep pace with the newsworthy happenings almost every day though exacting was exciting. The High Commission too provided inputs for interesting reports and of important historical events of which normally a journalist does not bother to learn. I had heard about the Magna Carta but forgotten all the details about it. I leant about it when Independence Day was celebrated by the Indian High Commission at the site where it was signed, 20 miles from London, near Windsor Castle.

It was enlightening to hear the speech of Michael Foot. He said that Kier Hardy, one of the founders of the Labour Party in the nineteenth century, was born on 15 August and was such a staunch supporter of India, in those days of the Empire, that he was called Member of Parliament for India. Call it a coincidence that 15 August, his birth date, became decades later the day India became free!

3

From Slums to Millionaires Row

> *And not by eastern wind only, when day light comes, comes the light; In front, the Sun climbs slow, how slowly, but westward, look, the land is bright.*
>
> —*Arthur Hugh Clough, poet*

The Treacherous Trek to Recognition

Who is Bhai Pritam Singh most Indians would ask whenever the name is mentioned. But, no story of the early days of Indian immigrants, who initially trickled in from rural Punjab, can be complete without recalling his selfless efforts to help hundreds of illiterates who just flew into Heathrow with almost empty pockets, dreaming of El Dorado. There was no one in those early years to properly guide them or give shelter and help them get jobs. They neither knew English nor the laws governing their eligibility for permanent residency and employment. They also could not anticipate taboos that segregated them from the mainstream.

But because the British had been in India for a long time, these early immigrants felt comfortable coming to Britain. They knew the sahebs and memsahebs. In those days there could not be any other destination outside India.

Many of them did not know much about Pritam Singh either. But he was one of the few unsung heroes who took upon himself to help these near stragglers to find their feet. Old timers, of whom very few are left, reminisce with pride about his pioneering efforts and personal sacrifices. It is difficult to imagine what the fate of these early immigrants would have been, or even of the generations that followed these carpenters and unskilled workers, if Pritam Singh had not taken upon himself to settle his fellowmen from Punjab.

The subsequent generations that followed them and attained success owe a lot to Pritam Singh, who, I am sure, as the last of elders fade would be forgotten. A flourishing community has little time to look back into the origins of its success.

The story of this semi-literate émigré, according to old-timers, from Taran Taran in Amritsar district was first told to me by the late Balwant Kapoor, a freedom fighter who himself came to Britain in early fities. Later Krishan Bhatia, who had come to Southall at about the time when skinheads and other right-wingers were up in arms against the Indians, stitched together the story from what he knew about or heard of Singh's background and his help to early immigrants.

Among a small batch of early settlers in Southall, Singh opened the first Indian grocery shop perhaps in early fifties there on the Station Approach Road, opposite British Rail's Southall Station, in a corner building. Now the offices of Britain's leading Punjabi weekly Des Pardes are situated there. A kind and helpful gentleman, he soon became known for his generosity, welcoming any new immigrant arriving from India or Pakistan.

Singh reportedly procured a near battered mini van, an eight to ten seater, and would religiously drive to Heathrow whenever a plane touched down from India. He would collect those who did not have any relatives or friends or some job offer and drive them to a small house, which came to be known as sarai (inn). It was in fact a transit home. The new arrivals were provided, free, roti, dal and a vegetable. Pritam Singh then got them work in nearby factories. Once they started to get wages, they were moved out.

'For any new immigrant to get employment the requirement of National Insurance Card was a must. Without it no employer recruited new hands,' said Bhatia. But Bhai Pritaim Singh was so resourceful that he would manage to arrange the National Insurance Card for the new arrivals within days so that they were able to start earning as soon as possible.

It is said that 10 to 15 lived in one room. There were very few toilets and they all pooled their wages for communal meals. Life was apparently tough, especially in winters. But they were a determined, hardy people. They had left behind their families with the promise to send remittances. Southall was then far off from becoming Little India.

These Indians found work in the same employment niches as West Indians, for example, 'in London hospitals, in the car and engineering industries, on the buses and trains and at the London airports' (Loury et al. [2005], 421). Some of their descendants could be seen at Heathrow even in the late eighties as cleaners and loaders.

Many also found employment in the more distant regions of the country, with municipal corporations, public transportation undertakings in northern cities such as Manchester, Preston, and Blackburn, as well as with British Rail (Loury, ibid). Northern engineering and metal companies in cities such as Sheffield, as well as the growing textile factories of Lancashire and Yorkshire were 'enthusiastic employers of Asian workers'.

As the number of arrivals increased, including family members, more and more Indian workers, both men and women, occupied jobs in the 'clothing and footwear industries of the East Midlands' making particular textile mills practically their own (ibid). In northern towns and cities such as Leeds, Bradford, Huddersfield, Manchester, Blackburn, Preston, Oldham, Bolton, Leicester, Nottingham, and Dundee, Indian and Pakistani labourers formed their own communities with the help of social and family networks.

After the Second World War huge numbers of manual workers from India were recruited in order to compensate for the labour shortage resulting from the war (ibid). Many of them were recruited to work on the railways as they did in India (ibid). 'Medical staff from the sub-continent was recruited for the newly formed National Health Service. These people were targeted because they spoke English and held qualifications which were recognized in the UK...(ibid)'.

The absence of agencies to organize immigrants from India was reflected in the problems they faced once in England, although with a large number of their people already settled, they did not need a Pritam Singh. It was far easier for them to get employment. But as they lacked education they could only get low-paid jobs.

Southall had begun to firm up and in Birmingham, Preston, Manchester, Lancashire, and north England cities Asian faces were beginning to become familiar. The news about the introduction of the Commonwealth Immigration Act 1962 (and later Immigration Act 1971) which largely restricted further primary immigration to the UK—although family members of already-settled migrants were still allowed to follow their relatives into the UK—triggered mass migration from India.

I met a number of Indians who became millionaires after they rushed to England before the restrictions came into force. According to The History of Asian Immigration 'The migration from India and Pakistan reached its peak in 1961 and 1962 with 49,000 and 47,000 people— most of them young males' (ibid, 420). Later in the 1960s their dependents would follow them and thus compensate the gender-related imbalance of South Asian immigrants.

The subsequent growth of the Indian community came from births. The number of Indian families increased but along with it grew resentment, especially in the young English, as jobs and housing were being increasingly taken up by immigrants. Racial discrimination led to humiliation and abuses, most settlers were regarded as scavengers and exploiters of the liberal society, although majority of the English were realistic and that helped.

Yet, the transition from the despicable discrimination these earlier generations faced chronicles a rather long struggle for rights and recognition. Krishan Bhatia, general secretary of the Indian Workers Association in the seventies recalls the difficult times for ordinary families. 'The fight back against discrimination and the effort to convince the English society that we were intelligent, hard working and innovative entrepreneurs was arduous. We wanted to prove that we were not angling for doles.'

Bhatia was involved in the tussle for getting legal status for the community. The information he gave me was a curtain-raiser to the difficult and complex situation in the sixties. He recalls them as extremely stressful years.

> *Having left their families behind, coming to a strange land with hopes of a better future, the immigrants in those days went through perhaps the most gruelling times.*

The immigration rules then were, although not as restrictive as now, such that many of the people arriving in the United Kingdom in search of job fell under the category of illegal immigrants. With the passage of time their number swelled so much that it became a complex socio-economic problem.

He recalled that because of their immigration status, the employers found them an easy prey, exploiting them to work for longer hours on measly wages. Separated from their families they worried about the future—whether they would be given permission to stay in the country or would they be compelled to go back. The uncertainties were sapping their energy and ability to work. Jobs were difficult to secure and Social Security benefits were not available to people belonging to this category.

This tricky situation continued for quite a number of years. It worsened in the latter part of sixties and early seventies when provisions of the new Immigration Act of 1971 were applied retrospectively, declaring immigrants who had arrived without valid authority as 'illegal immigrants'. This was the last straw, triggering widespread unrest among the immigrant community. Groups to lead resistance against such draconian rules spawned.

'Most of the immigrant organizations during the period were served by volunteers who had no resources, financial or otherwise, but were in fact a band of committed workers, concerned about the future of the people who had been in the United Kingdom for many years with sword of uncertainty hanging on the heads all the time,' said Bhatia.

It was about this time that the Indian Worker's Association of Southall (IWA) took up the cause of these distressed people. Many other organizations also mushroomed, but as it turned out IWA was most forceful and proved effective. It was led and 'run by a team of selfless, politically-motivated people who had been associated with various political parties back in India before migrating to the United Kingdom'.

IWA had some advantages. It owned a Cinema hall, The Dominion, by far the biggest of the few cinemas in the country showing Indian films at that time. 'The income from the cinema was all spent by the Indian Workers' Association on the welfare of community and the fight for a fair deal to it.'

The leaders of the Indian Workers' Association, championing the cause of 'illegal immigrants', did not limit their struggle to seek rightful status for people from India alone but worked hard to ensure that all those who had become victim of the retrospective effect of the Immigration Act, irrespective of origin of their country, were given leave to remain in the United Kingdom indefinitely.

A countrywide campaign was planned and launched. The IWA succeeded in involving in the campaign the Labour Movement, the Trade Union Congress, and a number of organizations of black community. Their struggle achieved a landmark success securing amnesty in 1975 for all those 'illegal' immigrants who had become victim of the retrospective provisions.

'The new 1971 rules contained a few provisions that offered certain relaxations to the "illegal immigration", but they were not put into practice because of the seemingly unwillingness and attitude of the Home Office bureaucrats. They were suspected of frustrating the cases of a large number of people applying to benefit from the amended rules'.

The discontentment boiled over when 16-year-old Gurdeep Chaggar was fatally stabbed, the first-ever racial murder, near the Dominion cinema in Southall. It ignited a nationwide agitation against discrimination. The IWA again intervened and took up the cause of those who were left in a lurch. 'A historic march was organization by it in co-operation with the Labour Movement, Trade Union Congress and several organizations of other communities, both black and white,' recalled Bhatia.

An estimated number of 20,000 from all over the country joined it. The demonstration was to start from the Hyde Park and was scheduled to terminate outside the Houses of Parliament. It was said to be the biggest gathering of ethnic community ever seen in London.

'Led by the IWA leaders and prominent Labour, Trade Union Congress, community leaders, it was joined by a number of MPs from all political parties,' recalls Bhatia. "The demonstrators had hardly marched through Marble Arch when the echo of their slogans seemingly reached the House of Commons.

'The then Home Secretary Roy Jenkins, declared Amnesty for all those who had arrived "illegally" before 1973, repealing retrospective implementation of the Immigration Act. Nearly 14,000 people benefited. Cases of majority of them were taken up and submitted by the Indian Workers' Association, without charging a single penny from the applicants,' says Bhatia with understandable satisfaction and pride.

The hapless immigrants of Pritam Singh days fought their way to legal status, in a country they had staked their future, with the help and encouragement of a legion of English liberals and politicians of all hues.

Another milestone in Indian immigration was the arrival of Gujaratis from East Africa. Their brutal ouster by Idi Amin in 1972 was set aside and the community just put its head down and dug in to make their home in Britain and revive their prosperity. Since they had British passports they could enter Britain easily. Their arrival changed the stature of the Indian community. Most being well-educated professionals, traders and businessmen they did not depend on doles.

Bhatia recounts, 'In the fifties and sixties it was impossible to get any jobs except in factories. The real breakthrough was made after Indians came from East Africa and started opening corner shops. The barrier was broken and small then medium-scale businesses mushroomed. The locals found the corner shop owners friendly and supportive. The social barriers began to crack.'

Lord Meghnad Desai was candid, 'They (those who came from East Africa) were not refugees. The British did not see or treat them as scavengers.' He added, 'The Gujaratis had a comfortable living in Africa. They were aspirational, educated, apolitical. Indeed it is in the seventies that Indians set on course to become the most successful and well-regarded of all other ethnic minority communities.'

They had all the qualities that the Tories appreciated, although for sentimental reasons most Indians were supportive of Labour. 'Indians were never demanding. No marches were taken out by them raising abusive slogans. Most had pride in themselves. These qualities were slowly recognized by the British and appreciated,' said Lord Desai. 'The word Paki was not meant for Indians. And moreover after 9/11 and 7/7 distinction crept between Indian community and other ethnic minorities.'

The 1971 social class profile of the white and ethnic minority populations (of males and females) show that Asian Indians were almost as successful as White people (op cit, 422). The other trait in the Indian community, especially among Gujaratis was preference for self-employment. By late 1970s and eighties, most middle-class Indians started to regard achieving social class status on par with the White people as the real success.

The importance of self-employment among Asian Indians, especially Gujaratis, grew.

> *The movement from unemployment in 1981 to self-employment in 1991 was made by approximately 17 percent of unemployed Indian women and by 20 percent of unemployed Indian men. In the 1990s this trend continued. (op.cit, 429-30)*

It is believed that 'through self-employment, Indian men and women experienced an upward social mobility during the decade 1981 to 1991…' (ibid, 429) In her 1995 Oxford case study, Research in Ethnic Relations series, Shaila Srinivasan found that Asian business-owner appreciated self-employment for 'culturally specific reasons'. They appreciated their independence and enjoyed an enhanced status within the Asian Indian community being a business owner… (Srinivasan, 1995, 86).

'The Indians preferred self-employment because, as Lord Desai said, education was a priority for Gujaratis who came from East Africa, and moreover, the second generation British Indians who had struggled and won the legal right to stay indefinitely, too, realized that education was the only way for upward mobility and integration. This stress on education and family tradition led to the immigration of Asian Indians becoming a success story.'

The move towards affluence had begun from the eighties but gathered pace with the arrival of Indian newcomers between 1991 and 2001. They excelled over Indians who had settled in Britain decades earlier, in terms of economic performance. 'These new arrivals are usually well-qualified and often find employment in IT and banking (ibid.). Therefore, 18 per cent of Asian Indian settlers who arrived in Britain during the last decade of the 20th century are 'high earners', earning more than 750 pounds a week, whereas only 7.9 per cent of earlier Asian Indian settlers do so (ibid).'

I was very happy to notice that the Indians in the UK are no longer considered a liability but are seen as irreplaceable contributors to Britain's economy. By and large, they do not live on social welfare, and do not indulge in unnecessary violence and demonstrations. Instead, they have proved to be major contributors in all fields. They are gainfully employed and work hard. The third generation is in most ways English—while retaining their distinctiveness.

There has seldom been any demand by the Indian community for either more privileges or for the English society to adapt itself to their social or religious customs. No separate parliament has been set up, because it is accepted by the community that they have to live within the parameters of laws and rules of their adopted country. No attempt has ever been made to impose their taboos and traditions.

It is now impossible to imagine England without Indians. What would happen to Leicester, if the Gujarati businesses in the Golden Mile, shut their shops, what would be the fate of Harrow, which enjoys prosperity because of the Indians there? What would happen to Tesco, Sainsbury's, Marks &

Spencer and Asda if Indian-origin women—most drive to work—who manage tills and supervise floors, left.

Lord Desai summed up, 'The India craze is good, it's more recognition of India, more recognition of Indian people and it's partly because of the recognition of the contribution of the Indians living here.'

Reaching the Success Post

It took nearly four decades, from the trouble-filled times of Bhai Pritam Singh, but now success story of Indians reads like a near fairy tale— of riches and acceptance as part of the national fibre. Undoubtedly, Indians are contributors to building of post-war Britain and making it one of the most industrialized and economically resilient countries.

The English and the Indians, I feel, should be obligated to each other for what Britain is today. My belief was further strengthened after studying the history of the post-war revival and rebuilding of England and the part Indians played in it. When the early batches of Indians came to post-war Britain— a war-ravaged land, with rationing of food, power cuts and shortage of labour— it was reeling under the havoc caused by German Luftwaffe. The future was uncertain. The Raj, the jewel in the crown, was slipping out after their two-hundred year-long rule. The sun had begun to go down on the Empire.

However, only a few decades later, Britain started to enjoy the feel-good factor that a thriving economy inevitably brings in. The country regained its stature internationally, despite the loss of colonies and its world ranking. The quality of life improved not only of the English, but of the ethnic minority communities as well. In the subsequent decades Indians went on to become the most flourishing community amongst all the ethnic minorities, a reiteration of their enterprise and entrepreneurship, glimpses of which were visible in their forefathers who came to England.

Architects of post-War Britain

The reason behind the awesome achievements and the acceptance, albeit grudgingly, of Indians, almost as equals today, I believe, is that the Indians who came or were encouraged to come, post-war, in a sense became associates at the basic level, in rebuilding the heavily bombed country. Ironically, however, glass ceilings inhibited them from gaining any social acceptance. They encountered deplorable living conditions, even then considered 'natives' by quite a few, but were needed as there was an acute shortage of workforce. They were as much a help in rebuilding the country as the English. That is why I feel that the Britain of today owes them too for the groundwork for what it became in the eighties when Margaret Thatcher started her long term. They also, if one looks back, possibly laid the foundations of the good relations India and Britain have now.

The Indians' success and prominence, which we all wonder at and admire, now, are essentially built on their contributions to the economy and equally due to the liberal, tolerant English society. It provided them the opportunity to prove their merit and climb up the social ladder. The racists are very much there but are fewer in numbers. "Anyone who has been to Britain will be aware of the huge role Britons of Indian descent play in the economy..." said Professor Paul Wellings, Vice Chancellor, Lancaster University. This is why I reiterate that Britain owes its remarkable accomplishments to both the English and the Indians.

The Indians, starting from the late fifties, helped create many iconic institutions. First, and most notable, was the invaluable role of Indian doctors and medical staff in the setting up of the National Health Service and nurturing it. It grew into a unique medical heath network, not to be found anywhere else in the world. People who return back to India from Britain know how wonderful NHS is. Here in India, any middle class person who needs regular medication has to pay almost ten per cent of one's salary. Anyone over sixty does not have to pay even for the prescription under the NHS. The old Indian GPs talk with pride about their input in running the surgeries under NHS. I saw the respect and goodwill Indian GPs have earned among their patients, even in the areas where most patients are British. In fact, once I suggested to High Commissioner Ronen Sen that the High Commission could interact with some Indian GPs. They do not need money or any such assistance but some recognition. I talked with a few of them and they were more than willing to help put to their patients the Indian stance on important issues, in right perspective.

The IT Indian professionals, one of the principal mainstays of the communications sector, financial institutions and operations in the city, have enhanced the respect for the talent and intelligence of Indians. They have bolstered the esteem which was earned by Indian-origin doctors and professionals. They have also raised the average income of the community, since they began to come to the country from mid-nineties.

Many Indian IT professionals, primarily from the south of India, set up their own businesses in Harrow, making many locals call the area they were clustered in as Harrow's Silicon Valley. I do not know whether they are still there or they have gravitated to bigger companies. I know that some of them went to Belfast where a huge call centre is run by an Indian company. Once I went to this call centre and was surprised that Indians were only in some supervisory and training posts. The entire operation was otherwise manned by the locals. The homogeneity was apparent. In fact one local girl asked me to take a few calls and she would help me answer the queries. I later learnt from Barry Gardiner, then ,minister for Northern Ireland, that the company was doing so well that it expanded further creating over 250 jobs for the locals.

In fact IT experts from India were in demand all over Europe. A German junior minister, I met while in Bonn, once rued that despite the 'most' alluring concessions to Indian IT specialists, they were reluctant to come to Germany. The IT graduates were offered permanent residency status within a short period of time and extremely lucrative emoluments. I explained to the minister that most preferred to go to the UK or the US, because of the language and also most had friends and relatives living in those countries.

Another factor that has made Indians almost an integral and vital part of Britain is the deluge of Indian companies into the country, along with acquisitions and investments, second only to the US. Many Indians told me how nice they felt whenever they saw the British prime minister pass by in a 'Tata' Jaguar, to find the Sunday Times rich list naming L.N. Mittal as the wealthiest person in the UK year after year, and to find scores of English people literally from the Who's Who present at Indian social and festive events like Diwali and charity dinners. They come happily because Indians by their useful role in all spheres of national life have developed homogeneity and close contacts with the senior politicians and corporate heads. The British media too has changed its editorial priorities, the news about India and Indians is carried regularly by all dailies, barring one or two. They have obviously their own reasons, possibly if you cannot criticise at least do not praise.

Some glass ceilings persist but they might not withstand for long the determination of the 'new' immigrants (the IT professionals) and the third-generation British Indians to breakthrough. They have accelerated the pace of assimilation and integration. New organizations have also spawned that have helped Indians to organize and become more visible and their voices heard. These forums also showcase their talent. The Indian success and prosperity has become discernible.

> "Many Indians told me how nice they felt whenever they saw the British prime minister pass by in a 'Tata' Jaguar, to find the Sunday Times rich list naming LN Mittal as the wealthiest person in the UK year after year, and to find scores of English people literally from the Who's Who present at Indian social and festive events like Diwali and charity dinners."

The doors of the most powerful and eminent in the Establishment and in the corporate sector are open to many, many Indians. Some of them have set precedents by becoming members of important British business bodies like the Chamber of Commerce or appointed to the Office of the High Sheriff of London, which was established over a 1000 years ago, much before the Norman conquest. Baroness Prashar was appointed member of the Lords Committee for the Appointment of Judges and later member of the War Inquiry Commission. Lord Navnit Dholakia was the first Asian to head a British political party when he was elected President of the Liberal Democrat Party. Indians were paid compliments for their useful role in Britain by Patricia Hewitt, chair of the Indo-British Business Council and a former cabinet minister. 'Britain has benefited enormously from the contribution that the British Indian community makes to its cultural, social, economic, political and sporting life.'

Govardhan Browns and Devdas Camerons

The increasing social interaction that followed riches and influence led to easy familiarity. Prime Minister Gordon Brown, a Scottish Presbyterian, happily became an honorary Hindu, taking the name Govardhan Brown, during a

> "The British media has changed its editorial priorities, the news about India and Indians is carried regularly by all dailies, barring one or two. They have obviously their own reasons, possibly if you cannot criticise at least do not praise."

Hindu Forum of Britain-hosted ceremony to mark the Diwali festival. He obviously knew about the festival of lights and goodwill and when and why Goddess Lakshmi is worshipped. He created history by lighting the diya to celebrate Diwali at 10, Downing Street.

The Tory leader David Cameron too was happy to be renamed Devdas Cameron at a function at Bhakitivedanta, Hare Ram Hare Krishna Iskcon temple near Watford. In fact, he remarked that having become Devdas he hoped to meet Aishwarya Rai (Paro in the film Devdas) when next in Mumbai. Unfortunately, he did not know that the Devdas-Paro romance ended in tragedy.

There is hardly any Englishman who does not know the Diwali festival, and Londoners even know what it signifies. Boris Johnson, Mayor of Greater London, speaking at the Diwali dinner hosted by Raj Loomba to raise funds for educating children of widows in India, said that his son and daughter knew all about the rituals and significance of the festival. I have cited these to illustrate how ingrained the diaspora and its culture is in the British life.

The Indian culture has been crucial in helping the Indian community in integrating in the British society as Calypso helped the West Indians. Earlier it had an exotic influence in films like My Beautiful Laundrette but now it is increasingly becoming part of the British cultural world. It could be seen so vividly and seemed a familiar feature in films like Bend It Like Beckham, East is East, while TV serials like Goodness Gracious Me and Kumars at Number 42 are part of the Coronation Street culture. Indian food is now regarded as part of the British cuisine. 'Foreigners' generally outnumber Indian diners at most top of the range restaurants. It is also nice to find mixed audiences at recitals by the likes of Ustad Amjad Ali Khan at Royal Albert Hall or at the Nehru Centre. In fact, events where Indian writers, poets or classical musicians and dancers participate seem to attract most English literati and cultural buffs.

Cultural Assimilation

Indians are also important influencers of Britain's pop culture. I always slow down at Selfridges whenever its in-store piped music resounds with the songs like Kudiye Bachch ke in between popular western pop. Who could imagine in the eighties an 'English' store celebrating Bollywood by revamping all its floors Bollywood style. Equally astonishing was the sale of a maroon kurta-pyjama worn by Amitabh Bachchan in the film Major Saheb for £700 and the sale of Dimple Kapadia's ornate bed for an astronomical price. The absence of the name of any Indian writer in the long or short list for Booker Prize is noted with some surprise.

Even now I often see Salman Rushdie's Midnight Children or Aravind Adiga's The White Tiger, which won him the Booker Prize in 2008, being read by commuters in the Tube or bus. Indra Sinha's Animal's People, which was short-listed for Booker Prize in 2007, was another widely read work. Dealing about the tragic after effects of the Bhopal gas disaster, it ultimately won the Commonwealth Prize. Many of us Indians were happy for him. Most knew that he had invested his life's savings in not only studying the misery of the families destroyed by the disaster but also in setting up a charity for their help.

In retrospect, I wonder why I never thought of studying and learning about the nightmarish experiences of the early immigrants during my years of posting in London. I used to go to Southall quite often to meet the late MP, Piara Singh Khabra, and his successor Virendra Sharma and other friends like Krishan Bhatia, who in fact briefed me on the early immigrants. Unlike now the pockets of Indians then were not bulging with notes and on top of it they were illiterate and could not reach the 'sahebs' who could have eased their difficulties.

As I sat down to write this book I realized that now life for most Indians is as good and comfortable as it is for most English. I never really felt I was in a foreign land. This feeling surfaces naturally in Europe and even in America. But in England, despite occasional racially-tainted incidents, no Indian is any longer uncomfortable. The young, of course, consider it their right to be there and are ever willing to fight for their rights as British.

Naturally, all about the early immigrants from India, the memories of the indignity and slum-dweller like treatment they faced in their efforts to acclimatise to the alien land, culture and people, and their struggle to overcome lingering prejudices of the British Raj about their supposed inferiority and backwardness have faded. Whatever bitter memories remained and haunted the older generation has been swept away by the approbation and even a bit of awe the diaspora has earned within less than 40 years. It is like a dream come true after a horrendous beginning.

At Home in London

London, especially, has grown on Indians, and Indians have grown on London. When I was once flying from Brussels to London, I had the same feeling that I used to have while flying from Kolkata to my home city Delhi that somehow the plane should reach me home early. I could only wonder how London became 'home'. It is no surprise then that for those Indians who are settled there, London or any other place where they are settled in England is home. I am unsure about Scotland, for I could not meet many Indians settled there, except for Bhashbi Fraser, poetess and lecturer originally from Bengal, and married to a Scot who is a lecturer too. She is settled in Edinburgh. Whenever I met her, I found her a typical Bhadralok Bengali, soft-spoken, very considerate and helpful. She surely is 'at home' in Edinburgh although I have a sneaking feeling that she would have been more at home if she was in London.

In fact, meet any Indian–origin MP or Peer or businessmen— they seldom talked about problems one encounters in a foreign land. They were more likely to discuss British politics, economy or gossip about the latest rumours. Most would ask me, as I represented an Indian newspaper, about politics or current affairs in India. At all private get-togethers or major dos most Indians look a contented lot, much at home.

This I noticed at one of the first Indian functions I attended, the annual dinner at the Portman Hotel by the Bharatiya Vidya Bhavan. I looked around in the huge hall to find that the number of prominent Indians on the Top Table was rather impressive—a minister of state, three Lords and Baronesses and two senior MPs, apart from an English minister and a Lord and two MPs. At other tables it was a mix of the English and Indian invitees. They all seemed to know each other well. The function was a blend of the East and the West too—toast to the Queen, toast to the President of India followed by an invocation in Sanskrit by Dr Nandkumar, Executive Director of Bharatiya Vidya Bhavan.

The food, apart from the Beaujolais Nouveau, Cabernet Sauvignon or Chardonnay, was all Indian. There were Kathak and Bhartnatyam performances. It all seemed so natural, as if I was attending a function not in Delhi or Mumbai, but in smaller cities. In these two cities I find more westernized than most events held during festive seasons in London; except the dress code: Black Tie.

Over the years I never felt like a stranger, whether walking in neighbourhood shopping areas like in Golders Green or Oxford Street reputed to be the street with the highest retail sale in the world. In fact, we would often try to identify if an Indian family walking by were Londoners or tourists. I wonder how I would react now when in London.

The reason for developing such a comfort zone becomes obvious if one goes back a bit about how they settled and took to different vocations. By late eighties, Indians had got into politics, academics, local governments, public utility services, educational institutions, and from the nineties they entered financial institutions, the city, in large numbers health services, the hospitality industry, retail and music. Indian drivers or Conductors in London buses do not get a second look. But, it is certainly noticed if the number of Indian young women, especially Gujaratis, is less some day at any retail outlet of Sainsbury's or Tesco. I have often asked at my local Sainsbury's where Malti or Dimple, the girls at the cash tills, were— if they were sick or something, if I would not see them for a week or so. I would similarly ask about Kirit Patel, its owner, greeting customers with a broad smile at the famous Warman Freed store if I could not spot him.

Indians do tend to talk with each other, even if they have met for the first time, exchanging notes about the places they came from and since when they have been living in Britain. Regular meetings at social or business events lead to familiarity, which makes one feel more at home. I found that because they are 'settlers', Indians are more friendly with each other—barring some NRIs who for no conceivable reason seem to despise each other. Since I lived in one area for years, most people in the market recognized me, even if they did not know my name. The Jewish couple that runs a launderette would always say hello, how are you, whenever we met on the street. At Yarok, a chain of vegetable and fruit stores, the manager, a Gujarati, would often discuss India and the senior cashier Ramila, a pleasant young lady, would invariably welcome with a smile and 'kaise ho'.

If I felt so much at ease in England, it is no wonder that the third generation would probably not even believe some of the stories I heard about the state of their grandparents and the treatment meted out to them when they initially came into the country. This is understandable. Having grown up with both eastern and western values, this generation of Indians live largely like their White peers. They favour a more independent and individualistic life over a traditional Indian family life.

Their most important task has been of compromising and adjusting between eastern and western values, between their cultural heritage and their British 'host's' culture. Most have accomplished that equilibrium admirably. They are indeed true British Indians and they are destined to take the diaspora success story to new heights. I met a few of such young people, L.N. Mittal's son Aditya, Joginder Sanger's son Girish, Gopi Hinduja's son Sanjay,

Raj Loomba's son Rinku and Ajitabh Bachchan's daughters, Namrata, Naina and Nilima all of whom are as British as any of their English counterparts while retaining their Indian identity. Sometimes I felt they were more into the Indian family culture than what I now see in Delhi. These ambitious, intelligent and hardworking young would surely break all the remaining glass ceilings soon.

THE NEW JEWS

The perceptive Lord Jeffery Archer once said, 'Indians are the "new Jews" and are taking over Britain. Now what you [Indians] are doing is what the Jews did 30-40 years ago when they came to England after the war.' True, I lived in a predominantly Jewish area and found that they were a very cohesive community— rich, adventurous and very modern but observed their rituals and traditions strictly. I used to see a family that lived next door to my house—extremely nice people—quite often doing prayers and reciting in a wooden shed in their back garden. It used to be lit up and decorated. There used to be many family get-togethers, possibly celebrating some festivals. I could easily relate their lifestyle to any well-to-do Indian family.

Lord Archer, thus, admitted by his observation, albeit obliquely, that the Indian community's incredible pace of upward mobility and its unbelievable achievements that gave it pre-eminence over all other ethnic communities earned them esteem and secured the acceptance that they are now indispensable.

I would reiterate the adherence to the customs and values of the country of their origin and the pride in their heritage as the greatest achievement of the Indians in Britain. Baisakhi in Southall is as festive and enthusiastically observed as in any Punjab city. The huge gathering on Diwali at the Swaminarayan Temple and the Bhaktivendata Mandir near Watford year after year makes me wonder how the young Indians, born and brought up in a western society, are so 'Indian'. At Puja time, idols of Durga are set up at various places, most prominent being at Camden and Hampstead Town Halls. There a large number of Bengali families and even non-Bengalis like, I used to go for prayers. Everyday from 'sapthami' (the seventh day of the nine-day navratri festival), some family or the other brings food for the entire gathering. The accent of the devotees is British, dress typically Bengali and the pundit recites in Sanskrit and the rituals are the same as at Kali Bari in Kolkata. All this sounds odd, but it does not appear incongruous to the environs of the city. Such adherence to one's culture while adjusting to the norms of the western society has, I suppose, given the Indian community an edge over some other ethnic groups whose identity has got blurred.

I remember an incident which was most instructive of the third generation. Darcus Howe, known for his acerbic comments, had discussed the episode of the stone idol of Ganesh taking milk at Channel 4 'Devil's Advocate' programme. Over 150 people were invited to the programme. When a comment was made denigrating multiple Hindu gods and allegation that all sorts of machines were set up in a long tunnel that had been dug during the construction of the famous Neasden-based Swaminarayan Temple, from which milk was pumped out, we were startled to see a young girl of around 19 or so jump up from her seat.

She spoke angrily protesting the denigration of her gods. She said she had never been to India but she would not tolerate insult to her faith. An engineer around 27, a Sikh, then joined her in protesting the remarks that had been made. I heard that this portion was edited from the programme telecast later.

This incident and many such others highlighted the general knowledge and intelligence of Indians. Lord Archer hit the nail on its head when he said, "They (Indians) are generally intelligent... (but) I don't think the indigenous population will put up with being exploited by them when they are short of bread but may well vote for them for the time being in the circus of a talent show, " during an interview with an Indian daily. True, they are more talented and able than the average.

Breaking of Barriers

The ability, grit and stamina to break barriers of prejudice, racism and intolerance are the main elements in their success story, a senior diplomat commented once. Despite Enoch Powell's infamous 'rivers of blood will flow' speech against immigrants, Southall graduated from being a 'Punjab Pind' to be a thriving part of Greater London. Wembley and Harrow are symbols of Indians' achievements in an adopted home. So are cities like Birmingham and Leicester. This could not have been possible without intelligence, hard work, ambition and the determination to succeed against all odds as the diplomat assessed.

But it has also to be admitted that the system they found themselves in helped too — it gave them the space, due recognition to merit and the opportunity to achieve and succeed. I would always remember what Gopi Hinduja told me once. He said, 'Have you ever wondered why those Indians who could not accomplish anything back in India could do well here.' The reason, he said, was that merit was recognized and encouraged in the British system without any extraneous biases and considerations.

'All of us who never queue in India at a bus stop, and never listen to the conductor's "no more please", never follow "keep in lane" rule, but automatically discipline ourselves here to stick to the rules. We can't become different just by coming here. It is the system that cannot be broken by 'sifarish or rishwat' that makes everyone rule-abiding and disciplined, the basics for success on merit.'

The truth in what he said can be found in what the generations that followed— carpenters, unskilled labourers and illiterate workers who came as first immigrants— have achieved in Britain. Is it possible, in India, for someone, like a simple graduate in refrigeration, employed in a plant to be able to own it in a couple of years and become a tycoon? Is it possible for one who used to cycle to give airline tickets to become a multi-millionaire in less than 30 years? Hopefully it would be in time to come!

The Gujaratis who came from East Africa added to the Indian success story. Their business acumen and industry revived Leicester. They also illustrated the resilience of the people of Indian origin. The shopping area called the Golden Mile because of the thriving business there, glows golden during Diwali. The county's premier daily the Leicester Mercury has pages full of news about the Asians.

It had to be from Leicester not surprisingly that a woman of Indian-origin was for the first time in Britain, elected Mayor. The Mayor, Manjula Sood, was born in Ludhiana and it was indeed a remarkable journey for her from there to Leicester. The politicians never tire of saying that people from India and those of Indian-origin who came from East Africa have 'played a huge role in changing UK into an all assimilating society, transforming it into multi-cultural nation'. They echo the truth.

Tony Blair recognizing what asset the diaspora was to Britain termed them 'British Indians' way back in 1996, while his wife Cherie describing India as a country that shares the democratic values of Britain, credited the nation for helping UK — through its migrants — transform into a real multicultural entity. She added pointedly, and rightly, that Britain of today was vastly different from that of the late seventies. It indeed is!

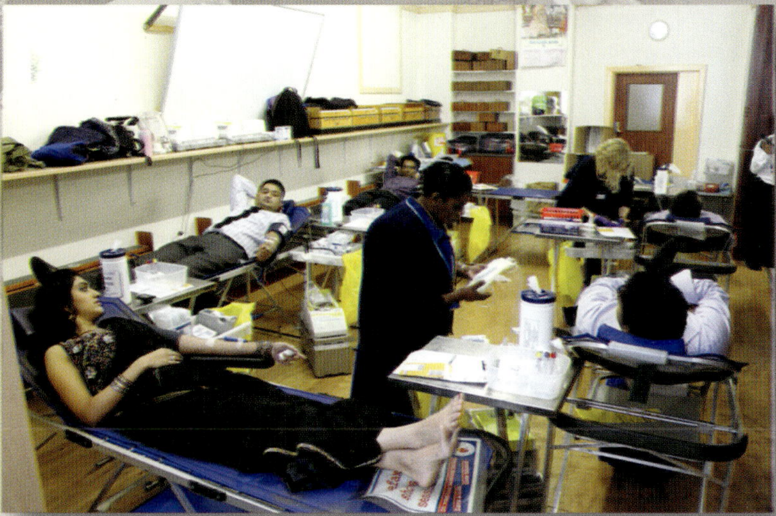

Blood donation: community contributing in every sphere

Cameron at puja: from David to Devdas

Tony Blair lighting Diwali Diya:
the festival has become truly national

Mayor Manjula Sood: A long journey from Ludhina to Leicester
(Pic Credit: Raju Vyas)

Diwali festival: Extravagant celebrations attracted the media

Could one imagine in the seventies or even the nineties that Asda, the supermarket chain, owned by Wal Mart, would be launching sales from its retail outlets of saris, salwar kameez and shawls under its George fashion label at comparatively cheaper prices, between £7 and £25. These Asda clothes could also be seen later on British soaps like EastEnders. The fact that a well-known High Street retailer embraced ethnic cultures to offer authentic Indian outfits at affordable prices, was another milestone in the fusion of the eastern and the western cultures in Britain. Cherie Blair was right about the country being different from the seventies.

Neither could one believe in the seventies and eighties that an Indian would own a house on Bishops Avenue in north London, known as Millionaires Row, with mansions of the likes of the Saudi princes in the neighbourhood. Or own a 'palace' in Kensington Palace Gardens, London's most expensive street, with ambassadors and high commissioners as his neighbours and the late Princess Diana's mansion within a stone's throw. Could one believe that an Indian family would buy a large tract of the Queen's estate in London or an Indian would be living in the exclusive and expensive Manor Park, for long the preserve of the English gentry?

Value Added Elitism

The Indians, quite a few of them, are now in the elite band— rich, influential and more essentially accepted as the upper class. Britain's new class of super-rich Indians has changed the British society in many ways. Their immense financial clout is obvious from the fact that Northwood, a quiet west London suburb, has become the country's first 'Millionaires' Row' and that too for a single ethnic minority — Indians. Homes worth more than one million pounds on Astons Road were being snapped up and then demolished to make way for mansions worth up to five million pounds, complete with indoor pools, sweeping marble staircases and extravagant landscaped gardens.

The popularity of 'The Astons' touched a new high, so much so that the very mention of the road's name was considered to impress both potential business partners and brides-to-be. According to locals, nine out of 10 new buyers on Astons Road were Indians, eager to take advantage of the area's respected private schools and some of the best golf courses near the motorway.

The wealthy Indians are naturally better known, their contributions are public knowledge and they wield considerable influence but I believe that there are innumerable silent, unsung "heroes" who have contributed no less to the British society and to the community. One has to just visit a surgery of an Indian-origin GP and it will be immediately clear how well they are regarded and the influence they have. They can be the best ambassadors for India and its interests because of their personal contacts with hundreds of people and the trust and goodwill they have built.

Many GPs in Birmingham, its suburbs like Walsall and Solihull, are active in community service and most sought after for important events. This is in fact true for most Midland cities.

The number of councillors and the growing number of mayors being elected is also emblematic of the near-complete acceptance of the community. The constituency of Middlesbrough and East Cleveland, which 1956-born Indian Dr Ashok Kumar had represented as Labour MP since 1997, has a minuscule number of Indian voters. Dr Kumar once told me he had the picture of Gandhiji on top of the main door to his constituency surgery. This 'Indian', a follower of the Mahatma, had been chosen repeatedly by the English constituents to represent them. Can there be a better example of the trust and esteem Indians have carved for themselves and the community?

In the report by the Government-appointed committee to inquire into the racial riots—the worst after two decades of Brixton riot— in north England cities like Bradford, it was noted that the least divide between the ethnic communities and the whites was observed in Southall and Leicester both Indian-dominated areas. The late Piara Singh Khabra, who represented Southall for decades in the Commons, reacting to the committee's noting said that it was not surprising that the Government realized that "we have been a stable society". The Sikh community in Southall and the Gujaratis in Leicester were not interested in causing trouble and were more focussed on education and their professions. This is true of almost every Indian family.

British Tolerance and Liberalism

The family cohesion and the respect for law, lauded by successive prime ministers, are the key to the rise to prominence of the diaspora in Britain, and to their indubitable success story. Their comfort level, as I said earlier, is astounding. This, I would repeat, is due to the tolerant and liberal British society, notwithstanding the racial incidents from time to time.

A Southall pub, the Glassy Junction, was the first to openly accept Indian currency for the pints, and no questions were asked. Many others on Broadway also do the same. Festivals are celebrated with as much abandon as in India, some within a stone's throw from Buckingham Palace or in Whitehall area near10, Downing Street, and no eyebrows are raised. Toast is raised at such functions for both the Indian President and the Queen. She was most amused and did not frown when residents of East London surrounded her during her visit in a cavalcade led by a chariot as part of her Golden Jubilee tour of England—mechanized elephants, Sikh drummers, women in their finest saris and salwar-kurtas thronged around her. The Times headlined its report on the visit, 'East End puts the pearl in jubilee crown'. Rather appropriate! Indians have indeed helped the homogeneity in the multicultural, multiracial Britain and are not only happy with its outcome but have benefited too. In the process many have moved from slums to millionaire's rows. And why not? They have worked hard. Others like GPs or smaller businessmen may not live lavishly, but are comfortably off.

The joke for some years now is that those Indians who make their first million want to own a Merc and those who have made a couple of millions want to be given Peerage. Many now yearn for Pravasi Bhartiya Samman. This is possibly a manifestation of their success in Britain and their ever increasing contribution to good causes back home. But it is also because they want more recognition and acceptance both by Britain and India. For they say openly they are both British and Indian.

More 'Samman' Please

I believe that the Indian Government should give more than one 'samman' to Indians in the UK and the US every year, not only because of their large presence in the two countries but also because they have been doing remarkably well in their adopted countries while keeping India's flag flying high. In recent years, there has been a race to be recognized by India and the Pravasi Bhartiya Samman or Padma Shri etc have become the route to fulfil this desire. Unfortunately, it has caused jealousies within the ambitious and the Indian High Commission gets unnecessarily dragged into their tussle. This is why I feel that more than one from these countries should be honoured, or do away with it.

However, the services of many of them do need to be acknowledged. Lord Navnit Dholakia fought and defended India's interest in the Lords while others like the late Piara Singh Khabra and Virendra Sharma took up cudgels for India in the House of Commons. It is also the efforts of Indian councillors, apart from those of some Indian diplomats in the nineties that the pro-plebiscite and anti-India lobbies, aggressively vocal until the late nineties, faded into oblivion. The MPs and a Lord who kept assailing India over Kashmir too were compelled to refrain from Early Morning Motions and interventions.

The NRIs might have in earlier years after liberalization been expecting too much from India. But now we in India should not regard them as too demanding and behaving— as once Yashwant Sinha, then India's foreign minister, remarked 'like sons-in-laws'. Having earned well in Britain, many have taken up good causes to help the under-privileged in India and have also been helping in setting up schools and improving living conditions in the regions from where their ancestors or they themselves migrated in recent years. They have spent millions in such missions, not because they were asked to but because they felt it was their obligation. Dr Karan Singh told me he could sense for some time that Indians abroad were likely to give back to India a share of what they have earned, because in the heart of their hearts they continued to feel for the country. He was absolutely right.

Many Indians I came across seem to get worried whenever some natural calamity affects people in India. Dr Murli Sinha, who is settled in Walsall for decades, was so moved by floods in his state of Bihar that he set up a charity to collect blankets, medicines etc. He was helped in this by the British too. Like in this case, the English have been very generous in helping the Indians who have charities for causes in India and the Indians too have been coming forward to contribute to causes in Britain. I would say that many Indians, through their contribution to their adopted country and to their natural home India, are now great assets to both.

It is possible that for some of my observations, I might be accused of 'native prejudice', but I have written what I genuinely felt over the years living in Britain. I do not claim that every Indian is meritorious or successful but that is true of a lot of them. They have done both the countries proud.

Why then should anyone in India or Britain (I mean the racists) grudge or be surprised if a large number of Indians in the UK have moved from slums to Millionaire Rows.

4

An English Springboard for Bollywood

> *Indian film is a phenomenon that in its ambition and inventiveness rivals the film industries of America and Europe*
>
> — *Ismail Merchant in Bollywood Saga*

The Queen hosting a party with Bollywood style dances and songs for Asian achievers at Buckingham Palace, the first ever, marked another milestone in Indian cinema's goal of captivating the world. Though known for her love for sticking to conventions that the Queen chose to make an exception for Bollywood was an acknowledgement that even the Royalty knows how much it has enchanted her people in the UK.

Britain has indeed become a Mecca for Indian films and the box-office collections in the UK are noted by the Indian film industry which considers it a benchmark for measuring the financial success of a film. It was news that *Rocket Singh*, heavily advertised in India could not collect much either in the US or the UK. That I am afraid made many in India decide not to see the film. This is true of every movie. I have written this to stress how much a success or failure of an Indian film in the UK decides the overall fate of a Bollywood production.

Many of its stars are in London more than even in Indian cities apart from Mumbai, where, of course, they live. Some like Shah Rukh own apartments. He never tires of saying how much he loves London and is happy to be there and how much welcome he is there. Karan Johar, one of the most successful producers and directors, reportedly stayed put in London while writing the story of Shah Rukh starrer *My Name is Khan.* Many films with big stars like *London Dreams* and *Namastey London* have been made with locations in the UK. It would not be wrong to say that Britain, in many ways, is an extension of Mumbai for film producers and actors.

All this has led to the impression that the country is sold on Bollywood movies. This notion is substantiated by the fact that box-office collections in the UK of Bollywood films are the biggest outside India. Most premieres are sell-outs; hysterical fans mob stars. More and more Indian films are shot on locations in the country—movies shot in London quadrupled from 10 in 2001 to 40 in 2006, and a further 160 films were shot at locations across Britain. The number of Indian films released in 2005 was 74 compared to 61 of those produced in the UK. The box-office collections keep breaking records.

The number of cross-over movies has multiplied too and more and more British actors have been flying to Mumbai for acting in Indian films. Any advertisement for selection of aspirants for a role in Bollywood films leads to long queues of all age groups and sizes—from lissom young ones to obese aunties. I once saw on television a lady pushing forty accompanying her daughter in her teens for one of the selections for possible roles in Indian movies. I thought she was chaperoning her daughter but to my surprise both went for the interview and screening. Indeed, the mother was the first to go. I need not say what happened! Like her, there have been many who present themselves for screening, hoping to fly to the fantasy world of Bollywood.

A film critic once told me that the temptation for hugging Shah Rukh, Salman Khan or Hrithik, blinds such women to their obvious lack of figure and talent. But now more serious and eligible aspirants have got an opportunity to hone their talent at Anupam Kher's academy which prepares and trains for a role in Bollywood. It is not surprising that it has a waiting list.

There never is, indeed, any need in Britain to explain what Bollywood means. The illustrated Oxford English Dictionary in 2003 incorporated for the first time the word Bollywood—a blend of Hollywood and Bollywood— finally recognizing the Mumbai film world and putting it on par with Hollywood. So anyone who wants to know what in 'cinema's' name Bollywood is needs to just check the illustrated Oxford English Dictionary. It was among the 500 new entries of 2003, along with Botox, Lap dancing and Viagra, and is accompanied by a picture of Aishwarya Rai (from the film *Devdas*) holding a lamp.

Bollywood: A Limited Appeal?

Despite Bollywood being so deeply entrenched and being a part of life and culture in Britain, I believe, from what I saw, that while it has had mesmerizing impact on the Asians—it provides an instant and easy link to their origins, heritage, values and family life—Indian cinema has enthralled only a minority of the English and it is nowhere near the enchantment of the west for the Indian cuisine. Only British businesses see in Bollywood pots of gold and in that commercial sense it dominates.

Anyone who wants to know what in 'cinema's' name Bollywood is need to just check the illustrated Oxford English Dictionary. It was among the 500 new entries of 2003... and is accompanied by a picture of Aishwarya Rai (from the film Devdas) holding a lamp.

This near-nonchalance of the English audiences is obvious from the fact that no Indian actor is ever mobbed while shooting near places like Parliament or Windsor where Asians do not generally go in large numbers. Once, I happened to be in Leicester Square in the early afternoon—when most tourists are not there— having fixed a meeting for coffee at a restaurant with a colleague. A film buff and critic, she spotted Salman Khan and Mahima Choudhry in the park. It was obvious that some movie was being shot. We went there and I found only a handful of Asians, about 15 or so, watching the shooting. They too were not acting crazy, chanting the actor's name or jostling him for an autograph. Later I learnt that it was a scene from the movie *Baagban*.

I have sometimes seen actresses in major High Street departmental stores, and rarely anyone approaches them. Once I spotted Rani Mukherji in the lobby of Sanger's Hotel Washington on Curzon Street in London. She was standing alone, no one was around to fawn on her or take an autograph. It is only Shah Rukh who, surprisingly, has an awesome hold on the Fraulein. I was witness to their adulation for him.

I was at a reception for the premiere of the Shah Rukh-starrer *Chak De India* at the Somerset House, a beautiful neo-classical historic building overlooking the Thames. It was a very upper crust affair with invitees from the Who's Who list. As could be expected, they were in formal dresses and conversing in muted voices while sipping champagne and relishing delicious Indian canapés. Suddenly there was a noisy distraction.

A horde of well-dressed middle-aged ladies were disgorging from two luxury coaches and moving towards the reception area, their faces flushed with excitement. The advance group asked anxiously whether he had come and gone, and 'have we come late?' On being reassured that 'he' had not come and that they were not late they were relieved enough to introduce themselves.

The forty-odd ladies were members of the German Shah Rukh Fan Club and had travelled across Europe and crossed the Channel to witness the 'historic' moment— the screening of the first Indian film at Somerset House and the first ever premiere outside India. The Fraulein then nudged past to arrange themselves along the red carpet, with champagne filled flutes. Their leader directed them to take vantage points. Shah Rukh was decidedly happy to see them. They were, one was told, the most devoted fans of the star, and we did not doubt that.

More followed to affirm the love affair with Bollywood and its leading stars. Almost 2,000 fans, most Asians except the faithful Fraulein, braved the chill to see the premiere of *Chak De India* which unlike other movies that are generally released in theatres was in open space. I am sure they waited patiently for two hours for the screening, because it was to start only after Shah Rukh was to come on the stage. Fans wanted to see him as much as if not more than, the movie. But obviously the non-Asians who came for the cocktail reception earlier had left.

The audience did not mind that the superstar made them wait. Sure of the loyalty of the fans the likes of Shah Rukh do not see the need for breaking the Bollywood habit of letting their fans sweat for their hero. So

> Films from Mumbai studios have successfully broken the language and political barriers between peoples of India, Pakistan, Bangladesh and Nepal.

apart from the music from Shah Rukh films, for over two hours, we heard his fans including the German ladies repeat the lyrics, clearly keeping in sync with the tune.

Breaking Ethnic Barriers

What that evening also showed was that films from Mumbai studios have successfully broken the language and political barriers among peoples of India, Pakistan, Bangladesh and Nepal. I remember vividly another incident that removed all doubts about Bollywood's harmonizing influence.

Journalists from the subcontinent based in Britain were waiting at the side entrance of Madam Tussaud's Museum for doors to open. We were there to cover the unveiling of his wax figure by Amitabh Bachchan. It was early morning, chilly and drizzling. We were huddled together under a small cover and chatting about Bachchan, the first Indian star to be chosen by popular voting for the installation of his wax figure.

It was there that one tall and slim person, claiming to be a Pakistani journalist, said loudly, 'I bet you all Indians here that none of you have the number of posters of Amitabh films as I have.' He in fact challenged any Indian anywhere to beat his record of over 2,000 posters of Amitabh movies. He added that he and his mother were the biggest admirers of the 'super star'. He had written on the posters the titles of each film and dates of release. We, the Indian media persons, were really amazed at his adulation for Amitabh.

> They were from Australia and had come to see London. The young girl had since the age of nine wanted to marry Salman. As I left I saw them move towards the exit to lay siege of the star.

I must also mention the hypnotic effect of Salman Khan, which goes beyond the borders of India. I met a Pakistani family at Madam Tussaud's as I came out after the unveiling of his wax figure by Salman Khan. They stopped me to ask why there was a crowd there and on being told that it was because of Salman, they seemed to freeze. 'Is he still here?' asked the daughter about 14 years of age. On being assured that he was still there, the girl told her father 'let's wait'. I learnt that they were from Australia and had come to see London. The young girl had since the age of nine wanted to marry Salman. As I left I saw them move towards the exit to lay siege of the star.

With such starry fascinations of Asians, it is easy, indeed, to believe that Bollywood has bewitched Britain. But in fact it has only captivated the over three million people from the subcontinent. Their number swells up with relatives and friends who come on visits from other countries and Asian tourists like the Pakistani family from Australia. But even then, unlike the kind of fan following a Raj Kapoor had in Russia or a Dilip Kumar in the Middle East, no contemporary Indian star has been able to enamour the English.

I would, therefore, reiterate that Bollywood has been unable to captivate the English. Only the Indian food can claim that. That in fact is a good benchmark to appraise the popularity of the two in Britain. The good Indian restaurants always have more English and European diners than Indians. But Indian films attract only a scattering of English audiences. The exceptions have been Gurinder Chadha's *Bend It Like Beckham* and Danny Boyle's *Slumdog Millionaire* and, of course, the evergreen Attenborough's *Gandhi.* But they all had what could be called the English connection. As far as I know even some cross-over films like *East Is East* that dwelt on the effect of the western culture on Indian families, could not attract what might be termed as sizeable number of the English.

The same is true about actors. English as it is are not generally as crazy about their stars as Asians are. In India, I learnt that there are hundreds of film magazines in almost all regional languages. All newspapers, except one

> In England, a Hugh Grant is seldom mobbed, a Julia Roberts gets admiring looks but nothing more, quite unlike the demented crowds of Asian fans that converge on Shah Rukh or any other Indian actor.

or two, have special pages for latest gossips and starry news. These stimulate young readers, and even the not-so-young ones, to go hysterical about the stars they fancy. We often read about how Preity Zinta was molested by crazy fans at some location or Bipasha Basu was allegedly groped at a temple. She faced a similar situation in Southall while shooting of *Dhan Dhana Dan Goal*. The rowdy fans, no need to tell, were of Asian-origin.

In Britain, on the other hand, most serious British papers have news about actors only when there is some 'news', like Liz Hurley going round with Arun Nayar or Jemima seeing Hugh Grant. Their antics in boudoirs are the preserve of tabloids. Thus, in England, a Hugh Grant is seldom mobbed, a Julia Roberts gets admiring looks but nothing more, quite unlike the demented crowds of Asian fans that converge on Shah Rukh or any other Indian actor.

I used the word demented because I do not think there is any other suitable world to describe the behaviour of some fans at functions where popular stars are present. Shah Rukh was literally mobbed when he was coming down the stairs in Nehru Centre at the end of a function. Luckily he did not tumble down because of his security men but it was a sight to watch the hoity-toity ladies pushing forty, trampling on each other to 'grab' him to get his autograph or get photographed with him.

At another film event in Grosvenor House the invitees were startled to see a lady on the wrong side of 60 sprinting like a teenager with a photographer in tow. She jumped on the podium where Amitabh Bachchan was speaking after receiving an award. The 'grandmother' bear-hugged a red faced Bachchan while the photographer captured the moment of her triumph. She was escorted away by security leaving behind a rather flustered Bachchan. It must have been amusing for Shweta Nanda to see her father embraced by an old lady. I think it was Gopi Hinduja sitting on the same table as I was who brought normalcy back by initiating a discussion on the strides made by the Indian film industry.

The one Indian star who has been widely focused by the British media and the English movie-goers is Aishwarya Rai, especially after the screening of *Devdas* at the Cannes Film Festival where her beauty left the onlookers breathless. She drew even more attention following the ad blitz for the film *Bride and Prejudice*, an adaptation of Jane Austen's novel. When rumours of her being cast in a new Bond film surfaced, almost every daily carried reports about her, informing readers that she had been Miss World and was one of the most beautiful women in the world. The media also informed their readers that she belonged to a traditional conservative family. This kind of detail is rarely given about Hollywood stars.

Tabloids described her as a virginal beauty, and one journalist asked me in all sincerity whether I had ever heard about her being kissed as she never allowed it on the screen. It did not surprise me that the Oxford Dictionary chose her picture from *Devdas* to embellish its explanation of the word Bollywood. I must say that she captivated the British media far more than any other star including Shah Rukh. For some months she was very 'special and newsworthy" for both English mainstream papers and the tabloids.

Shilpa Shetty, another Indian actress, became a household name in England and caught the attention of the British media not because of her acting or stature in Bollywood but basically because the English felt ashamed and developed guilt-complex after Jade Goody's infamous racial diatribe against her. Even Tony Blair and Gordon Brown welcomed her in Parliament to express their regret. Amitabh Bachchan is another Indian star who has been invited to dinner in Parliament.

I once attended his press conference in one of the Member's committee rooms, which was packed. He is the only other Indian known to a large number of people in Britain. I recall Jack Straw, a senior minister, saying in the House of Commons that he had just come after meeting a famous personality, Amitabh Bachchan. There are others who draw more crowds of fans than Bachchan but the crowds are basically of Asians.

This chasing and cheering of Indian actors by Asians has also given an impression that Bollywood has become part of the British milieu, but it is not entirely true. Yes, the people from the subcontinent love to see any film from Mumbai studios and adore the stars. Although lately, even the British Asians have become discerning. Reports were that the UK collections from films like Akshay Kumar-starrer *Blue* and Salman and Kareena's *Mr and Mrs Khanna* were poor. This was not very good news for Bollywood. It has depended on the Asian moviegoers in the UK to salvage films that did not fare well in India.

> The joint Hollywood and Bollywood movie planned to be made on Mrs Indira Gandhi or Sir Ben Kingsley's ambitious plans for the Taj are indicative of such a trend.

A few films that did not do well in India recovered money for the producers from collections in the UK. This setback could lead to a few films being made in Mumbai with the English audiences in mind. The joint Hollywood and Bollywood movie planned to be made on Mrs Indira Gandhi or Sir Ben Kingsley's ambitious plans for the Taj are indicative of such a trend.

Diversifying for an English Market

I tried to assess why Bollywood directors and producers, while attracting English and Hollywood stars, have not been able to draw English audiences. Even the famous ones like Kylie Minogue, who made her Bollywood debut in the scuba-dive caper *Blue*—dancing with its star Akshay Kumar—could not help bring in English film buffs to see the film. She was expected to breathe some fresh air and more importantly help box-office collections to rise.

Several other Hollywood icons have come to Mumbai, including Steven Spielberg, but for making films like *Slumdog*. He brokered a deal likely for his next film, the remake of *Harvey*, the classic 1950 tale of a man who befriends a giant invisible rabbit. It is said to be funded by Anil Ambani, who is now referred to as a movie Moghul. The two-way traffic of business between Bollywood and Hollywood does seem to be picking up. Since Danny Boyle's award-winning *Slumdog Millionaire*, the British too are looking into 'possibilities' of fame and success from films based on Indian themes. The fall-out of the world success of Boyle's movie totally shot in Mumbai with an unknown cast has reportedly made Indian producers, too, to conceive of films that would attract non-Asians as well.

The forays by young directors to America and Britain for shooting films and then taking the initiative of interacting with English audiences is another good omen for Indian movies reaching beyond the diaspora. I once met director Tanuja Chandra at a dinner at the residence of Monica Mohata, Director, Nehru Centre. She struck me as an imaginative film maker. She appeared to have the ambition and courage to try to break (and succeed) the conventional mould, risk being adventurous and reach the audiences untapped so far, all without money in the pocket.

She was in London in connection with her new film *Hope and a Little Sugar*, which was screened at BAFTA theatre, a matter of pride for any film maker. Mahima Chaudhry who acted in the film was also there. The question and answer session after the screening with an audience mostly English showed

> Tourists from the world over thronged the store and saw the glamour and extravaganza of Bollywood in the best of environs. The fantasy about India had been translated into objective reality. Bollywood at Selfridges was indeed Bharat Darshan, 'filmi-style'.

that they could be lured to see Indian films—as much as Indian audiences accept foreign movies like *Slumdog Millionaire*. Snoop Dogg had become the first hip-hop artist to contribute to the Hindi film *Singh Is King*. 'This is just the beginning. I'm coming to take over Bollywood,' he had said at the time.

Mahima was asked, 'What gives you hope?' after the screening of *Hope and a Little Sugar* at the BAFTA theatre in London. She did not give standard philosophical answers, instead said, 'My little daughter. She has brought back my innocence…if that's still possible, after having a daughter!' The predominantly English audience burst into appreciative laughter. She and director Chandra were, as it is, feeling happy at the warm response to the film. Tanuja recalled, 'We had a packed house, much of which surprisingly, was non-Indian.'

Then again Mahima was disarming with her kissa kiss ka (story of the kiss). She had everyone giggling away as she related the kissa of the kiss. It is such funny little anecdotes that are liked by western audiences, especially in Britain. She narrated,

> *I was in a relationship with someone when I was approached for this film, so I was uncomfortable kissing on screen. Tanuja was in talks with a few other actresses as well, who incidentally did not have problems with the kiss. However, her producers changed and things didn't work out with those actresses. And coincidentally, my relationship too broke off! So upon finding out that Tanuja hadn't finalized a heroine, I called her and announced, I am ready to kiss! And so, I sit in front of you today, gathering accolades all because of a little kiss!*

The audience clapped at Mahima's wit. They felt disappointed that the film did not find a distributor in the UK.

When I asked Tanuja what kind of Indian films could attract English movie goers and how, this is what she had to say.

> *(Most mainstream Bollywood films) are made primarily for Indians here and abroad. They're not pitched to the tastes of Western audiences. Bollywood is a huge, sturdy, self-sufficient film industry that does not depend upon foreign territories for its survival, other than the NRI community abroad, which is huge too.*
>
> *But, having said that, I would add that lately film makers have taken an interest in making diverse kinds of cinema. Some of which are the kind that Western audiences like too. These niche films cater to those tastes. Other than that only films by Mira Nair or Deepa Mehta are made for English or European audiences. Mine too was one of those because it was made in the English language and produced by Americans. But by and large, our Hindi films or regional films are made for Indians.*

She suggested that if Bollywood film makers 'would like to gain the non-Indian audience too, which no doubt is huge, they will have to give up on some of the Indian film conventions, which they might not want to do. Even a film like *Lagaan* which was nominated for the Oscars wasn't typically the kind that mainstream American or European viewers would flock to.'

> *So it's really a creative choice. It's the same reason* Slumdog Millionaire *was a bigger hit abroad than in India. Basically it comes down to a creative decision, and most Bollywood film makers are happier making films for Indians. I personally find it exciting to make both kinds. Ones that may be more off-beat and find takers abroad, as well as those that primarily Indians will like. I would not like to be limited to any one kind. However, I can recognise the simple fact that since my experience of life and sensibility comes largely from an "Indian" upbringing, any work that I may make for an English audience cannot have an indigenous feel of a Western country. So my subjects will necessarily have to be about Indians abroad or the style will have to be less Hindi film, without song and dance or melodrama, but the subject matter will probably deal with Indians.*

Marketing Strategists' Bolly Dream

It is a different story in the marketing and advertising sector. Bollywood is a magical wand to seduce the Asian community that has been growing in prosperity. So, utter the word Bollywood and British businesses start dreaming of and calculating commercial gains. The marketing pundits and advertising strategists have read rightly that with the increasing purchasing power of the Asians, the best bait for them to induce them to lighten their wallets is through linkages with Bollywood.

The British Tourism Authority realizing that Indian tourists—who are Bollywood addicts and spend more than the Japanese (approximately 300m pounds) — printed for its 'Visit Britain' campaign a *Bollywood map of Britain*, detailing 22 locations used for 30 Bollywood hits. A Scottish company immediately began offering holiday packages taking in tours of film locations.

I learnt that over 50,000 Bollywood location maps were distributed not only in India but also in the Middle East. This map details many known and some lesser-known locations. Among the lesser-known were an obscure Surrey football ground (for a scene in *Bend It like Beckham*) and a Slough Queensmere shopping centre (backdrop for a scene in *Yaadein*). It also showed Bicester Village shopping centre in Oxfordshire, which featured in the 2001 film *Kabhi Khushi Kabhie Gham*, and Dolbadarn Castle in North Wales, used in *Kyun Ho Gaya Na*, in 1998. Apart from 'traditional' locations like Windsor Castle, Trafalgar Square, Tower Bridge and Princes Street in Edinburgh were also shown.

The map was released at the International Indian Film Academy (IIFA) in Sheffield. It helpfully gave details of how to reach the locations and places to stay. The BTA said, 'Britain's popularity as a Bollywood backdrop can only help us raise our profile among this growing audience and we are confident that this campaign will help them to see it as Bollywood Britain.'

The initiative for the map campaign was supported by Shah Rukh. It is significant that, in this connection, a daily considered Shah Rukh being called King Khan by his Asian fans, news—for hardly any English cinema-goer would know about his 'kingship of Bollywood'. This testifies to what I said in the beginning that it is the Asians who with their passion for Bollywood movies and adulation for its stars have created the impression that Indian films have enamoured the whole of Britain.

Salman with "Salman" at Madam Tussaud's

Slumdog Millionaire: films based on Vikas Swarup book

Fans shout for Shah Rukh at London premiere of
Om Shanti: Indian films' premiere draw huge crowds
(courtesy Eros International)

Tanuja Chandra with Mahima

Kher taking a class

Bollywood allure: Anupam Kher with students of his academy

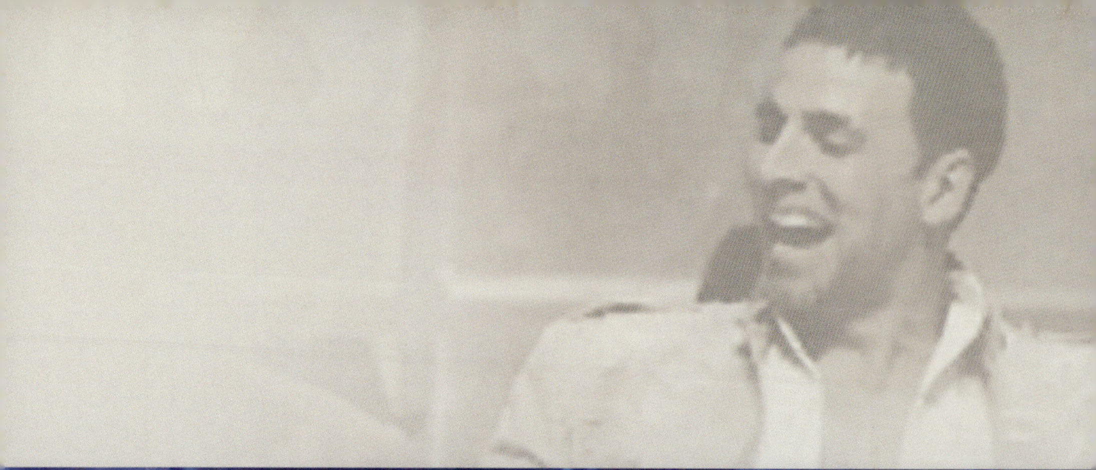

Akshay Kumar with Kylie Minogue: she could not lift the film

I did go to a village where some scenes of the Amitabh-starrer *Mohabattein* were shot. The local pub imbibers seemed to have been very happy with the crew members, who they said used to drop in occasionally and were very friendly. 'They were quiet and nice.'

During the British Film Institute's Asian festival, tour operators courted Indian visitors offering personalized tours of the Lake District— which was the location for the big budget production, *Mujhse Dosti Karoge*. Ideas had also been developed for Bollywood-inspired Indian marriage and honeymoon packages in the Highlands and Windsor, but that did not take off as much as was presumed.

High Street B-Celebrations

Another milestone of Bollywood's grip on the commercial sector was reached with the upmarket departmental store Selfridges in Oxford Street deciding to hold a three-week long 'Bollywood Celebration'. It radically transformed all its floors showcasing Indian cinema and its stars. During the period over a million people—many Asians arriving in special coaches—visited the store. The management was in high spirits. Its managing director, James Bidwell, said, 'What we have is the authentic Bollywood experience, fantasy made even more thrilling by the possibility that the real thing may be close by.'

Executive director of the store, Vittorio Radice, added, 'Everybody has access to the world of dreams of stars and celebrities, of impossible love and extraordinary riches. And just as everybody has access to these dreams through the silver screen, at Bollywood at Selfridges is a scene for people of all ages, and all tastes, to wonder at for free'. He proved right.

Asians proved to be avid addicts and were thrilled to see the bed and wardrobe of Dimple Kapadia, taste special dishes prepared by the chefs of the Taj Hotels, who were flown from India and looked at antique jewellery, lehangas, cholis and chunris from Rajasthan, colourful tiklis, bangles and saris from Bengal, Maharashtra and South India. A red kurta worn by Amitabh Bachchan in *Major Saheb* was another great attraction and someone paid 700 pounds for it. A Rajasthani antique jewellery shop-owner stayed back for a few months. He told me that interest in his items was tremendous. So was the interest in the mehndi stall. A few girls were there for quite some time. They charged five pounds for each palm. One could see the excitement on the faces of ladies, even European, getting designs drawn on their palms and even arms.

'Bollywood at Selfridges' was a story of consumption and fantasy, said a columnist. 'Capitalizing on the notion of fantasy and play, Selfridges recruited new and existing consumers to partake in a Bollywood adventure by playing off the appeal of consuming films.' Authentic dishes from various regions of India, clothes and curios, in fact name anything from rural or urban India, it all was at display.

It was the best promotion Bollywood could imagine. 'This event shows the reach of Indian cinema across the globe,' said Amitabh Bachchan. True, tourists from the world over thronged the store and saw the glamour and extravaganza of Bollywood in the best of environs. The fantasy about India had been translated into objective reality. Bollywood at Selfridges was indeed Bharat Darshan, 'filmi-style'.

Amitabh Bachchan, Dimple Kapadia and Madhuri Dixit came for the opening and Hirthik Roshan, then at the peak of his popularity following his film *Kaho Na Pyar Hai*, came later to perform. The sequences of dances, star visits, and music kept crowds coming in. The celebration's legacy included old Indian film songs and Punjabi pop music which became a regular on the in-store piped music system.

B-Manna for Media and Advertisers

The British mainstream papers and advertising agencies are other beneficiaries riding on the Bollywood wagon. *The Times* started with Bolly news, reviews and gossips, titillating and glamorous pictures on its online edition, and it has drawn Asians to claim record hits. The information on it is really update and upfront and no-holds-barred. *The Telegraph* followed and BBC too went in for it in a big way. The Asian publications have a number of pages devoted to Indian cinema and stars. But most, except one weekly, which has an editor looking after its cinema pages, generally carry syndicated reports. If you have read gossip in one then you do not have to read any other Asian publication.

The successes of Indian film festivals, increasing number of releases of Indian films and many getting into Top 10 lists—not only led to big theatre chains like Cineworld, Veu and Odeon assign one of their screening halls for Indian films— in fact in Leicester one theatre screens only Indian films—but enthused advertising agencies and potential advertisers to use Indian films and stars to lure Asian buyers. Aishwarya Rai's face could be seen on the adverts for *Bride and Prejudice* mounted on the sides of London's red buses plying even in Central London. Madam Tussaud's marketing team hit upon the idea of installing wax figures of Indian actors to attract not only the Asians in the UK but also tourists from the Middle East and the subcontinent. A spokesperson told me that the number of Asian visitors increased significantly after the unveiling of Bachchan's wax figure.

His wax figure and that of his daughter-in-law Aishwarya Rai and Bollywood colleagues Shah Rukh and Salman Khan now stand along with Brad Pitt and other all-time greats of the cinema world. The scene in the 'Garden Party', which a visitor sees first on entering the wax museum, with a frock-coated waiter offering a glass of wine at the entrance, is so realistic that many are momentarily foxed and think of picking up the wine glass.

As one admires the wax figures of the great and beautiful stars, with many getting photographed along with Elizabeth Taylor, Hugh Grant or our own Aishwarya Rai, one realizes that films are the universal medium binding people together.

Hollywood's El Dorado

The English or Americans might not be obsessed like the Asian fans about Indian films but the global impact and influence of the Bollywood brand has set on course Hollywood and others in the west on a long love affair with Bollywood, for they believe that it is the real El Dorado for them. And I think for this Britain has contributed significantly. Danny Boyle's *Slumdog Millionaire*'s eight Oscar awards, the sweeping at BAFTA and huge box-office collections along with several other Indian hits– *Slumdog Millionaire* was 14th in gross collections in the world in 2008, *Ghajni* 117th with 38.3, *Rab De Banadi Jodi* 130th with 29.5, *Singh is King* 132nd with 29.32 and *Jodha*

"...the global impact and influence of the Bollywood Brand has set on course Hollywood and others in the west on a long love affair with Bollywood, for they believe that it is the real El Dorado for them. And I think for this Britain has contributed significantly.

Akbar 139th with 26.9 in a table of 500—impelled the best directors and production houses in the west to look at India and Bollywood. Many of them want to make films with Indian themes and locations. This pursuit has also changed and will continue to change the western view of India and its people.

Anurag Kashyap's *Bombay Velvet*, being presented by Danny Boyle, and Paul Schrader's *Extreme City*, to be produced by Bollywood director Anubhav Sinha, is inspired by success of *Slumdog Millionaire*, but its focus had reportedly shifted to more timeless aspects of India. A documentary was also made by an Australian filmmaker *Yes, Madam Sir* on India's first woman police officer Kiran Bedi, whose sincerity and courage clashed with the authorities wrapped in red-tape.

The Dutch-born French filmmaker Jan Kounen made *Darshan— The Embrace*, which extolled the healing power of touch as demonstrated by Kerala-based spiritual leader Mata Amritanandamayi, known to her followers around the world as Amma. In 2006, veteran French director Benoit Jacquot's *L'Untouchable* told the fictional story of a young Paris actress who learns that her father is a low-caste Hindu.

The fascination for spirituality and search for peace brought to India known producers who have been making films from adaptations of novels based on Indian philosophy. Julia Roberts, with her three children, their nannies, eight cooks and sturdy security men stayed for a fortnight at Pataudi Palace, near New Delhi, for the India leg of the shoot of Ryan Murphy's *Eat, Pray, Love*, an adaptation of writer and journalist Elizabeth Gilbert's 2006 spiritual travelogue of the same name.

Searching for inner peace after a contentious divorce and a bout of depression Gilbert had gone to Italy, India and Indonesia on a year-long voyage of regeneration. Julia plays the protagonist who spends many months in a Hindu ashram to master the art of meditation. Many of her scenes were shot in an ashram there. The priest gave her the name Paravati and likewise her children were given Indian names, Balram Krishna, Laxmi and Ganesh.

> Many of her (Julia Roberts) scenes were shot in an Ashram there. The priest gave her the name Paravati and likewise her children were given Indian names, Balram Krishna, Laxmi and Ganesh. Julia learnt to eat simple dal, rice and vegetables with her hand and chant Sanskrit shlokas.

Julia learnt to eat simple dal, rice and vegetables with her hand and chant Sanskrit shlokas. She endeared the hotel staff by her no starry-nakhras that the Indian actors are notorious about. A paper, in fact, reported how an Indian star came to stay in the hotel at the same time and was whisked away to her suite by her security guards.

New India through Films

The well-known film writer and critic Saibal Chatterjee rightly observed that 'regeneration, spiritual and otherwise, seems to be the new buzzword driving the Western gaze on India'. He also pointed out that several films at the 34th Toronto film festival showed India in a new light. 'Western filmmakers are increasingly tapping India for inspiration and locations and perceiving it in a new light. ... a spate of new films is going beyond the much flogged India-as-a-land-of-slums-and-squalor syndrome.'

He mentioned three major films which were in the official line-up of film festival— *The Waiting City* (Australia), *Google Baby* (Israel) and *Cooking with Stella* (Canada) — that narrated Indian stories while eschewing the clichés associated with the country.

He contrasted the old cinematic view of India and its society with the prevailing modernistic values. He noted, '*The Waiting City*, written and directed by Sydney-based Claire McCarthy, is set in bustling, chaotic Calcutta (Kolkata). But it is a far cry from Roland Joffe's 1992 cinematic rendition of Dominique Lapierre's *City of Joy* and Nicolas Klotz's *La Nuit Bengali* (1988), based on Romanian philosopher Mircea Eliade's doomed love affair with a girl from an aristocratic 1950s Calcutta family.' Chatterjee quotes McCarthy, '*The Waiting City* is like a love song to Calcutta, one of my favourite cities in the world....I was determined from the very outset not to perpetuate Western misconceptions about India.'

> Britain has indeed been, to sum up, the gateway for Bollywood's overseas gold rush. Directors and actors like Shekhar Kapur and Kabir Bedi have become an integral part of the British film fraternity.

Renowned photo-journalist Dilip Mehta, a Canadian citizen of Indian origin and director of *Cooking with Stella*, was also mindful of how he was going to project the city of his birth, New Delhi. 'I was sensitive to the images of this city. I wanted to show a rather different India ...Of course poverty and despair are huge parts of life in India…but that is not the world that *Cooking with Stella* sets out to explore,' he told Chatterjee.

'With the culturally condescending, poverty-fixated, cliché-ridden Western vision of a populous nation of a million contradictions undergoing marked dilution, a new India is beginning to emerge in the cinema of the world.' This is the most pertinent observation made by Chatterjee in an article published by many papers including BBC online.

This new trend in the west of presenting India's spirituality, deep-rooted belief in the triumph of good over evil and optimism despite hardships and above all the story of the emerging India would not only give the world the correct perspective of the contemporary India and its people but could supplement the efforts of some Indian film-makers to put across to the world the changing social values and ethos of the young Indian.

The highly successful *Kabhi Khushi Kabhi Gham* and *Hum Dil De Chuke Sanam* show the traditional, patriarchal family and the Indian women in the evolving society while films like *Kabhi Alvida Na Kahena* show India's international jet-set, dilution of middle class hypocrisy and the courage to try and live one's life according to one's own desires and rules.

Going Global

Excess and success have an incongruous linkage. Bollywood's success in Britain and generally in the west has much to do with the excess flow of funds and inflow of investments from overseas that followed liberalization in the nineties which enabled producers to invest in best technology and come out with films that competed with Hollywood films. Then the extravaganza of colour, music, themes based on family traditions, overdose of emotion that evoked nostalgia, foreign locales and hero in the west falling in love with a desi heroine, immediately connected with the diaspora. The likes of *Dilwale Dulhaniya Le Jayenge* and *Pardes* brought Asian audiences repeatedly to cinema halls. I heard that *Dilwale* has been running for 14 years in a cinema hall in Mumbai in the morning and matinees shows, and the ticket price is what it was 14 years ago. Old people come to see it, impelled by nostalgia and the younger ones come to see the young Kajol.

Bollywood producers were thrilled to find its films a favoured product in the affluent NRI market earning it huge amounts of hard currency. They realized that it was the opportune time to go globe-surfing on the crest of the wave of prosperity of the Asians abroad. The linkage was clearly evident in the excited voices of some at Odeon when they saw Bluewater Shopping Complex in *Kabhi Khushi Kabhi Gham*, just like back home we are thrilled to see in some movies familiar landmarks in London. In *Baagban*, when I saw a song sequence of Salman Khan and Mahima Choudhury, I too was thrilled to recall that I had seen the shooting in the park in Leicester Square while I was going to meet a friend for coffee.

Producers, because of the growing global market and some NRIs putting in money, developed the financial viability to shoot more and more overseas. *Kabhi Kushi Kabhi Gham* or *Mohabattein* were shot for weeks in England, which could not have been possible in the seventies. Several films from the mid-nineties have also been largely, or entirely, shot in New York, Los Angeles, Vancouver and Toronto. The west is keen to welcome more Indian productions.

Leicester University has been trying for years to induce Indian producers to use its studio. It promised to provide the latest technology, state-of- the-art studios, facilities like best cameras, cameramen, editing facilities and extras too from the huge population of Asian in Leicestershire. It sent a team to Mumbai for negotiations. 'The director could come with the hero, heroine and a few leading actors and we will take care of the rest,' said the team leader to me. 'We have all the technicians and extras needed and would arrange stay at the hotels and transportation at discounted rates.'

It is thus natural that the overseas circuits are most prized, and Britain, despite being just an island beats America in box office collections. I would say that Britain and the Asians there have provided the base for Bollywood to boldly venture internationally.

Several NRIs in Britain continued to finance and also shared in the distribution of films. The Indians present at the mahurat of Subhash Ghai's *Yaadein* in London were easily worth over 25 billion pounds. A few had interests in distribution and some in financing Bollywood films.

Global Bolly-influence

The new millennium was a major milestone in the growth of Bollywood's global popularity. A few in the industry confirmed that in the 2000s, Bollywood began influencing the western world. 'This helped the nation's film-making to attain new heights in terms of quality, cinematography and innovative story lines as well as technical advances such as special effects, animation etc,' said a well-known critic. Films like *Devdas* and *Koi Mil Gaya*, amongst others, won critical acclaim for photography and special effects—as good as the best from Hollywood. I remember how producers, critics and stars at Cannes Film Festival went berserk when Aishwarya Rai arrived for *Devdas*'s screening in a colourful Indian costume.

The commercial value of crossover films has further firmed up links between Bollywood and Britain. Quite a bit of connecting and familiarization of Bollywood to non-Asian audiences was done through songs and dances by Lord Andrew Lloyd Webber's Bollywood-themed musical *Bombay Dreams*. A.R. Rahman who provided music became an international maestro— Lord Andrew told me even before the opening of the musical that he was the best composer in the world. Parminder Nagra, the heroine, was grabbed by America. Dilip Tahil also in the musicals got a major part in the *East Enders*, BBC's most watched soap opera. I found him mostly living in London and so much work started coming his way.

The predominantly English audience on the opening night of *Bollywod Dreams*—including the likes of Peter Mandelson— was an indicator of how it would percolate the magic of Bollywood into the higher echelons of the British society. It was the first Indian-themed musical in the West End but was lapped up by the notoriously snooty and critical English audiences. The gates opened and a musical version of *Hum Aapke Hain Kaun* also played in London's West End.

It is thus nothing surprising that the awareness of Hindi cinema is far more in Britain, albeit the English are yet to be lured to theatres. But, the fact that many Bollywood movies are dubbed in German and shown on the German television channel RTL IIRTL II could be one of the reasons for Fraulein's love for Shah Rukh.

Britain has indeed been, to sum up, the gateway for Bollywood's overseas gold rush. Directors and actors like Shekhar Kapur and Kabir Bedi have become an integral part of the British film fraternity. The reason for such a ' magnificent obsession' for Bollywood films and the people from its world, I would say, is that in all its evolutionary and transitional phases it has stuck to 'emotion', its most precious story ingredient. It needs no words and thus has helped break the lingual, political and geographical barriers. The audiences in the west yearn for emotional support, which Bollywood films portray in ample in colour and music.

Bollywood in the UK: Key Facts

United Kingdom has the largest audience for Indian cinema outside India according to Neilsen EDI. Of the 527 films released in 2008, 76 (14.4 per cent) were from India, while films of UK/UK co-productions were 82 (15.6 per cent). But, almost 16 per cent of all films released in the UK in 2005 were Indian films. This was higher than the number of British films, approximately 13 per cent.

Bollywood films grossed £12.4m in the UK in 2005, up from £8.1m in 2003. This was 1.4 per cent of the gross UK box office in 2005, a niche certainly, but higher than the total box office of all European releases combined (UK Film Council). But, box office collections from Indian films in the UK and the Republic of Ireland witnessed a minor slip in 2008 accounting for 1.4 per cent of the total collections in this region in 2008, from a 1.6 per cent market share in 2007. Collections from Indian films in the UK had peaked in 2006, when its overall collection accounted for 1.8 per cent, according to the UK Film Council Statistical Year Book 2009. Movies made by US production houses, which accounted for 65.2 per cent of total gross box office collection in 2008, also slipped from the 2007 level of 67.7 per cent.

Bollywood produced 11 of the 20 most successful foreign-language films released in the UK in 2005. UK Asians are big cinema consumers, with 42 per cent going once a month or more Apart from the US, India is the only country to be listed in this year's book as a standalone category on the basis of films' country of origin.

Shah Rukh Khan starrer, *Rab Ne Bana De Jodi*, was the second largest grosser (£1.5 million) among all foreign films released in the UK and Ireland, followed by *Singh is King* (£1.4 million) starring Akshay Kumar. In fact, films with Indian origin or co-produced by Indian production houses accounted for half of the top 10 grossing foreign films in the UK and Ireland in 2008.

Global Ranking in the UK

According to a report, notwithstanding the popularity of Indian movies in the UK, the Indian film industry ranks low among its global peers. At 2.1 per cent of the global box office collection, India is ranked 13 among the global markets for 'filmed entertainment revenue'. Citing a PricewaterhouseCoopers' report, the UK Film Council year book said UK, with a 7.7 per cent share, is

Typical comments

Films of the year 2007: *Chak De! India* (Go for it India!), King Khan is back on the big screen and this time he has 16 women under his wings.

Guru, Ratnam's film is a warm, intimate and moving portrait of a perhaps flawed visionary who may have been both a genius and a thug.

Cheeni Kum, Some ingredients are unsubtle, but as a whole, this Amitabh Bachchan starring dish is delightful.

Gandhi My Father, Much is known about Gandhi's non-violent ideals. Little is known about his family life, until now.

the third largest market for films in the world. U.S (41.5 per cent) and Japan (10.4 per cent) are the top two markets.

'The world filmed entertainment market is still dominated by the largest developed economies. Although the Indian market is vast in terms of admissions and both India and China have huge populations and are growing fast economically, their filmed entertainment markets still count in US dollar terms below Australia (population 21 million) and Italy (population 59 million),' according to the 2009 Year Book.

When BBC asked its online readers to describe Bollywood in five lines, the responses were tongue-in-cheek but fascinatingly representative of different views about the movies from the biggest film industry in the world.

One message said, Elaborate, FANTASIA land, alluring, seductive, sometimes nonsensical in a way that makes it comical, A union of beauty... however which way u see it. Another message was, glamour from actors to the set, masala, colourful clothes the sets etc, beautiful just to look at on screen well some movies anyways, songs! Message 3 summarized it as: cheesy, plagiaristic, predictable, blingy, different.

5

Watchdog with A Bite

"*Who watches the watchman*"

—*A commentator*

Nonchalance, Negativism, Goof-ups

It was quite an experience, for me as a journalist, to be able to analyse and 'understand' for a decade and a half the reporting style, editorials, choice of columnists and stress on investigative stories by the British mainstream dailies and tabloids. I was also fortunate to be able to interact and make friends with some eminent journalists and columnists. The first one to call me home for a drink, as I mentioned earlier, and to brief me on reporting from London was Sir Simon Jenkins, who lived not far from where I rented an apartment. After that I went to *Daily Telegraph* and *The Guardian* offices and met their Foreign Editors.

I found most media persons helpful. Whenever I needed information or background about some politician or such like, it was promptly given. Occasionally I got calls from the BBC Asia Today asking for background of a politician who was slated for an interview. But most interesting was to watch the role of the dailies in formulating and influencing public opinions. It was evident that the impact of their reports and editorials on the society and politicians was considerable. True they have unlimited resources and licence to investigate, scrutinise and do follow-ups, unlike in most developing countries. I was also amazed at the freedom the media had for undercover operations.

Editors, correspondents or columnists are not handed over lists of subjects or of personalities who must not be touched and censured. No one is sacrosanct. This has given the British media the power to act as watchdogs. I was, however, most impressed by their concern for the ordinary people. Their 'human touch' in defending or espousing causes of most ordinary people and their passionate defence of national interests were, I found, something to learn from.

But in the early years of my posting what I did not feel very happy about was the media's lack of interest in Indian affairs. Most dailies would hardly spare space for properly reporting visits of even an Indian prime minister. There would seldom be a follow up even if a meeting of the Indian and British prime ministers was reported. The only exception used to be *The Independent* and *Financial Times*. *The Independent* was one paper that reported on P.V. Narasimha Rao's official UK visit in March 1994 extensively.

The first report it ran was of Rao's scheduled meeting with John Major and then added, '..... India's controversial policy of liberalisation— some call it Thatcherism— has benefited foreign firms more than Indian as the government pins its hopes for economic success on enticing capital from abroad'. The interest in India was growing with opening up of the economy. But, I am not too sure how other dailies covered the visit.

> I was however most impressed by their concern (media) for the ordinary people. Their 'human touch' in defending or espousing cause of most ordinary people and their passionate defence of national interests were, I found, something to learn from.

In some papers, for days, and in a few others for weeks, no news about India was carried. I recalled A.N. Varma, principal secretary to Prime Minister Narasimha Rao, telling me on telephone a year or so earlier when I was based in New Delhi that the papers in the West had hardly any space for visiting Indian prime ministers. So why was the news about the visit of Robin Raphael, then US Under Secretary of State to New Delhi was splashed on the first page. She could have been simply ignored. I protested that the write-up was quite critical about her attitude towards India.

All this came back to me when I saw the casual, and often negative, coverage about India even in some mainstream broadsheets. I would describe as somewhat barmy the views of sections of the media about India then, to use the British slang. India was not some banana republic. I thought British media would have been more knowledgeable and interested in India than papers of any other country because of the long Indo-UK association.

I tried to find reasons for such lack of interest from a few Indian friends living in Britain, who felt that India was not important enough for Britain, unlike the US, Europe or China—and that the reader interest was dismal. They were more upset at their functions and achievements being generally blanked out.

For most of the British media, I am sorry to say, it was the Indo-Pak dispute over Kashmir, tragic incidents or natural disasters that stirred interest. One of the first detailed reports I saw way back in the early nineties was about a train accident in the northeast. Such disasters and abhorrent customs like sati seemed to be of 'reader interest'.

One paper had extensively reported on the outbreak of plague in Surat along with a picture of an Air India Boeing with the caption 'Plague Plane'. The report bared pre-conceived notions about the country and a lack of effort to find out the ground realities. On asked by my paper to write about the impact of such media reports I began my article with a quote from what Samuel Pepys wrote on October 16, 1665 in his diary about England then facing the epidemic of plague.

'But, Lord how empty streets are, and melancholy, so many sick people in the streets, full of sore.' And then I wrote, 'A section of the media here must be ruing that they could not write a similar elegy about India.. ..the glee at the reports of new cases outside Surat was quite evident, as if transmission of the disease established their impression of India still struggling to come out of the state of mediocrity, and the rope trick era.'

Much prominence was given to the banning of flights and import of food items by Gulf countries, which they bought worth £112 million annually. The Old Aunty, the *BBC*, however, maintained a balanced reporting in all its telecasts. One noted daily criticized Narasimha Rao for not addressing the nation or holding a Press conference. Had he done it, possibly the paper would have concluded that the situation was critical.

With such little focus or misplaced impressions about India it was no wonder that news about Indians in the UK was of little consequence except for some regional dailies or weeklies. A few tabloids would be enthused only when some alleged or imagined misdemeanours or scandals involved Indians.

I was shocked to see on the front page of a large-circulated daily of tabloid size a picture of a few prominent Indians including the Hindujas, LN Mittal, Joginder Sanger with the then Asian-origin Minister Keith Vaz and producer Subhash Ghai splashed across the centre of the first page with a damning caption. I do not recall the exact sentences but the accompanying report tried to insinuate things that damaged their credibility and reputation.

The fact was that they were invited by Subhash Ghai for the mahurat of a movie starring Jackie Shroff, which had taken place months before the article was published. There was nothing sinister about the gathering. In fact all those present in the picture had links and interest in the film industry. 'The gathering was not one of Mafioso,' said one of the 'victims' to me. The picture was taken by an Asian photographer who freelanced for an Asian weekly (it became a daily later) published in London. I heard rumours that he was paid about £3000 for the picture. But this could not be confirmed.

It also became evident to me that many journalists had not only pre-conceived view of the Diaspora but about India as well. Some reports were unnecessarily judgemental. Quite a few media persons had scanty knowledge or information about how fast India was modernising. During the popular *BBC* Dateline *London* discussion, I got into a rather stimulating exchange with a formidable Dowager-like correspondent of a large-circulated daily who said that Indians would hardly know about pubs.

Another correspondent of a Middle Eastern newspaper made a sweeping statement in the same programme that all Indian businessmen dished out expensive gifts to politicians and bureaucrats for favours. He added for effect that it was almost a customary tradition. I pointed out to the lady that she should visit Bangalore or Mumbai to enlighten herself. I asked the other correspondent whether British firms doing business in India were giving gifts too.

In retrospect I feel that the reason for the lack of interest in India in the late eighties and early nineties was that the politics and social ethos in the sub-continent were not understood by most writers. There was not as much interaction between British and Indian journalists as would happen later and neither visits to and from India were as numerous as later by 1998.

In the early nineties, for instance, they were seemingly ignorant of the history of the Kashmir dispute, although it had literally become part of British domestic politics due to organized campaigning by Pakistan-supported pro-plebiscite lobbies and many constituencies, where the election outcomes could be affected by pre-dominant Pakistani or Mirpuri voters.

The impact of concerted campaigning and politicking was apparent in some reports and analyses of the Kashmir dispute. I realized then that the media in Britain too was not immune to pressure lobbies. I was told that the pro- plebiscite groups had excellent public relations and forced their briefings on correspondents, who as it is did not have any clear picture of the geo-political situation in the region. During elections in Britain I also felt that papers and political correspondents by and large displayed distinct political biases. It would be rather facile to say that only the Indian media is politically slanted and journalists alleged to be in different camps. There may be a difference in degrees or in the way reports are presented but in the British media too papers appear to have definite ideological preferences. And so do political commentators.

One glaring example of this lack of understanding and the impact of concerted and vocal campaigning building pressure on organisations and the media and colouring its views was a report in the *Campaign Journal* Amnesty International of British section. It severely indicted India of human rights violations.

On its cover was the picture of a young woman covered with a black shroud praying before a tomb. The caption said, 'Kashmiri woman in mourning' and on the cover the title was 'Kashmir: Where India has turned Heaven into Hell'. It was alleged that the woman's husband was shot by security forces and she was mourning at his tomb. Another picture in inside pages showed a child sitting near his father's dead body crying.

It was claimed that an Italian freelance photographer had risked his life in taking the pictures. The reporter who wrote the text was said to have asked that his name be withheld. There were several photographs including one in which a number of young Kashmiris stood in a line facing policemen with their rifles aimed at them. It gave the impression that a firing squad was about to shoot the youth.

The then Minister of Press and Information, Rajiv Dogra, drew my attention to the journal. I was sitting with him in his office in India House and he gave the magazine to me saying 'read it, there is a most damaging story on Kashmir'. I looked at the cover picture. It was a dark-complexioned young woman who was keeping her head over a tomb, covered by a black shroud on which excerpts from the Koran seemed to be written. I was intrigued how a Kashmiri woman was so dark. Dogra told me it was worth investigating. Disturbing facts tumbled out.

I met an official of the Amnesty's British section near his office in Angel who promised to clarify after talking with the photographer whose name I learnt was Gabrielle Torsello. It ultimately transpired that the picture was taken at a mazar 10 km from Kanyakumari in Tamil Nadu. This explained why the woman, a Hindu, was dark complexioned. She was praying at a 'mazar' for a child. Her husband was alive.

I sent the report to my paper. But my problem was transmitting the cover photo. There was no computer. But Chandan Mitra, who was then Executive Editor, sensed that we had a scoop which would cause tremors internationally. He said 'fax the cover'. I was told that he stood with the layout person to see that the faxed copy was made good enough to be printed. The story was splashed on the first page.

The Amnesty's British section had seemingly goofed up. I met the photographer at a hotel opposite the High Commission and he showed me the colour slide of the cover picture. The location where the picture was actually taken was written on its side by him. I was told that the Amnesty apologised to the Indian Government. A year later I met a cousin of mine, then Minister Political at one of the Indian Embassies, and he said my story helped them considerably to blast the false propaganda by Pak lobbies.

The investigation also led to the ripping off the tight lid over the identity of members of Amnesty International, which was kept secret. It was shocking to learn that the Babbar Khalsa International was reportedly an institutional member, and various anti-India individuals were members too. Reports were that the ISI encouraged such membership which then cost just £7. The messing up of the Kashmir article was possibly due to the induction of the wrong sort in the Amnesty.

Thankfully, Amnesty's obsession over Kashmir, and looking at India all the time through the Kashmir prism ended after the exposure. The incident also showed the good and constructive work that could be achieved with confidence and cooperation between the Indian journalists and the High Commission.

Another instance I remember was the recall of a BBC correspondent from Kashmir in 1995. He reported from the Valley that some people had boycotted the on-going polling and thrown stones at some booths. But Dogra and another minister, Ajit Doval, found after inquiries that the scene recorded by the correspondent was allegedly a staged one. The two then met the then BBC Director General. Dogra told me, "Possibly that was the only time that BBC recalled its correspondent overnight".

Whatever could be the reason for that correspondent to send that report, in those days the coverage on the Kashmir dispute in the British media was far more than in India. It was apparently biased because they were seemingly based on the regular 'feeding' by Kashmiri lobbies.

The views of the Labour Party's then shadow foreign secretary, the late Robin Cook, his deputy and of about a dozen MPs and Peers, mostly of Labour Party, were also responsible for the tainted attitude of the media towards the Kashmir issue and for disparaging criticism of India over it.

Anti-India groups and pro-plebiscite lobbies, allegedly encouraged and funded by the ISI, had unbridled freedom to assail and criticise India. Their activities were at peak in early and mid-nineties. Some British MPs and Peers orchestrated their demands for referendum and repeated their exaggerated and made-up allegations of human rights violations by the Indian security forces. Early Day Motions on Kashmir were routine. Prime ministers of the Pak-occupied Kashmir were special invitees of some MPs to address in committee rooms of the House of Commons.

Allegations oscillated between the absurd and the defamatory. How could anyone logically accept that over 50,000 had been killed and thousands of women raped. But then the constituencies of such parliamentarians had sizeable segments of Pakistani and Mirpuri voters. They possibly succumbed more to constituency constraints than faith in the veracity of those allegations.

Early Day Motions on Kashmir were routine. Prime Ministers of the Pak-occupied Kashmir were special invitees of some MPs to address in committee rooms of the House of Commons.

A few had also allegedly enjoyed warm hospitality during their trips to Muzaffarabad, capital of the Pak-(occupied) administered part of Kashmir.

The fringe meetings at the annual conferences of all the three parties, Conservative, Labour and Liberal Democrats were religiously organized by Kashmir lobbies where accusations against India would be voiced and demand made for British Government to intervene and resolve the dispute. These meetings were addressed by Pak politicians as well as some British MPs and Peers. As an Indian journalist I would always be keen in those years to learn about the goings-on and listen to the speeches at these fringe meetings.

I had reported from Brighton in 1995,

> *Near invectives were used for 10 minutes by two Labour councillors (of Pakistan origin) from Bradford and Luton ... in vilifying India's record in Kashmir...They blatantly lied...to the delegates and leadership crowding the conference hall in Brighton which made one doubt whether the leaders... were letting the downright unethical attack on a friendly country with the sole objective of ensuring a few seats in the Midlands.*

> *This had finally stirred the Indians and a group of over 100 from Hounslow, London and Southall, led by the late Balwant Kapoor, a freedom fighter and president of the Overseas Indian Congress had marched on the streets of Brighton and protested.*

But the late Robin Cook had succeeded in pushing through the party's national executive a policy on the Kashmir issue during that annual conference in Brighton. It was possibly the first instance of a political party to have a Kashmir policy.

These meetings and statements of pro-referendum MPs and Peers and even of Kashmiri leaders invariably made it to the newspaper pages. The PoK leaders who addressed meetings in London would get a couple of paragraphs in the dailies. So did regularly tabled Early Day Motions on the dispute in Parliament.

Fortunately, after Labour Government under Tony Blair came to power, the official policy was clearly stated that the dispute had to be resolved by the two countries India and Pakistan through negotiations. Britain would not mediate as it was unacceptable to one of the parties of the dispute. Since then the media interest died down, most of the lobbies packed up and are now hardly heard of.

The British media slowly grasped the truth about India's complaint of the terror export from across the Kashmiri borders after 9/11 and 7/7. They were very fair in reporting and even demanding in editorials that cross-border terrorism must be eschewed. I now feel that it was not prejudice that made some dailies carry allegations of human rights violations and "obstinacy" of India in refusing to concede to plebiscite but the lack of factual information.

The 'Discovery' of India

A flourishing, successful community could not be glossed over for long. The media attitude started to change as the century was closing. Gradually, the Indian community, its younger generation in particular, became more socially and politically active and upwardly mobile. With greater participation of the Indian-origin persons in politics, the diaspora and India got increasing attention of the media. Meanwhile, the number of Indian-origin MPs and Peers and of Indian executives in the city and in public services consistently increased.

The Friends of India groups in all the three major political parties that were formed in the late nineties also helped focus on India. I could find some report or the other relating to India in at least one or two newspapers, like *The Times*, *Daily Telegraph* or The *Independent* and *The Guardian*. *Financial Times* invariably carried detailed reports on economic policies, investments by Indian companies in Britain. One or the other paper always published in advance an interview of an Indian Prime Minister on the eve of his visit to Britain.

The laudable attainments of Indian students in education, more Indian writers winning the prestigious Booker Prize along with latent affluence, increasing Indian investments, second only to the US by 2007, increasing number of acquisitions and mergers, influx of 'new' generation Indians and cultural assimilation, popularity of Indian films and stars all contributed to the swelling of reader interest in India and Indians and greater coverage of India.

When Selfridges converted all its floors in 'Celebration of Bollywood' it was news that had to be covered. Many new entrants each year to Rich Lists are of Indian origin. They have to be listed along with their profiles. A research analysing the wealth of Britain's 200 richest Asians between 1998 and 2005 revealed that Asian wealth increased by 69 per cent compared to the overall GDP growth figure of 22.8 per cent.

The numerous charities and fund-raising functions by trusts and institutions like the Bharatiya Vidya Bhavan, Loomba Trust, Pratham and Consortium for Street Children are always attended by politicians, financiers, foreign envoys which developed greater awareness about India and the culture and heritage of the community in Britain. All this naturally made it to newspaper pages. I noticed that with deeper knowledge about culture and festivals some of which the journalists covered in London, many dailies and even television channels started covering festival celebrations in India. The navratri celebrations and the burning of the 'demon king' Ravana found spaces along with related pictures.

The Beginning of India Interest

If I had to give a date since when interest in India started to grow, I would say it was after the signing of the Indo-British Partnership (IBP) trade agreement by Narasimha Rao and John Major. The realisation, albeit slowly, that the feel good factor in the country owed much to the increasing bilateral trade stoked respect for India's economic sinews. The liberalisation made investors and companies look India-wards.

Soon after the IBP agreement, the general elections in India made the commentators concede that the country was mature and democracy was as good and thriving as in the UK. The 'concern' about failing democracy and likely chaos, harboured by a few in the early years, gave way to faith in India's parliamentary system.

> *My dispatch on May 20, 1996 is pertinent:*
>
> *The coverage of the poll process by both the print and electronic media (UK) has been unprecedented but more remarkable has been the stress in the reports and analyses of the psyche of the rural voter. ...*
>
> *The condescending note and the smirking sympathy in the reports of the past polls... have given way to awe and admiration for the maturity of the voter in far-flung villages." I concluded that India has been rediscovered by the west and has emerged taller in its eyes.*

It was for the first time that a large number of reporters from Britain monitored the election and many of them travelled into interiors to watch the voting. They realized that democracy in India was safe in the hands of the rural voters, notwithstanding their poverty and illiteracy.

In retrospect it is clear that the increasing bilateral trade, touching £10 billion, Indian investments in the UK, over 500 Indian companies setting up there, and, of course, the IT revolution, were catalysts for bringing a sea-change in the attitude of the British papers— from nonchalance to positive awareness and their increasing focus on India and Indians. This was an encouraging development that has mutually benefited both the English and the Indians.

For the British media India is no longer a backward nation wrapped in the snake- charmers and rope trick times, but a country moving fast towards becoming an economic superpower. Some may be doing it grudgingly, but more space is now given to India-related news. In fact, the mainstream dailies sometime cover events which were unthinkable a few years ago. For instance, when Mukesh Ambani took a 66 per cent pay cut, the news was published along with the praise for that by the Indian Government. It was also mentioned that he was India's richest man.

In fact, the coverage of political developments, economic growth and technological strides has been razor-sharp in papers like *The Times*, *The Guardian* and *Daily Telegraph*. And the latest news, gossip and reviews from Bollywood are a regular feature in most mainstream papers. The description of Bollywood makes most Indian readers smile. Bollywood is explained as the world's largest film industry based in Mumbai, India, and home to stars such as Shah Rukh Khan, Aamir Khan, Amitabh Bachchan, Aishwarya Rai, Priyanka Chopra and Shilpa Shetty.

I saw in Britain a news about 'Bachchan to lend voice to Mumbai attack song' within 24 hours of it becoming known in India. It said, 'Veteran Bollywood actor Amitabh Bachchan will lend his voice to a song commemorating those who died in last year's militant attacks on Mumbai.' The news that Barack Obama celebrated 'Hindu festival of light' by lighting a traditional Indian lamp at the White House was published with picture. The apology by Karan Johar for using the word Bombay and not Mumbai was also big news.

In fact, India has been rediscovered by the media. It has also been fair in its reports and analyses, although a few of my journalist friends accept this with ifs and buts.

> It was for the first time that a large number of reporters from Britain monitored the election and many of them travelled into interiors to watch the voting. They realized that democracy in India was safe in the hands of the rural voters, not withstanding their poverty and illiteracy.

Diaspora on the Media Radar

Even better, now that the diaspora is in media radar, coverage of Indian festivals celebrated in the UK, NRIs' grouse and fights over stricter immigration and employment rules, racism and job opportunities, have substantially improved. Most, by and large, report without any bias. This has resulted in the wider appreciation of the community's contributions and the relevance of its grievances. It has also helped closer Indo-British relations and encouraged investments both ways.

I wondered why it took so long for the media to take note of the diaspora. I got some inkling about the reason when I met a political columnist who was then with the *Evening Standard.* I asked him why Indians in Britain were not considered newsworthy, except for a couple of very prominent ones like the Hindujas or Swraj Paul. He explained that timely reports concerning the diaspora rarely reached the newsrooms. 'There is the need for better communication.' I do not think many in the community fully agreed with such reasoning.

From what I heard it was true to some extent, that most Indians were rather insular until the eighties. Generally activities and events by the diaspora were confined to the community. Diwali, for instance, which is now ritually celebrated in a huge hall in the House of Commons and attended by the prime minister, scores of parliamentarians and corporate heads was largely observed by Indian families within their homes. The English had no inkling of how important the festival was and what it symbolized and that its message was of relevance to the world of today.

The media interest continued to mount. Gradually, the Indian community asserted itself and entered the Big League through notable achievements. It hosted more functions on festive and other occasions where participation of the English and a few media persons was noticeable. They also organised themselves to be able to orchestrate their demands and rights, in short demand fair play.

Forums, like the BAPIO (British Association of Physicians of Indian Origin) and for those who came under the Highly Skilled Migrant Programme (HSMP) fought at great expense the 2006 decision by Government to apply new qualifying criteria for extension of those under the HSMP and permanent residency (ILR) to existing resident Highly Skilled Migrants and doctors.

Both BAPIO and HSMP succeeded in getting support from leading English figures and contested successfully the immigration rules that adversely affected the Indian-origin doctors and highly skilled migrants. This attracted media attention regularly. The support by the British to HSMP and BAPIO found wide media coverage and sympathy—except one or two who, it seems, noticeably avoid these successes. But thankfully they do not criticise either. I did notice that statements of anti-immigration groups would be carried very subtly. But I do not think these affected anyone. The media certainly backed the cause of young doctors and other professionals. There was no bias in the reporting.

Another reason for the increased media interest in Indians is that the young, whether in Hounslow, Wembley or Harrow, are no longer tolerant of the attitudes their grandparents endured and have got membership to elite clubs. Leicester and Birmingham largely owe their prosperity to the diaspora and papers like the *Leicester Mercury* or *Birmingham Post & Mail* carry news about it in every edition. Most young Indians are now used to reading English mainstream papers. This is reflected in the fact that the circulation of weeklies in Indian regional languages has become static.

In fact a senior editor of *The Times* I met at a dinner in Nehru Centre a few years ago said to me that he wanted to reach the paper to more Asians in Britain and what would in my view interest the community. I told him that the only way to do it was to carry more incisive and original reports from the sub-continent covering politics, economy of Punjab and Gujarat and, of course, Bollywood. *The Times* now has a portal especially for reviews of films and news from Bollywood. Some others have followed.

The increased frequency and better researched reporting on India and the focus on the community by the UK media were crucial, for they are very powerful in shaping opinions. More the news about the 1.6 million Indians in the country, better it would be for integration, assimilation and harmony in a multi-racial and multi-cultural society that Britain is so proud of. Media's influence can be understood by circulation figures. In a country of 56 million people in 1995, the combined circulation of broadsheets and tabloids was in millions, *The Sun* leading with sales of over 3.2 million.

Indians: A Medium of Political Onslaughts

With greater media recognition of the diaspora and their importance in the society and some of them reaching within striking distance of powers-that- be, there was a period when a few top Indian businessmen came under concerted onslaught by the media. Fortuitously it did not drag on for too long. L.N. Mittal was alleged to have secured Prime Minister Tony Blair's recommendation in acquiring the Sidex steel plant, the biggest public undertaking in Rumania. Blair favoured him, because the media said, Mittal gave large donations to the Labour Party.

The facts were slightly different. Much before the letter was sent by Blair, the then Indian Ambassador in Bucharest Rajiv Dogra had told me that the Rumanian government had almost decided to sell Sidex to Mittal. Ambassador Dogra had during a call from Mittal mentioned to him that there were opportunities for Indians to invest in the country.

Mittal had flown in his private jet from London to Galati in the Danube delta to see the plant. He decided that it was a good proposition and approached the Rumanian Government.

With Blair the main media target leaving active politics it seemed as though they 'adopted' Mittal as their own. When he fought a bitter battle to acquire Arcelor, he was fiercely supported by the very papers that used to complain that he hardly employed the British workforce and that he was not even a British citizen.

The sudden appreciation of Mittal significantly coincided with Tony Blair being out of Downing Street and British politics. Mittal was no longer needed to be a 'cause' to attack him. Similarly, the assailing of the Hindujas stopped too when Peter Mandelson left the Cabinet. Many other Indians were investigated too but no dirt could be dug out about them.

I then subsequently realized that the media aggression, seemingly to "expose" some leading Indian businessmen, was primarily aimed at discrediting British politicians that the media would be targeting at a particular time. Blair was the target and Mittal a handy medium. Likewise, the media had more Peter Mandelson in sight than the Hinduja Brothers.

But apart from this exceptional phase, I reiterate that for the British media, no one is sacred. In fact, the high and mighty is more vulnerable. This bespeaks of the freedom of press and speech, the hallmarks of democracy that functions well in the country. The manner in which Blair and other public figures were attacked and the near-libellous comments about MPs who were

Selfridges: Bollywood celebrationa could not be ignored
(pic courtesy: The Nation)

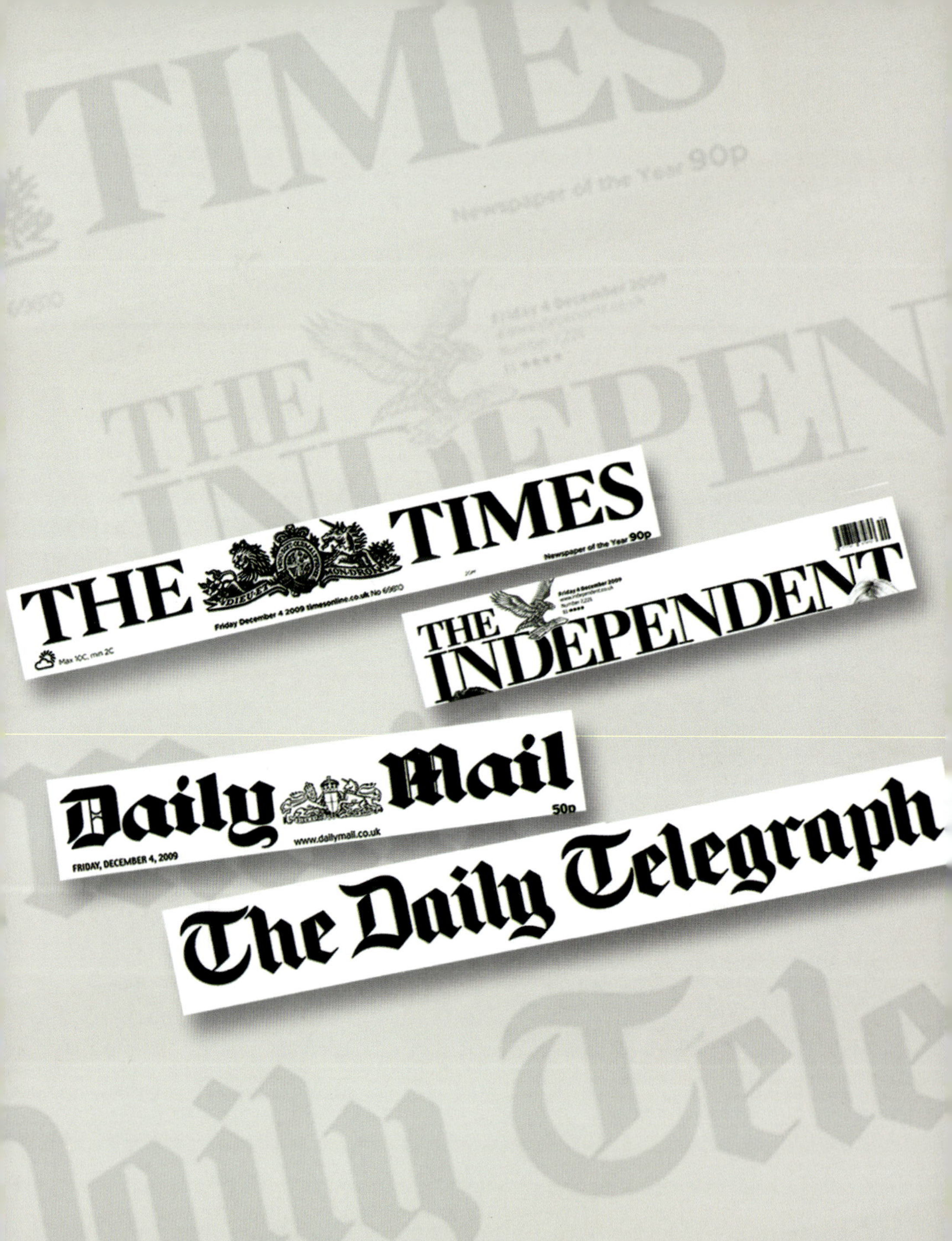

Watchdog: All get united in national interest

exposed when they systematically manipulated their expense accounts were proof enough that the press was a self-appointed watchman but approved by the people, which spared no one. Indians were not necessarily the black sheep by design.

In fact, Ratan Tata rather quickly became a household name. The British media backed his bid for Corus, the biggest steel plant in the UK, and were not unhappy when his company took over the Jaguar and Land Rover plants. The media along with the Unions pressed the Government to give financial assistance to Jaguar and Land Rover hit by recession. It did not matter that they were promoting an Indian company's cause.

One of my fellow Indian journalists, however, remains convinced that a few publications take pleasure in being over-censorious and critical of prominent Indian-origin persons. But without being a devil's advocate I would say that the British media does not spare anyone — just recall how David Beckham, nominated icon of the youth and an ideal family man—was lampooned over his intimate squeezes with Rebecca Loos. Also recall Camillagate and Squidgygate tapes and several other such exposé, widely published with lurid and salacious details. The shamed were Prince Charles, Camilla Parker Bowles and Princess Diana.

Then there was the ripping off of the respectability of the MPs and Peers who manipulated their expense account. Even the Home Secretary Jacqui Smith's account showing a few pounds spent on porno DVDs bought by her husband was played up.

It is indeed possible, and instances are there, that the media often crossed the Rubicon in its haste to reveal, exclusively, a wrong-doing and become the sentinel of the society. But as one commentator asked, 'Who watches the watchmen'!

One aggrieved politician quoted Benjamin Disraeli in an agitated emotional state, 'Today they blacken my character tomorrow they would blacken my shoes.' I did not have the heart to tell him that tomorrow may be a mirage.

Ratan Tata rather quickly became a household name. The British media backed his bid for Corus, the biggest steel plant in the UK, and were not unhappy when his company took over the Jaguar and Land Rover plants.

Qualities Worth Emulating

Years of reading the papers and watching television channels in the west made me understand and appreciate the depth of news coverage and editorial priorities of the broadsheets which were refreshingly different, from the keyhole, chequebook journalism and tattles of tabloids. I may say that the reports in the mainstream papers were quintessentially English of public school – many seniors are Oxonians or Cantab. Their editorial gamut was, and is, truly international. I remember S. Nihal Singh once telling me that Indian papers carried very little international news. This has become truer over the years.

Dailies like *The Times, Daily Telegraph* and *The Guardian*, seriously cover and give primacy to political news, which are quite often more incisive in content than is generally found in the Indian media. Commentaries are well-researched and balanced. Investigations by them are meticulously done and are devoid of sensationalism. They are also mostly in public interest. *The Times* for instance has regularly carried reports on security, fundamentalism, radical Islamization, after the 7 July bombings in London underground trains and a double-decker bus.

There are of course political preferences- like in *The Guardian* which is Left-oriented and *Daily Telegraph* which is said to generally support policies of the Tory Party. Likewise mid-market *Daily Mail* and others like *Daily Mirror*, *Daily Express* and *The Sun* have their own editorial policies. But then *The Guardian* also took the lead in the chastisement of Blair over the Iraq war and the suicide of the scientist Dr David Kelly. Likewise *Daily Telegraph* spared no MP or Peer, even if a Tory, in its exposure of the expenses scandal.

The cardinal editorial rule, more often followed than broken, is seemingly to forget the political preferences in public interest. This is what has made the people largely believe in what is reported. They do believe it is a watchdog for their and Britain's interest.

Another remarkable fact is how quickly the media reacts to the views and sentiments of the people. It became a vehicle for the millions of mourners who poured out on streets to grieve over the death of Princess Diana. The reports of the anger of the nation at the Queen not publicly participating with her people in their hour of sorrow compelled the royal family to come out of the gates of Buckingham Palace and mix with the mourners lining up there.

> The cardinal editorial rule, more often followed than broken, is seemingly to forget the political preferences in public interest. This is what has made the people largely believe in what is reported. They do believe it is a watchdog for their and Britain's interest.

During the bombing of the underground trains and a double-decker bus in London on July 7 and post the terror attacks, the media again was quickly in sync with the people. Most although emotionally drained and angry did not wish any retaliation. The media too refrained from inciting hatred and in fact blended its responsibility for social harmony with the need for security extremely well.

The other trait that needs to be emulated is that which is subscribed to by broadsheets and even tabloids—the expose all, spare none editorial culture. It zealously upholds and defends rights of individuals, campaigns for justice of the most ordinary people, and often spends huge amounts of money to help find the perpetrator of any crime and help the victim, even if he is no VIP. Indeed they do not distinguish between an ordinary individual and a very important person.

There are various instances of dogged pursuits and investigations by the media to get the wrong righted. Both electronic and print media have taken up cudgels for the man on the street. Hundreds of thousands pounds have been spent by them to bare illegal trades and practices apart from huge amounts spent, particularly by tabloids, in spying on boudoir romps and indulgences by celebrities.

The illegal gender-testing of unborn babies and induced abortions in India were exposed by *Daily Mail* team. It is said that the team stayed in the country for quite some months and travelled extensively. It was backed by another set of reporters who collected information from couples in the UK who travelled to India for tests and abortions.

> There are various instances of dogged pursuits and investigations by the media to get the wrong righted. Both electronic and print media have taken up cudgels for the man on the street.

After one person was killed in a train accident near the Southall station, the media did not rest until the Government sanctioned to change the signal system at a steep cost under tremendous pressure. A girl in a village, the name of which could not be known to most, was raped and murdered. She went out at around eight in the evening to drop a letter her mother gave her in a nearby mailbox. The girl never returned. Her body was found in a park. The media pursued the investigation into her murder for months. Rewards were offered by a few papers, all for an unknown girl in an unknown village.

Later events like the shooting of Brazilian youth Jean Charles de Menezes at Stockwell tube station in London by police, misidentifying him as a suicide bomber about to explode a device on the London Underground and the July 7 bomb attacks on underground trains confirmed again that newspapers and tabloids give up all their slants and biases in demanding justice and public disclosure of omissions and commissions by any individual or authority. The Press did not hesitate to demand justice for the Menezes family although they were from Brazil and castigate its own country's top police officers. It almost hounded the then Police Commissioner out of his high office.

Way back in the late seventies when bride-burning cases began to be noticed in India, I suggested to the publisher-editor of a magazine which was being recognized as one of the best newsmagazines, to start a campaign against the rising incidents of brides being burnt for dowry. He turned it down saying that the reader interest would not last long. I was disappointed but later realized he was right to some extent. Within months, all newspapers pushed bride burning reports to inside pages and gave just a paragraph or two. They were routine and not newsworthy.

The campaign by NDTV and *The Indian Express*, not too long ago, for retrial of a highly connected accused alleged to have shot a young model showed how the media campaign could secure fair justice.

It was heartening to find the Indian media, both print and electronic, taking up the alleged misuse of power by one Director-General of Police accused of molesting a minor girl who was so traumatised that she committed suicide. Slowly, like the British media a number of Indian newspapers and TV channels are acting as watchdogs. Call it the effect of globalization or the people revolting against corruption and misuse of power, such developments augur well for democracy.

The contrast, however, between British broadsheets and most Indian newspapers in their editorials has widened in recent years. The former still believe in giving primacy and importance to serious news and focus on entertainment, music, culture, and such light reading stuff is mainly on weekends, whereas in India the stress is more on social interactions ('Page 3'), light easy reading items and 'filmi' news, although separate pages are given for these. Possibly the new generation of readers in India like to read about personalities rather than politics. So believe the younger crop of editors.

The Tabloids' Royal obsession

Unlike in Britain India has no monarchy. The pursuit of the royals by the tabloids was new and amazing for us from the Indian media. Everyone will recall how John Hewitt, Diana's lover, was chased out of the country for giving details of their affair to Anna Pasternak for the book *Princess in Love*. Roundly called the Royal Rat he fled to the continent to escape from the fury of the Press that aroused murderous hate in the people. I think the *Mail* had announced a cash award to anyone ferreting out Hewitt, who was in hiding.

The Hewitt incident also revealed to me the media interest, indeed near-obsession, for the royalty and the money raked in from sleuthing them. It far exceeds the focus on any family or personality in the Indian press. Most papers had, and still have, royal correspondents, who in those days seemed to tail Princess Diana, 24x7. She was the surest bet for boosting the circulation of the papers. A royal correspondent of a daily was said to be a counsellor and friend of Diana and she often confided her problems to him.

I am told that one tabloid had deputed correspondents and photographers, who worked in shifts, to catch Diana coming out of a gym with Will Carling, then England rugby captain. The daily's team, it was said, hid behind a hedge—rain, cold no worry— and did succeed in catching them. The spin off, Carling's wife divorced him.

I was not surprised that even after her death for years Diana remained the best bet for boosting circulation. It took over 10 years for the media to stop publishing something or the other about her. Her two sons must be relieved that their mother's name was not sullied by various "revelations" by the likes of Hewitt.

Infectious Tabloid-ish Journalism

I had not read any tabloid before coming to London. I did not know much about them, except that they were more interested in lurid details of footballers' flings and indulged in "breaking" stories about sexual escapades of celebs. But I did not have any inkling either that many carried serious articles and also initiated investigations of public interest (and curiosity).

I was told about *Daily Mail* at a dinner by a Tory Baroness. On learning that I was reporting from the UK, she advised me to subscribe to it. 'You must read *Daily Mail*, if you want to know what is happening in this country. Its editorial content is comprehensive and tells you all about people, society and its investigations are constructive and most revealing. It's the most complete daily.' I followed her advice.

But her preference for *Mail* also indicated that most readers wanted a mix of the serious and the sensational. This has in my view gradually affected broadsheets as well. But they do not indulge in chequebook journalism, yet pick up scandals and sleaze details that tabloids go hysterical about, albeit they publish them more soberly, devoid of melodrama. The tabloidish touch is now apparent. I fear it might increase as circulations spiral down.

But unlike in India, most British editors still believe that serious political reports and news about society are what most readers, even the young—you can't ignore the young executives and entrepreneurs who are avid newspaper readers— prefer to read.

Another marked difference I noticed was the manner and language used by media commentators. There is no restraint in onslaughts on even prime ministers, no one is sacrosanct. For sample I cite what Nick Cohen once wrote, "Gordon Brown would be better. David Blunkett would be better. Charles Clarke would be better. My bloody gran would be better. Face it, he's (Blair) got to go. Let's drain the swamp." There have been even more scathingly worded comments for other politicians, including Gordon Brown. But I have always wondered whether such steamy expressions hurt the target at all.

Media Introspection

I have had, as I have been saying repeatedly, great admiration for British journalism. Except that sometime it appeared that tabloids, at least a few of them, pursued couples doggedly— publishing details about their trysts (so and so was spotted at the night club dining cosily and often holding hands, they left together in the same car), sometime pressurizing them to come out openly about their relationship, even get married. But once this happens, sooner than later the snooping starts looking for any cracks in the couple's feelings. Any 'straying' is published with seeming delight. Such tactics are fun for readers but not for the 'victims'. This has, I believe, resulted in more searching within.

In fact, as I was leaving the country I noticed an increasing introspection by the media. Is everything not alright with it? 'We all know there's something deeply wrong with Britain today. A sense of dissatisfaction and dull resignation haunt the country. For months now we've savaged politicians. That problem is still very, very far away from being fixed. But it's unfortunate we've isolated our anger in one area,' noted Ian Dunt in politics.co.uk .

The British press has also been accused of drinking in the Last Chance Saloon. Fear has been expressed time and again that 'broadcasters are also getting a taste for the commercially-popular cocktail of sensation and intrusion that it sells'.

The questions increasingly asked are like, 'Are journalists doomed to ignore stories about important public interest issues in favour of titillating tales that pander solely to the public's prurient curiosity? 'Are docusoaps and current affairs series based on questionable evidence replacing the award-winning documentary programmes of past years?'

The Press Commission and the Media Ethics and Self Regulation look closely at the moral dilemmas facing journalists in their day-to-day working lives and examine the self-regulatory bodies that police the various codes of practice.

The Guardian had also accused the *News of the World*, about an apparent culture of law breaking and privacy invasion. Dunt said that this allegation 'could give us the opportunity to look closely at the British media, and ask ourselves how it is failing us. We'll be lucky. The trouble with scrutinising the media is that it's the media who have to do the scrutinising. And people tend not to defecate in their own backyard'.

The questions increasingly asked are like, 'Are journalists doomed to ignore stories about important public interest issues in favour of titillating tales that pander solely to the public's prurient curiosity?

> *'For years, commentators would write nosey, judgemental stories on politicians' sex lives while pursuing highly dubious embraces of their own. But who would write about it? Only themselves! And they were the last people who would.'*
>
> *'But now things are infinitely worse. The media failings are legion. Too many Westminster journalists accept small exclusives in exchange for good behaviour. Too many of them are genuinely friends with those they report on.'*

Isn't this true in most democracies? The reason for mud-raking is attributed to the decline of newspaper sales. A few journalists that I spoke with, sounded familiar when they commented that many of the stories are based on press releases or one of the news feeds, like Reuters, rather than their verified account of an event.

Indian editors would possibly agree fully to the observation by some journalists in Britain that there is an outcry (by the public) for increasingly populist subjects covered by broadsheets and that editors do not commission work which doesn't sell. 'I have personally felt the sinking feeling in my stomach as a serious political story I spent hours working on was outperformed ten times over by a fluffy piece I scribbled up with the word 'celebrity' in the title,' complained Dunt. Many of us would recall similar experiences. But, I agree that commercial consideration is supreme.

Although this commercial need is camouflaged in saying that it was all in public interest. But then Dunt asked 'was the sexual mores of the head of Formula One a matter of public interest.... It is something which is interesting to the public, which is a different matter entirely'.

'That we should have editors arguing for the legitimacy of this kind of journalism when serious political coverage is lying dead in a ditch is deeply humiliating to my profession. The case against the media is so severe

Indian editors would possibly agree fully to the observation by some journalists in Britain that there is outcry (by the public) for increasingly populist subjects covered by broadsheets and that editors do not commission work which does not sell.

it appears conclusive. We desperately need to give it the kind of scrutiny politicians receive.'

This I noticed did start. There was a lot of soul-searching and the awarding of a prison sentence to a senior journalist in 2007, as detailed below, triggered a constructive debate in the press itself of what was wrong and what was the limit to investigation and its techniques.

Self-discipline was also imposed. The broadsheets and tabloids do not intrude into the privacy of the Royals any longer, following an understanding between the palace and the editors. The chequebook journalism has been criticized by the courts. Investigative journalism is now focussing increasingly on exposing scandals and misconduct that need to be uncovered and are in public interest.

Sting Operations: Pros and Cons

There has been much hue and cry over a few sting operations in India. Reporters involved faced prosecutions. But in Britain all agree that sting operations that are in the public interest are needed. A sting operation against a few MPs suspected of taking bribe, as it happened in India, or in unearthing plots by Islamic terrorists or exposing people in authority whose behaviour run against statements they have made, or positions they hold, is held to be in the public interest.

But the much-denied techniques used by many newspapers to obtain personal information have been questioned in the UK. According to one British commentator in the 15 years since the industry launched the Press Complaints Commission (PCC) hundreds, if not thousands, of ordinary people and 'celebrities' have had personal details splattered over intrusive and often inaccurate stories.

'Many lost relationships, jobs, and even homes after publication of prurient stories based on illicitly obtained information from employers, phone

There has been much hue and cry over a few sting operations in India. Reporters involved faced prosecutions. But in Britain all agree that sting operations that are in the public interest are needed.

companies, banks or public authorities," noted Mike Jempson, Director, The MediaWise Trust (UK). Worse, the aggrieved have never been compensated although ironically those supplying 'inside info' are paid handsomely. One Mulcaire reportedly pocketed four times the national average wage for supplying information exclusively to just one newspaper during one year.

In May 2006, Information Commissioner Richard Thomas claimed to have a list of 305 journalists who had obtained information by illegal methods. They were customers of a single private detective who specialized in delivering details of criminal records, telephone accounts and other personal information. No prosecutions followed the publication of his report 'What price privacy?'

The Information Commissioner issued a follow-up report, 'What price privacy now?' in December 2006 that provided more detail, but no names. It found that journalists had improperly obtained well over 3,000 separate pieces of personal data. Such intrusion mounts immense pressure on individuals.

Indian media, on the other hand, does not believe in pressuring people to do something like making couples get married, then trail them and start digging about how they are doing, hoping to catch them doing something wrong for another exclusive. Nor does it snoop around for digging dirt. In fact, some time it eschews revelations that need to be exposed, just because there is reluctance to hurt or damage someone.

One journalist of Hamburg-based *Bild* had, when I was in the city, asked me half jokingly, 'Have our British counterparts (tabloids) slowed down or going full steam breaking into bedrooms?' The fact is that like in India in most European media gossiping about personal life of politicians is avoided. In France, of course, affairs of politicians are *cause celebre*. The British tabloids however maintain, and to some extent rightly, that one important aspect of journalism is to expose scandals and that misconducts need to be uncovered.

The Case with Salutary Effect

The arrest and imprisonment of an assistant editor of the UK's largest-selling Sunday tabloid for illegally intercepting celebrity telephone calls have had a salutary effect. In January 2007, Clive Goodman, 48, who specialized in gossip about the royal family for the *News of the World* had begun his four-month sentence. His associate, Glen Mulcaire, 35, a private investigator hired by the newspaper, got six months. Immediately after they were sentenced *NoW* Editor Andy Coulson announced that he had tendered his resignation weeks earlier.

Accepting 'ultimate responsibility' for the crimes committed in his paper's name, Coulson said, 'I feel strongly that when the *News of the World* calls those in public life to account on behalf of its readers, it must have its own house in order.' This is the ethics that most dailies seem to be following.

The Guardian commentator noted, 'Perhaps this sorry saga will encourage editors to invest more in quality investigative journalism and jolt politicians into asking more pointed questions about the management style and commercial priorities of the newspaper industry.

'No one wants to see the regulator given power to jail or sack editors, but unless the industry owns up to its failings and gets tougher on those who let the public down, news media could find pressure mounting for legislation.' A lesson to remember, perhaps!

Press, Politicians and the Government

To quote Max Weber, 'Indeed, it is above all the successful journalists who find themselves having to face the onerous inner challenges. It is no small thing to consort with most powerful people... apparently on the basis of equality, to be flattered because you are feared, while all the time knowing that no sooner has the door closed behind you than your host may have to defend himself to his guests for having invited the "scoundrels of the press".'

Reporting on politics and politicians, I knew from my own experience, was not an easy job. I remember a minister whom I knew well calling me early one morning and complaining how I could let go an item which hurt him. My reply that he was not mentioned at all failed to convince him. But there were a couple of very senior ones who laughingly would say "Your criticisms would not affect our personal relations." This was proved to be true in some cases. But by and large what Webber wrote was and is the fact. Journalists as a tribe are welcomed because they are feared not because they are liked. Some young, impressionable ones get the wrong impression that they are close to a minister because he gives special time to them or takes him in his car. It is not he but his paper that is befriended.

I have seen such relationships among the press, the government and politicians, change with times. This is true everywhere. I have heard stories of special political correspondents in New Delhi being the most sought after during the Nehru era. After speaking in the Lower House (Lok Sabha) MPs would request these correspondents covering Parliament to mention their names—at least once-- in their reports. For the mention of the name even with one line about that MP could catch the attention of Panditji. Things drastically changed during Mrs Indira Gandhi's tenure- not many could claim any special favours from her. When Rajiv Gandhi succeeded her, a few journalists were given special access courtesy his advisers. During Atal Behari Vajpayee's years too, some journalists became powerful because of their supposed proximity to senior ministers.

Correspondents of British papers who report on the House of Commons proceedings have also been special ones for ministers and senior MPs. Way back in the eighteenth century Edmund Burke is said to have pointed at the Press Gallery and remarked, 'And yonder sits the fourth estate, more important than them all.' Now BBC, in fact, the broadcast media in general, constitutes a fifth estate.

I, therefore, always thought that journalists in Britain were given much more importance than in most other countries because the media was genuinely free. During John Major's years, there were a few journalists who had access to 'scoops'. But mostly his opponents--and they were in a surfeit—who assiduously cultivated the press for reporting against Major and ran a campaign to discredit him.

I found most have had ideological preferences. A journalist belonging to a paper backing, say, Labour policies would thus have quicker and easier access to Labour ministers and politicians. Not that the others would be blocked out. But those 'liked' would scoop up 'breaking stories'.

There are many such instances. The reporter with 'inside' access would invariably score over the one who did not have such privilege. But what did he, the insider, gain for himself? Nothing, except job satisfaction! I never heard any name dropping. This is by and large true of our media too, except that some get a wrong sense of power by being close with powerful politicians.

In Britain, the relations between the media and the government apparently underwent a radical change from Major's days during the long Blair era. Peter Oborne has given some instances in his book *The Triumph of the Political Class* in a nearly 40-page chapter titled 'Client Journalism'. He says that over the last twenty-five years a new type of government has emerged—affecting

British democracy direly--in which the political class, the new ruling elite evolved and triumphed, and it has made party-political differences non-existent in pursuit of power and patronage.

He demolishes my belief that the British media is a watchdog against any act of the government that affects the independence of the great institutions—Parliament, the judiciary and the civil service. He charges the media with being lured by the political class. He alleges that the political class along with its 'counterparts and collaborator, the media class, has changed the very nature of government in the twenty-first-century Britain'. I have confined myself to what he says to prove this charge of his.

His observations and accounts of what went on between some media persons and Downing Street occasionally made me compare the relations between the Indian media and the Government. He falsifies the belief I also had while in London that generally the Press tries to take on the role of opposition. I remember Vijay Dhar, then a very close adviser of Rajiv Gandhi, complaining that the press published only negative stories. It ignored positive achievements of the Government.

But I then felt that it was more necessary to highlight the shortcomings so that corrective measures could be taken. In any case balancing the two would be more ethical. I often did read reports praising the Government's efforts, for instance, in securing deals which would generate employment. But the media in England too focuses more on the slip ups and omissions by the government of the day.

6

Indian Curry's Hold Over Britain

> *While British took India by gunpowder, India has captured Britain with curry powder*
>
> *—Lalit Mansingh, former Foreign Secretary*

Nothing could be truer than this perceptive comment made by Lalit Mansingh when he was India's High Commissioner in Britain. The over 9,500 curry houses— some of them are now institutions and favoured destinations for London businesses— in the small isle with a turnover of 4.3 billion pounds a year and employing 70,000 people, more than the steel and coal sectors bracketed together, symbolize the enduring 'love affair' of the British with the cuisine of their former Raj. Rough estimate is that three out of ten British families dine at least once a month at an Indian restaurant. Many top corporate houses try to clinch deals over exotic Indian dishes. 'Currying' favour, Gordon Brown served up an Indian feast at Chequers as he held talks with top trade union chiefs. Scots are said to consume on an average over 50,000 curry dishes every week. It must be going down well with their single malts and beer.

This awesome rise in popularity of the Indian curry houses is particularly remarkable considering that Britain had just six nondescript eateries serving Indian meals after the Second World War. The Punjabis, who settled in Southall and Hounslow, had a few family-run restaurants in these predominantly Indian areas which were unostentatious, and without any décor or fitting one associates now with the Indian restaurants. They were little better than the dhabas in Punjab. But the food used to be superb, authentic Punjabi, no chicken tikka masala curry.

I still remember the good meal and warm, homely welcome I got at one such Southall restaurant way back in the early eighties. While staying at Sheraton near Heathrow on my way to New York, I was taken by a friend to the restaurant just off Broadway in Southall. It was run by a family where the father was cashier, mother and daughter-in-law cooked in an open kitchen and the son doubled as a server and cleaner. The 'kali mirch chicken' was delicious, rotis crisp and hot. I never ate a better kali mirch chicken at any of the five-star Indian restaurants during my over 15 years posting in London. I regret that I forgot the name of that place and the friend is no more. Most probably that small, apology for a restaurant, was bulldozed by the growing prosperity. Southall is now dotted with restaurants that are jazzier and modern. Dishes have fancy names. But 'that' chicken is no longer to be found.

Outside these 'Indian' areas, curry houses were at best serving a small number of dishes. They survived because of the growing number of Indians coming to the country and the fascination for the curry of the English families who had returned from the subcontinent. The meals we get now at most restaurants serving Indian cuisine were available at very few restaurants, like 'Veeraswamy' or 'Gaylords International'. Mostly the food was not 'refined' to suit the English palate. Jiggs Kalra, who helped open 68 restaurants across the world, too told me an interesting anecdote. In 1980 or 1981, a few secretaries in an office had excitedly gone to lunch at an Indian restaurant in central London. When they came back one of them showed her nails to him. First he thought that she was showing her nail polish, but then he spotted her turmeric-stained fingers. "See, this is the proof that we went to an Indian restaurant".

Jiggs' pride was hurt and he explained to her that they must have gone to some joint which might be falsely claiming to serve Indian cuisine to draw English diners. This is true to some extent even now, although no nails get turmeric -stained.

In fact, knowledge about Indian food now is phenomenal. I was amazed at many English diners discussing dishes with chefs, just like we do in India. This is partly due to the cookery books written by Madhur Jaffrey or Pat Chapman and television shows. An Indian food critic said it was after 1982, when Chapman, called 'the ambassador of Indian food' by Derek Cooper, the 'Curry Leader' by Fay Maschler and 'a Missionary seeking converts to curry' by Lloyd Grossman, founded The Curry Club to share information about recipes, restaurants and spices that awareness grew about Indian food . The number of admirers of the curry also went into an upward spiral.

Two decades later Indian cuisine became so much an integral and essential part of the English eating habit that many dishes are possibly quite often served at family dinners. Camilla, the Duchess of Cornwall, while visiting the Brilliant Restaurant on Station Road in Southall with Prince Charles had taken special interest and watched the dough being kneaded for making naans. Who knows naans might be on the royal menu. The Queen had got Indian canapés cooked by Veeraswamy chefs for her party for Indian achievers at Buckingham Palace.

The BBC, too, contributed to reaching Indian recipes to households through a number of television shows. One of the recent BBC2 'Indian Food Made Easy' series showed Indian-born TV chef Anjum Anand explaining that Indian food was only about curries was a myth. A very affable young lady who lived in Hampstead once told me that she wanted through her dishes to persuade viewers to get out of the habit of takeaway tikka masalas. She believed that most English had a misconception about Indian food on many levels – 'that it's unhealthy, which it's not, and secondly, that it's complicated, which it isn't.'

Comfortably married into an affluent Indian family, Anand took to cooking because her 'family' told her she was too thin. So did it mean that some Indian dishes help to put on weight? She did not think so, unless the food was prepared specifically with such an aim. In her case, she shed the pounds she added because 'it didn't suit me', she said.

The popularity of such shows was evident from the amount of press write-ups about her culinary skills and her dishes. They were indeed very interesting. The media and connoisseurs of her recipes named her Nigella Lawson of Indian cuisine. This was a big tribute as Nigella has been one of the most famous cooking diva with her own website. Anand must have been flattered but said that she did not ooze sex appeal like Nigella. Whatever it might be, I found that her passion for searching new recipes and experimenting with different ingredients were as much as those of Nigella.

BBC has also over the years a number of other TV shows and posted several features by the likes of Roopa Gulati who explain what spices are essential ingredients and how to make different dishes. Chapman regularly appears as a celebrity chef at major food shows abroad and in the UK. In 1999 he hosted his own 'Rice and Spice' theatre at the BBC's 'Good Food Show' at Olympia. He takes culinary tours to India, runs Pat's Cookery Courses, and although to date he does not own a restaurant, from time to time he guest chefs at Indian restaurants, Hilton Hotels, Taj Hotels - India, Selfridges, Club Med, Cordon Blue Cookery School, British Embassy - Berne, and Cunard's flagship the QE2.

The *Daily Telegraph*'s Max Davidson said, 'Chapman is to curry, what God is to the Old Testament!' Sarah Jane Evans in *BBC Good Food Magazine* said of him, '...it would be difficult to find anyone who matches Pat Chapman's enthusiasm for spicy food'. Madhur Jaffrey's recipe books too are bestsellers. The viewers' ratings are high testifying to the fact that housewives have taken to cooking curry and tandoori dishes for dinners at home. These 'chef masters' have contributed immensely to reaching the Indian dishes to English households.

The Sway of the Indian Curry

'London is the food capital of the world', according to Rohit Khattar, owner of a chain of highly popular restaurants. This is true, cuisine from every country in the world is available in the city and that makes it more multicultural than the people of different nationalities. But the Indian curry has definitely stolen a march over all of them, be it Chinese, Italian or Turkish. It did, however, take some time before I could realize how much Indian cuisine had become part of the British dining habit and how they had adjusted their palate to the spicy food. Some rugby players, recalled Jiggs Kalra, would take the hot curry and then drink a few pints, to sweat out their tiredness. Hearing such stories I often wondered what magic had Indian eateries woven to mesmerize the English. Everyone seemed to relish going to an Indian curry house.

'If you have to meet an Englishman urgently, invite him for an Indian meal,' was the advice given to me half-jokingly by the then Press Counsellor Ian Hughes in the British High Commission in New Delhi, on the eve of my leaving for London. I found his advice quite helpful. It was indeed always a pleasure to offer dinner or lunch meeting with columnists and politicians. Most saying they would be delighted would generally add, 'I love Indian

> "London is the food capital of the world", according to Rohit Khattar, owner of a chain of highly popular restaurants. This is true, cuisine from every country in the world is available in the city and that makes it more multicultural than the people of different nationalities.

food'. I would often be surprised by the knowledge some of my media friends had about Indian dishes. They invariably discussed the origin of the Chicken Tikka Masala Curry (CTM). One even remarked, 'It is our contribution to the Indian cuisine'.

> The 'takeover' by the Indian food is apparent from the fact that now most typically English pubs have the hot curry, rice and pappadom on their menus—14 per cent of all gravy consumed out of the home is in pubs.

The 'takeover' by the Indian food is apparent from the fact that now most typically English pubs have the hot curry, rice and pappadom on their menus—14 per cent of all gravy consumed out of the home is in pubs. The business of the packaged Indian meals and dishes, both non-vegetarian and vegetarian, too has a multi-billion pound turnover. These readymade meals are not only sold by chains like Sainsbury's, Marks & Spencer, Asda and Tesco but exported too. High-brow departmental stores like Harrods and Selfridges have several dishes on offer in their food halls. I was told by an Indian-origin person serving at the Indian counter in Selfridges, 'We sell very well, lamb curry and sheekh kebabs are hot sellers'. The buyers generally are English or tourists from Europe.

> 'If you have to meet an Englishman urgently, invite him for an Indian meal,' was the advice given to me half-jokingly by the then Press Counsellor Ian Hughes in the British High Commission in New Delhi, on the eve of my leaving for London. I found his advice quite helpful.

Britain's Historic Curry Links

The astounding fascination of the English for the curry has often been ascribed as manifestation of the English rule. Most British posted in India grew to like many things Indians, especially the cuisine. One Lieutenant Governor of 'Oudh' was said to have fallen in love with the biryani and rogan josh (mutton curry) prepared by a Nawab's head chef. The astute Nawab always arranged a mujra (music and dances) whenever the 'laat' sahib craving for the biryani and the curry invited himself for dinner at Nawab's place. He was well-versed in Urdu and had come to like Thumri (a sensuous semi-classical Indian music) as well. It is said the Nawab became one of the most influential persons of his times, thanks to the biryani and mujra.

The khansamas and ayahs who were brought to England by civilian and military officers from India too cooked a few Indian dishes which their saheb and memsahebs liked. Naturally, their friends and relatives who came to dinner with them tasted those Indian preparations. I happened to meet a gardener at a temple in Midlands whose great-grandfather from Bihar had come to England with the family of a civil service officer, who retired from Patna, the state capital. He would occasionally prepare dal and curry which the children of the retired officer had grown to like. The gardener said that according to his father the Indian preparations were often served for relatives and guests who came for a meal at the officer's residence somewhere near Brighton. No wonder the English were familiar with curry.

I also heard that Queen Victoria after the death of John Brown, a Scot whom she was reportedly very fond of, became similarly attached to an Indian servant, Abdul Karim, one of the two people who had come to work for her in late June 1887, days after her Golden Jubilee celebrating her first fifty years on the throne. She called him the munshi, and he came to be hated more fiercely than John Brown for the same reason—the warm regard she had for him. It is rumoured that he could also prepare some good Indian dishes, but

He (Lt. Governor) was well-versed in Urdu and had come to like Thumri (a sensuous semi-classical Indian music) as well. It is said the Nawab became one of the most influential persons of his times, thanks to the biryani and mujra.

this has not been confirmed. However, it is said that his family back in India was given some land as 'bakshish'.

Cancer Fighting Curry

The curry's popularity and acceptance by the English have led to scientists and researchers study its ingredients and effect. One doctor was foolhardy enough to allege that the Balti curry could lead to high blood pressure, obesity and even heart attacks. The Balti restaurant owners in the Curry Mile in Birmingham were outraged and went on a verbal onslaught. Other doctors were urged to highlight the benefits of the curry. The doctor who committed the 'blasphemy' could not take the heat and surrendered. He declared that it was only everyday intake of the curry that was harmful but that too if taken for a long time. He also said that in small quantities, curry was actually beneficial to health. I never heard of him after his clarification. 'Possibly he was drowned into buckets of curry poured on him by the restaurant owners. Or he became a permanent invitee by Balti restaurants on the Curry Mile', joked Dr Murli Sinha, a heart specialist in Walsall near Birmingham.

Undaunted curry marches on. In fact, several medical reports have testified that certain properties of turmeric help develop immunity, especially against cancer. BBC homepage carried a write-up about this.

> *A good rule of thumb is that a curry is a dish containing sautéed garlic, onions (unless religion or culture forbids their use) and varying amounts of most of the following spices: turmeric, cumin, coriander, ginger, chilli, cardamom, black pepper, cloves, fenugreek, and fennel. .... In fact, the combination of spices in these dishes changes from country to country and even from house to house. Their origin, however, does not diminish their incredible medicinal value.*
>
> *Believe it or not, each ingredient of the common curry has a medicinal use. In fact each ingredient has been used for thousands of years to treat a variety of ailments from stomach cramps to throat infections (although some believe curry has caused more stomach cramps than it has cured).*

Claim of Scientists

Scientists have claimed that an extract found in the bright yellow curry spice turmeric can kill off cancer cells. The chemical—curcumin— has long been thought to have healing powers and is already being tested as a treatment for arthritis and even dementia. According to a BBC report tests by a team at the Cork Cancer Research Centre show it can destroy gullet cancer cells in the lab. Cancer experts said the findings in the *British Journal of Cancer* could help doctors find new treatments.

Dr Sharon McKenna and her team found that curcumin started to kill cancer cells within 24 hours. The cells also began to digest themselves, after the curcumin triggered lethal cell death signals. Dr McKenna said, 'Scientists have known for a long time that natural compounds have the potential to treat faulty cells that have become cancerous and we suspected that curcumin might have therapeutic value.' Dr Lesley Walker, director of cancer information at Cancer Research UK, said, 'This is interesting research which opens up the possibility that natural chemicals found in turmeric could be developed into new treatments for oesophageal cancer.

Rates of oesophageal cancer rates have gone up by more than a half since the 70s and this is thought to be linked to rising rates of obesity, alcohol intake and reflux disease so finding ways to prevent this disease is important too.

Another impetus to popularity of curry was provided by an Anglo-Indian chef Gurpareet Bains. He claimed to have cooked up the 'world's healthiest meal' a cancer-fighting curry. The chicken and blueberry curry with goji berry pilau rice is full of natural healthy superfoods that can help fight cancer, claimed the 32-year-old creator. He further claimed that the spicy chicken meal could help fight off carcinogenic cells while other traditional ingredients such as ginger, chilli, turmeric and garlic, 'are known for their antibacterial and antiviral properties'.

The Bedford-based Bains, the Indian superfood innovator and nutritional therapist, averred that eating the curry just once-a-week could "deal a devastating blow" to the onset of cancers and other diseases like Alzheimer's.

It has long been known that some foods including spices and fruits have exceptional health benefits. So combining these two genres of food stuffs seemed logical in any quest to find the world's healthiest meal. Thus the curry I have created [it took him two years to perfect it] is brimming with health-beneficial ingredients that could, if eaten regularly, deal a devastating blow to many diseases.

He reportedly researched the best natural superfoods and calculated the exact quantities of each ingredient needed for optimum health results. His finished meal is full of antioxidants, anti- fungals, anti- virals, analgesics, and anti-bacterials. Each plateful contains 25,000 'ORAC' units— the scientific measurement of antioxidants in foods.

Experts were quoted saying it was up to 20 times more nutritious than any specially-formulated 'healthy' meal. Foods higher on the ORAC (Oxygen Radical Absorbance Capacity) scale have been proven to counter the onset of cancer, Alzheimer's, coronary heart disease and diabetes. Almost a quarter of antioxidant-rich foods are spices— a single teaspoon of cinnamon is the equivalent of two portions of grapes or a glass of fresh pomegranate juice.

The Recipe (For healthy living)

Chicken Curry with Blueberries and Goji Berry Pilau

(*Serves four*)

To cook curry

1. Blend 20g of chopped coriander, 200g of fresh or frozen blueberries, two tablespoons of freshly grated ginger, and 3/4 of a teaspoon of salt with 500g of low-fat Greek yoghurt, and set aside.
2. Place four cloves of chopped garlic into a saucepan with three tablespoons of olive oil and heat on a low-medium flame until the garlic starts to turn brown — this should take no longer than one or two minutes.

3. Add one teaspoon of turmeric, mix well and heat through for 20 seconds. Mix in two tablespoons of ground cinnamon and one teaspoon of chilli powder and cook for 20 seconds.
4. Add 500g of chicken breast, cut into bite-sized pieces, and seal, stirring frequently— this should take no more than five minutes.
5. Now slowly pour the yoghurt mixture, mixing into the chicken, and bring to a simmer on a low heat
6. Simmer for 10 minutes uncovered, stirring from time to time. Mix through one teaspoon of garam masala. Garnish with extra coriander.

To cook Pilau

1. Place two teaspoons of cumin seeds and two tablespoons of olive oil into a saucepan and heat on a low-medium flame until the seeds begin to pop—this should take no more than three minutes.
2. Add one small sliced onion and cook until soft. Then add one teaspoon of turmeric powder, stir and heat for 20 seconds. Add one grated carrot. Cook for two minutes.
3. In the meantime, boil 1 3/4 cups of water.
4. Place the onion mixture, one cup of basmati rice, 1/2 tsp teaspoon salt and the boiling water into a large microwaveable bowl and mix with a fork.
5. Cook uncovered in the microwave for 4 minutes (700W), 3 1/2 minutes (800W) or 3 minutes (900W).
6. Mix and cook for 4 minutes (700W), 3 1/2 minutes (800W) or 3 minutes (900W).
7. Cover and continue to cook for 4 minutes (700W), 3 1/2 minutes (800W) or 3 minutes (900W).
8. Add 50g of goji berries and a handful of peas and let stand covered for 10 minutes.
9. Fluff the pilau with a fork, and serve.

CURRY, SEX ON THE PLATE

There was another twist to the curry success when a team of researchers at Nottingham Trent University, not too long ago, came up with the finding that the curry was like sex on a plate. They said that curry was as addictive as sex. The leader of the team Prof. Stephen Gray reiterated that the psychological effect of the curry led to addiction as it gave more high than favourite British dishes. The bodies start to crave for the dish just like for sex. The researchers had compared the effects of tikka masala, korma and rogan josh with those of fish and chips. The finding was scientifically explained. Whatever it might be, sex on the plate, or the curry's own hypnotizing qualities, the fact is that it is the hottest favourite of Britons as well as Scots. The phenomenon has come to be known as 'currification'.

The knowledge about the Indian cuisine and its nuances, which since the nineties percolated to the inner most cities, ironically appears to be much more than in India, where food in different regions radically vary and there is hardly much interest, say, in south India to know about Bengali machhar jhol or Rajasthani gatta curry. In Britain, on the other hand, the interest in Indian cuisine developed partly due to the habit-forming tasty spicy curry, which nudged out the bland English dishes, and also partly because of the advent of books and literature on Indian cookery, which encouraged housewives to try out Indian dishes at home. Chapman alone has written 34 books with sales topping 1.5 million. Rosemary Stark complimenting him wrote in *Daily Mail* that he was responsible for Baltifying Britain.

The tentacles of the Indian food have spread wide and deep. In Newquay, seaside resort and fishing port on the north Atlantic coast of Cornwall, I was struck by signs for fish and chips along with offer of kebabs at small kiosk-like outlets near the beach. Moreover, like fish and chips on a paper, kebabs too were served on small napkin-size paper plates. There could be no better proof of how much Indian food has taken over Britain. I had been to most sea resorts and invariably spotted a number of restaurants claiming to serve Indian meals. Even in Inverness in Scotland, when I asked the manager of Thistle Hotel (where I was staying to do a story on the Loch Ness monster) about Indian restaurants in the city, he gave names of three which he said were good. Even along the lake I found a small Indian Balti curry house. Its owner told me that many tourists attracted by the mystery of the monster passed by. 'Thanks to Nessie, I am doing rather well.'

I wonder if sometime in the future one will come across Indian curry houses, westernized dhaba style, on motorways.

Aishwarya Rai at the launch of Gautam Rajadhyaksha's Bollywood exhibitionat Sitaaray: Fun n Food

Javed Akhtar and Shabana Azmi: at opening of Sitaaray

Chutney Mary: ever-changing decor, keep diners coming

Masala Zone: Interior attracts

Khattar's Tamarai Resturant: Always a waiting list

Restaurant Openings on Social Calendars

Since the late nineties the opening of an up-market Indian restaurant is always an 'event' and the elite are invariably seen happily tasting the new eats. Most restaurants have something to entice either through new dishes or even by themed interiors. Sir Michael Caine and his wife Shakira's high-class Deya in Portman Square claimed to serve the hottest curry. It boasted one of the capital's most admired Indian chefs, Sanjay Dwivedi, formerly of Zaika.

Rohit Khattar's Chor Bizarre that opened in 1997 near the Ritz Hotel in Mayfair was the only one outside the Kashmir Valley that had access to the secrets of the 'Wazwan'— the legendary ceremonial feast of 36 courses. It was also the first restaurant in London which has a branch of the same name in Delhi. Khattar had stuck to the concept of chor bazaar (thieves' market), all the chairs and tables were of different shapes and designs, as if each one was picked from flea or from stolen goods markets. He had hit the jackpot.

But he too has over the years been changing the menu, enticing people with fashion shows, painting exhibitions and arranging poetry sessions or discussions. I have met many film stars, artistes, fashion designers and poets there as well as Lords, Baronesses, corporate heads, ministers and diplomats.

He went on experimenting and opened Tamarai (lotus) in Drury Lane. The menu of pan-Asian dishes took one year to prepare—the result, it won the prize for the best wine list. His third, Sitaraay, with a Bollywood theme as the name suggests, introduced exclusive tandoori dishes. It was appropriately opened in the presence of Javed Akhtar and Shabana Azmi. Around the same time Aishwarya Rai inaugurated 'Faces', a photographic exhibition by the legendary lensman Gautam Rajadhyaksha. It really drew a big crowd.

The serving style was also fascinating. It is always difficult to get a table at Tamarai and no wonder it won the prize for restaurant with best value for money. "I had gone to London with trepidation" said Khattar. 'London had already many established, well-known restaurants. It was like carrying coal to Newcastle.' But I can say that he brought to London a unique dining experience, full of exciting events and exciting people, poets, drama personalities, writers, fashion czars and, of course, beautiful Bollywood ladies.

> I wonder if some time in the future one will come across Indian curry houses, westernized dhaba style, on motorways.

Ways of Enticing

The established ones, despite doing brisk business, also refurbish their restaurants and change their menus to keep ambience of a freshly opened one. Veeraswamy, one of the oldest restaurants in London—about 90-year-old— was completely refurbished by Namita Panjabi and old and new clients tempted with a revised menu offering several delicacies from India. I had been there before it was taken over by Panjabi, her husband Ranjit Mathrani and sister Camillea. It looked as if it had seen its best days. But after its complete makeover it became a rather alluring place. They also started a chain of middle-range restaurants called Masala Zone. The first one that opened on Marshall Street in Soho, apart from novel cuisine and thalis at very reasonable rates, had drawings by Rajeev Sethi of the journey of a villager from his rural countryside to the urban, industrialized Mumbai on its walls—reminiscent of the sketches on the thatched walls of huts in rural India. It became an attraction for both Londoners and tourists who flock to the place.

Many prominent Indians were invited to its opening with a novel lunch menu as bait. Lord Swraj Paul, Lord Bagri, and several other known NRIs had come and all of them were amazed at the items, including the famous Lucknowi chaat. Namita Panjabi told me that she brought one member of the family owning the most popular chaat house in Lucknow and took me to the kitchen to meet him. She cautioned me not to write about him in my report. 'Chefs like him are stolen shamelessly'. She was right. I know the case of one tandoori specialist who was enticed away by an Indian-origin multi-millionaire when he opened his own restaurant, without the least concern that he was luring him away from a friend's eatery.

But back to how the Indian restaurants keep their flock of customers and rope in the new. Bombay Brasserie in Kensington— where Stevie Wonder sang live as also singer Macy Gray, where all three Godfathers Marlon Brando, Al Pacino and Andy Garcia, were hosted, where a takeaway was sent on a private jet to Italy for Tom Cruise and Sir Anthony Hopkins celebrated his

> Rohit Khattar's Chor Bizarre that opened in 1997 near the Ritz Hotel in Mayfair was the only one outside the Kashmir Valley that had access to the secrets of the 'Wazwan'— the legendary ceremonial feast of 36 courses.

sixtieth birthday—is regarded as one of the classy Indian restaurants. The restaurant was closed for five months to reinvent itself to offer the original Bombay Colonial feel with contemporary elements. It brought the Taj Group of Hotels' executive chef Hemant Oberoi to overhaul its menus and opened with a pan-Indian menu.

Likewise, Chutney Mary has been a landmark for connoisseurs of good food since it opened in 1990 with its English décor serving seven main cuisines of India— Lucknow and Punjab in the north; Gujarat and Parsi in the west; Hyderabad in central India; Chettinad in the south; and Goa and Kerala on the south- west coast. Namita, Mathrani and Camillea brought chefs over from each of these regions to recreate the flavours, textures, spices, cooking techniques and ingredients of each region. Namita and Camellia go back to the roots of Indian cooking, and prise recipes from 'gourmet homes and the palaces of maharajah, and from the roadside cafes and street stalls that were the one real, vibrant form of public food'. But they too refurbish to keep the clientele coming and to meet challenges from newly opened curry houses.

In fact, the three of them have done yeoman service in the currification of Britain and in the process built a multi-million pound empire—possibly more apt to say created a Raj in reverse. The list of celebrities who are regulars there is imposing—they come from across the Atlantic as well.

Dr Kartar Lalwani came out with a novel concept for his Indali Lounge restaurant on Baker Street. He (Dr Lalvani made his fortune selling vitamins) claimed that his was the world's healthiest Indian restaurant, where cholesterol 'is kept under control by not using butter, ghee and cream. Sunflower and olive oils with fresh herbs and spices are used to give the flavour'. Naan is blended from barley, oat and wheat for extra fibre. Its theme is we look after your health while providing you tasty north Indian meal. You can see the curiosity on the faces of diners there. There is apparently no dearth of weight watchers.

These upmarket restaurants have supplanted to some extent clubs and hotels where important social and business meets were normally held. The

> The three of them (Namita Panjabi, her husband and sister) have done yeoman service in the currification of Britain and in the process built a multi-million pound empire—possibly more apt to say created a Raj in reverse.

Confederation of Indian Industry hosted its annual evening get-togethers in London at Bombay Brasserie and Banaras where British CEOs and investment bankers enjoyed Indian snacks. I have attended at least two or three meals hosted by visiting Indian ministers at Atul Kochar's Banaras, and Air-India hosted its dinners at La Portes Des Inde. British CEOs have often been spotted at Chor Bizarre or Chutney Mary or Bombay Brasserie entertaining their business guests.

The stories of the likes of Brad Pitt ordering Indian curry to be flown thousands of miles are now no longer considered newsworthy. The British politicians, MPs and ministers, often gather at Cinnamon Club, an Indian restaurant, located in a building that once housed a Victorian Library in Westminster. Another restaurant Kundan, near Parliament, has the division bell because many MPs lunch there and they can rush when it rings to alert them of voting to take place. I was told John Major was one of its regular diners.

The list of clientele to a few top Indian restaurants is elitist and reads like a Who's Who. I soon realized the truism of Press Counsellor Ian Hughes' advice on the eve of my departure to London, 'If you have to meet an Englishman urgently, invite him for an Indian meal.'

Elite, Exotica, Exotic Prices

I did not have much idea of the popularity of Indian cuisine or curry houses until while staying at Taj Baileys in 1985 I went to have dinner at its restaurant Bombay Brasserie. I was astounded to see Prince Charles and Diana dining there. Completely at ease, they looked like any young couple on an evening date.

I recall Diana munching some nibbles and Charles placing the order. Curious about them being there, I asked the waiter serving me about the royal couple and was informed that they often dined there. 'They like the biryani here.' So I too ordered the same. And realized why the biryani there had the royal stamp of approval. Come to think of it, it was the first and last time that I personally saw the two together. By the time I was in my London posting the cracks had appeared and they were moving inexorably towards divorce, each declaring his or her extra marital affairs with bravura on television.

Another mystery for me was the popularity of the top Indian curry houses despite their 'exotic' prices. One manager said it testified the extent to which Indian food was liked by the English. But Namita Panjabi was more candid. 'It's about sophistication of the curry for the elite. Everyone is willing to pay a huge amount for his pot of curry. The good Indian restaurants are very, very expensive.' It takes her chef three hours to prepare an exotic spread of which the cost is 40 pounds. Tamarind in Mayfair had charged 40,000 pounds for 100 guests and that was the cost sometime ago. Andy Varma, of Vama, London's new-age restaurant, was quoted saying, 'whoever said, Fish 'n' Chips was London's staple diet, curry and rice is our first cuisine. At Vama, guests spend almost 70 pounds every night on one curry dish. I have Robbie Williams walk in every other day, because he wants his lamb pasandas. He's not the only one, there's Naomi Campbell, Jodie Kidd who've discovered Kerala curry'.

Obviously those who love the curry from classy joints can afford such prices. The list is never ending, Prince Philip, Victoria and David Beckham, Hugh Grant, Liz Hurley, Tom Cruise, Rupert Murdoch, Cliff Richard, Brad Pitt and Steven Spielberg. And, of course, the Indian stars. Politicians too have soft spot for the curry. I have always found Indian meal at all the functions hosted by Labour Friends of India.

Once I invited the shadow Home Secretary Dominic Grieve and his wife, a QC, to Sitaraay. The restaurant has on its walls pictures of heroines, heroes, villains and playback singers. Where we sat the pictures were of heroines and my guests spent quite some time admiring the beauties of the past and the present. They obviously did not understand the words of the songs played, mostly from old films like *Andaz* and *Pyasa*, but did seem to understand the pathos and longing in them. 'The music seems to blend with the ambience,' said Grieve.

I have compared prices at restaurants in five-star hotels in New Delhi. Although it seems exorbitant when one is paying in Indian rupee but they are less than the prices at most good Indian restaurants in Central London. But even then I found that there would always be a waiting list at restaurants like Chutney Mary, Veeraswamy or Chor Bizarre, especially on weekends.

Anything Indian goes

The chronicle of how Indian cuisine became part of British dining habit, how they adjusted their palate to the spicy food and the magic that Indian eateries have woven to mesmerize the English reads like a romantic fiction. It indeed is amazing that even those who have little knowledge of the cuisine revel at all kinds of combinations. I could not help noticing at a restaurant in Inverness, a stout baldish gentleman having pappadom and naan with chutneys. No wonder he kept wiping sweat from his head. I asked the waiter why it was not explained to him that he needed a curry too. 'Sir, he comes at least once a fortnight and he likes only what he is eating. He thinks curries are too oily.' So everyone to his own taste, like the German diner at a London restaurant eating, ostensibly with relish, salad and naan.

Otherwise, apart from a few exceptions, the English or for that matter many in European capitals know the dishes they like and invariably try to find out about new additions on the menus. I saw a Lord with his family discussing in detail various items with the steward at Veeraswamy. I was delighted to overhear that he ordered a curry which was a speciality of Avadh cuisine—Gosht Hara Salan. I belong to Lucknow. I noticed at Chor Bizarre that most English diners were regulars and often did not refer to the menu while ordering. Obviously no one suffers from the dreaded Delhi belly after eating at famous, genuine Indian restaurants. The danger might lurk in some pseudo- Indian restaurants.

I recall a rather hilarious case wherein a curry dish caused quite a stir in a court. The wheels of justice had to be halted at Guilford Crown Court in Surrey when lawyers of both prosecution and defence, after lunch recess, had to make frequent visits to the toilet. The jury was amused to learn that the two learned counsels had conveyed to the judge that they enjoyed a curry with naan at a nearby curry house and since then their trips to the loo were irritatingly frequent. The defence lawyer was first to start the journey to the toilet but the prosecution counsel was soon afflicted and followed him. The masala curry led the judge to postpone the case for a week. But this was a rare case.

The health officers have increased their scrutiny over the years. In fact, I was struck by the honesty in scrutiny when a very popular bar of a five-star hotel, which I frequented quite often to meet friends, was sealed. I had gone to meet an Indian VIP who was staying at the hotel one evening. After the meeting, I went to the bar to meet a journalist friend. But I saw him standing outside the bar that was shut. When I had passed it earlier it was open. I wondered what had happened in the meanwhile. Though the hotel staff was quiet about this we remembered a couple of mice used to be regulars at the bar. In fact most human regulars there were quite fond of them. The mice would scurry from under one table to another and nibble parts of canapés and cheese that fell on the carpet. They caused no fright even among the ladies. But the health officers supposedly were not that friendly.

It was then no surprise that the health squad caught a popular curry house in Curry Mile in Manchester where cockroaches ruled the kitchen. It was fined over 30,000 pounds and closed for six months. I thanked my stars that I was not sick after eating there once when I had gone to Manchester. Such inspections have had salutary effect and the curry is where it has been, at the top. The CTM remains the nation's delight. The later findings that turmeric helped prevent malignancy and a few other herbs had Viagra-like qualities have driven away all inhibitions about the curry.

The CTM's New Rivals

I was lucky to be initially briefed on the history of Indian restaurants by Mr Mahendra Kaul, then the co-owner of the well-known Viceroy of India restaurant on Glentworth Street off Baker Street and one of the pioneers in introducing Indian cuisine in Britain. He was not enthused much about the chicken tikka masala curry, affectionately called CTM, and I recall an anecdote he narrated about this 'tandoori' gravy. He had invited the Indian High Commissioner, a Kashmiri and a connoisseur of good Indian food, for the opening of his Gaylords International in Mayfair decades ago. High Commissioner TN Kaul agreed with the proviso that if there was any tandoori dish like CTM he would rather dine at home. But that CTM and tandoori dishes now make for almost 65 per cent of the turnover of curry houses.

The statistics of the sales of CTM are fascinating. Marks & Spencer claim to sell 18 tonnes a week, while 27 million portions a year are sold in Indian restaurants and about 12 tonnes of it a day are produced by Noon Products that are supplied to supermarkets. The Bangladeshis claim that most schools and charities in Sylhet—from where most chefs come to work in Balti curry eateries are run by proceeds from its sales. No wonder Chef Iftekar Haris from Newport, Gwent wrote a musical in praise of it.

> In fact most human regulars there were quite fond of them. The mice would scurry from under on table to another and nibble parts of canapés and cheese that fell on the carpet. They caused no fright even among the ladies.

The National Curry Week organizers claim that if all the portions sold in one year in the UK were stacked they would constitute a tikka tower 2,770 times taller than the Greenwich Millennium Dome—165ft. Now we know why the late Foreign Secretary, Robin Cook, declared CTM to be Britain's national dish, replacing the ubiquitous fish 'n' chips. Even after a decade of being so crowned CTM remains the most desired dish but Indian restaurants have not depended on it to be their till-movers.

Spicy Newcomers

The Indian restaurant owners have quite ingeniously kept diners coming to them with their new cuisines and regional dishes, which become popular in quick time. Arun Harnal, executive operations director of Bombay Brasserie, said people were now trying different dishes as 'they get more knowledgeable although chicken tikka masala will always be popular' but seva batata puri, the legendary lamb chops with ginger, Goa fish curry and Prawn balchao are all his restaurant's iconic dishes and are much in demand.

At Tamarai, owner Rohit Khattar, who seemingly believes in continuous innovation and experimentation, introduced pan-Asian fare and hit the jackpot. The name itself has a meaning. Says Khattar, 'The lotus, a symbol of the sun, of creation and rejuvenation, is considered to be the first flower to appear on earth and is intrinsic to the folklore of some of the world's ancient civilizations; symbolizing the eight-fold path to enlightenment in Buddhism, as well as in Hindu mythology, the lotus is a form that has inspired art and emotion through the ages and is the design and cuisine inspiration for TAMARAI.' Rare among London restaurants, guests dining at Tamarai are able to enjoy a late night license and complimentary parking in the building.

Anshuman Saxena, general manager, Tamarai, talking about the English diners said that 'Now the palate of an average Briton is becoming more used to higher spice levels. There was a research done recently which proved that on Scoville scale (the measure of spiciness), British palate has become more and more desirous of spicy foods, whether it's Indian, Chinese or popular Peri-Peri Portuguese (Nandos).' Elaborating on the Britishers' experiments with new cuisine he added:

> *Not only spice, Britons are experimenting with innovative cuisine that takes Indian food to new boundaries, using European ingredients,*

local meats, mixed recipes and fusion food. The most popular dish no doubt is still chicken tikka masala and its variants. But, tandoori kababs are also more popular now.

Seekh kabab, chicken tikka, lamb chops are all becoming more popular as they go well with drinks and are easier to eat than a curry. Guests are also ordering more regional Indian dishes like South Indian, Kashmiri, Bengali, Hyderabadi– all these regional cuisines are getting reflected in most modern Indian menus.

He is right and is endorsed by what Peter Grove, editor, *Masala & Menu* commented in a magazine, 'We discovered tandoori chicken but that wasn't enough. Now, want to know about regional Indian cuisine, we're ready to try something new'.

A number of special festivals are held by restaurants where regional dishes, prepared by chefs flown from respective regions are served. Game birds-based Jodhpuri style dishes were served for a fortnight at Chor Bizarre, with the former Maharaja bringing in his personal chefs, and it attracted connoisseurs in hordes. Wines to go with each dish were suggested. In fact Rohit Khattar once collaborated with the well-known wine-taster Charles Metcalfe, vice-chairman of the International Wine Challenge, for a 'dine and wine' experiment.

It took a whole year for the two to prepare a guide for socialites on choosing the appropriate wine to serve with a particular dish. Aloo ki tikki was to be served with a dry Riesling as its accompaniment for gourmet delight. Metcalfe said he concentrated on spices used for an item and tried to match the flavour with a wine which made one savour the dish better. 'The tamarind and yoghurt in aloo ki tikki make it high in natural acidity which goes well with a German Riesling.' So he suggested the tikki to be enjoyed with sips of Devil's Rock Riesling. He matched chicken tikka with a Chardonnay and sheekh kabab with a white wine because of black cumin, garlic and lemon

Not only spice, Britons are experimenting with innovative cuisine that takes Indian food to new boundaries, using European ingredients, local meats, mixed recipes and fusion food.

used in its preparation. The list of good food with good booze was given to all invitees.

Many invitees including Tiger Pataudi tried the recommendations. None could last the whole list. But it was fun to taste a particular item and then sip the wine suggested to be drunk with it. We would try to nod intelligently as if we were able to distinguish the difference of taste between sipping say a recommended Australian Shiraz and a non-recommended Chilean Sauvignon. Frankly, by the end of the evening everything tasted nice. And Metcalfe kept grinning—possibly knowing our state—as we complimented him before leaving.

Rise of Regionalism

Some of the regional dishes became popular so quickly that they could command high prices. The likes of spicy Chettinad cost not less than 17 pounds, and yet it is much in demand. As once Jiggs Kalra said, the spices and aroma of Indian dishes is tempting. 'You wouldn't have had Kerala's Kozhikkari in Delhi … but you can get it in London.' Quite true! This is because the English are ever willing to try anything new. Saxena at Tamarai endorsed this. 'Guests like to experiment by ordering, maybe, one dish out of four that they have not tried before, so this satisfies the adventurous dining spirit.'

This is why food critics believe that in Britain Indian cuisine is continually being rediscovered. 'Everyone is finding it more sophisticated than French cuisine. But for god's sake it isn't about dal makhani and chicken tikka masala,' said Cameilla Panjabi to a critic.

The overnight success of Taj's 'Quillon' restaurant which serves Kerala food testifies to the popularity of regional meals. It got the Michelin star, and more foreigners than Indians dine there. I once took a German diplomat for lunch there, and she later told me that she went there quite often and

Jiggs Kalra said, the spices and aroma of Indian dishes is tempting. 'You wouldn't have had Kerala's Kozhikkari in Delhi … but you can get it in London.' Quite true! This is because the English are ever willing to try anything new.

all her German friends simply loved the food there. I would never forget one lunch hosted there by Omar Abdullah, when he was minister of state in external affairs ministry. About eight of us, of which five were journalists from television and print media, had just finished the starters, when one of the media persons, possibly from *The Independent* as far as I remember got a call on his mobile. He went out to talk and then came back and told me in whispers that a plane hit one of the World Towers. I told him it must be some silly amateur on a small flying club plane. But then the BBC man's mobile rang too and he returned to tell us in sombre tone that it appeared to be a major catastrophe. All of us got up. The tragic events of 9/11 had begun to unfold.

Whenever I went back to 'Quillon', it was difficult not to remember that day. But the food is so delicious that nothing can ever affect the dining experience. The chief chef Sriram Aylur reiterated time and again that he would use only authentic ingredients for preparing Kerala dishes. The result is that the English repeatedly go there because they have got attuned to the 'Quillon' taste.

Secret of Success

The very fact that curry has more English connoisseurs than Bollywood has managed to allure English fans—although Britain often saves many Indian producers from complete disaster at the box office— is the benchmark of the extent of the success of the Indian cuisine. Another amazing fact, and that adds to the 'glory' of the curry, is that despite Britain being multicultural with restaurants specializing in cuisines from almost all parts of the globe, Indian food has left most far behind. Chinese restaurants and takeaways were dominant for a long time but eventually the Indian restaurants—95 per cent Bangladeshi—and takeaways have 'raced' to the top.

Industry insiders reiterate that Britain has been easily captivated by the curry because of its close ties with the Indian subcontinent. A distant cousin of mine used to regale us with this story of an encounter at one of the London tea shops in the early fifties. He was enjoying a cup of Indian tea and an apology for samosa with another Indian friend who later became the Lieutenant-Governor of Delhi. My cousin looking towards an Englishman who was eating his samosa with much relish said to his friend in Hindi, 'What does he know about real samosas. He thinks it is the best. Poor fellow.'

When my cousin and his friend got up to leave the Englishman, speaking in Hindi, told them, 'Yes, this garib (poor) gora (white) does not know what a real samosa is. I commanded a unit in Ranchi for many years. The way you two becharas (simpletons) spoke I realized you are from Bihar. Don't think we are ignorant about how most Indian dishes taste.' My cousin said never again while in London he dared to denigrate the Britishers' knowledge of Indian cuisine.

Connoisseurs of Indian cuisine also often aver that the Indian restaurants in London serve superb, authentic Indian cuisine which is occasionally better than the food served at restaurants in India. One such instance happened at Tamarai. A famous Indian surgeon had gone to dine at the restaurant with his family. After looking at the menu and tasting the starters, he wanted to try most items on the menu as it seemed the starters were better than what he had had in India. But, he added he could not eat much. It was a tall order but it was complied with. Chef Manish, a personable fellow unlike some snooty ones, served him small portions, totalling 19 courses. He was amazed at the variety served. Back in India, he was full of praise for Tamarai food.

I would personally testify that one or two dishes at Veeraswamy that are from Avadh are far superior in taste than what is served at any eatery in Lucknow, the capital of the old Avadh. The kababs at Sitaraay or Amaya could, on their chefs' days of peak culinary form, give Bukhara a run for its money—my apologies to Bukhara, which has figured over the years in the top 50 finest restaurants in the world. I would not know much about the Kerala cuisine but a few from that region told me that some of the preparations at 'Quillon' were as good as, if not better, than at the best eating places in Trivandrum.

I think the way in which the items are served, the décor and general ambience in most London restaurants also contribute to the diners' bias for Indian preparations in Britain. The chefs and owners in the country know they have to continuously offer the best and serve in the most attractive way to keep a 'foreign' diner coming repeatedly. Unlike Indians back home, they do not habitually eat Indian food. They have to be enticed and addicted by offering the best. This is why the ingredients used are most authentic, original and utmost care is taken in preparing each dish. At Quillon, Namita Punjabi's Chutney Mary and many other classy eateries spices are imported if need be. Many owners and chefs keep travelling to India to find new regional recipes to offer both clientele— the English and the diaspora.

All top establishments also keep refurbishing the interiors to give a new look. When I went to La Porte Des Indes with some friends, we were intrigued to see the bar floor covered with peanut shells. Chor Bizarre was noticed instantly because all furniture and accessories picked up randomly from chor bazaar and thus nothing was in harmony.

But all success cannot be attributed to change in menus or decors alone. Sanjay Ghai's Gaylords on Mortimer Road near Regent Street has had its menu unchanged for years, yet it is always full house there. His clients are mostly English and Indians who have retained the taste for real Punjabi and North Indian fare that used to be available in Gaylords in Connaught Place in Delhi in the fifties. When I asked Ghai why he did not change the menu, his response was, 'for decades (he opened in 1963) my food has been popular. Most of my diners come repeatedly. They have got habituated and like what we have been offering. Why should I change?'

Right, why play with the golden goose. I too have repeatedly gone there with English friends like Peter Oborne, the well-known political columnist. I know any time I tell Peter 'Lets go to Gaylords', he would never say no.

The success of Indian cuisine is thus, surprisingly, also partly due to what Ghai said. Stick with the tasty dishes and get your regulars habituated to them. Sital Singh Mann, owner of the Punjab Indian Restaurant, one of the first Indian curry houses in 1947, would agree with Ghai enthusiastically. The recipes of the food there possibly date back to the favourite dishes available in Patiala or Amritsar in the last century. Pictures of the erstwhile Maharajas in Punjab adorn the walls with one caption helpfully telling us that the particular Maharaja had several wives, some of these Maharanis very pretty naturally, can be seen in the photograph.

These pictures of regal bygone days are themselves attractions for the English and tourists who throng Convent Garden. Whenever I have gone there with my friend Prem Prakash, chairman of *Asian News International*, I have invariably looked at each of the pictures that bring alive the era of princely splendour. There are no pretensions about the decor but the place is immaculately clean and steaming dishes are served by smiling waiters. The standard for the food was set by the father of the present owner. He told his son, 'The food should be such that you can eat it every day. Only then customers will keep coming again and again.' And they do.

Mann has followed the counsel and eats everyday the food prepared in the restaurant's kitchen. The recipe has hardly undergone any change since

1947 but you would have to wait to be seated during evenings. That old is gold is seemingly true for Mann and Ghai. Such continuity is, as I said, one of the paradoxes in the Indian cuisine's unbelievable success in Britain.

But what is its future? If fish 'n' chips could be challenged by chicken tikka masala curry, how can there be any guarantee about the future of Indian cuisine. The answer to this was provided, albeit indirectly, by *Daily Telegraph*. While reporting the move by the Department of Trade and Industry to inject a few millions in the curry industry, which it argued helped generate 1,000 more jobs, the paper commented that 'there is more future in making curries than in making pottery, and certainly more future than making steel with government money.' This must have been music to the ears of the Indian restaurant owners and those of manufacturers of packaged readymade meals.

The last word was said by an official. 'The investment backing only affirms the fact that Indian curry is now nation's favourite. It provides the maximum revenue and will soon become the most major export items.' So don't be surprised if Marks & Spencer stock packed chicken rogan josh and lamb masala curry in their Indian outlets. And I bet its demand could soar to become their fastest selling item in India. And to think, Khattar worried about carrying coal to Newcastle.

Genuine Indian Restaurants

There have been many arguments over the number of restaurants serving the real Indian cuisine. Lately, the owners of Bangladeshi restaurants, which account for over ninety per cent of the total number of those serving Indian cuisine, have been demanding a separate identity. Many of them, whether in London, Glasgow or Manchester and Birmingham, are famous for good fare and built a large number of regulars. Several of them have been winning awards for the best curry since several years.

I asked around. Anshuman Saxena of Tamarai gave a reasoned answer. 'Because now most good Indian restaurants employ chefs who have been trained in India, the authenticity of restaurants is high even if they are not owned by Indians.' He is right. The recent immigration rules have made it impossible to get visas for chefs from Bangladesh. The owners have made innumerable representations to the Government that their businesses have been going down as they are unable to get chefs who know the recipes of the country. Some even closed down. The Government has been insisting that

A short list of elite diners

Sultan of Brunei, Tom Cruise, Sharon Stone, Mel Gibson, Nicole Kidman, Chelsea Clinton, Bryan Adams, who has a personal Indian chef, Johnny Depp is a chicken biryani freak, Uma Thurman, Minnie Driver, Boris Becker, Mahesh Bhupati, and the King and Queen of Jordan, who like low-cal, non-spicy Indian dishes.

those from East Europe could be trained but that is indeed ridiculous. For one there is the language barrier and it would take ages to train them. The recipes are very complex. This has forced many restaurants from Bangladesh to look at other options, like employing an Indian chef. It would be easy to train them.

But despite these problems a massive 95 per cent of the remaining Indian outlets are run by Bangladeshis who mostly hail from the Sylhet area in the north-east of the country (the pattern is a legacy from the time that Sylheti seamen became galley hands and cooks on British merchant ships and established cafes and tea-houses in waterfront areas when they settled in the UK. (Source: *New Statesman*)

In cities such as Bradford, Birmingham, Manchester and Glasgow the trade is dominated by Pakistanis, Mirpuris, Bangladeshis and some Indians; and London suburbs like Wembley and Tooting have large Gujarati Hindu populations with their own distinctive, often vegetarian, restaurants (over 145 vegetarian restaurants) in London.

Mother of all Controversies

When, how and where? The controversy over the origins of chicken tikka masala (CTM) has become a part of the Indian curry saga in Britain. The interest in CTM is quite unbelievable, according to BBC. It is estimated that it forms the subject of well over 60 per cent of all enquiries from the media both in Britain and internationally. Only one thing is clear that in India the dish had been comparatively unknown until it was declared by the then Foreign Secretary, late Robin Cook, to be Britain's true national dish, deposing fish and chips. Many outraged voices were raised.

Cook was said to have suffered from Tory xenophobia. But it all was to no avail. Its sale in its various mutations is awesome— Sainsbury's sell 1.6 million CTM meals every year and stocks 16 CTM-related products including chicken tikka masala pasta sauce and other derivations CTM crisps, CTM pizzas, CTM Kievs and Marks and Spencer's famous CTM sandwiches (18 tonnes devoured every week) according to BBC.

But it is also a fact that there is no mention of it or recipes given of how to cook it in most Indian cookery books, of which there is a surfeit. A report said Alan Davidson's *Oxford Companion to Food* did not even consider it deserving of a listing. It is true that many chefs ridicule the preparation. I know at least three in London who said CTM, what CTM, it's just a mixture of oil and spices, absolute mutilation of genuine Indian dishes.

A 1998 survey by *Real Curry Restaurant Guide* found there were 48 different CTMs. The only thing common in them was chicken. Jiggs Kalra told me that a friend of his had brought twelve different types of CTM. 'Their colour varied from red, near yellow, saffron and pinkish. Thank god there was no green coloured CTM,' he said disparagingly. Apart from its sheer 'weight' of the sales its delectable taste swept away the fish and chips, which did not have a chance against the CTM.

It is such a 'jewel' of the Indian cuisine that many claimants have surfaced from time to time claiming to be CTM's innovators. I had initially no idea about the importance of the dish among the gourmets or food critics, but one evening at a dinner Mr Mahendra Kaul related to me the story of the CTM. He did not have very high opinion about it, adding that the real things included tandoori chicken— brought to India by Kundan Lal of 'Moti Mahal' after partition—and chicken tikka. I am told that it was first priced Rs.5 (4p). Unbelievable!

He was candid in saying no one for sure knew how it originated. But the story doing the rounds was that a brigadier retired from the Indian Army had gone to an Indian curry house and wanted a Mughlai (Jiggs Kalra calls it Mughalia) dish. The cook-cum- proprietor prepared chicken tikka but when he brought it to the brigadier saheb he was stunned. The armyman ranted, 'where is the damn curry'. Seething with anger, the cook poured a mixture of oil and water over the tikka. It is said that the saheb was delighted. And thus seeds of the CTM were sown.

According to an article, the shape of things to come might have been a recipe for shahi chicken masala in Mrs Balbir Singh's *Indian Cookery* published in 1961. Many other stories about its origin have been published.

Journalist and restaurateur Iqbal Wahhab's version was almost like Kaul's. He was quoted saying that it was created when a Bangladeshi chef produced a dish of traditional chicken tikka only to be asked 'where's my gravy?' The response was, supposedly, a can of cream of tomato soup and a few spices and the 'masala' element was born. Charles Campion refers to CTM as 'a dish invented in London in the seventies so that the ignorant could have gravy with their chicken tikka'.

Award-winning restaurateur Amin Ali of The Red Fort and Soho Spice in London's Soho claims to have served CTM when he first arrived in London in 1974. A lowly waiter at the time he remembers wondering just what the dish was.

According to another report, 'the descendents of Sultan Ahmed Ansari, who owned the Taj Mahal in Glasgow, claim he invented it in the 1950s'. But no claims have any proof. In any case the tandoor was hardly known even in India until Kundan Lal Gujral of Moti Mahal brought to Delhi his famous tandoori and butter chicken after partition in 1948. It is unbelievable that tandoor could have been known in Glasgow that early.

But more recently another version was given in an Early Day Motion moved by Mohammad Sarwar, MP from Glasgow, along with four other MPs. The EDM demanded that Glasgow be declared the curry capital.

> *That this House records its appreciation of the culinary masterpiece that is chicken tikka masala; notes that it is Britain's most popular curry; recognises that it was invented in the great City of Glasgow by Ali Ahmed Aslam, proprietor of the Shish Mahal restaurant in Glasgow's West End in the seventies; further notes that Glasgow is three times winner of the curry capital of Britain award; and supports the campaign for Glasgow to be given EU Protected Designation of Origin of this most popular dish.*

Chicken tikka masala was most certainly invented in Britain, probably by a Bangaldeshi chef, and is so popular it is even being served in some hotel restaurants in India and Bangladesh. So the mystery about the CTM continues. But as I said earlier it certainly did not originate from India. There is no evidence to suggest that chefs of Mughal emperors had known anything about the CTM nor the khansamas of the Burra Sahebs during the Raj did.

But its testimony lies in the fact that millions love it. A writer put it well, 'chicken tikka masala is very much a Cinderella of culinary creations.' What

BBC noted CTM origin was similar to other exotic dishes/culinary styles that belie their assumed origins, Eg., chopsuey (origin San Francisco); deep-pan pizza (Chicago) and Balti (Birmingham).

more can one say about the 'great' CTM. There is no way to dislodge it from its lofty heights. Many are sorry.

The BBC news feature page said breakdown in traditional British values and rise of multicultural Britain (CTM is most popular dish in UK according to Food Service Intelligence) was synonymous with the rise of chicken tikka masala curry.

It also floated a new 'provenance' saying it was hazy: 'Somewhere in the UK. Various stories abound. Said to have originated between 1950s and 1970s and birthplace is sometimes cited as a Glasgow curry house. Legend has it one obstinate diner demanded gravy on tandoori chicken. A bemused chef responded by adding a tin of Campbell's tomato soup and a pinch of spices, unwittingly partaking in early example of fusion cookery'.

BBC noted CTM origin was similar to other exotic dishes/culinary styles that belie their assumed origins, Eg., chopsuey (origin San Francisco); deep-pan pizza (Chicago) and Balti (Birmingham).

The last word of BBC on CTM was Exportable: in supreme example of 'coals-to-Newcastle'-style international trade, several British firms now sell CTM to India.

The family of Sheikh Abdul Kahlique, owner of the Polash in Shoeburyness, according to a report, benefited from the success of CTM. The report said, 'His father, Haji Abdul Razzah, returned to Bangladesh in 1985 having made sufficient profit to build the Polash Hotel in Sylhet and a mosque and the Polash Sheba Charitable Trust were added after his death.' The family firmly claims its fortunes were largely down to CTM, the mysterious Indian-British hybrid.

7

Delights and Demons of Democracy

> *Sir Christopher Kelly's recommendations are a form of bereavement counselling for expenses-stricken MPs.*
>
> —*Alex Stevenson*

It sounded funny but understandably it could not have amused the MPs who were advised to put the 'abuses of the past behind them' and 'simply get on with it'. The ban on spouses as secretaries must have been especially depressing and to top it the recommendation for ending resettlement grants would make many pockets empty. "The idea of renting in Camberwell or Walworth rather than SW1 will not be welcomed. Most MPs are gnashing at the teeth," said Alex Stevenson, deputy editor, politics.co.uk

The Kelly report on reforms in the system for claiming expenses following the expenses scandal that tainted almost half of the parliamentarians was, I felt, the mechanism for self-introspection and correction. It was the hallmark of an effective democracy. The appointment of Sir Christopher Kelly, within a few months of the exposure of the abuse of expenses' claim procedure in the *Daily Telegraph* and his report in less than six months after that cleared the way for healthier polity and ethical conduct of the elected representatives.

Prime Minister Gordon Brown's demand to shut up and stop causing trouble and the advice to MPs to 'simply get on with it' added to my belief that even if aberrations affected British polity, there were enough mechanisms to pull them back on the right track.

The respect and observance of the rule of law is one of the bulwarks of a working democracy. I heard voices and comments alleging that even at the highest levels of British political life, 'liberties are being taken that affect all our freedoms' though.

Peter Oborne, the noted political columnist of the *Daily Mail*, seemed to be even more disparaging.

> *A new type of government has emerged in Britain over the last twenty-five years. The long tradition of integrity and duty that characterized British public life for much of the nineteenth and twentieth centuries has been abandoned and replaced by a form of capital cronyism----the independence of our great institutions---Parliament, the judiciary, the civil service—has come under attack.*

I was, to say the least, extremely surprised to read such a damning summation of the contemporary British politics. But it deepened my interest in delving further into the system there because the Indian parliamentary system is to a large extent based on the Westminster model. Its democracy not only survived but strengthened despite chaotic collapse of democracies in India's neighbouring countries. There was, however, the dark period of emergency that threatened to uproot democracy in India. However, that was averted by the same person, Mrs Indira Gandhi, who had imposed it and had thrown out civil liberties enshrined in the Indian Constitution. She came back with a thumping majority, voted by the same people who vanquished her less than three years ago. She became more popular and was accepted as one of the avowed democrats in Indian politics. The outpouring of grief when she was felled by the bullets of her personal security guards in 1984 was testimony to the regard and love that she had earned. Sentiments expressed for her on her 25th anniversary only cemented the high pedestal she has been put by the people.

I can only liken, albeit to a very limited extent, such a swing with the political graph of Blair during his over 10 years at Downing Street. I recall what Tony Blair said to his MPs just after his massive victory over the Conservatives in 1997. He was hailed all over Britain as the crusader who would cleanse British polity of the mess left by John Major government. He struck the right note. 'You are not here to enjoy the trappings of power but to do a job and to uphold the highest standards in public life.'

It had sounded a bit familiar. I soon realized that generally in democratic countries newly elected leaders love to promise paradigm shift in policies and politics from that of the vanquished predecessor and in the euphoric ambience they are invariably believed. Likewise people put faith in Blair's claim for cleaner politics and politicians.

The charisma of young Blair indeed had had a mesmerizing effect. His rhetoric and ebullience was a refreshing change from the staid John Major, jaded and worn out from the sleaze and infighting in his party. People were obviously sick and tired of their feuding and the outrageous conduct of quite a few of them.

The déjà vu, due to the Blair effect, was evident. His sense of timing, so crucial, in democratic polity, was perfect. He named Princess Diana, People's Princess within hours of her death which further endeared him to the grieving masses—he was echoing their feeling. Editorials and political columnists expressed belief in him. He brought out people on the streets where they, abandoning the tradition of mourning in private, sobbed uncontrollably for the world to see.

He was credited with savoir faire. That within a couple of years the mood would change and he, until then regarded to have Teflon touch, would be charged with perfidy and betrayal leading to the outcry for him to be tried for war crimes, was unimaginable.

Such dramatic changes in the public mood and even swifter shift in power equations within the Labour Party were revealing to me. It was so different from Indian politics, although both the countries have similar parliamentary systems. The party functioning in India, I realized quite early, was different because of the social and other factors like regional and caste considerations affecting Indian polity. I do not recall any drastic change in India in the public mood, unlike against Blair's policies and style of functioning, except for the tide of disappointment that led to the ouster of the Janata Party government.

I could also compare the change in public sentiment— almost overnight— against V.P. Singh following his 'Mandalization' that had led to a couple of immolations by young men with the sudden rise of resentment and hostility against Blair following his decision to join the American offensive against Saddam Hussain.

But the deluge of protests and demonstrations against his Iraq policy, the near- abusive language used to question his veracity in declaring that Saddam Hussain had weapons of mass destruction that could hit Britain in 45 minutes, ironically strengthened my belief in the democracy in the country. Freedom of expression, the right to protest, which are axioms of democracy, were in full play. There was no attempt by Blair to suffocate dissenting outcries.

Even after the July 7 bombing of underground trains and a double-decker bus in which 52 people lost their lives, there was no evidence that dissent was being suppressed or Muslims were discriminated against. Likewise in India too one has to credit V.P. Singh for not coming down heavily and suppressing the anti-Mandal campaign.

I could favourably compare the independence of institutions like parliament, judiciary and civil services of the two countries. If the importance given by Jawaharlal Nehru to Parliament was missing under some successive prime ministers, so it was during the tenure of a few British prime ministers. There were many other similarities. Except that, maybe, the freedom to write against and criticize the government of the day is more obvious in Britain than in India. But it is hard to say whether it is due to the intolerance of the governments or the control by managements that for various self-interests wish to be in the good books of the ruling party.

It was, anyway, instructive to read columnists and political commentators who had initially pinned faith in Blair turn against him and his new Labour Government with uncharacteristic venom and bitterness. They despised him so much that years later when he emerged as a front-runner to become President of the European Union, one writer commented that another Napolean was not wanted in Europe. In India, usually, such turn-around has been less noticeable. The British media seemed to publish reports about his diminishing chances with glee.

But when he was the prime minister, columnists and political commentators could not dislodge him by their tirades against him. In fact, Hugo Young wrote in *The Guardian*, in June 2003 that when political columns began, 'which was just about when I first got a job in Fleet Street, each paper tended to have one of them, which thus acquired an oracular authority no journalist deserves. In our case, at *Sunday Times*, it was William Rees Mogg. He seemed to be stupendously important. His demand in 1964 that Sir Alec Douglas-Home should quit the leadership of the Conservative Party was met with instant obedience—Home openly admitted that Rees Mogg's piece had pushed him over the edge'.

Today no political columnists, and there are now over 200 of them, can get anyone ousted from office. 'There are no oracles, only a cacophony of rival voices. But I can't think of many other virtues in a state of affairs that has so reordered the space and, often, the prestige afforded to columnists on the one hand and reporters on the other. Reporting is the bedrock of journalism, while columns seem more like the shifting sands of tide and fashion: indisciplined, unreliable and possibly, in the basic scheme of things, unnecessary.' Young rightly pointed out, writing in *The Guardian*, that columnists criticize but do not make decisions. Unlike in the US they are no players in politics of Britain. He gave the instance of President Lyndon Johnson actually going to Walter Lippmann's house in 1964 to ask him what to do about the Vietnam War.

I have included here what Hugo Young wrote to underline that columnists whether in Britain—and in India too I may add —can only criticize and be happy that they got their feelings off their chests but they can hardly force any politician to resign or even mend his or her ways. The writings probably make the politicians more cautious. The barrage of calls by them for Blair to resign has had no effect. He left according to the time he chose. Similarly, Mrs Indira Gandhi ended the Emergency when she thought it was the right time. The protests in some sections of the media have had no effect.

I have sometimes wondered if the downswing in Blair's popularity and credibility in just a few years reflected the power of the public opinion. But he did not leave even at the zenith of his unpopularity that the media made known. Even the huge protests in Hyde Park—one staged by the anti-war campaigners was claimed to have brought in 100,000—against his Iraq policy failed to dislodge him. Was it because these demonstrations did not correctly reflect the public opinion?

It is difficult for me to comment on this. But one thing is sure that as per the British convention, Blair could not be ousted unless his party wished it. And apparently the majority of Labour MPs did not want to. The other thing is that despite the supposed anti-Blair feeling in the people, he won for his party a record third successive term. How could he achieve such a feat if the majority of people were against him? I sometimes wonder if we in the media are good judges of people's views. So did the media's wish for him not to become the European Union President reflect what the British people desired?

The opinion polls which we publish routinely are no better in reflecting the ground reality. An opinion poll that suggested a ten-point Tory lead when comparing David Cameron to Brown was proved pointless. There were nearly a hundred such polls and ratings published since Brown took over from Blair and despite the gloomy forecasts about him and the supposed attempts by his ministers and party to force him to resign, he continued to be at 10 Downing Street. And he seemed to be enjoying his stay there. Columnists and commentators, however, never feel embarrassed and continue to express what they feel. This too is right: the Press is the watchdog after all.

The reason for the columnists who fawned on Blair but turned deadly against him illustrates the necessity of their continuing to write as they feel is in the national and people's interests. They were livid with Blair for risking the lives of the British soldiers in Iraq. His repeated assertions that he took the decision to join the Iraq War because he genuinely believed it was the right thing to do could not convince his critics. They had thus every justification to be up in arms. Anyway, the media vs. Blair ended when Blair resigned. Cherie Blair was the one who silenced them all, and while the family was leaving Downing Street for the last time she looked at the media corps gathered on the opposite pavement and said 'we won't miss you'. I could see the startled faces of the journalists.

I often try to introspect if we in the media abhor a leader who gets too powerful? Blair was in fact very powerful for quite some years after his election in 1997. He was accused of being an autocrat and of acting like a President. But it is also true that he took Britain to new heights and in the process became a world leader. It was he who brokered the coalition to fight the

I often try to introspect if we in the media abhor a leader who gets too powerful? Blair was in fact very powerful for quite some years after his election in 1997. He was accused of being an autocrat and of acting like a President. But it is also true that he took Britain to new heights and in the process became a world leader.

The Queen on her way to open Parliament:
Its exclsuively her day (pic: courtesy The Nation)

Scene outside: Mourners at the Palace gates;
forced Royals to fly flag half-mast (pic: courtesy The Nation)

Dr David Kelly: His suicide almost brought down Labour Government
(pic: courtesy The Nation)

Taliban in Afghanistan. He befriended both Bill Clinton and George Bush on equal terms. He did become a bridge between Europe and the US. Did all this go to change his political psyche and his understanding of his role as the prime minister? I suppose in a way Brown would be happy that he never could become as powerful as his predecessor. That could have been his undoing.

I remember one seasoned British political columnist who seemed to have had some sort of premonition. Only a few days after Blair's stunning victory, sipping cognac after a biryani and kabab dinner at Cinnamon Club near Parliament House, he had a word of caution. 'You must have heard the old saying power corrupts. We have to wait to see how Blair handles his massive mandate. In a democracy you must always expect the unexpected. It's only in autocratic regimes you can be sure of whatever the ruling junta says.' He was prophetic. Yet he never put his views in his columns.

I dare not sum up politics under Blair or later when Brown succeeded him— both because despite staying in Britain for over 15 years I do not understand the psyche of the people nor what has happened in the past. I have a rudimentary knowledge of political history. Margaret Thatcher was said to be very powerful too, possibly much more than Blair, but she was undone by her own party. That I suppose is the crux. No British prime minister can be thrown out however much he or she might become unpopular both with the people and the Press unless the party throws him or her out or the voters do at the election time. Lord Meghnad Desai told me that the removal of a leader is through such a complex procedure that it is nearly impossible to oust him or her, even if a section of the party too wishes that. This was proved when party dissenters moved a motion for throwing out John Major.

I think it is true of all democracies. In India it is similarly impossible for a leader to be touched. V.P. Singh and Chandra Shekhar had to resign because they lost majority. Charan Singh had to go without facing the Lok Sabha (the Lower House) because the Congress Party which had lent its support to ensure majority for him withdrew it. No other prime minister had to go midway.

Freedom to Dissent

In Britain the liberty to express one's feelings, however much against the government, is more than in any developing democracies I feel. The dissent against Blair's Iraq policy or agitations over the mysterious suicide of Dr David Kelly were never smothered. Even the fear of terror attacks, post- 9/11 and 7/7, did not manifest into curbing the right of expression of one's views. Only whipping up hate was made a criminal offence. The massive protests in Hyde Park by the anti-war campaigners and the march by Muslims on the London streets were neither banned nor were any arrests made. It was much later that a few were rounded up for inciting hatred.

When I went on a Sunday to Hyde Park and sauntered near the Speaker's Corner, I was convinced that the right to protest— discouraged even in quite a few democracies— and practice one's belief was not just supercilious pronouncements. I had heard many anecdotes about the often inflammatory and libellous speeches there, but could never imagine what was usually said there and how much immunity speakers enjoyed.

There was a bearded Maulana standing on a soap-box kind of contraption and he seemed to have had attracted a good number of listeners. He was holding forth against western leaders and also denouncing the ones in the Middle East whom he had adjudged as 'dalals' (stooges) of the west. People were all attention. He seemed to be more amusing than a terror mastermind: possibly because of that he was frequently cheered and egged on. He worked himself to a hysterical pitch and his denouements became more lethal. Then, the piece de resistance; he bellowed, 'I would put President ... in the WC and pull the flush.' He paused for the cheering and he got it in ample measure. Two police officers strolling nearby did not show any reaction.

Such liberal attitude irked many in the aftermath of 9/11 and 7/7, but the Muslim community continued to demonstrate and protest and follow their religious practices without any legal or social restraints. In fact, both the media and the judiciary acted as watchdogs for them. Such freedom, defence of its open society combined with tolerance and ostensible equality of all people, despite threats of suicide bombers and home-grown jihadis was proof enough that democracy in Britain preserved its ethos.

He worked himself to a hysterical pitch and his denouements became more lethal. Then, the piece de resistance; he bellowed, 'I would put President ... in the WC and pull the flush.'

All this convinced me that there was value politics and clean politicking, aberrations from time to time notwithstanding. My good friend Peter Oborne would not agree. In his book *The Triumph of the Political Class* he argues that the political class, along with its collaborator, the media class, have changed the very nature of government. But, of all that later.

I have produced a few editorials on the suicide of Dr Kelly, the British UN weapons inspector to illustrate the freedom the media enjoys. Kelly's discussion with BBC Radio 4 Today programme journalist Andrew Gilligan about the British government's dossier on weapons of mass destruction (WMD) in Iraq inadvertently caused a major political scandal. He was found dead days after appearing before the Parliamentary committee charged with investigating the scandal. The *Sunday Times* Editorial said, 'The tragedy of David Kelly's suicide will leave most people in Britain with a sense of sadness mixed with anger and disgust ... He was, it seems, driven to the blackest despair by being the unwilling pawn in a game being played between Downing Street and the BBC. ... Now it has become a matter of life and death and all those involved - Downing Street, the Ministry of Defence, an unusually hostile foreign affairs select committee and the BBC - should be ashamed ....'

It did mention that Alistair Campbell went on the offensive against the BBC over suggestions by [the BBC reporter Andrew] Gilligan ... that Downing Street had 'sexed up' last September's dossier on Iraqi weapons. Had Mr Campbell not done so, the stories about government doctoring of that dossier would have faded away rather than dominating the news agenda for the past seven weeks. And had Mr Campbell not done so, with Mr Blair's authorization, Dr Kelly would still be alive today.' *The Observer*, considered Left-oriented, said in its editorial,

> *The events leading to Dr Kelly being called to give evidence deserve close scrutiny, as does the wider question of the use made of scientific and intelligence material in putting the government's case for war. But the [judicial] inquiry must also examine the behaviour of all the protagonists. Why did Mr Campbell feel it necessary to raise the stakes so high in his exchanges with the BBC?*
>
> *The integrity of the prime minister and his government do not turn on one disputed report. Why did the Ministry of Defence allow the name of Dr Kelly to enter the public domain, an apparent abuse of confidentiality and of his accepted role as someone who could give off-*

the-record briefings to the Press? Why did the Foreign Affairs Select Committee allow its investigation to descend into a witch- hunt for a journalistic source? And what is served by the BBC's dogmatic insistence that each and every one of its broadcasts is unimpeachable?

The Independent on Sunday commented in its editorial:

A political sideshow has resulted in a tragic death, a death that now overshadows this government, yet also illuminates the shoddy way in which politics - even politics that take this country to war - has been constructed in recent months ... Mr Blair went to war arguing that Iraq posed an imminent threat. It is not scientific advisers, or Mr Campbell, or the BBC journalist Mr Gilligan, who should be in the dock, but the prime minister. The judicial inquiry into why a decent man like Dr Kelly took his life is to be welcomed. But we need a wider inquiry: into the real reasons why this country was taken into a war that has claimed not only too many lives as its victims, but the nation's trust in its leaders as well.

The News of the World editorial lashed out at BBC:

Are there no limits to the BBC's arrogance? Traumatised by his ordeal, Dr Kelly - a decent and inoffensive man - has killed himself. And still the BBC plays holier than thou with hollow words of sympathy ... And what of Mr Gilligan's own deafening silence? For a man who seemed to have a great deal to say, he appears to have been struck mute ... Could the truth be that Dr Kelly entrusted Mr Gilligan with facts - and Mr Gilligan sexed them up? Almost certainly...

The Mail on Sunday commented:

With that amazing nerve that has taken him so far in life, the prime minister pleads for restraint and respect in the national debate about the death of Dr Kelly ... But Downing Street has been at the very centre of the elaborate, ruthless operation that has led to his wretched death. Mr Blair, his servants, agents and toadies showed neither restraint nor respect in their behaviour ...

The Sunday Mirror, supposedly Labour-friendly, said:

> *There is a cancer at the heart of British public life that is paralysing government, poisoning genuine debate and, if allowed to rage on unchecked, will eventually threaten democracy itself. ...The business of politics has been polluted by a new brutality that eats up and spits out human beings, sacrificed to the great God soundbite.*

These editorial comments, now years later, recapture the mystery--which led to various rumours and allegations---that surrounded Dr Kelly's suicide and how it affected the credibility of the entire government and more so of Blair. Yet, he and his Government survived. Not only that, just two years later, Blair led his party back to power. What can we surmise from this? One, that apart from the charges of pressure on BBC, no paper was cowed down. Freedom of Press and expression could not, or was not, curtailed. Second, nothing short of conclusive proof or substantive doubt can convince people to favour or turn against a political leader. This again is true for India too.

Parliamentary Democracy

During the first four years of my posting, before the dawn of the Blair era, I had been closely following the party system, politicians and the role of the media in politics; I was also following the debates in Parliament especially on Kashmir and how ministers and MPs conducted themselves. I was amused to see on the television one or two MPs in the blissful state of drowsiness, and occasionally a near-empty chamber. All this was of much interest to me. I do not think the whips in Indian Parliament would ever be envious of their British counterparts.

Fortunately, I got a unique opportunity to compare India's parliamentary system based on the Westminster model and the actual British parliamentary system and its working. My initial impression was that although the system was adopted in India but values were not. However, with scandals involving ministers, MPs, Peers and reports of manipulation of the Press and vote politics and the lobbyists' hold I became unsure.

Lord Bhiku Parekh drew the distinction between the parliamentary democracies in Britain and India excellently. He said there is a long tradition of parliamentary discipline in Britain. There are no shouting and fisticuffs or members holding the session to ransom. The second thing is that while being loyal to the political party they belong to, members retain a sense of independence. Labour or Conservative MPs, while remaining faithful and loyal to their party, can voice their dissent about a policy or action. Their views are heard.

But there is something that Britain is learning from India. There is a 'watertight separation between the two houses' there. The Prime Minister cannot go to the House of Lords to speak or answer questions. This leads to having separate ministers and leaders. They in turn cannot come to the Commons to be questioned. 'It (the separation) is so tight that I cannot go to dine in the Commons dining room, unless I am invited by an MP,' added Lord Parekh. In India, the prime minister could go to either of the Houses. Britain is learning from this now. It was suggested that Lord Mandelson, leader of the House of Lords, should be allowed to come to the Commons.

Many other things we criticize in politicians in India and the belief that sections of the media and journalists tend to ingratiate themselves with the ruling party is also true in Britain, if one is to believe what the likes of Oborne have written. Possibly, it differs in degrees. But, one major difference I did notice was that politicians in Britain were never treated as superior class. There is no hero-worship, no feet touching and *jai hos*.

British politics does not suffer nor does it have to contend with divisive factors like those of caste, communalism, religious fanaticism and regionalism and, more importantly, the rural and urban biases. The attitudes and approaches of MPs in India who come from a rural background differ sharply from those of their colleagues from urban constituencies. These handicaps have possibly impeded democratic values and polity in India. That despite of all these fractious issues the country has managed to ensure its democratic credentials is remarkable.

The watchdog role of the media in Britain and India is also somewhat alike. But the media there, despite reports of manipulations especially during the New Labour regime has shown amazing courage and daredevilry for

> Lord Bikhu Parekh.. "while being loyal to the political party they (MPs) belong to, members retain a sense of independence. Labour or Conservative MPs while remaining faithful and loyal to their party, can voice their dissent about a policy or action. Their views are heard.

exposing the mightiest. This is often considered perilous by many of us here. Although in India whether such constraint is due to the fear of the politicians or is self-imposed for some reason or the other is difficult to comprehend. After all, many powerful chief ministers and cabinet ministers at the Centre have been attacked and exposed in the past. Arun Shourie, as chief editor of *The Indian Express*, could politically disrobe three powerful chief ministers with impunity.

This is why I feel that shameful outrages, greed and depravity would not be able to mar democracy in either of the countries. I think Nehru's legacy, although some are critical of many of its lingering effects, ensured that democracy in the country would never be obliterated. The Emergency that did destroy the tenets of democracy could not last for more than 19 months. Mrs Indira Gandhi herself felt suffocated and went for elections, although she could have waited for more than a year. And the voter taught her and her party such a lesson that no leader in future would dare commit the mistake of playing with democratic roots.

I think that the British electorate also ensures that no prime minister develops dictatorial traits. Why did it vote Winston Churchill out despite his extraordinary victory in the Second World War? I did try to ask some political scientists and most said that as his role was over, people wanted someone who could then lead the reconstruction and recovery of the bomb-ravaged country. In India Mrs Indira Gandhi, the most loved prime minister was herself rejected by her voters in Rae Bareli, almost a fiefdom of the Nehrus and Gandhis because she had imposed Emergency. The lesson to her would never be forgotten by any politician in India. That is democracy at its best.

The Not-so-Privileged and the Privileged

The first thing that struck me in London was the absence of the lal batti (flashing red lights over cars of ministers) syndrome and Black Cats escorting VVIPs, and many who simply have pretensions of being VVIPs, as in India. I never saw in Britain a road sealed for the cavalcade— of maximum three cars at that—of a prime minister. I never spotted armed police officers lining routes to ensure the safety of the VVIPs, nor ever heard sirens blaring for a minister's or a senior police officer's car to get the right of way. In fact, once Keith Vaz, then Minister for Immigration, had given me and Raj Loomba a lift from the inaugural meeting of the Labour Friends of India in Bournemouth to London past midnight. I was quite surprised to find that he was driving himself and there were no armed-toting security officers to protect him.

I asked Sir Paul Stevenson, the Metropolitan Police Commissioner and head of the Scotland Yard, why the prime minister and other VIPs were not accompanied by armed security guards and why they do not travel in a cavalcade of cars and the routes they pass are not lined up with police. 'The best security is one which is never seen,' he said in answer to my first question. About the absence of a number of cars following that of a Prime Minister's he smilingly said, 'Large number of cars and policemen posted along the route of Prime Minister is the best way to tell terrorists that their target is passing through such and such route.'

It is not that danger did not lurk in Britain. First, it was the Provisional IRA and then the home-grown suicide bombers, Al Qaeda and Taliban. Britain has been the prime target of jihadis for over a decade. Is then India more violence-prone? Possibly!

After all two prime ministers have been assassinated and Mahatma Gandhi too had fallen to an assassin's bullet. The security perceptions, and even politics, too, to some extent, then naturally changed. This happened in Britain as well after the IRA attempt on Margaret Thatcher's life in Brighton. It was a well-planned assassination plot.

On 12 October 1984—just a few weeks before Mrs Gandhi was shot dead by her two personal security guards— the IRA bombed the Grand Hotel in Brighton during the Conservative Party's annual conference. Five people died and 34 were injured in the attack. Margaret Thatcher, who was working on her conference speech, escaped uninjured. It was later said that she had come out of the bathroom barely five minutes before the bomb exploded, and that possibly saved her life. But, her colleague, Norman Tebbit, had to be rescued from the rubble. His wife, Margaret, was left paralysed.

Michael Dobbs, a former senior adviser to Margaret Thatcher and John Major, was at the Grand Hotel when the bomb detonated. He believes its

About the absence of a number of cars following that of a Prime Minister's he (Police Commissioner) smilingly said, 'Large number of cars and policemen posted along the route of Prime Minister is the best way to tell terrorists that their target is passing through such and such route.'

legacy has had a profound impact on British politics, especially at party conferences and Westminster. It has had an impact on security concerns as well.

Some of us Indian journalists had a bitter experience because of the near-paranoia during Labour's annual party conference in 2008 in Manchester. A couple of us were invited by the Indian High Commission to attend the dinner hosted by the then High Commissioner Shiv Shankar Mukherjee in the very building in Manchester where the Labour's annual party conference was being held. The security personnel refused to let us enter despite a senior Indian diplomat identifying and vouching for us. They said that our names should have been registered and cleared by the security by a certain date.

I returned without hanging around along with Mr Prem Prakash, chairman of the *Asian News International*. We were lucky that we did not have to go without a meal, thanks to the generosity of a senior doctor Murli Sinha who woke up his wife, near midnight, to cook dinner for us. The following morning we learnt that a few journalists who refused to budge, a sort of Indian version of dharna (sit-in), were allowed in but by then all the ministers had left the dinner party. There was nothing to report.

We never had such unseemly experience at previous conferences, possibly because the venue of High Commissioners' dinner was never fixed where the conference was held. In 2008, there was an apparent oversight and miscalculation.

But such instances are rare. The tightness of the security in Manchester was unprecedented and police officers were nervy, we were told that, because there was information about Al-Qaeda likely to use some locals to attack the venue of the conference. Otherwise I never saw anything like Z, X or other categories of security for ministers which in India is decided by the home ministry for every VVIP.

It is so different in Britain. Once I spotted Norma Major – when her husband John Major was prime minister —standing in a queue waiting her turn to pay at the cash till at Sainburys' Victoria Street outlet. No one was paying any attention to her nor did I see security officers lurking near her. Years later, I was equally astonished to see Tony and Cherie Blair standing alone at a railway station, within hours of leaving Downing Street, to board a train for his constituency Sedgefield. To me they looked forlorn without the trappings of office and security. Blair, in fact, needed security because the radicals always threatened him.

The near-obsessive demand of most politicians and even bureaucrats to be surrounded by a possé of gun-toting sharp-shooters here is rather strange—is it a hangover of the Raj imperialism? Even in the sectarian-torn violence in Northern Ireland, I did not see the kind of security that is seen here even when a prime minister visits a social event. I had gone to Belfast before the Republicans voluntarily declared ceasefire for understanding the sectarian war that ravaged the province and to find whether there could be any comparison with the situation in Kashmir.

Once there, I felt insecure and feared that I might be a victim of cross-fire or bombs that were thrown unexpectedly. It was unnerving to see the city almost besieged by armed soldiers and armoured vehicles, their guns looking menacing, at every important junction. In fact, while going round the Catholic and the Protestant areas, I requested my guide, a very charming young lady from the Northern Ireland Secretariat, to ask the driver of the car provided by the Secretariat 'so that I might not venture into a wrong place at a wrong time and get caught in cross-firing—to stop as we entered Shankill Road. But to my dismay the driver refused.

I wanted to speak with some shopkeepers to find out how they paid the weekly protection money and how it was collected. I also wanted to know how fearful they were of attacks by the IRA. During briefings in London I had learnt that Shankill Road was the location of several bomb and gun attacks and in the 1993 bombing suffered the highest casualties that resulted in numerous revenge attacks by loyalists. A pub was also destroyed in the attack a few months before I went there. Nine people had been killed in the bombing.

The driver explained that he would stop only when he was sure to be able to speed away quickly in case of an attack. He gave me various instructions what to do and how to clamber back into the car in case of bombs exploding. 'I will keep the engine running.' It all sounded rather dramatic. But such was the fear then.

Yet, when I went a few weeks later to Belfast again to cover a meeting of the then Prime Minister John Major with the corporate heads and bankers in the conference hall of the four-star Europa Hotel, I was surprised not to see the place swarming with security men. The Europa was damaged 33 times by Provisional IRA bombs between 1972 and 1994, and was known as 'the most bombed hotel in Europe'. Yet no security cover was visible. Standing on the mezzanine floor I saw Major arrive in a greenish Jaguar. There was only one other Jaguar behind his car and I did not see armed personnel jumping out and surrounding him. I have never been able to understand how the cover was provided to him. He was there for almost two hours.

During the red alert days due to the threat from Al-Qaeda, I attended a meeting by the Hindu Forum of Britain where the guest of honour was the then Minister of Home. I did not spot security officers either patrolling the vast grounds outside the building in the hall of which a large audience was present. I saw only one officer in civvies come with the minister when he arrived. No one looked at me, as if I was a potential bomb-thrower. Likewise, I saw Gordon Brown, moving freely and meeting the invitees at a dinner meet hosted by Labour Friends of India during the Labour's annual party conference in Manchester. Many of us talked with him but there were no police officers looking at us suspiciously.

It is not that the ministers are without security, its degree depending on the assessment by intelligence agencies and Scotland Yard but it's not overtly visible. Lord Swraj Paul, genuinely bemused, once mentioned that he was surprised to find during the (first) Pravasi Bhartiya Divas in New Delhi that after he had gone through metal detector at the entrance of the venue, another scrutiny was done inside the hall.

I believe that the VIP areas, like Westminster, Buckingham Palace, Downing Street, nuclear installation sites and even sensitive cities are sanitized so well that the need for possé of security personnel to protect a prime minister, ministers or other important politicians is not required. I was told by a minister for security that there was continuous monitoring of suspected would-be terrorists and jihadi groups. Such surveillance has helped in pre-empting plots which, if they succeeded, would have caused devastation similar to 9/11 or 26/11.

Lord William John West, a Parliamentary Under Secretary of State at the British Home Office, with responsibility for Security, and the Security Advisor to Gordon Brown, once told me that after the Mumbai terror attack, special measures were taken to seal the sea routes so that terrorists would not sneak into England. Over three billion pounds had been already spent in the fight against terror. Such measures had an effect but I also noticed certain anomalies which I think are the result of the inherent English attitude to trust anyone who is a British citizen, even if his original nationality was different.

I have read many reports questioning the selection of an individual for anti-terror operations or in security and intelligence units. I read a report titled 'Returning to the terrorist danger within Britain's shores', which said "Whitehall descended to a Bertie Wooster-type caper when it drafted a Treasury official, one Azad Ali, to join its counter-insurgency panel to advise Mr Keir Starmar, the Director of Public Prosecutions, on cases involving Muslim suspects with extremist leanings. It wasn't as if the man was a closet jihadi. He operated in the open, his blog in which there was praise for the spiritual head of Al Qaeda and denied that the 26/11 Mumbai attack, which claimed 173 lives, was an act of terrorism.

> *The appointment of a man such as this to help guide policy on terrorist prosecutions has alarmed some of Mr Starmar's senior legal colleagues. Quite so. They are clearly not in the business of making an ass of the law. This lunacy is surely rooted in history. Islamism was for long a hand maiden of empire and an Anglo-American ploy in the Cold War. There is every likelihood that, in the closing decades of the 20th century, Islamist groups from around the world were permitted to hibernate in the safe haven of London courtesy the nation's great and good provided they kept the peace. What they did abroad was permissible free enterprise", wrote Premen Addy in The Pioneer.*

He added,

> *...small wonder that Mr Charles Pasqua, a senior French Minister at the time, dubbed London 'Londonistan'. But the chickens have come home to roost in Britain's times of trouble. Throwing money at Pakistan or covering up for its errant rulers with the Scotland Yard's questionable autopsy into the death of the country's cricket coach Bob Woolmer and the assassination of its leading Opposition politician Benazir Bhutto offers no respite. The murderous show goes on.*

Whatever it be Britain has been able to pre-empt terror attacks and potential suicide bombers lying low because it has been able to virtually seal its borders and also because the number of people who could aid and abet in terror carnage is not too large. Unlike in India!

With India the problem—which Britain does not have-- is of infiltration from not-too-friendly neighbourhoods and of the still inadequately available sophisticated technology for surveillance. In Britain, the airports and ports are so well monitored and rules of entry so difficult that the inflow of jihadis mainly from Pakistan almost dried up within two years of 7/7. This is why

British ministers do not need possé of armed men around them and overt security measures. This helps their image. Whereas back home the Black Cats and lal battis tend to alienate people. The feeling of the people is that the lives of those they elect is more valuable than theirs. Even if this view is taken as over-reaction, it is true that such security puts the politicians in a privileged class, an anomaly in democracy.

> Politicians in Britain were never treated as superior class. There is no hero-worship, no feet touching and Jai Hos.

The Self-correcting Polity

The more I observed British politics, the more I was convinced that even if the values that made Britain the mother of democracy were sometime diluted, due to exposures like the humiliation of over 300 Peers and MPs after being caught of fiddling with their expense accounts — and even ministers including reportedly Prime Minister Gordon Brown, who was said to pay back 12,000 pounds and Speaker John Bercow a 1,000 pounds— the democratic structure and the parliamentary system remained strong. This was possible because of the immediate corrective measures undertaken and implemented. The House of Commons Commission said that since *The Daily Telegraph* began revealing details of their claims in May 2009, 260 MPs and former MPs returned a total of £637,000 by early October, which means within five months. The number of MPs is expected to rise as some of them have not yet complied with an independent audit which has asked them to repay some claims.

If one goes back a few decades, the Profumo-Keeler sex-escapades or even a prime minister suspected by intelligence and more recent tainting of the likes of David Blunkett or Jacqui Smith, all failed to adversely impact independence of democratic institutions. Smith had to publicly apologise for

> The manner in which the biggies could be exposed and the prompt punitive measures that were taken against them ensured that the British polity largely remains ethical. Its institutions, pillars of democracy, have not lost their freedom.

claiming money for her second home. She subsequently resigned. Blunkett, considered one of the toughest eggs in the Blair cabinet, had to resign twice, the first time when it emerged that he used his position as Home Secretary, to have the visa of a nanny of his ex-lover— she was later named as Kimberly Quinn, the American publisher of *The Spectator* magazine--fast tracked. Peter Mandelson too had to leave cabinet twice.

The manner in which the biggies could be exposed and the prompt punitive measures that were taken against them ensured that the British polity largely remains ethical. Its institutions, pillars of democracy, have not lost their freedom. Oborne would again not agree with me. According to him a new type of government has emerged in Britain over the last twenty five years and its traditional institutions are in danger.

But I still believe that apart from some aberrations Britain has been able to retain the attributes that Robertson wrote in 1986 that a democracy had to have. The word democracy, he said, only starts to mean something tangible in the modern world when it is prefixed with other political words, such as direct, representative, liberal and parliamentary. I think that Parliament is representative and most members know their responsibility to their constituents.

Institutions have been able to retain their freedom, to a large extent. The executive has not been able to influence them. For instance, following the humbling of ministers, MPs and peers over allegedly making false claims in their expenses account, Parliament itself went into introspection, the media remained apolitical in exposing the wrong-doings, police could not be pressurized not to investigate 27 MPs and the judiciary could not be deterred by people in authority.

There was no let up even after months of the first investigative reports about the alleged fiddling with expense claims appeared in the *Daily Telegraph*. The media and party leaders kept the pressure on the erring MPs. The Committee for Standards in Public Life, which with the House of Commons Commission and the Government producing a 'nuclear option' – within months—for hauling rebel MPs into line, amid growing anger at their failure to pay drew up strict new rules. Those MPs who refused to pay back 'excessive' expenses claims would have the money clawed back from their salaries – or even the lucrative 'golden parachutes' they get when they leave the House of Commons, the committee proposed.

I never heard of commissions and committees set up to probe allegations or scandals taking such a long time that people forgot what it was all about. The regulations to prevent claims by MPs and Peers by circumventing rules were put in place in less than a year of the media exposure of the falsification of accounts. Moreover, a few who tried to bluster their way out of exposures fell on their swords.

A senior Tory MP and Minister Jonathan Aitken vowed to use the 'sword of truth' against T*he Guardian* and sued the newspaper for libel in a row over his dealings with Saudi arms traders. But instead of fixing the daily, he went to prison for seven months for perjury. He was revealed to have lied repeatedly. Likewise Lord Jeffery Archer too tried to take on *The Daily Star* and filed a libel case against it. But instead of the paper getting punished the millionaire novelist was jailed for four years. He was found guilty of perjury and perverting the course of justice. Such instances were possibly the reasons for most politicians avoiding fracas with the media.

Moral Turpitude no bar, Corruption is

In India, we are so cynical that even when a politician is accused of corruption, moral turpitude or criminal act, we take it for granted that nothing will affect him or her—although the complete wipe-out of criminals in the 2009 general elections would surely have a salutary effect. In Britain, too, there were some astonishing paradoxes—a couple of Tories with besmirched reputations, ironically, went on to become more affluent and popular, albeit outside political arena. The one accused of receiving brown envelopes crammed with pound notes—although vehemently denied by him of any such wrongdoing— metamorphosed into a public speaker and was most sought after. His earnings shadowed his loss due to de-selection. He and his wife were invited for television appearances. His shame was soon forgotten.

Likewise, the Tory MP, who during campaigning, was caught smooching a young girl, ostensibly a campaigner for him, on a bench in a park—*The*

> I do not think survival of the so tainted is unsavoury in the least. It might not be very appetizing to puritans, but this too is a facet of democracy. Even the disgraced have the right to reform and rise.

Sun called it open-air sex romp—went on to win in a constituency generally anti-Tory. I do not think survival of the so tainted is unsavoury in the least. It might not be very appetizing to puritans, but this too is a facet of democracy. Even the disgraced have the right to reform and rise. Much later, in fact after a decade, it was alleged that the MP was a victim of a sting operation. The girl was planted to lure him so that a media photographer could catch him in the act. Such a dogged pursuit of the politicians not too careful about their sexual escapades was, however, something new for me.

In India, like what I found in France or Germany, in fact, most western countries, moral turpitude is no bar in politics – I suppose the hue and cry over Silvio Berlusconi in Italy was because he was over indulgent. Corruption, on the other hand, even if unproven, is fatal for politicians in Britain, whereas in India or in fact in South Asia such corrupt mostly survive and thrive on the assumption by the people that it has been institutionalized and infected all parties and so there is no getting away from it. Corrupt are seldom caught and thus continue to 'serve' their constituencies. This might well, hopefully, change with the rise of the young in politics.

But the slightest suspicion of corruption in Britain costs politicians their positions in the government and the party. Most MPs caught in the expense claims scandal either voluntarily declared to retire or were deselected by the party leaders. The tax affairs of 27 MPs were also investigated by the Inland Revenue after checks on their expenses claims. The investigation followed a warning from the head of HM Revenue and Customs after the expenses scandal came to light.

Any politician suspected of corruption is generally abandoned by his own party. He becomes hapless, family connections or links with the powers-that-be, or bribery, nothing helps in salvaging him. I never found any one tainted with corruption becoming important again in politics.

Democracy under Monarchy

D. Robertson's saying that, 'Democracy is the most valued and also the vaguest of political terms in the modern world,' is apt for Britain. It is monarchical, yet a very much functional democracy. As Clement Attlee discussing powers of the Queen, said, 'A monarch is like a referee, although the occasions, when he or she has to blow the whistle are nowadays very few'. Prince Philip summed it up in his own inimical style, saying monarchy had become an old-fashioned institution.

But the British device of giving it an aura of mystique, I believe, has evoked curiosity about its monarchy across the world. It has no role in running the country. The Palace and, in fact, all the royal palaces like the Windsor Castle are major attractions for tourists from the world over. There is always such a huge crowd, with many Japanese clicking their Nikons, during the changing of guards in the forecourt of the palace that I never tried to pass through to the Buckingham Gate Road between 11.30 and 12.30 in the mornings.

But the reverence Queen Elizabeth II inspires and the almost fanatical loyalty towards her is unique. There was just a quiver and a ripple of anger when the Queen did not come to the Buckingham Palace to mourn Diana's tragic death nor was the flag flown half-mast there. It seemed that at last people might openly censor her, even become rebellious enough to demand she join them in mourning. But the moment she came to the Palace and the flag was lowered all was forgotten and forgiven.

Admiration for her, even in these times when the young have little regard for their elders or for any authority, is exceptional. It was a treat to watch the faces of the people who crowded in front of Buckingham Palace as the Queen and her family emerged on the balcony on the 50th anniversary of VE-Day. Young children on shoulders of their fathers, old women hanging on to their younger family members, couples clasping each other's hands cheering and tapping with the music and then breaking into ecstatic clapping. Emotion and sentiment for the memorable day and the Royals were in full play. And when Sir Cliff Richard sang 'Congratulations', a favourite of the Queen Mother, all eyes seemed to rivet on her. She did not disappoint them. On the TV screen one could see her clearly ad- lib the song. The Queen could hardly suppress her smile. I realized how deep the bond was between her and her people.

The very first act of Tony Blair, after his sweeping victory, must have served as a warning to him, not to encroach on the Queen's turf. He and Cherie had walked from Downing Street to Parliament for its opening by the Queen. They were greeted and cheered by crowds lining their route. But, this seemingly commoner's touch raised the hackles immediately. It was said that this diluted the focus on the Queen, the opening of Parliament being traditionally the day of the Monarch. I did see on television the two walk towards Parliament and I thought it was a nice gesture, a people's representative going about his business like the people.

But, obviously, it riled the monarchists and also the traditionalists who seem to have veneration for the Queen ingrained in them. I experienced that personally. A couple, the husband, a retired military officer, and his wife, both nearing 70, were standing behind me at the Queen's Summer Garden Party on the sprawling grounds behind Buckingham Palace.

We were all in a line waiting for the Queen and her party to pass by. I saw the officer's wife adjust his ties and pull his coat as the Queen neared and then she said to me, 'Sir, would you mind if my husband stands in front of you. You see he is much shorter than you, and this is the only and last chance for him to see the Queen from close quarters.' She explained that they were invited to the party because some officers of a certain regiment were chosen that year by the palace. The look on her husband's face as the Queen smiled at him while he bowed to her bespoke of the loyalty and respect she commands. That moment, I am sure, would be lived and relived in their family for a few generations.

It was no surprise that when the expenses account tainted almost half the members of Parliament, demands were made that the Queen must interfere. She is the last resort, someone to whom people can turn to if their chosen representatives cross the Rubicon line of democracy. Monarchy as an institution has been given a long life by Queen Elizabeth II while democracy flourishes too.

Elections and Electioneering

When I went to cast my vote for the first time at a polling booth in a small hall in a Church in Golders Green in north London, I expected long lines, agents and policemen and identity checks followed by the ink put on my finger. Instead I was welcomed by two elderly ladies sitting in the front room adjoining the hall where ballot boxes were kept. They asked my address and then directed me to a girl inside the hall to get my ballot paper. I realized that different girls and young men were assigned for handing over the ballot papers to voters residing in different areas.

The girl asked me my name and voter I/D number and then gave me the ballot paper. No identification was sought. I cast my vote and left. No indelible ink was put on my finger. It had taken me hardly ten minutes to vote. Trust seems to be the guiding principle. And it is seldom betrayed; unfortunately instances of violations and riggings allegedly involved people from the sub-continent. It is rather shameful that a few imported the electoral malpractices rather common in their countries.

A report alleged that first-generation Pakistani and Bangladeshi Muslims as well as their political masters helped fuel widespread rigging of postal votes and other electoral malpractices in Britain. Although the majority of those booked for electoral malpractices have been white males, the report by the Joseph Rowntree Reform Trust, a national charity promoting democratic reform and constitutional change, said half of those convicted were Pakistanis and Bangladeshis.

The 94-page report, *Purity of Elections in Britain: Causes for Concern*, said that half of the 42 people convicted for electoral malpractices since 2000 were British Muslims, their religious identity assuming significance because of their disenchantment with the Labour Party following Britain's invasion of Iraq. Convictions for electoral fraud were brought against representatives of all the three major parties, as well as minor parties such as the anti-immigrant British National Party.

'Significantly, these convictions of British Muslims have emerged alongside anecdotal evidence of more widespread, and long-run, practices associated with Pakistani, Kashmiri and Bangladeshi traditions of Biraderi (brotherhood) clans in influencing voting behaviour,' said the report written by Stuart Wilks-Heeg, a local democracy specialist at Liverpool University.

I fear that the free from all cumbersome process of identification and proofs of one being a voter might not last long, if the alleged rigging and registration of false names in the voting lists continue. I heard that at a polling booth in Scotland one minor tried to cast vote more than once. One MP was reportedly investigated on the suspicion of malpractices during his election. He was cleared after a trial lasting nine weeks.

But except these minor lapses elections in Britain are free and fair, parliament is assertive and MPs regularly attend their constituency clinics and interact with their voters. I have often seen MPs meeting their constituents in the visitors' area during the session of the Commons.

Once I went to the constituency surgery of the Foreign Secretary Jack Straw in Blackburn. I had decided to meet him there as he would be a bit more free than in London and be able to discuss his participation in the Hindustan Times Leadership Summit. It gave me an insight into how the MPs interact with their constituents.

There was no heavy security arrangement. I did not see any electronic machine for visitors to pass through. Only two police officers stood at the main entrance, but they did not frisk any visitor. The constituency secretary came out and asked each one waiting to meet Straw what their purpose was. Thereafter Straw met them with officials of his ministry, parliamentary secretary and personal assistant who took notes of the conversation between him and each visitor. Such meetings are generally held every week.

I was told that the constituency selection committee keeps records of such interactions, satisfaction of the voters with their representatives and the overall conduct of the local MP in Parliament and outside. The committee has the power to deselect a sitting MP. Although I heard that in one or two cases the party leadership pressurized the committees to change their decisions.

All this sounded familiar. In India too, until selections were centralized by all political parties, a similar selection process was followed. The district committee of a party used to recommend nominees for parliament and assembly and it was generally accepted by the party leadership.

Electioneering is very different. It cannot be similar to that in India for various reasons. One the constituencies in India are large, there are considerations like caste and local biases, factionalism, factors alien to Britain. Candidates in Britain can cover their entire constituency in just a few days. This is why I found door-to-door canvassing and corner meetings. I used to get appeals to vote in the post. Then two or three people would come to meet and generally leave from the door itself after requesting that I give a thought to the merits of the candidate they were canvassing for.

No loudspeakers are used, no processions taken out, and no actors are brought in to appeal to the electorate. In any case there are no actors who are hero-worshipped. I admired the conduct of John Major during the 1997 election in which his party was routed. Even his worst critics conceded that he was a gentleman. But even that asset of his could not save Tories from the ignominy of a total wash-out. At a dinner Major hosted for prominent members of the South Asian communities just before the polls, I asked about the odds of his party returning and his answer was not as I expected from a party leader leading his members in an electoral combat. He said he was doing his best and results should be favourable. He did not sound very optimistic.

The scandals had obviously taken their toll. The party was reduced to a rump. Major gracefully retired to enjoy his cricket at the Oval. He faded away soon in the glitz of the Blair effect. Unlike in our country where no politician ever retires, and if he passes away, his kin take over his mantle, the family continuity is seldom broken. But fortunately the reign of the families has not so far dented democracy in India. It has indubitably remained as strongly embedded as it does in Britain. If one ignores what has, or had been happening in a state or two. But I fear that dynastic successions in politics make it impossible for others, possibly more talented, to get an opportunity to enter politics. I do not know what effect it would have on Indian democracy in the long run. But there are no such fears in Britain. Nicholas Soames, grandson of Winston Churchill, a Tory MP, is a rarity in British politics.

When I asked Lord Bhiku Parekh, he immediately said dynastic succession has both good and bad points. The bad effect is that it limits the choice of the leader – as I have said—and the second thing is that a family becomes important. "People look up to baksheesh (reward) from the family rather than try through their services for a reward from the electorate." This affects the very ideology of democracy.

But he added that the advantage of dynastic succession is that at least the family guarantees a stability point and keeps out shifting, ever in-fighting alternatives. We can see in India the truth in what Lord Parekh said. But while demons of democracy are dealt with summarily in Britain, in India they generally survive until the elections.

8

Lessons in Political Correctness

> *Politics is the art of the possible*
>
> —*Lord R.A.Butler*

I had never heard the word political correctness in India; nor did I hear it in the early years of my London posting. So I was naturally unaware of its origin or its concept. In India we had an unwritten rule not to offend anyone's religious feelings or beliefs in one's customs. Politicians and the Press apart, common people stuck to this. When political correctness became a fashionable word in the British political lexicon, I was, therefore, unable to foresee that it would become a creed for politicians and influence the politics there to the extent of restricting freedom of speech and expression of one's views. It also sounded the death-knell of the famous British wit.

Its deadly impact dawned on me as I heard and read reports of a frontline Conservative Party member Ann Winterton removed from the front bench because of a joke she related at a rugby club private gathering. It was a joke which was no more offensive than the hundreds we have been reading for decades about the miserliness of the Scots. But the Tory Party was trying hard at that time to appear politically correct in race matters. Its worry was over the far-right British National Party winning its first council seat.

I wondered what would have happened to comedian Mehmood in India, who mimicked a South Indian music teacher in the box-office record-breaking film *Padosan*, if political correctness of this extent haunted the Indians too. The local bodies, civil service, businesses all had to fall in line. Teachers trembled lest they attracted the political correctness police for uttering anything in their classes.

Once I rang up a councillor in Bradford, whom I knew a little, to learn about the reasons for riots there and in nearby cities. He said he could tell me in general terms but if he got to the specifics and I wrote them, he could be hauled up for not being politically correct. I realized how stifling the passion for political correctness was—to the extent of being an impediment to information.

I tried to find out what it was all about. What is political correctness, how did it start and how did it become so successful? I got the answers while searching on Google. I have picked up the following through Wikipedia. Political correctness is first and foremost an attack on free speech, clear thinking and discussion. Political correctness is perpetrated by the left in politics as a cover for their flawed ideology — a sort of cultural Marxism.

> *By cloaking their strange ideas under the cover of not wishing to offend anyone (which naturally appeals to peoples' better nature), they try to bypass debate and give a 'received wisdom' which must not be questioned. And anyone who disagrees with this 'received wisdom' must therefore be a really nasty person and deserves to be ostracised by their peers. This peer pressure is instrumental in enforcing and expanding political correctness"-- from the notes of the panel in Political Correctness—the awful truth (info@politicallyincorrect.me.uk).*

I also found on the net the way it started. According to it,

> *Political Correctness started in a think tank (called The Frankfurt School) in Germany in 1923. The purpose was to find a solution*

> *to the biggest problem facing the implementers of communism in Russia. Why wasn't the wonderful idea of communism spreading? The Frankfurt school recommended (amongst other things): the creation of racism offences, continual change to create confusion, the teaching of sex and homosexuality to children, the undermining of schools and teachers' authority.*

I wonder if this was some sort of joke itself. I never heard of anyone being pulled up in Germany in the nineties for violating this dogma. But then my knowledge in such a sensitive matter is limited.

But seeing the impact of political correctness on British polity—which kept frighteningly swamping the national psyche as well— I could never understand why the whole onus for it was put on the Left, because the Right, in fact everyone, whether believing in it or simply out of fear, practised it scrupulously. There came a stage when anyone who disagreed with the 'received wisdom' was promptly ostracized like the poor lady belonging to the Conservative Party; by no means could the Tories be said to be Left-oriented.

The craziness for political correctness has, of course, ruined the famous British sense of humour. But worse, it has tempted some to hold it as a threat to get their demands, however illogical, conceded— whether in the government, the corporations and particularly in the police which has been 'judged' to be institutionally racist as it is. The Human Development Director in a multinational corporation, who was sitting next to me at a dinner, said to me after ascertaining that I was an Indian that politicians, police and businesses were in constant threat of being 'bamboozled' by anyone; even 'offensive, mean little twerps' for violating the code of political correctness. I got a sneaking feeling that he had been subjected to some sort of 'torture' by his employees who accused him of political incorrectness.

I believe this total surrender to the extreme creed of political correctness has upset relations among different communities, the ethnic minority communities and the English apart from affecting the liberal, tolerant British polity. The multicultural bonhomie has lost some of its sheen, when due to political correctness an individual, institution or community was favoured, others felt alienated. But the politicians, I suppose, have to worry about their votes and the police its already half-battered image.

The BBC reported that the then Home Office Minister John Denham had been criticized by the police for using the phrase 'nitty gritty' because of

Among the everyday sayings that have been quietly dropped in a bid to stamp out racism and sexism are 'whiter than white', 'gentleman's agreement', 'black mark' and 'right-hand man'. Black bear toys are endangered species and so is black Barbie Doll.

race relations rules. Denham used the phrase during a debate at the Police Federation conference in Bournemouth. He was told that police officers could face disciplinary charges for saying 'nitty gritty' because it dates from the slavery era. Some rank and file officers said the rules about language 'have become "a minefield" and have made them inhibited in doing their job'.

Dozens of quangos and taxpayer-funded organizations were ordered to purge common words and phrases so as not to cause offence. Good Friday, the most important Christian Festival commemorating the anniversary of Christ's crucifixion and death, was either watered down or rephrased by some schools, I heard, so as not to hurt sentiments of any ethnic community. It was not amusing to read a columnist lamenting that Good Friday might disappear from the calendar. He said, 'celebrate it this year for you may not be able to next year'.

Among the everyday sayings that have been quietly dropped in a bid to stamp out racism and sexism are 'whiter than white', 'gentleman's agreement', 'black mark' and 'right-hand man'. Black bear toys are endangered species and so is black Barbie Doll. The Northern Ireland Human Rights Commission had reportedly advised staff to replace the phrase 'black day' with 'miserable day', according to documents released under freedom of information rules. This is maddening craziness. It points out that certain words carry with them a 'hierarchical valuation of skin colour'. The commission even urges employees to be mindful of the term ethnic minority because it can imply "something smaller and less important".

Once I had a laugh at the joke that feminists demanded that Manchester be renamed Itchester, because the word Manchester glorified men. I hope this joke does not become a reality and political correctness does not lead to the city being rechristened.

Once I had a laugh at the joke that feminists demanded that Manchester be renamed Itchester, because the word Manchester glorified men. I hope this joke does not become a reality and political correctness does not lead to the city being rechristened.

Many Indians and their organizations get concerned when a crime, rioting or criminal activity involving people from any of the countries in the subcontinent was attributed to 'an Asian or Asians'. The anxiety among the Indian diaspora deepened because in riots in cities like Bradford in north England. No Indians were involved but reports about these incidents were always referred to as clashes between Asians and Whites. When in Birmingham some youths rioted against the police, reports spoke of clashes between Asian youths and the police. When I met a senior official and a few councillors in Birmingham they first swore me to keep their identity secret and then said that the youth of such and such community had clashed with police.

Such use of the generic word Asians to describe anyone from the subcontinent became a norm. I also sent many dispatches on this controversy. Umbrella organizations like the Hindu Forum of Britain, I was told, petitioned the Government in this regard. It was when the government appointed a committee to inquire into the causes of Bradford riots and to make suggestions to pre-empt such violence in the future that one came to know the real facts. In its report it discussed the alienation between the whites and the Muslim youth.

Why did the importance or I should say the dread for political correctness hit the Government and politicians? Even most media reports were punctilious in following the code. In retrospect, I think the government and politicians started to stick to its creed more zealously in the aftermath of terror attacks of 7/7 and the continuing threat from within Britain. There was no doubt that the Muslims could have been unnecessarily made to feel alienated and discriminated against. They feared backlash as it is. But in the long run it seemed to be carried to the extreme. More so, it did not help in improving relations with the young Muslims who continued to feel discriminated and alienated.

But the immediate result was that everyone in the country had to toe the line. Murmurs —I should say grumblings—could be heard that it restricted

> The National Gallery in London believes that the phrase 'gentleman's agreement' is potentially offensive to women and suggests that staff should replace it with 'unwritten agreement' or 'an agreement based on trust' instead.

free speech and the right to express one's genuine beliefs or to deal with issues impartially. I have always wondered why the Maulana who hit out during his fiery speech in Hyde Park on 'dalals'" whom he named fearlessly was not hauled up.

An explanation to that could itself be politically incorrect. An Indian-origin owner of a stationery and greeting cards shop in Golders Green market related to me how two youth from an Eastern European country barged into his shop and tried to break the till and take out cash. They were clearly caught on the CCTV camera. He reported the incident to police officers on beat and told them from which country the two youth were. But the officers said he should not call them as belonging to a particular country. Political correctness was at work. Needless to say, they were never caught. Anyway, they could not steal anything. But the shop-owner said he continued to live in dread. He used to see the two youth quite often strolling past without any fear.

Similar is the English complaint that one is branded as a nasty racist if they question as to whether a free flow of immigrants is good or bad. The National Gallery in London believes that the phrase 'gentleman's agreement' is potentially offensive to women and suggests that staff should replace it with 'unwritten agreement' or 'an agreement based on trust' instead. The term 'right-hand man' is also considered taboo by the gallery, with 'second in command' being deemed more suitable.

Many institutions urged their workforce to be mindful of 'gender biases' in language. The Learning and Skills Council, I read, wanted staff to perfect their brief rather than 'master' it, while the Newcastle University singled out the phrase 'master bedroom' as being problematic. Advice issued by the South West Regional Development Agency, according to what I spotted on the website, stated, 'Terms such as "black sheep of the family", "black looks" and "black mark" have no direct link to skin colour but potentially serve to reinforce a negative view of all things black'. Equally, certain terms imply a negative image of 'black' by reinforcing the positive aspects of white. I suppose the term White Christmas could also be erased. And what about the term white collar worker?

Political correctness has made common sense a thing of the past. If you catch a burglar in your house then it's probably best to help the poor soul by carrying your possessions to the front door lest he should trip up and hurt himself and it's you that end up in court!"

These instances make one laugh. But by no means it is a laughing matter. Even good things carried to the extreme can hurt. You can't just swallow a large number of vitamin pills to benefit from them.

Marie Cure of the Plain English Campaign rightly advised that while political correctness 'has good intentions but things can be taken to an extreme. What is really needed is a bit of common sense'.

This seeming lack of commonsense and, if I may add logic, has made interactions and dealings complex and difficult. There is, even without meaning it, a change in political outlook. I was not surprised to see on the net that the application of this creed in the public domain had angered some of Britain's most popular writers. Anthony Horowitz, author of the *Alex Rider* children's spy books, was quoted saying:

> *A great deal of our modern language is based on traditions which have now gone but it would be silly — and extremely inconvenient — to replace them all.…An 'able seaman', under new regulations, could well be neither. 'Spanish practices' can happen all over Europe. We know what these phrases mean and we can find out from where they were derived. Banning them is just unnecessary.*

Unfortunately for the Labour Government, political correctness entering the political code of conduct made it bear the brunt whenever things went wrong due to it. Concessions were granted for most illogical demands. *News Panel* (www.politicallyincorrect.me.uk) noted:

> *The basic idea is to make the country wholly dependent on the State. By dumbing down of education, the creation of huge state sector employment and large scale immigration, New Labour has effectively created a captive audience to vote for them or Blue Labour, should the Conservatives actually get back to power.....*
>
> *If the Conservatives did get back into power, nothing much would change. David Cameron has already shown his true politically correct credentials many times but none so shamelessly as when he sacked the well respected Patrick Mercer, just for speaking the truth. Patrick Mercer wasn't being a racist, he was just commenting on how in Army life you get picked on if you have some different feature whether it is black skin, ginger hair, being fat or just lazy. My Father did me a*

great service many years ago when pointed out that 'sticks and stones would break my bones but names would never hurt me'. Thanks for instilling some common sense in me, Dad!

Another comment was even more acrid. ".. political correctness has made commonsense a thing of the past. If you catch a burglar in your house then it's probably best to help the poor soul by carrying your possessions to the front door lest he should trip up and hurt himself and it's you that end up in court!" He was right. One farmer was locked up because in the pitch darkness he shot at two burglars who had broken into his home. He was frightened because attempts to break-in had been made several times and he lived alone in a secluded area.

I wonder what would happen to those who ask for black coffee or term a particularly nice August in England as Indian summer. Can we, the Indians, take offence at this? After all an Indian summer means 40 to 45°C and hot winds and dust storms. Does using that term mean we are being taunted for the severity of our climate?

I heard a shoplifter who was pinned to the ground by two staffers of the Sainsbury's outside the retail outlet in Golders Green threatening that he would sue them for using unnecessary force and calling him 'you…(they named him from the country he immigrated to Britain).' The manager, who knew me as a regular customer, looked at me and lamented, "I suppose we should give him a glass of wine and some cheese and biscuits until the police come. And call him William Shakespeare and not a …nian."

I wonder what would happen to those who ask for black coffee or term a particularly nice August in England as Indian summer. Can we, the Indians, take offence at this? After all an Indian summer means 40 to 45°C and hot winds and dust storms. Does using that term mean we are being taunted for the severity of our climate?

The reality is that the overzealous politicians by using political correctness as a means to get votes have diluted many invaluable virtues of British politics. As I said earlier, it is good and it has done good but politicians have drained it of all commonsense.

9

Weaving Mindsets: Politics and Racism

> *Immigration is not an issue for fringe parties, nor a taboo subject. It is a question to be dealt with at the heart of our politics, a question about what it means to be British.*
>
> —*Gordon Brown*

Prime Minister Gordon Brown appeared to be echoing the concern of many politicians about the alleged adverse social and economic effects of immigration. What was surprising was his sudden interest in the controversial issue after two years in office and five months after the right-wing British National Party won two seats in European Parliament. It seemed that he was spurred to speak at length about immigration and assure strict measures to not only make the entry of professionals from the non-European Union countries but also of students—who are keeping British universities financially viable—near impossible, was the General Election, just a few months later around May 2010.

The effect of such statements on social homogeneity and on the over three million people from the Indian sub-continent—not counting people from other non-EU countries—did not worry the Prime Minister. Such statements give wrong message to racists. Their patent hatred against immigrants tends to become latent.

I would not have thought that stricter immigration rules could stoke racism, if I had not read Ruth Brown's well-researched write-up 'Racism and Immigration in Britain' in the *International Socialism Journal* (Issue 68, 1995). She had shown through various instances connect between elections, parties vowing for strict immigration controls and racism. Her observations set me thinking about the action and reaction between racism and immigration as a political issue.

I tried to analyse various reasons that Brown gave and the assurance he made to restrict the flow of immigrants. His saying that there were 'significant variations' in how it affected different parts of the country, that people living in towns with lots of new arrivals would worry about falling wages, fewer jobs and the supply of housing and that 'immigrations is.. a question about what it means to be British', reminded me of the racist problems in the aftermath of some new immigration measures that Ruth Brown cited.

In fact, what Gordon Brown said was somewhat akin to what the right-wing British National Party (BNP) with avowed anti-immigration agenda had been saying for years. Ironically, it was condemned by all including Brown's Labour Party as racist. Was then Brown trying to wean away BNP's fringe sympathizers? As much as I knew about Brown, I do not think he would ever think of causing racist ripples. But then the wish to retain power is irresistible.

In another chapter I have written about the discrimination immigrants faced for years following the Commonwealth Immigration Act (1962) because it stoked unparalleled racist feelings. But even then I was taken aback by what Ruth Brown noted in the *Journal*. Hard words!

> *The main effect of Britain's first overtly racist Immigration Act (of 1962) was thus to institutionalise racism within the machinery of the state, rather than to prevent the recruitment of necessary labour power.*
>
> *It was the first legislation to introduce state regulation of Commonwealth immigration and introduced the first ever entry*

restrictions on British Commonwealth citizens, by making primary immigration dependent upon the possession of a work voucher. Given that the intended targets of the Act were all black or Asian (and few ever even attempted to deny this), the 1962 Act also marks the first of a series of racially discriminatory pieces of legislation which have combined to lay the basis for the notoriously racist immigration laws for which Britain is so famous today.

But this also reminded me of what Krishan Bhatia told me. He said the new settlers from India in the fifties and sixties were unaware of the laws and could not get work vouchers. Later, officers for no reason delayed decisions on applications of many for regularizing their stay. Bhatia said they were seemingly influenced by racist feelings. This is supported by what Ruth Brown wrote. She further added in the *Journal*, 'The 1962 Act enshrined in law for the first time the completely false, yet no less insidious, notion that immigration equals black immigration, a notion upon which all successive immigration legislation has been built.....' Alan Travis, home affairs editor of *The Guardian* wrote on 1 January 2002:

The government knew it would face charges of racism when it clamped down on the flow of "new Commonwealth" immigrants to Britain while introducing "open door" concessions for citizens of the "old Commonwealth" — Australia, New Zealand, Canada and South Africa— who were "of British stock". "The secret cabinet minutes show that, in agreeing to the 1971 Immigration Act, which still forms the framework of much British immigration law, ministers agreed that their decision to exempt from the clampdown "old Commonwealth" citizens who had a UK-born parent or grandparent would "probably attract some criticism as being discriminatory in favour of the'white" Commonwealth".

He disclosed that the then Home Secretary, Reginald Maudling, said such racism could be defended on the grounds that Britain had a special relationship with Australia, Canada and New Zealand and 'from Gallipoli to Inchon there are enduring monuments to its reality.'

He also told the cabinet that tougher restrictions on the inflow of Asian immigrants were 'necessary and defensible given their propensity in contrast to aliens to settle permanently and bring in their dependants'. Travis quoted

Seargent Gurpal Virdi; fought hard
and long racism in the force
(pic: courtesy The Nation)

Asst Com: Tarique Ghaffur;
highest ranking Asian Met officer—
victim ofracism? (pic: courtesy The Nation)

BNP winning first council seat made Government tilt towards visa restrictions (pic: courtesy The Nation)

from the state papers which were released that day by the Public Record Office. It revealed that one faction in the cabinet actually wanted to extend the right to settle in Britain to all 'old Commonwealth' citizens regardless of whether or not they were from 'British stock' but this proved too much for the Prime Minister, Edward Heath, who blocked the move on the grounds that it would be 'contrary to the concept of the Commonwealth as a multiracial institution'. Many would not buy that argument.

The files showed that under growing pressure from Enoch Powell, Mr Maudling told the PM that the new immigration law was needed because 'we are also expected by our supporters to take visible action further to reduce the number of immigrants'. So that is the crux of the stricter immigration rules, they eventually impact on the people from the sub-continent.

The Travis article further reported that Maudling told the prime minister secretly it was vital to 'defuse politically the problems of immigration ... as soon as possible. I am sure it would be helpful if the admission of new Commonwealth immigrants could be immediately reduced by administrative means'.

Travis commenting on 'language which may astonish readers 30 years on', quoted what Mr Maudling said:

> *The number of aliens who want to settle here is relatively few, and for this reason— because they come from a cultural background generally fairly akin to our own — it is not difficult to assimilate them.*
>
> *But of those wishing to come here to work from the Commonwealth, particularly the new Commonwealth, the vast majority would want to settle permanently and by reason both of this factor and of the fact that they come generally from a different cultural background, the task of assimilation— as experience so bitterly shows—is all but impossible. If we put the Commonwealth citizen on the same basis as what at present is the practice for aliens, and abolish the quota which presently applies only to Commonwealth citizens, the result would be a great increase in coloured immigration.*

Cabinet Secretary, Sir Burke Trend, the article revealed, had made clear that the main motive behind the act was 'to avoid the risk of renewed "swamping" by immigrants from the new Commonwealth'; and that such a 'resurgence would inflame community relations in Britain'. The new legislation, which had been introduced by the 1945 Labour government, ended the right of Commonwealth workers to settle in Britain. It followed a series of inflammatory speeches from Powell including a prediction in February 1971 that there would be 'an explosion' unless there was a massive repatriation scheme for immigrants.

Sir Burke Trend said opponents to the clause either feared opening the door to 'the alleged hordes of Anglo-Indians'; or, if they were liberals, believed it was wrong to discriminate between the 'Zanzibar republican and an Australian with a direct family connection.'

So we learnt that 'colour' mattered and so did the views of the supporters, who are in effect the voters. Ruth Brown was proved right once again. It is evident that the curbing of immigration, more than containing racism, mattered most at election times. This would be especially true in the times of economic downslide, which is what Brown was faced with as 2009 drew to an end and the worries of the forthcoming general elections began to haunt him. This could have been the reason for Brown to assume charge and promise to plug the flow of immigrants.

In a write up, 'Immigration', in *Global Issues* by Anup Shah, Matthew Randall has been quoted as saying that, when 'economic conditions get harder', 'empathy and understanding for the situation and conditions immigrants face is easily lost… mainstream media coverage in some countries, even places like Britain, makes it easy to stir up hysterical stories about immigration which helps direct the conversation and policies towards who can be "toughest" on immigration'.

He also cited the poll on immigration conducted for *ITV News* in the UK (April 2005) — 73 per cent of people thought too many immigrants were allowed into the UK and just 3 per cent believed that not enough were allowed; 75 per cent believed immigrants put a strain on public services; 39 per cent of people believed immigrants bring disease to the UK; 25 per cent felt migrants made Britain a thriving multicultural society; 'Immigration can become a social/political issue, where racism can be used to exploit feelings or as an excuse for current woes of local population; Where there is a perception

It is evident that the curbing of immigration, more than containing racism, mattered most at election times. This would be especially true in the times of economic downslide.

> Brown in laying open his plans for stricter immigration rules was obviously trying to shore up the chances of his party-- just like many of his predecessors had—at the General election.

that immigrants and refugees appear to get more benefits than local poor people, tensions and hostilities can also rise'—a perception which triggered the worst race riots in Bradford in 2001.

The poll statistics of 2005 could have been even more damning for immigrants in 2009. Brown in laying open his plans for stricter immigration rules was obviously trying to shore up the chances of his party-- just like many of his predecessors had—at the general elections. I am sure he did not have any racist intent. But the problem as stated in the article 'Immigration' in the *Global Issue* is because 'immigration can become a social/political issue, where racism can be used to exploit feelings or as an excuse for current woes of local population…'.

I am sure that most MPs were never motivated by crude racism or bigotry. They have been genuinely worried about the pressure on social services, hospitals and educational infrastructures. And they have been concerned about the greater number of jobs being taken up by 'foreigners'. This is understandable and justified. In India, too, such considerations have spurred state politicians in Maharashtra, the financial hub of India. They could be alleged to suffer from misplaced chauvinism against people within India and for a state which is part of India.

So why blame Brown? Come elections all parties since late fifties have brought into their campaign the issue of immigration hoping that it would help them increase their tally of votes. But it is also true that talks about immigration controls and hyping up the alleged unmitigated disaster because of the immigrants had invariably sparked racist feelings in the past. The

> .... talks about immigration controls and hyping up the alleged unmitigated disaster because of the immigrants had invariably sparked racist feelings in the past. The consequences could be graver in the present multi-cultural and multi-racial make-up of the British society.

consequences could be graver in the present multi-cultural and multi-racial make-up of the British society.

A large number of families from non-EU countries are now living in Britain and statements of Brown like it was 'lazy elitism' to portray people with worries about immigration as racist could raise fears in Indians and others of radical right-wingers opposed to immigration of getting overly active. The reiteration by such right-wingers of pressure on the resources and taking up of jobs by immigrants has in the past resulted in racist feelings.

I would, however, reiterate that Brown or any other politician from the three main parties do not intend to fan racist passions, for parties also need the votes of ethnic minority communities all of whom come from non-EU countries. But the report that the range of jobs available to skilled foreign workers would be reduced by tens of thousands and from next year all vacancies for hospital consultants, civil engineers, aircraft engineers and shipping officers would have to be filled from within Britain and the EU did unnerve professionals and skilled workers who came under the Highly Skilled Migrant Professionals (HSMP) scheme. Soon engineering posts, skilled chefs and care workers would be put on the same list, it was said.

Employers knew the potential economic impact of limiting skilled workers. The Institution of Civil Engineers said restrictions on engineers could affect major infrastructure projects such as new nuclear power stations

What then could happen to the nearly 30,000 Indian professionals who were permitted into Britain under HSMP scheme and to the 9000 Indian curry houses? Many skilled workers have faced problems, whenever immigration rules were tightened against them, with racial overtones at their work. And worse, with the recession not yet over, many of them were apprehensive of losing jobs and thus failing to get enough points enabling them to stay on. The fear in the skilled workers was justified. Many Bangladeshi restaurants have been facing closure with the immigration rules making the knowledge of English language compulsory for visa applicants. Chefs from Sylhet hardly know English, thus the Balti restaurants have been unable to bring them into Britain.

> All of a sudden the pride of the politicians in the multi-cultural society, apparently, disappeared. The fear of an electoral debacle bulldozed every other consideration.

Yet the plans for more restrictions were announced. The skilled workers in the country who were allowed entry under the HSMP feared fresh wave of discrimination at their workplaces, because attempts could be made by others to force them to quit. All of a sudden the pride of the politicians in the multi-cultural society, apparently, disappeared. The fear of an electoral debacle bulldozed every other consideration.

The HSMP Forum had voiced its concern immediately. Its worry was that as in the past the new rules would be implemented with retrospective effect.

> *...We would like to raise the concern that introducing new laws often results in targeting existing migrants who have been responsible tax- payers and law-abiding residents. Migrants enter the UK only after they get the 'permission' to do so. Migrants have to satisfy the demanding nature of the authorities and the particular requirements of the points-based system before they can even think of building a life in the UK.*
>
> *However, in view of the current economic climate, there could be instances of migrants losing their jobs and we believe that these circumstances must be taken into consideration when deciding on whether or not they will be 'permitted' to continuously live in this country.*

The Executive Director of HSMP, Amit Kapadia, pointed out that the new shortage occupation list was to significantly reduce the number of foreign employees, which would affect many existing migrants' immigration status.

> *It is not justified on the government's part to exercise its powers of expulsion indiscriminately especially if these migrants were unaware of the changing circumstances when they first made their applications. For instance, many applicants who may have applied a couple of years ago would not have foreseen the subsequent changes in the shortage occupation list which could thwart their aspirations to continue to work and settle in the UK.*
>
> *It is our concern that the new draft bill, which intends to introduce the new streamlined power of expulsion, would further abuse human rights laws and would unfairly penalise honest and hardworking migrants just as the Citizenship and Immigration Act which was passed in July 2009 will do.*

> It is least surprising that the once most-preferred British universities by Indian students have been supplanted by the American colleges. The figure of Indian students in the US crossed hundred thousand whereas in the UK it has been crawling up slowly from 27,000.

Non-EU Students under Scanner

Brown and his ministers also knew that Indian and Chinese students have helped universities to be financially viable. Yet, they went ahead and outlined plans for restrictions on students from non-EU countries. This was surprising too considering that just two years ago Brown's government had relaxed rules for students, allowing them to stay back, take employment, albeit for a limited period. But, seemingly, a clampdown was suddenly planned. It was said to be aimed at bogus colleges offering non-EU nationals an easy route into Britain. But many steps were taken to shut these bogus schools. Such arguments convince no one. It could not be the reason for ministers reportedly preparing to raise the minimum level of a course for which visas are granted and to introduce English language tests before they are given out. Brown also raised the prospect of tougher rules on foreign students taking part-time jobs that 'would be better filled by young British workers'.

This meant that only those students, whose families could afford to pay over 20, 000 pounds a year tuition fee apart from the living expenses, would seek admission in British universities. And if the rule was given retrospective effect, it would financially ruin most of the over 27,000 Indian students and many thousands from countries like Pakistan. With what kind of feelings these students would leave Britain? They could not be blamed if they felt ostracized because of the colour of their skin.

> I believe that any democratic government should watch the interest of its people but it is a bit complex in Britain. People in Britain also mean a sizeable number from the non-EU countries. They were allowed to come into the country and live or work legitimately.

It is least surprising that the once most-preferred British universities by Indian students have been supplanted by American colleges. The figure of Indian students in the US crossed hundred thousand whereas in the UK it has been crawling up slowly from 27,000. The planned restrictions on jobs, apart from the fee disparity between them and the EU students by over three times could in the near future dry up the number seeking admission in the UK universities. But consideration for winning the election was naturally paramount. The financial viability of educational institutions could be tackled once back in power.

I believe that any democratic government should watch the interest of its people but it is a bit complex in Britain. People in Britain also mean a sizeable number from the non-EU countries. They were allowed to come into the country and live or work legitimately. They could genuinely fear racist reprisals. True, the Labour Government, starting from Tony Blair, had taken measures to drive out racism and make incitement of hatred a criminal offence. Blair rechristened Indians, Pakistanis and Bangladeshis British Asians, which distinguished them from the category of immigrants. He and his successor Brown never tired of commending their contributions in all fields and taking pride in the multi-ethnic society that prospered through diversity.

But Timothy Wood in his article 'Britain's Race Relations Problem: Reasons for the Unchanging Racial Divide in the UK' (5 May 2008) looked at the 'state of race relations in Britain today, from the government's insubstantial proposals to ease tensions, to what needs to be done in future'.

> *The face of Britain is becoming less like the multi-cultural utopia that it aspires to be, and more like a nation divided among its different peoples. The UK government is constantly making grand statements about how it intends to bridge the racial divide. It has pursued a set of measures aimed at resolving this issue, such as bringing schools of different faiths together to promote understanding. However, to see real progress occur the government needs to get to the root of the problem.*

Pointing out 'inadequate Government proposals' he noted that 'instead it seems to repeat the same generic statements. In a Downing Street speech in December 2006, former Prime Minister Tony Blair said, "Multicultural Britain was never supposed to be a celebration of division but of diversity, to allow people to live harmoniously despite their differences. We need to reassert the duty and need to integrate". While he may be correct, is it really enough to see the kind of breakthrough that is needed in easing racial tensions?'

Wood said,

> *For real change to occur, the process needs to work both ways. There are proposed initiatives designed to encourage integration among different groups of society, such as an English language test for new immigrants. But do the British public know anything about the people who come here to find a new way of life? For example, the national controversy that erupted because of the Muslim veil arose because Western values and teachings allow people no real understanding of why it is worn, and indeed the Muslim way of life in general.*

So the debate has continued. Although I did not ever feel out of place during all my years in England, I did report several cases of racist slurs and even violence. Yet I always felt that these were isolated incidents and the government and police were doing their best to root out racism. Until I recalled Ruth Brown observation ' ....Labour attempted to complete its about turn on immigration during the early 1960s by attempting to hide behind an argument first mooted by the right wing of the Tory party, namely, that immigration controls are needed to preserve good "race relations" in Britain'. Was history repeating itself?

This forced me to think more seriously about the racist effect of immigration controls. There were different, contradictory thoughts. No country can leave its borders open for unrestricted access. But then one reads, 'This completely insidious notion—that racism in Britain is best eradicated by inviting immigration officers to practise it at the point of entry into Britain'—is best summed up by this syllogism from Roy Hattersley in 1965: 'Without integration, limitation is inexcusable: without limitation, integration is impossible'. But Lord Dholkia once pointed out to me that more crucial than integration was assimilation. Limitation, as has been shown by many, triggers racist feelings, albeit unintended.

Stricter immigration rules imply that people from non-EU countries would be kept out. But whether it would also keep out racism is rather difficult to answer. In this context, I feel it is ironic that there have been long periods when immigrants were encouraged and brought into the country, although they were always made to feel inferior. I was indeed surprised to read that among others even Enoch Powell (famous for rivers of blood would flow if immigrants were allowed) 'actively encouraged the migration of medical staff from India and the West Indies during his time as Minister for Health'. But once the subsequent generations toiled and became successful, the prejudices inevitably followed to dog them. This annoyance of the majority was possibly the reason for the 1971 Immigration Act, wherein ministers decided to exempt 'old Commonwealth' citizens who had a UK-born parent or grandparent from the clampdown.

The Indians, who have constituted the majority of professionals and students, naturally felt that they were the target every time the immigration rules were tightened. This might be so. Liam Fox, when the shadow Health Secretary, had once demanded that the examination of doctors from the non-EU countries be made more stringent. He feared that doctors from such countries could be a risk to the health of patients. He possibly forgot that Indian doctors and other health workers were the backbone of the National Health Service (NHS). That the Plab test—for entry to practise in Britian—is very tough and medicine in India is taught in English. I wrote about it in my paper. I did ask what about doctors who came, unrestricted and without sitting for any test, from the EU countries. They are taught medicine in their national languages and seldom have much knowledge of English.

So it is natural that whenever any measure restricting immigrants from the non-EU countries is considered, Indians do feel as though they were the bigger targets. Although one senior Indian doctor near Birmingham, to my surprise, was all in favour of restricting new crop of young Indian doctors from coming into the country. He argued that it would affect the young Indian medical graduates living in Britain as much as it would make it difficult for the English doctors to get jobs. "What about my son? He would face stiff competition from his Indian cousins. Then why blame the British if they feel that jobs meant for them are taken up by 'foreigners'."

But that does not by any means justify racism. Incidents of racism occur regularly. The police was branded as institutionally racist by the judge who enquired into the police investigation in the murder of a Black youth Stephen Lawrence allegedly by five English youth. Later, Sgt Gurpal Virdi of the Metropolitan Police was accused of sending racist hate-mail to himself. One of the letters to him and a few non-white officers said, "Not wanted. Keep the police force white. Leave now or else." It was signed: NF.

I realized the trauma such incidents cause. I met Virdi at his house and he just poured his heart out. His wife's face was ashen, children were not playing. He told me that a police car was spotted outside his house several times. Soon after, officers who were tailing him caught up with him while he was taking his children to the dentist. He was swamped by police officers and dragged and bundled in one of the cars, he alleged. He felt it was done to humiliate him.

When it was discovered that although the mails were sent from his computer, he could not have been present at the time they were sent, the police sent a terrorist team to their employee's house. 'They started ripping the whole house down. Seven hours it went on. They searched every single inch of the house, taking off shelves, pulling apart towel rails, every single packet, even sealed ones were opened, chapati flour, carpets, floorboards, the shed.'

His wife was told not to speak in any language except English. His daughter's computer was taken. He said it was just a week old or so. It was a present on her tenth birthday. But the team said it was a lie.

Although traumatized and troubled Virdi swore he would fight the injustice alleging that he was framed. It took him four years to get justice, but he did get it fair and square. I have always had, and continue to have, great respect for the judiciary in Britain. The Rule of Law is held tenaciously by judges both in letter and spirit.

Virdi was not only awarded a hefty compensation but the Metropolitan Police was also directed to write an apology to him. A plaque was presented to him by the Black Police Association—which fought his case. It said, 'Presented to Mr Gurpal Virdi for your courage and tenacity in fighting for justice.'

The 200-page Virdi report detailed how Sgt Virdi had been falsely accused of sending racist hate-mail to himself and other ethnic-minority officers; how he had been 'convicted' by a kangaroo court who then turfed him out of the force; and how an employment tribunal had ruled he had been falsely dismissed by a racist employer for an offence that he couldn't have committed. Though it was justice to him the officers who allegedly victimized him had not been named and shamed, and it was said that there had been no formal investigation into the true identity of the culprits behind the hate-mail.

Ironically lessons were not learnt by the racist elements. A few years later the assistant commissioner Tarique Ghaffur, Britain's most senior ethnic- minority officer, also alleged racist discrimination. Much earlier he had told Virdi, when he asked him why many non-white officers had been under investigation. 'Look at their backgrounds. They're all the officers who challenged racism in the Met. We're targets. Any opportunity and they'll get us.' Well they got him ultimately. Although at a price! I met him often even after he left the service and I found that although he never mentioned what happened to make him feel racially discriminated, he was trying to forget the ugly phase in his otherwise distinguished career, and get on with his life.

These are a few instances to illustrate that racism, whatever might be the reasons for it, continues to be a pest. The consequence of that is that any move to control professionals entering the country or of those who are already in Britain under various schemes causes alarm in the non-whites and raises racist feelings in right-wingers.

It was interesting that while Gordon Brown was announcing his plans for controlling immigration, parliamentarians like Nicholas Soames called for a compulsory "English test" for those applying for UK visas, a move that could impact thousands of Indians seeking to move to the country. Former Labour Social Security Minister Frank Field and Soames also stressed the need for new restrictions on spouses coming into the country. So far English test was necessary for those seeking citizenship. These MPs wanted even immigrants applying for UK visas to undergo an English test. I did not see anything objectionable in that. If someone seeks to come to Britain, knowledge of English is vital for getting along there. As the MPs too said, English would help immigrants to understand their rights and responsibilities and would help get employment easily and integrate better. But with racism still surfacing from time to time, any restrictions make some see red.

In retrospect I feel that although racism-related incidents continue to occur, they are less now—as against in the sixties and seventies — due to the colour of the skin. The reason for annoyance with the Indians, in particular, is because of economic reasons. Most are educated, are either in good jobs or are in family businesses. The inner city psyche of seeing them as usurpers has lingered. A similar psyche possibly afflicts the police force. However, translated in simple terms, such prejudices seem to be due to the colour of the skin.

Things did start changing with the influx of East Europeans. More incidents of locals objecting to their usurping jobs surfaced. I heard such murmurs in Southall and Birmingham as well. It is like what I was taught in sociology.

Those sitting in a train compartment, all strangers to each others jointly hate newcomers at the next station. Then these newcomers join the others to feel uneasy about the newcomers at a later station. It's the group feeling.

Likewise the Poles, Rumanians and others, all white-skinned, who came to Britain after the East European countries joined the EU, caused unease. Indians who had been complaining about discrimination lamented about these new immigrants. They took jobs at cheaper wages, displacing others from work in restaurants, hotels, pubs and in construction, plumbing jobs.

So I feel that racism due to the colour of the skin could in future be swamped by the economic problems. I quote again Randall in *Global Issue*, 'Immigration can become a social/political issue, where racism can be used to exploit feelings or as an excuse for current woes of local population'. In the case of immigrants from East Europe, immigration has no relevance. They cannot be stopped from coming and taking up jobs. This could ultimately be a bigger political and economic issue than the Indians. I have not mentioned Pakistanis or Bangladeshis who had been unable –so far—to develop the economic sinews like the Indians.

> Racist feelings would, I hope, diffuse. Of course it would never go away completely. It would possibly be not overt and blatant. Maybe in a few organizations and businesses too! But you cannot make a home in someone else's country and then complain, I suppose.

I think the upward mobility of the new generation of Indians would lead soon to their integration and assimilation in the English society, whether some right-wingers and those who believe in Powell's philosophy like it or not. I have seen some young Indians who would be as intolerant of any discrimination as the radicals were of their older generations. And they have the financial muscle and reach to make themselves heard. I am not saying this with any feeling of perverse satisfaction. I believe that these successful

> Indians who had been complaining about discrimination lamented about these new immigrants (from East Europe). They took jobs at cheaper wages, displacing others from work in restaurants, hotels, pubs and in construction, plumbing jobs. So I feel that racism due to the colour of the skin could in future be swamped by the economic problems.

youngsters would convince those who still nurse dislike of the skin colour that they have and are contributing to the country as much as the best white. Racist feelings would, I hope, diffuse. Of course, it would never go away completely. It would possibly be not overt and blatant. Maybe, in a few organizations and businesses too! But you cannot make a home in someone else's country and then complain, I suppose.

Coming back to Brown's planned measures it is a fact that if they became laws they would surely affect Indians most. But I feel that with the world class educational standards in Indian colleges and universities, Indians wanting specialization or higher education can go to many other countries. Businesses would continue to get a red carpet treatment in Britain. The Tatas, the Mittals and the like are unstoppable, and so would be the executives and management staff they send to Britain. As for professionals, the opportunities are many in India itself. Closed doors in Britain would not be any loss. stricter immigration rules for political reasons would not matter if those settled there are not affected.

10

Shame of Honour

> *Honour is about a collection of practices used by the family to control behaviour, to prevent perceived shame, but there's no honour in murder, rape, or kidnapping.*
>
> —*Detective Chief Inspector Gerry Campbell*

Gerry Campbell, head of the Community Safety, part of the Violent Crime Directorate, who investigated several cases of 'honour' killings in South Asian families, has obviously observed the most despicable, inhuman behaviour of families and at the same time the unbelievable tragic and pitiable end of young women. I am an Indian, but I failed to understand how the families from the subcontinent despite living in a western society for decades clung to their obsolete traditions to the extent that they could turn beastly and murder their own.

A father stabs his desperately pleading daughter 18 times and slits her throat thrice while her mother watches. When a neighbour hearing the screams of the girl comes to inquire he is told by the father that his daughter is having fits.

An aged mother-in-law takes her daughter-in-law Surjit Athwal to Punjab on the pretext of attending a wedding. The daughter-in-law simply disappeared. It took nine years of dogged effort by Scotland Yard to prove that the mother-in-law and her husband got Athwal murdered by contract killers in India.

A mother was apprehended at Manchester airport while trying to board a PIA flight to Pakistan with her daughter who had been drugged. One girl was reportedly murdered for a love song dedicated to her on a community radio show. An eight-month pregnant woman was murdered when she ran away to marry against the wishes of her family. A 28-year-old Sikh woman, Geeta Aulakh, was killed and her right hand, on which Sikhs wear the kara, was severed ostensibly to dishonour her by excommunicating her from the faith and save honour of the family and the community.

These are just a few instances of barbarism in modern Britain. At least 12 women are killed every year for honour according to the police estimate. But many others would be hidden— forced suicides and murders made to look like suicide. They are widely believed to take place undetected. The family pressure on young women is so much that those aged 16-24 from Pakistani, Indian and Bangladeshi backgrounds are three times more likely to kill themselves than the national average for that age. It is also impossible to tell what pressures some must have been under. And for every woman who dies, it seems certain that there are many, many more living with honour-related abuse and hidden away in shuttered communities.

The Centre for Social Cohesion claims that 25 (more than 12 claimed by police) are killed every year by their families for saving their so-called honour. These are generally the result of forced marriages or attempts for it. According to government figures over 3000 cases of forced marriages take place annually. This is beguiling. Some apparently lead to killings and suicides. Mystery shrouds many deaths of young women.

Of 240 suicides on rail tracks in Britain three years ago, 80 were by women in Southall, reportedly most were Sikhs. Reports revealed that these women from Punjab were more educated in comparison to their husbands.

A young mother, Navjeet Sidhu, had committed suicide by flinging herself on the track along with her five-year old daughter and two-year old son while the Heathrow Express was speeding past the Southall Railway station at over 125 mph. Six months later her mother committed suicide at the same spot in a similar way. Her reason for suicide remained a mystery.

Of the 240 suicides on rail tracks in Britain three years ago, 80 were by women in Southall, reportedly most were Sikhs. Reports revealed that these women from Punjab were more educated in comparison to their husbands. In case of Geet Aulakh, for instance, her husband was jobless. She was working as a receptionist at the Sunrise Radio, the biggest Asian radio network in Britain.

Unfortunately, according to a social worker such tragedies did not stop forced marriages. Once a wife dies, the opportunity opens up for her husband's family to get another dowry. I talked with Virendra Sharma, MP Southall, who said that the problem 'arises from the fact that once married the women have no one to turn to'.

I recalled Lord Bhiku Parekh's suggestion. I had telephoned him after the incident of the Heathrow Express to get his views on why such suicides recur among women from India. He gave me many reasons including the one that women, mostly from Punjab, found themselves helpless once they came to their husband's house in Britain. In some cases women born and brought up in England were married to men from India. They could not tolerate the western lifestyle of their wives. He suggested that a committee should be constituted comprising of senior people from diverse backgrounds within the Indian community, on the patterns of the panels set up by Jews, to deal privately and offer counselling to young women in family matters. They would understand the problems better as they would know the customs from different regions of India. But this could never take off and I left London some time after.

He (Lord Parekh) suggested that a committee should be constituted comprising of senior people from diverse backgrounds within the Indian community, on the patterns of the panels set up by Jews, to deal privately and offer counselling to young women in family matters.

Navjeet Sidhu; Young Sidhu committed suicide with her children
(pic: courtesy The Nation)

Surjit Athwal: victim of honour killing

Geeta Aulakh: victim of honour killing?
(pic: courtesy The Nation)

Such a committee is needed. So far no amount of measures has been able to stop honour killings or forced marriages. The Government appointed a special committee of three, Baroness Uddin, Lord Dholakia and Lord Nazi Ahmed all of whom travelled across the country interacting with families. Special police and community support units were set up. But the scourge continues.

The reason for the maximum number of victims being of Pakistani and Bangladeshi origin can be attributed to the fact that in their countries such obnoxious practices have continued, with many practising outdated beliefs. One said that the concept of women being property was one of the contributory factors for honour killing known locally as karo-kari. Aamir Latif, IOL Correspondent, wrote that 'according to official statistics in 2006, as many as 1,261 women were murdered in the name of honor killings in Pakistan....Official data presented in the country's Upper House Senate shows that more than 4,000 people were killed during last 6 years in the name of honor killings.' The United Nations Population Fund estimated that 1,000 out of 5,000 victims of honour killings in the world were from Pakistan.

The Surprise

Pakistani and Bangladeshi families came much later to England compared to the Indian families and their women are not well educated. Nor many are allowed to work. But the frequent shameful killings in families from India are a bit confounding. What surprises me is that the comparatively prosperous, well-educated and socially mobile third and fourth generation Indian families are so intolerant about old customs of marriages within caste or community being violated by their young? Their young have grown up in two cultures, but more western. They have lived in a western liberal society since birth and befriended non-Indians in colleges and work places. Campbell too was surprised that the worst problems lay in third or fourth generation families.

> Why would such parents, who have lived in the western ethos for decades, put the clock back when it comes to marriage? I could not understand their ostrich -like attitude. But then I found over the years a sharp difference in the attitude of the more urbane Indian and those who remained in clusters.

'People who actually are hanging on to traditions that in the country of origin have gone, things have moved on back home but they don't know that', he was quoted saying. Such extreme reaction to out-of -caste marriages has almost disappeared in urban India.

Why would such parents, who have lived in the western ethos for decades, put the clock back when it comes to marriage? I could not understand their ostrich -like attitude. But then I found over the years a sharp difference in the attitude of the more urbane Indian and those who remained in clusters.

During puja at the Camden Town Hall or at Hampstead Town Hall where the idol of Durga is installed and rituals are performed from sapthami to navratri, I saw a few Bengali young women with English husbands. They helped as much as Indian husbands in preparing for the puja. The families of these girls seemed happy and well-adjusted with their English sons-in-law. I also attended the wedding of the daughter of my friend Kailsah Bhadwar with an English young man at the historic Café Royal on Regent Street. Not only the Bhadwars but also their relatives too seemed happy and comfortable. The lavish wedding itself showed how much the family accepted a 'foreign' son-in-law'. There are many other instances.

No case of forced marriage or suicide or honour killing has taken place in any Gujarati family. Nor has it happened in upper middle class or wealthy Indian families. Almost all cases of forced marriages or suicides were reported within families living in Indian-dominated areas like Southall, Hounslow or Greenford. I heard of only one case of alleged killing of a pregnant Sikh woman from Scotland, who had fled from there and settled in London with her husband. Witnesses alleged that an old Sikh was seen fleeing from the house, about the time the woman was murdered.

Another case of a suspected dowry death in Glasgow was alleged by the parents of a woman who was electrocuted around 1997, as far as I can recollect. They met Executive Editor Chandan Mitra at the *Hindustan Times* office in New Delhi and told him that they had written to the Home Office, alleging that their daughter was being harassed for dowry. She felt tortured and had written a letter to them hinting about it. But she was unwilling to return because she felt that would shame them.

Mitra called me and faxed a copy of the letter. I telephoned the Chief Detective Inspector in charge of the case and explained to him the complaint and suspicion of the parents. I must say he was most cooperative although he could not fathom, understandably, what was dowry death. He told me that the death was confirmed due to electrocution but he would look into again. He said he would stop the funeral which was set for 4 pm the same day. Nothing transpired, no evidence to the contrary could be found. I do not know what the parents did later.

The incidents of alleged forced marriages or honour killings are generally reported in families whose socio-economic level is on an average much lower than that of the Indians we see at the Durga puja and at most NRI gatherings.

The Government and police, I have to acknowledge, have been doing their best to pre-empt, forced marriages. When the Government's forced marriage unit was set up, it received 5,000 calls and rescued 400 victims in its very first six months. But they are handicapped. The incidents are hidden within the four walls of these homes, and the communities too feign ignorance since many believe that girls should be married according to the wishes of their elders.

British policemen had been initially— and some still are— wary of intervening and booking the family elders. One, it might not be politically correct and, secondly, charges of racism or communalism could ensue. The policemen of South Asian origin who do not have to face such accusations, too, hesitate to take strong action against the family members. Many religious bodies while condemning the ghastly murders cloaked as honour killings have never taken any step to stop the evil.

I investigated into reports that families hired taxi drivers, bounty hunters, and enlisted support of councillors and police officers belonging to their communities to trace and bring back any woman who managed to escape. In the process they were reportedly quite often molested, raped or beaten up. I learnt that near Sheffield, a group of hunters charged anywhere between 10,000 pounds to 25,000 pounds for their 'efforts'.

I was told that in one case bounty hunters traced the runaway girl by keeping vigilance at several post offices. They had learnt that she was living in a safe house but used to come to collect weekly social dole at a post office. She

I investigated into reports that families hired taxi drivers, bounty hunters, and enlisted support of councillors and police officers belonging to their communities to trace and bring back any woman who managed to escape.

was spotted at a post office and then followed to the place where she lived. They then kidnapped her and reportedly raped her, and then a taxi driver in league with them took her to her family.

Campbell confirmed that police knew about families using bounty hunters. He said it was not uncommon to hire them to hunt down people who left forced marriages or fled from a family where they were at risk. 'It's rare for [one person] to take unilateral action, it's all done in consultation and there is logistical support and collusion in the extended community.'

This is why the coming up of support groups, apart from the Black Sisters in Southall which has been helping and rescuing women for a number of years has been a welcome development. The menace is too widespread for one group to provide help everywhere. The oppressed women do not have much time. Their families are invariably in hot pursuit and have the resources to mobilize the hunt, whereas the runaway woman has not much means to keep running.

The Cardiff-based Henna Foundation and Jasvinder Sanghera's charity Karma Nirvana in Derby are actively involved in helping women. Jasvinder Sanghera, too, had fled a forced marriage and made a new life for herself, after her sister Robina killed herself to escape the misery of a loveless marriage. When it opened its helpline in April 2008, Karma Nirvana received 4,000 calls in the first year and is now taking 300 calls a month from people under threat of honour-based violence, often linked to forced marriage. Sanghera wrote about the tragedy in her own life in her book *Shame*, which became the bestseller in 2007 in Britain. She was honoured as Britain's Woman of the Year and the Forced Marriage (Civil Protection) Act became law, giving the state the power to pre-empt forced marriages. The ensuing Forced Marriage Unit is contacted by about 5,000 people a year.

I talked with Sanghera who said that possibly 3 per cent of women manage to escape forced marriage. But they live with fear and rejection of not only their families but also their communities and sometimes their friends. I heard of a case in which the sister and mother of a young woman, who left home when being forced into a marriage, would cross the street if they saw her.

Campbell was perceptive when he said that 'honour-based violence is complicated and a sensitive crime to investigate. Its fathers, brothers, uncles, mums and cousins and the victim, or potential victim, have a fear of criminalising or demonising their family so they can be reluctant to come forward.'

He said the force did not know how many victims 'are out there suffering in silence but as an example in the financial year of 2008-9 we had 132 forced marriages and honour-based violence offences reported to us.... We've been learning about this for 10 years and have been really galvanised over the past four years so while we are not complacent we have come on leaps and bounds.' The Met Police reopened files of 81 women who were killed in past 10 years to try and ascertain whether the deaths were due to attempts for forced marriage or were they victims of honour killings.

Diana Nammi, who runs the Iranian and Kurdish Women's Rights Organization in London, has also been trying to persuade women to seek advice and assistance if they feel they are in danger. She once pointed out that the number of women about whom one heard or the cases dealt with in court were just a handful of the full picture. She added that it was unacceptable that a woman could be killed for her make-up or having a boyfriend or for refusing to cower down to a forced marriage.

She reiterated what I mentioned earlier. In the UK younger people were at risk because they had grown up in England and wanted to adapt and live in the modern world, without barriers to who they could be in love with or not be in love with. She also correctly pointed out that honour was a very old tradition but it could not operate in Britain. Many young do not even understand it.

Hopefully the efforts of the authorities, support groups and individuals like Ram Gidoomal CBE of the South Asian Development who has devoted time, spent money and put his energy in trying to evolve ways to save women from forced marriages, would eventually bear some positive outcomes. He too said that many young had real problems in trying to cope with this clash of cultures. In extreme cases, the clash of cultures results in young people wanting to take their own life or people engaging in honour killing or murder of the worst kind.

He suggested that the authorities needed to look further than murder cases to get to the bottom of honour crimes. 'Suicide, attempted murder and

> 'Wearing lipstick, owning a mobile phone, cutting your hair; any of these things could be said to bring dishonour on a family because those are all signs that a girl is getting Westernised, which is what Asian families fight so hard against.'

injuries can all fall into the category of honour killing.' Experts on family issues believe that honour-based violence could be a socio-economic issue. There was a strong correlation between violence against women and issues such as inequality between men. 'In deprived communities where men are struggling to earn a living they can feel subordinated and lacking in respect, and so try to get their authority back by dominating anyone below them, usually women,' said Gidoomal.

But what was disturbing was that despite the wide publicity of cruelty to young women by their own families, a 2006 BBC poll for the *Asian Network* in the UK found that 1 in 10 of the 500 young Asians, including Hindus and Sikhs, said that they could condone the murder of someone who dishonoured their family. It is impossible to believe that at least some of the polled did not know about the sequel to *Shame*, *Daughter of Shame,* which Sanghera wrote two years after. The book written in a racy narrative style revealed Sanghera's experiences with other Asian women, through her Karma Nirvana women's centre. 'Wearing lipstick, owning a mobile phone, cutting your hair; any of these things could be said to bring dishonour on a family because those are all signs that a girl is getting Westernised, which is what Asian families fight so hard against.' She cited the case of one Sajida Bibi, who was murdered on her wedding day, because she, not her family, chose her husband. I was appalled to read about several such incidents. I secured details and reported many cases in my paper. I would assume and hope that as the new generations learn to cope with the cultural divide and get the courage to come out openly about pressures within their families and seek help, the shame of honour killings, which has stigmatized the South Asian families, would be obliterated.

The Government measures and support system provided by private organizations apart, awareness about the issue in the UK is being raised in Punjab by the likes of Langar Hall. Most have come to know and are alarmed that some NRI families have been hiring contract killers in India. BBC reported these contract killers were asked to carry out up to 100 murders in India each year. We know the case of the unfortunate Surjit Athwal who

> Pav Athwal, Surjit Athwal's teenage daughter, who was very young when her mother was killed, later launched a helpline to help victims of forced marriage and honour-based violence. 'There is no honour in the murder of a loving mother.'

disappeared in Punjab in 1998. It was established by the investigating officers that she had been murdered in a so-called honour killing after her in-laws discovered that she planned to divorce her husband. They had hired criminals in India to kill her. She was strangled and her body dumped in a river. Her brother, Jagdeesh Singh, now campaigns for other victims' families.

Pav Athwal, Surjit Athwal's teenage daughter, who was very young when her mother was killed, later launched a helpline to help victims of forced marriages and honour-based violence. 'There is no honour in the murder of a loving mother.' As a community it is important to speak up about these injustices – raising awareness is simply the first step.

Judge Giles Forrester, who convicted Surjit's mother-in-law and husband, summed up the issue well. He told them, 'In reality, however, you murdered her for no other reason than the existence of matrimonial difficulties and the likely breakdown of the marriage. You decided the so-called honour of your family name was more important than the life of this young woman.' This is the reason for most honour killings.

Ann Cryer, the Labour MP for Keighley, whom I met several times, welcoming Judge Forrester's finding too said that 'in most communities people would condemn domestic violence, but in Asian communities, the religious and secular leaders were either turning a blind eye or actually condoning it.'

Within the Indian community, religious leaders have not said anything to condone violence in families. But the problem would not be resolved until the community seniors take the issue seriously and help the Government and Police in their efforts to pre-empt forced marriages. Only then honour killings would stop.

I was initially hesitant to include in the book the issue of forced marriages and honour killings. But on hindsight I felt that it might make the Indian community introspect and ensure that in future young women are not tortured, tormented and murdered in their community. I suppose those who have made it in their lives owe that much to their own.

11

Altruism from Abroad

> *A couple of million pounds are raised annually by Indians in Britain, and a few Britons for good causes in India.*

When the Indian economy opened up in the early nineties, incentives were offered to non-resident Indians (NRI) for investments in the country and to put money in Indian banks at high interest rates and low taxes on them. As expected there was a mini rush to invest and take out fixed deposits. The NRIs for the first time were treated as an extended family and welcomed warmly. They were bringing in foreign exchange which was most needed and thus welcome at that time.

It was not uncommon to see NRIs converging on New Delhi, Mumbai and Ahmedabad to study sectors for starting businesses. Money transfers to Indian banks too gathered momentum. They were the new 'VIPs' and as befitting VIPs they could secure immediate appointments with senior ministers and bureaucrats in economic ministries. Likewise, Indian ministers flew west to encourage them to invest in India. The word NRI was like magic, it opened all doors. But when some of the NRIs started to expect concessions and favours in return, the cordiality started to turn frosty.

The general impression in India of NRIs was of being excessively affluent and having an easy life while their cousins suffered turbulent times and deprivation. The country seemed to want a one-way traffic—give but don't ask. The theory being that the NRIs left the country so they did not have the right to ask for anything. So when some NRIs pressed for a few more concessions they became Non-Required Indians. I heard many visiting ministers in London say that NRI demands were unreasonable. One finance minister even told a gathering of prominent Indians in London that some NRIs were behaving like sons-in-law. 'Please be a son and not a son-in-law.'

The realization came late—and that too not to most— that many NRIs, especially following liberalization, had begun to help the deprived or underprivileged sections in India without asking for anything. It was Atal Behari Vajpayee who, for the first time, recognized the spirit and passion of many NRIs to undertake projects ranging from education for the poor children, better living conditions and for the malnourished. The Pravasi Bharatiya Diwas was started to convey the country's pride for what they achieved in their adopted countries and to accord them honours for what they were doing for their home country.

I remember the excitement in the diaspora in UK when the first Pravasi Diwas was scheduled. Every Indian seemed to want to attend it. Its success led the Manmohan Singh Government to create a ministry for overseas Indians. He acknowledged while addressing people of Indian origin in Port of Spain the capital of Trinidad and Tobago that Indians abroad were the most visible symbol of the country's globalization process. He hailed the role of people of Indian origin in foreign countries.

I think Dr Singh, with the increasing number of NRIs raising money for charity work in India, might soon acclaim the contribution of people of Indian origin to their country of origin—India. In Britain I know personally how much NRIs there have been trying to do to help and take up projects for the families that need help. I was, indeed, amazed to see the enthusiasm and determination of many Indians to reach out to India. These were not sons-in-law but sons of the soil. The more time and money they spared or raised for the Indian causes the happier they seemed to be. I know a few who having made money the hard way— commendably rising from cleaning floors and delivering tickets or earning daily wages in low-paid jobs—to become multi-millionaires. They never forgot their homes and the people they grew up with.

They resolved, once their struggle was over, to help the underprivileged or deprived people in India. They have not limited themselves to donating to temples or dargahs, like many rich in India do once their prayers for greater success and wealth have been answered.

The one-way traffic expected by the country is not only overtly visible now but also getting increasingly recognized! In fact, they are an example to wealthy Indians at home. As one NRI who spends a lot of time and money in India for philanthropic purposes said, 'Panditji had said that the likes of Bokaro Steel Plant and Bhakra Nangal Dam were the new temples of India. I think adopting villages and floating schemes to help the empowerment of poor women should be the prayers in today's India. Some funds can always be spared from building multi-million rupees worth residences and buying fleet of jets and cars.'

Saga of Unconditional Care

While caring, educating and empowering poor children and widows are worthy causes to pursue them knowing that it brings no material returns needs determination, devotion and sacrifice. Success and affluence create hunger for more and the successful have no time or thought for the less fortunate. We see this everywhere. It is usually a personal loss or tragedy that becomes a lesson that one never forgets even when one is flourishing. These sagas indeed inspire.

It was such a personal loss and his mother's struggle to bring up her children single-handedly that were the raison d'etre for Raj Loomba to conceive of the Shrimati Pushpa Wati Loomba Memorial Trust. Set up to educate children of poor widows, the Loomba Trust, as it is popularly known, is established in his mother's memory. Raj Loomba's mother was only 37 when she was widowed. Loomba, who was just eleven at the time, says he could sense the strain his traumatized mother was going through in bringing up her seven children all alone. Luckily, his father had left enough money that helped educate the siblings. However, after the marriages of his two sisters there was nothing left.

Loomba was sent by his mother to the US for his studies. He came to Britain, after completing it, to join his elder brother there. There was nothing left at home to come back to. In England, he cleaned floors, drove ice-cream van. A few years later with some money he had saved, he set up his business from a market stall in the north of England. Since then Loomba never looked back.

With success and business growing, he sat back and introspected, what if his father had not left enough funds for his mother to be able to provide education to him and his siblings. 'Possibly I would have been plying rickshaw in a Punjab city.' He had seen poor widows struggling to survive and bring up their children. Most often such children had no future. That is when Loomba thought of doing something for poor widows back home. He set up the Trust in the name of his mother in 1996. 'She was my inspiration'.

I am sure when he set up the Trust, Loomba could not have envisaged that within a few years its humanitarian causes and its success would stir up the eminent and powerful to encourage and support him. Their cooperation and partnerships helped the Trust achieve, in less than a decade, its target of educating 100 plus children of poor widows in each of the 29 states in India.

Fortuitously, the encouragement Loomba needed when he registered the Trust in 1997 came from Cherie Blair, wife of British Prime Minister Tony Blair. Once when I had gone to meet him for some comments on an Asian issue he told me that he had written to Cherie Blair about the Trust's mission. Later when he met her, he told me she showed great interest in his objectives. He said she was so motivated by the aim to educate children of poor widows in every state of India that she agreed to become its first patron. A few years later she became the president of the Trust.

Within a year the Charity was established in the UK, and the official launch was attended by many prominent politicians and corporate heads and Prime Minister Tony Blair. The Trust was inaugurated in India in

With success and business growing, he (Loomba) sat back and introspected, what if his father had not left enough funds for his mother to be able to provide education to him and his siblings. 'Possibly I would have been plying rickshaw in a Punjab city.'

1999, its country in focus then, by Prime Minister Atal Behari Vajpayee. The association of Cherie Blair and many others like Lord Navnit Dholakia, Sir Richard Branson, Mayor Ken Livingston, Countess Mountbatten of Burma and Sir Sigmund Sternberg, and, of course, the unstinting support of Raj Loomba's wife Veena has helped him take the Trust quickly towards its avowed objectives. Cherie Blair's devotion to the Trust has been remarkable. In course of time she has become its international face. However much she might be busy, I do not think she has missed any event, be it in India, Africa, the US or Britain.

It was no surprise that such a humanitarian objective not only attracted philanthropists who donated towards educating children selected by the Trust but also galvanized organizations such as Virgin Atlantic, Oxfam and the Prince of Wales' International Charity to become partners. In India, the Trust was helped by most state governments for the cause was such, according to Lord Karan Bilimoria.

The Trust's fund-raising events especially its annual Diwali Charity dinners became one of the most important dates in London's social calendar and attracted the royalty, ministers, diplomats, bankers and Asian entrepreneurs. They have been held at historic venues like the Mansion House, the Whitehall Banqueting Hall and even the 800-year-old Guildhall, where before the Trust's charity dinner, no Indian function was ever held in its history. At these dinners attended by Princess Royal, Foreign Secretary David Miliband and Mayor of Greater London Boris Johnson, funds have been raised for educating children of poor widows in India. At Guildhall, I learnt that rupees three crore was raised. That's hope for a lot more children in India.

I attended several of these charity meets and noticed that the undercurrent of bonhomie and informality at these otherwise formal events put every guest at ease and inspired them to join the Trust's charity missions. They also helped the English and other foreign guests to understand and appreciate Indian culture for invariably the dinner would be followed by Indian music and dances. And for Indians like us unknown aspects of English history would be unveiled. During the dinner meet at the Whitehall Banqueting Hall, while Mayor Boris Johnson revealed that his two young children not only knew all about the significance of Diwali and its rituals but also lit diyas and enjoyed the festivities, Cherie Blair told us the history of the Hall itself.

There was much flutter among the Indian invitees when Kajol, the famous Indian actress, was escorted to the podium to accept a memento from Blair who declared her the Trust's Ambassador for the Empowerment of Women. It was announced that 150,000 pounds were raised that evening.

With the mission for education of these children successful, Loomba did not sit back but turned his focus on the plight of widows who were poor, neglected and oppressed across the globe. This was a more complex and major undertaking, for it meant reaching out to countries like Rwanda, Kenya and South Asia, and, of course, India, all of which have different customs and laws. It is indeed not an easy task with over 245 million of them, mostly suffering unimaginable torture, oppression, indignity and poverty. And above all stigma!

Loomba said he was passionate about the issue. He reiterated that his mother was luckily left with money by his father, but he had seen the inhuman treatment of poor widows. He was determined to put in time, effort and money. He planned for the Trust to expand into far-flung countries, attract the attention of the governments of various countries, the United Nations and of the central and state governments in his home country.

Loomba, along with a few other members of the Trust, started devoting a lot of time and making concerted efforts to reach help to widows, especially in countries like South Africa, Uganda, Rwanda and Kenya apart from India. The Trust also launched campaigns to raise awareness about the widows' despicable state and the social and economic travails they have been enduring. 'Their plight is compounded by the fact that the society and the governments have ignored them so far. In most developing countries they are seemingly ignored, as if they do not exist—the living dead.' The solution, Loomba said, lay in empowering women. This is why Blair in particular has been travelling to different countries along with Loomba to garner support from women organizations and authorities to devise measures for the empowerment of deprived women.

The Trust decided to make June 23 the centre of its awareness campaign and designate it as International Widows Day. Now an established annual event it has helped highlight the issue, bring together countries, companies and individuals in a coordinated public demand for action and change. 'More importantly, the day gives widows' groups the opportunity to share their experiences with an international and influential audience, as well as engage political leaders in discussion about ways in which effective action can be taken.'

I attended the major Loomba Trust's International Widows Day Conference in the Locarno Suite at the Foreign and Commonwealth Office in 2006. The participants included well-known personalities like Yoko Ono, and a number of NGOs from different countries. I realized then how serious was the problem of widows worldwide and why the Trust's mission was given so much importance. Yoko Ono, who flew from New York to attend the one-day conference, commended the Trust for providing a platform for individuals, corporations, governments and NGOs to raise international awareness of issues affecting widowhood. I heard frightening stories about the sufferings and often torture of widows from speakers from organizations dedicated to alleviate the suffering of widows and orphans in the developing world.

Cherie Blair and Yoko Ono made impassioned appeals for help and a united effort to make a success their campaign to tackle poverty and deprivation, social stigma, legal discrimination of widows and the impact of HIV / AIDS on them. Hillary Clinton also addressed the conference via a video link. The appeal for helping widows reached across the globe.

The most promising sign for its success was the enthusiasm with which women joined up to take the campaign forward. It also amazed me how quickly 'June 23' and the campaign picked up since its launch in 2005. In 2008, 'June 23' was observed in seven countries across four continents. A Trust member said, 'Every year these events highlight the plight of widows and the need for immediate measures to help them. All over the world the awareness is growing.'

The Trust has expanded into far-flung countries, attracted the attention of the British Establishment, the United Nations and White House, governments in African countries where due to genocide and strife the number of widows is huge and their condition deplorable. In India, the central and state governments and private organizations have joined the Trust's campaign.

Loomba cautions that although the campaign is gathering momentum there is still more to be achieved. 'It is an unfortunate reality that the plight of widows and their dependants is hugely under-represented on the international stage. Widowhood is a global issue. A social stigma continues to surround women who have lost their husbands.'

> The Trust decided to make June 23 the centre of its awareness campaign and designate it as International Widows Day. Now an established annual event it has helped highlight the issue, bring together countries, companies and individuals in a coordinated public demand for action and change.

The Trust is campaigning for official recognition by the United Nations for International Widows Day. 'With this endorsement, the plight of widows would be thrust permanently into the global consciousness, helping to focus attention on the issue and acting as a catalyst for change. It is a global issue.'

Hopes have been raised since the United Nations designated the Trust itself as an official Associated Non-Governmental Organization (NGO), while a growing number of countries from Nigeria to Nepal and, in particular, Ghana, is championing the Trust's initiative.

The Trust has made inroads into Rwanda, Kenya among other countries in Africa, and India and Nepal in South Asia. It is also exploring many other countries. Loomba and partners have criss-crossed several time zones to hold seminars and mobilize local volunteers to educate widows, help children, many of whom suffer from HIV/AIDS. Blair once said with understandable pride that in conjunction with Oxfam and the Mayor of Kigali, the Trust initiated a project to help widows in Rwanda—a country ravaged by war and genocide. Almost in quick time, 10 widows in India too were trained in Beauty and Hair Care — free of charge— with the aim of providing the impetus and skills for them to start their own business.

The Trust has presently sister charities in India and the US, and supports poor widows and their children in Uganda, Sri Lanka, Bangladesh, Kenya, Rwanda, South Africa, Syria, Nepal, Malawi and in India. Loomba was joined by Blair in the appeal to societies and the privileged to take care of the poor widows, educate their children and generally help women demand and achieve equal status in society. 'With the assistance of international community real change can be effected and the lives of thousands, if not millions, of widows will be transformed,' said Loomba.

He told me that the Trust was trying to establish a dialogue with businesses in India as well. 'Their resources could be the key to many future projects.' I was quite surprised that seminars and other meets, which were helped by Sir Richard Stagg, the British High Commissioner in India and his wife, Lady Stagg, stirred many people. This was a good omen. Aruna Oswal and the former governor of Sikkim and Uttrakhand, Sudarshan Aggarwal, at a seminar in New Delhi were so moved that they donated Rs 500,000 and Rs 200,000 respectively.

The UN gives humanitarian aids in millions of dollars but most of the 245 million widows have been passed by as if they do not exist and do not need to be treated as human beings. With their children, who too are reduced to begging and subjected to exploitation this number of the forgotten touches nearly a billion A comprehensive report prepared by the World Opinion Organization in conjunction with Chatham House and the well-researched study by Risto Harma, gives information about the condition of widows in all countries. It was sponsored by the Trust and cost thousands of pounds. It brings to fore the miserable existence of widows in many societies, and their brutal treatment.

The Trust has been able to achieve its objectives and get an international platform due to the efforts of Raj and Veena Loomba and the support of Cherie Blair and many governments that were enthused by the Trust's objectives and its efforts. A major accomplishment, indeed, for one who started off with odd jobs but is now pioneering a new dawn for poor widows and their children. Raj Loomba never forgot the hard lessons he learnt at the age of eleven. It has possibly earned him the unspoken thanks and gratitude from thousands of poor widows and children.

Wells for India

I had heard from Lord Bhiku Parekh about Dr Nicholas and his wife Dr Mary Grey. He told me that the Greys, who lived near Winchester, had set up a Trust registered in the UK as Development Organization. Through this Trust they were working with the poorest communities in Rajasthan since 1987. Lord Meghnad Desai also mentioned once that some Englishmen have been doing charity work in the country for quite a number of years.

I found out about the work that they did and their efforts to help poor villagers in various districts of Rajasthan. The couple merits a special mention and thanks from all Indians because they are not the usual rolling in millions philanthropists but academicians. Both professors and alumni of Oxford University could not normally 'dare' to start a project like 'Wells for India'. Apart from them the Trust includes three or four more Oxford University alumni. So we can say justifiably that it is an 'academic' enterprise, which succeeded remarkably well.

In 2007, on the 20th anniversary of the Trust, it was revealed that a million people in 700 villages spread over 21 districts had benefited during the two decades. The Trust also became part of a European Commission Humanitarian Aid Office (ECHO) Euro 3.0 million programme. This has been providing desperately needed support to four districts of western Rajasthan—Jodhpur, Barmer, Jaisalmer and Bikaner—along with other

Programme partners Oxfam, Save the Children Fund, and Church Auxiliary for Social Action (CASA), Dan Church Aid (DCA), CARE and Action Aid. The total Wells for India supporters' and ECHO contribution is £180,000.

When I talked with Dr Nicholas Grey I could sense his passion for helping villagers, especially, in the desert areas of Rajasthan, although they are far away from them. The Greys live in the picturesque Test Valley in Hampshire. It is so quaintly charming that I would recommend anyone visiting Stonehenge to visit the place.

Dr Nicholas Grey told me that he went to Rajasthan in 1987 to visit Dr Ramsahai Purohit, a follower of Vinoba Bhave, whom he had met earlier. There was severe drought then and Dr Grey said he was 'disturbed by the situation' in villages near Jaipur, which he visited with Dr Purohit. After they returned to England, the Greys decided to set up a charity 'Wells for India'. In 1988 the Foundation started its operation in Dudu block in Jaipur district with a Gandhian organization – Gram Seva Mandal Idan Ka Bas (GSMI). Fourteen irrigation wells were deepened.

The couple visited India frequently initially and despite getting on in years they now come annually to visit more villages and the desert. Once the deepening of wells and digging of new ones for potable water in a few villages in Dudu block was over, they expanded their operations over the years to 220 villages of Dudu block. The range of activities also diversified to include augmentation of water resources and access to safe potable water to the area during 1988 to 2001.

Dr Mary Grey wrote about their efforts in her book *Gender, Justice and Poverty in Rural Rajasthan – Moving beyond the Silence*.

> *The founding of the Wells for India was in response to the drought of 1987 when 60 million animals died, wells dried up and women were forced to walk still further into the desert in search of water.*
>
> *Since then we have expanded into three regions of Rajasthan loosely grouped near Jaipur, Jodhpur and Udaipur, and in each case working in partnership with Gandhian NGOs. The target has always been the poorest and most marginalized people, and the method has been that of empowerment...the focus has moved to health, education and gender issues.*

The real relief was provided when the Trust expanded its operations in the Thar Desert with another Gandhian organization – Gramin Vikas Vigyan Samiti (GRAVIS) and in south Rajasthan Aravali hills region with 11 NGOs. Most important was the building of 12 water storage tanks in the Thar Desert.

I was told that the Wells for India was providing support since October 2002 on a regular basis to over 10,235 most needy households, 57,700 people and 64,000 small animals (sheep and goats) located in 315 settlements in 105 scattered villages in five districts of Rajasthan. All villages were receiving drinking water supplies, while 36 villages food grain, 78 animal feed and fodder, and 36 were involved in cash and food for work programmes. "Programme is implemented in close collaboration with Rajasthan state government departments and managed by 11 project implementation partners in the state," said Wells for India's programme manager, Om Prakash Sharma. He added that the Trust was also focusing on rainwater harvesting bringing wide social and economic benefits to poor communities. Water is essential for all other forms of development. 'Our works in Rajasthan for last 21 years illustrated how safe potable water availability not only improves health and releases time and energy of women, but also improves poor people's income, education, as well as social and cultural well-being. Increased water availability through small-scale water harvesting structures has increased the productivity of crops, fodder and milk production.'

According to Jos Garbett, the Operations Manager for the charity at the Bishop on the Bridge in central Winchester, 'when focus moved to holistic development along with long-term water harvesting and livelihood enhancement activities, greater emphasis is also given on developing a long term action research and development component in all of our projects. Aim of this research and development is to bring out the results of our works in the form of scientific data so that achievements and experiences can be transmitted at international gatherings.'

Wells for India was providing support since October 2002 on a regular basis to over 10,235 most needy households, 57,700 people and 64,000 small animals (sheep and goats) located in 315 settlements in 105 scattered villages in five districts of Rajasthan state of India.

Greys are now old but Jos said they not only 'continue to work daily to sustain the programmes that were initiated in the past but are always thinking of new schemes to further help raise the survival level through health, education and living facilities'.

PAREKHS' NIRMAN FOUNDATION

I had been in contact with Lord Bhiku Parekh for over a decade while posted in London. We often talked about the diaspora and family-related issues. I would invariably telephone him for comments on happenings, seek advice and often request him to explain things of which I did not have much knowledge. He never disappointed me, in fact helped me send informative dispatches. Yet, he never mentioned anything about his own family Trust which I discovered was helping people in many ways.

It was while I began writing this book that he casually mentioned about it, when I asked him about Indians or Englishmen doing charity work in India. 'My family Foundation is called Nirman Foundation based in the United States. It was set up by my father, brother who lives in the United States, and myself. It does a number of activities relating to India and Indians.'

I asked him what motivated him to join the Foundation. 'I decided to give 20 per cent of whatever I earned for charity or constructive work in India.' He was quite modest, 'I earned much less than my brother in the US but all the funding for the various activities has been through our earnings.'

The list is impressive. It funds two D.Phil. students at Oxford, a three-month-long post-doctoral fellowship at the London School of Economics, and an annual lecture at the University of Westminster. In India it has donated a mobile hospital costing nearly Rs.30 lakh to a medical university in Vadodara, Gujarat. It also gives ten scholarships to post graduate students at Jawaharlal Nehru University. It has also instituted an annual lecture at the Jawaharlal Nehru University and a prize for the best Ph.D. thesis. It funds Wells for India as well. It also supports cancer camps in Vadodara and a camp for the disabled in South Gujarat.

I talked with Dr Jayshree Mehta, a Trustee of the Foundation in Vadodara where Nirman Foundation funds the study of prevalence of cancer in women in a rural district of Vadodara. A large team of health workers was trained for this research. I found that it has helped create cancer awareness amongst rural women. By assessing the prevalence of breast, cervix and oral cancers in women it must have saved a number of lives from suffering. All the patients with abnormal findings were sent to the nodal hospital for further investigations and treatment. Moreover, all these patients were registered in the hospital on a priority basis for their treatment without any cost. According to the results, the prevalence of breast, cervical and oral cancers in the rural district of Vadodara appeared to be about 88, 39 and 97 per 100,000 women respectively.

Dr Mehta said there was a definite cause for worry as the results showed that despite a significant number of participants having abnormal breast, cervical and oral symptoms they had never felt the need to get themselves examined, as they were totally ignorant as to how grievous their problem could be. 'Not only illiteracy and ignorance, but also fear of the cost of the medical consultation prevented them from getting examined.' She added that 'an important objective is to stress on the role of social, cultural, behavioural and psychological factors such as occupation, lifestyle, ethnicity, custom and habits. Social support systems, beliefs and attitudes, in the onset and precipitation of cancer, in coping with the illness, and in recovery and post-treatment readjustment were also studied.' I was amazed at the good work that was being done by the family Foundation of Lord Parekh. Yet he seemed reluctant to talk about it!

From London to Jaisalmer with Love

I had been to Jaisalmer—also called as the Golden City of India because the yellow sand gives a yellowish-golden hue to the city and its surrounding area—in the heart of the Thar desert a few times but never heard of the Jaislamer In Jeopardy (JiJ). I think it was in 1998, when I got an invite from JiJ to attend a fund-raising event at Cinnamon Club, near Parliament. I wondered what could JiJ mean. When I went to the historic city over 10 years ago I could not see anything alarming. But then I was just a tourist more intent on driving some miles away to see the sand dunes.

> It (Nirman Foundation) funds two D.Phil. students at Oxford, a three month long post-doctoral fellowship at the London School of Economics, and an annual lecture at the University of Westminster. In India it has donated a mobile hospital costing nearly Rs.30 lakh to a medical university in Vadodara, Gujarat.

A surprise awaited me when I reached the Club. There were over 50 guests, all of whom seemed to know each other, but there were hardly any Indians among them. I felt a bit lost until I met two media colleagues, Nabanita Sircar and Amit Roy. All the guests were mostly English except two or three Indian couples. I realized too they all were from the upper crust.

I was grateful to Veronica Hall, a Trustee of the JIJ, who took time off from looking after the invitees to brief me about the Foundation. She told me that it was a British-registered charity established in 1996 by writer Sue Carpenter, to raise international awareness and funds to protect and preserve the city's heritage. It was quite a revelation how an English person, just a visitor to Jaisalmer, resolved to save the heritage of the city she did not have any links with. Yet she overcame odds to convince strangers to join her in her mission.

Carpenter on a visit to India in 1994 went to Jaisalmer and the 'magic of the place took hold of her'. But being a writer she realized how the city's economy centered on tourism was taking its toll. It threatened Jaisalmer's post-mercantile relevance. She introspected, 'should expedient concrete constructions — bare-box tourist utilities— be allowed to elbow out hand-crafted pieces of old architecture. There was no doubt that Jaisalmer's tradition of water carriers from the nearby ponds in the desert needed to be upgraded; but should the planners and administrators not have taken lessons from other heritage towns around the world? Instead, their solution was a network of water pipes mismatched with the drainages. As a result excess water used was "literally drowning this gem of a town'.

Carpenter decided she would fight to save the town's heritage. The fact that she was readily published by *The Times*, London, the *New Scientist* and *Harpers & Queen*, helped. She began by writing about Jaisalmer's predicament. An early attempt to form activist groups in India had come to naught. I was embarrassed to hear that there was much bemused commiseration at her attempts at 'getting anything done at all in India'.

She was, however, determined to promote Jaisalmer as a heritage site and highlight the perils that faced it, along the lines of the campaign to save Venice, a city 'with which Jaisalmer's past and present have much in common.'

She said that a lecture at Nehru Centre drew two companions who stayed with her to fight and the campaign rolled on. As often happens with such committed endeavours, a chance connection opened the right doors: an aide of the Prince of Wales helped her establish contact with the World Monuments Fund [WMF] of the USA and then things moved fast. Jaisalmer

Fort was placed on the Fund's 'Watch List of 100 Most Endangered Sites in the World' and prompted WMF to channel $100,000 to Jaisalmer, the largest single grant that the fund gives to a single subject. Local support came from India's INTACH.

JiJ soon started to focus on bite-sized projects. Its 'Streetscape Revitalization' programme took two streets to restore them to their old world lineage. Sewerages were to be repaired, houses stabilized and lavatories constructed.

The idea was to establish Jaisalmer as a continuing, sustainable, living city and not just a collection of empty restored monuments. With this objective, Carpenter carried on her campaign to spread awareness and raise funds. In October 2000 and January 2001, she personally played guide to groups of concerned Indophiles, brought to Jaisalmer and Rajasthan, to see for themselves what needed to be done.

The colourful Rajasthan Tented Mela was organized in London to raise funds. Held at the Royal Geographical Society it not only helped raise funds but also JiJ's profile. More than 600 guests, dressed in glittering Rajasthani attire, flocked to the gardens of the RGS in Kensington, London, to experience Rajasthani folk music and dance performed by the gipsy troupe Musafir, while traditional Raj Tent Club canvas tents fluttered in the breeze. The Rajmata of Jaipur was the biggest attraction. The event was followed by a lecture on Rajasthani Style by Clarissa Mitchell, founder of the Raj Tent Club. Men donned vibrant rainbow turbans while women had their hands and arms painted with henna. Stalls in the bazaar sold Indian clothes, jewellery, antique prints, and pashminas. General Billy's wine and Cobra beer helped in 'intoxicating' the atmosphere.

The £30,000 raised by the Rajasthani Tented Mela was used to repair one wall of the Maharaja's Palace in the Fort that was in imminent danger of collapse. The JiJ also raised resources from grants, events, sponsorships, Friends of Jaisalmer, donations and JiJ merchandise to fund its projects. When I attended another event a few years ago, I could sense in Carpenter, Hall and other activists a satisfaction that the struggle was over and JiJ was

> She was however determined to promote Jaisalmer as a heritage site and highlight the perils that faced it, along the lines of the campaign to save Venice, a city 'with which Jaisalmer's past and present have much in common.'

one of the UK-based charities doing wonderful work for the people in the Golden City.

The nearly complete 'Streetscape Revitalisation' programme helped in fitting new toilets into 54 houses, and upgrading the sewerage and drainage systems and restoring it to its original plan. JiJ got a further grant of approximately £20,000 by the Staples Trust to continue the project in two more streets in the Fort.

Since the time the Streetscape Project was completed tourism and businesses have expanded within the fort. This has once again put the existing system under a great deal of strain. So Carpenter and other trustees felt that a complete overhaul was necessary once again. But it was universally acknowledged that the situation would have been dire if the Streetscape project had not been completed.

No wonder, JiJ received two major international heritage conservation awards for the Streetscape Project— An Honourable Mention in the UNESCO South-East Asian Cultural Heritage Awards and in association with Greaves Travel, outright winner of the Built Environment Section of the British Airways Tourism.

I know that some beautiful carved doors and such items were bought by antique dealers and sold abroad. I was happy to know that an entirely British foundation was saving or restoring the historic city's rich heritage.

Carpenter said way back in 2000, "We are not fighting an endless war, but a contained battle, and the finances — millions rather than tens of hundreds of millions— are attainable. Perhaps one individual can make a difference." She would not agree, but the individual turned out to be Sue Carpenter.

Taking Children off Streets

She has become a legendary fund-raiser for street children. Indefatigable and determined she crisscrosses across the globe to organize events to highlight the plight of such children and convince donors to be liberal in helping organizations that have been helping street children, estimated to be 100 million world over. Surina Narula has helped raise over 1.5 million pounds in a decade in the UK which has been channelled for the well-being of street children. She is involved with almost every leading organization in the world—and heads quite a few of them now--that help street children. Her dedication to help them is particularly commendable. A wealthy, elite member of the upper echelons of society, she could have lived in her luxurious Hertfordshire home with sprawling lawns and swimming pool and busied herself attending the upper crust parties London is famed for. A number of times I spotted the Mittals, Sethias, Sangers and the Hindujas at functions at her sprawling house.

But she put her 'comfortable living' and extensive network to use to build resources for numerous organizations devoted to salvaging street children, 'many suffering from HIV/AIDS, and exploited, abused and left to the vagaries of nature'.

There are no thanks for helping 'abandoned' children for a better living. It is indeed non-glamorous for it does not relate to the middle, or the upper classes. But when one asks Narula about her work, one can see how happy she is 'working' for these children. Her involvement is amazing. She spent a number of weeks amongst the street children near New Delhi station to understand their day-to-day problems and crises they faced. She used the experience for her dissertation and then her Masters in Social Anthropology. I reiterate all this is so non-glamorous that newspapers, at least in India, hardly consider it newsworthy.

Her dedication is still more remarkable for she knows that her objective would never be fully achieved. 'We will never be able to get rid of street children. What we have to do is to treat them on the streets and help them by finding shelters and facilitating medical help and proper meals and clothing for them.' She enumerates the reason, 'the phenomenon of migration, especially in India, will continue. Many of the children are of migratory workers. The number is too high.' Not surprisingly, India has the largest number of street children.

According to the United Nations Human Rights Commission, 18 million children live on streets in India of which 100,000 to 500,000 are in Delhi alone. This is why Narula focused on India and spends a lot of time here. But simultaneously she has been flying all over the world holding mega events for raising resources to help these children. It needs phenomenal energy and commitment to sustain and continue any work on this scale.

She could not have thought of such a role for herself when she went to Libya after her marriage with H.S. Narula, head of a construction company,

> She (Narula) has become a legendary fund-raiser for street children. Indefatigable and determined she crisscrosses across the globe to organize events to highlight the plight of such children

Surina Narula legendary fund-raiser for street children

Mobile fully equipped hospital for free treatment of villagers;
donated by Nirman Foundation

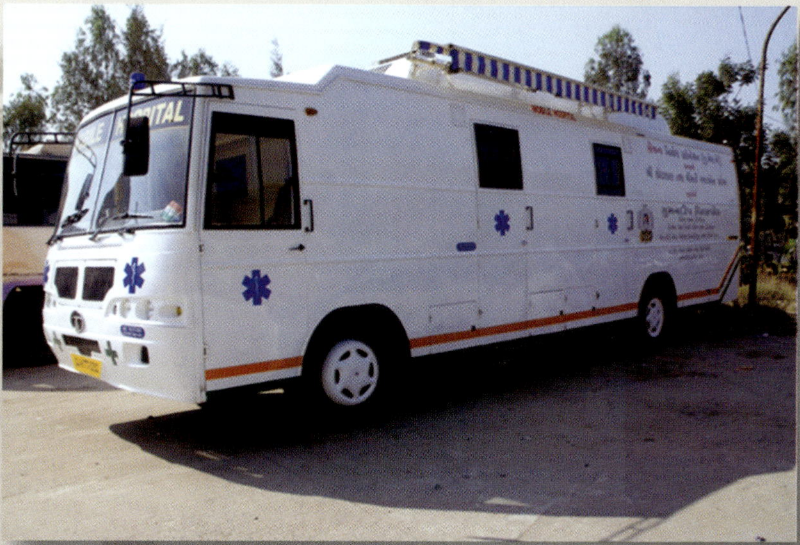

Surina Narula with "rescued" street children

The late Rajmata Gayatri Devi:
enthusiastic supporter of
Jaislamer in Jeopardy

Sue's mission for
better living conditions
in Jaisalmer is succeeding

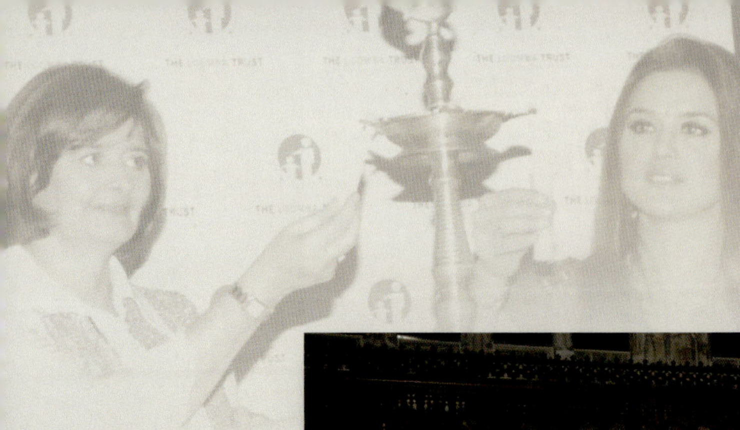

Charity dinners by Loomba Trust generate large funds for educating Indian widows' children—Nalin Surie, David Miliband, Cherie Blair, Preity Zinta and Loomba

Poor widows children in class room-- education thanks to Loomba Trust

Important Personalities flew in for Loomba Trust's first International Widows Day in Lucarno Suite in Foreign Office, London: Start of a global Campaign

Yoko Ono with Raj Loomba and UK ministers: joined for widow empowerment

Dr Nicholas and Mary Wells
— devoted life and money for reaching water to villages near Thar desert

which had then projects in that country. She was in fact caught up in the social swirl immediately. The wife of the Indian Ambassador in Libya had formed a group of Indian women and invited Surina Narula to join them. Young, but bold, after a few meetings which 'were more like a social get-togethers' she felt that their time and resources could be better used for some worthwhile causes. Her suggestion for fund-raising events was welcomed and she managed to collect 20,000 pounds in one year.

She decided to donate it for some worthy causes in India. But then she was told that according to rules, she could give money to only those organizations which had a foreign fund number. When she flew to Delhi with the money she did not know any charity organization to which she could donate the money. She scouted around and went to offices of some organizations. She recalls with a wry smile that she would wait and wait in the offices and would not be called to meet the organizers. They met her only after she conveyed that she had come to donate some money. Then she heard from a friend of Urvashi Butalia and Chander Chopra who were 'deeply involved in helping tortured and harassed women'. She realized how much good work they were doing for women in trouble.

Narula learnt from them 'how much there was to do in India' and decided to 'get personally more involved'. She joined the Board of Society of Friends of Lotus Children for street children in Bangalore and helped them for a year. That was her first step. She climbed fast, devoting more and more time and resources in helping these hapless children. She opened a small office in her residence at Hyver Hall. But there was a problem as there was no information, statistics or educational tools readily available in those days for these children.

It was Elizabeth Nunn— later honoured with MBE for her services to street children in India—who explained to Narula the problems of street children. She started to devote more time to the cause of street children and her efforts were soon recognized. When the Consortium for Street Children was launched in 1992 at Downing Street by John Major, then Prime Minister, she was made a member of its Board. 'It felt strange. I was the junior-most and would sit with Baroness Shreela Flather, chairman, and likes of her. It was intimidating'.

The UNICEF gave an office to the Consortium. Narula recounted representing it at various international forums and of starting to put up fund-raising events. I attended one of these, a Graffiti Ball at the Sofitel Hotel near Heathrow's Terminal 5. The huge hall was full. Her wealthy friends including the Hindujas were there and paid huge prices for items auctioned during the evening. She met the over 500 invitees, and must have lost her voice by the time it ended, having spent hours in narrating the miserable life of street children and the need to help them. It is no surprise that she helped raise millions of pounds for this cause.

She, indeed, grew with the Consortium. Narula became president in 2008 by which time the Consortium had grown into the biggest umbrella organization for children's charities— 60 NGOs, 40 UK-based development agencies and voluntary organizations spread over in 60 countries. 'One chooses three or four organizations that work for such children to concentrate and help them.' Narula chose four of them in India and her efforts brought immediate success.

She initiated a series of events, like DSC Soccer Balaak ki Khoj, around New Delhi to raise awareness for street children's rights and develop capabilities for realizing their potential. It involved underprivileged children to showcase their sporting talent. Former French football star and Ambassador for the Consortium, Vikash Dhorasoo, was present to spot talent among the street children. She also organized fund-raising premieres of *Bawander*, *Train to Pakistan* and *Asoka* for street children. .

It is difficult to keep track of the organizations she is associated with and helps in fund raising. She is Director on Board of Plan International UK, Patron of Plan India and Honorary Patron of Plan USA, also a Patron of Hope of Children –the first Indian, Patron of Motiroti and past trustee of Pratham UK. She is also working with Amol Kanth for street children in Guatemala, Brazil. She also helped with the Police Manual on how to treat and deal with street children in the UK. She told me that Bollywood could help a lot, because it has tremendous 'social impact, for instance *Slumdog Millionaire* created a great awareness about slum children'. She is now working full time for street children.

Pratham in London

The launch of Pratham UK in 2003-04 was a major event which attracted not only the NRIs, many of whom knew of Pratham India and were associated with it, but also young Indian executives and bankers. The objective of raising awareness and funds for Pratham India's programmes including the primary objective of educating every child in the country inspired Indians in the UK. A series of seminars, charity balls, sporting events and other programmes that attracted students helped raise considerable amounts in a rather short period of time. Its success in the UK was assured.

The annual charity balls in London, in fact, became a major event in the calendar of every Indian and helped not only collect huge funds but also were stimuli for Pratham UK's steady growth and consolidation in quick time. Young Indian bankers and those in financial sectors were so enthused that they organized events in other cities like Leicester and Manchester. Considerable funds were raised at such charity functions.

I attended a couple of the charity dinners in London. They were spectacular and invariably attended by the likes of the Hinduja Brothers and L.N. Mittal, who helped swell the kitty. The extravaganza, the cultural shows, a mix of the western and Indian and above all the bonhomie created remarkable ambience. It was no wonder that huge amounts could be raised which meant more children in India receiving education.

I particularly recall the 2005 Ball, a glittering event, held at the Grosvenor House. It was attended by 750 guests —a record number —from across the UK and Europe. Almost £400,000 was raised resulting in net proceeds of over £265,000. It led to the opening of various UK chapters. There was much buzz with Aamir Khan adding to the glitz. Everyone was anxious to see Mallika Sherawat perform.

Waheeda Rehman, as the Goodwill Ambassador for Pratham India, also worked hard to reach Pratham UK to every part of the country. She participated in a series of events including a dinner dance in Essex with over 300 people; a get-together in Leeds with 150 and in Harrow with 75; and an 'Introduction to Pratham' at the Nehru Centre with over 150 supporters from London. I attended one of the functions. It was a delight to hear the impassioned plea by Waheeda Rehman to contribute and help educate children in India. Her dignity and poise won many donors.

I believe that the success of PrathamUK is due to the initial spadework done by various prominent Indians in the UK and the attractive programmes and events which were organized. Some of them attracted the young. For instance, a group of students hiked and scaled 24 peaks in the Lake District in the Hike and Run for Pratham. It raised £3000. Over 50 volunteers ran to support Pratham in the London raising a total of £25,000.

Merrill Lynch chipped in, in a big way. PrathamUK was selected as the 'Charity of the Year' by Merrill Lynch's Global Markets and Investment Banking EMEA group. For a one-year period, it organized a set of fund-raising events. 'Pratham Club' students at London Business School organized live cricket broadcasts of India-Pakistan matches in the school including a special Valentine's Day event of Bollywood music.

I tried to inquire about some activities in India that ran with the help of funds collected in the UK. An important one was ASER (Annual Status of Education Report) 2005. Led by Pratham, it tested a representative sample of children in over 1,88,000 households in 485 districts in India. Competencies in language and mathematics were tested for all children in the 6-14 year- age group; schools were checked for pupil-teacher ratios and infrastructure. The results showed that enrolment levels were high in almost all states, however, the foundation of basic reading and arithmetic needed to be urgently strengthened. The survey indicated that 11 million children were not in school. Of the children surveyed in classes six to eight in government-run schools, 22 per cent could not read simple passages, while 40 per cent could not do simple division.

One of PrathamUK's newest initiatives is the Pratham Young Professionals Network, a platform that encouraged philanthropic endeavours amongst third and fourth generations in the UK.

I found that the funds raised by Pratham UK have been used almost all over India not only for educating children in schools but also through various other activities. For instance according to Pratham spokesperson, almost 270,000 pounds were allotted for Read India summer campaign in 20 districts of Uttar Pradesh, aimed at helping improve the learning levels of the children during their summer vacations. Pratham also partnered with the Sarva Siksha Abhiyan (SSA) in UP for a remedial learning programme which was targeted at children in class 2 and 3.

In winter, too, camps were organized during which the focus was on children from government primary schools studying in classes 3, 4 and 5 who could only recognize numbers in mathematics and in language could read only word.

The funds—56,409 pounds— received from PrathamUK were also used to support the direct programme activities conducted in approximately 307 villages in Tamil Nadu. It helped to provide pre-school education to approximately 4,500 children between the ages of three and five in Balwadi. In six month's time, according to the Pratham spokesperson, most of the Balwadi children learnt to count and pick anything up to 10. They could also do simple addition and subtraction within 10. They could identify many letters of Tamil and English languages.

Pratham UK's success within a few years reiterates the concern and passion of the diaspora, young and old alike, to help in whatever way the development of their own. And there is nothing better than enabling children to go to school. According to UNICEF there are 100 million children out of school. According to Wikipedia, the largest number of illiterates in the world is in India. The diaspora in the UK is definitely trying to help all those institutions which are working at removing this stigma.

More Charity Groups from UK

Many charities are being continually set up in the UK for raising funds for various causes in India. One such charity Food for Life Vrindavan UK was formed in 2007. It is the official UK partner to Food for Life Vrindavan Society, a non-governmental organization (NGO), with the Indian Government, having taken on this role from the trustees of Friends of Vrindavan UK Ltd since early 2007. The primary aim of the UK forum is to raise funds for Food for Life Vrindavan Society. It said that 95 per cent of the funds that it raises from donors are donated directly to Food for Life Vrindavan Society. The interesting fact is that Food for Life Vrindavan UK Ltd does not have any paid staff. All directors and trustees meet the majority of the running costs of the charity.

It arranged in 2009 a fundraising event at the time of Diwali where the special guest was Indian film star Vivek Oberoi. He was joined by some of the British-Asian talent like Nitin Ganatra of Eastenders, along with an exclusive gig by Niraj Chag and Navin Kundra. The aim was to raise funds for the building of the third and biggest educational complex in Vrindavan, which would educate 1,440 under-privileged children—project, cost £400,000. The school was scheduled to open in October 2010. The event held in Kadwa Patidar Hall, Kenton, London, raised around £200K including pledges.

There are many such quiet charities and individuals who too are working without expecting any thanks or awards for raising funds for numerous causes— primarily education and empowerment of women in India. India need not thank them, for they are, as Lord Bhiku Parekh once said to me, Indians abroad. However, the likes of Loombas, the Parekhs, the Narulas and many others who quietly go about doing their bit for a country they left behind years ago deserve recognition.

12

Friends of India: Lost and Gained

> *There is this immense nation, set in the midst of Asia, an Asia which has been ravaged by war. Here we have the one great country that has been seeking to apply the principles of democracy. I have always hoped myself that politically India might be the light of Asia.*
>
> —*Clement Attlee 15 March 1946*

Where did friends of India, like Clement Attlee and his colleagues, disappear? In the early nineties I was shocked to find a strong and hyperactive anti-India lobby in the Labour Party and also a couple of Conservative MPs decrying India for 'appalling suppression of Muslims in Kashmir valley'. In fact I felt more concerned when many English people in their conversations at social dos asked about 'killings and rapes' in the valley. Most appeared to believe that India was in forceful occupation of Kashmir and its predominantly Muslim population in the Valley was subjected to uncalled for violence. This kind of image weaved by a few prominent leaders and MPs, most in Labour, was intriguing. I was under the impression that Labour leaders were friends of India. But it seemed to me that India hardly had any friend left in the Labour Party.

Dinesh Singh, a veteran Congress leader and a senior minister, and some others used to tell me that leading Labourites like Herbert Morrison, Aneurin Bevan and then the young Michael Foot, were friends and admirers of prominent Indian politicians like Nehru, Krishna Menon and others from much before India became independent. Foot had remained the staunchest supporter of India. At Oxford Debating Society, Foot had moved a motion – this house prefers the Indian Congress to the American Congress'.

I used to see him on his morning walks in Hampstead Heath with his dog, until ill-health forced him to stop coming there. In conversations with him one could see his admiration for Nehru and feeling for Indira Gandhi. He was one British leader who welcomed Mrs Gandhi when she went to England after the Emergency , while the media assailed her for it. Foot considered Nehru and Krishna Menon to be heroes.

Such friends of India saved the Commonwealth. Dinesh Singh once related to me that India after becoming a Republic was ready to quit Commonwealth as Britain had been supporting the US policy on Kashmir in the Security Council. Nehru was livid. But then Morrison and Bevan were sent along with a few other Labour members to persuade Nehru and his colleagues not to leave the Commonwealth. Bevan was an admirer of Nehru. He once said, 'Nehru without doubt is the last of the great British liberals'. Their friendship of long years helped and Nehru agreed not to get out of Commonwealth. The 53-nation member body would have been nothing without India in it.

I had seen the bonhomie between Hugh Gaitskell, then Labour Party leader with the likes of H.N.Kunzru and a few other MPs—Tarkeshwari Sinha-- at a lunch hosted by my maternal uncle R.P. Sinha, then general secretary of the Congress Rajya Sabha parliamentary party at Delhi Gymkhana Club. I was very young, but I do remember Gaitskell repeatedly averring the closeness between his party and the Indian leaders across party lines. He was in a jovial mood and noticing me asked 'young man, do you have any girl friend'.

He (Bevan) once said 'Nehru without doubt is the last of the great British liberals'. Their friendship of long years helped and Nehru agreed not to get out of Commonwealth.

But the same Labour Party had changed with Robin Cook, then shadow foreign secretary and several senior MPs like Gerald Kaufmann, Claire Short and Max Madden. They openly orchestrated and supported the allegations made by pro-Kashmir lobbies. They said that it was Britain's moral responsibility to resolve the dispute between India and Pakistan, in plain words they wanted third-party mediation. In fact MacShane has kept flaying 'the atrocities being committed by Indian troops in the held Kashmir as well as the militaristic and jingoistic postures of India toward Pakistan', despite his party Government's clear policy that the Kashmir issue be resolved by negotiations between the two countries, India and Pakistan and its earlier messages that cross-border terrorism had to stop before resumption of any bilateral talks.

I was in Brighton in 1995 during the Labour's annual party conference and could sense the anti-India feeling pervading there. Labour councillors of Pak-origin and about six pro-Pak lobby MPs controlled the agenda on Kashmir. A fringe meeting hosted by these Labour councillors was attended by several MPs. Anti-India speeches abounded and the Indian Government vilified for alleged human rights violations in the Valley—50,000 innocents killed, thousands of women raped. Cook was ably supported by his deputy Derek Fatchett in his tirades against the alleged human rights violations in the valley.

The sustained campaign and activities of pro-Pak and pro-plebiscite in Kashmir lobbies led to the adoption of an ambiguous Kashmir policy by Labour's National Executive, which gave further fillip to pro-plebiscite and third-party mediation groups. Their representatives went religiously to the annual meets of the UN Human Rights Commission and tried to blast India. Rumours were that they were encouraged and supported by Pakistan. Once I wrote about this giving some facts and figures. I was threatened with criminal defamation, but possibly better sense prevailed and the detractors later became 'friends'.

But as I left London in 2009, the whole scene had changed. Over 300 MPs and Peers who were members of the Friends of India groups in the three major political parties not only understood the geo-political situation in the region but came to the forefront to put their viewpoints without bias. There was awareness of the facts and ground realities in Kashmir. The pro-plebiscite lobbies became redundant and the regular meetings which MPs used to sponsor for the Prime Minister or any other senior cabinet member from Muzaffarabad at committee rooms of the House of Commons became

Deputy PM John Prescott, Lalit Mansingh and KM Singh: at the launch of LFIN at Bournemouth (pic by Raju Vyas)

Barry Gardiner with Atal Behari Vajpayee: on a goodwill visit with LFIN members to India

Lib Dem Leader Charles Kennedy, Lord Dholakia, High Commssioner Nareshwar Dayal: at launch of Lib Dem Friends of India

Michael Foot with Dr LM Singhvi: Since his young days Foot had been staunchestfriend of India

His (Lalit Mansingh) efforts to bring together MPs and make them take interest in Indian issues succeeded remarkably well. There could be no better contribution to India's cause by an ambassador.

irrelevant. A few MPs like Kaufmann, who still flay India, get the opportunity to do so mostly at Pakistan High Commission or Pak-sponsored meetings. No one now gives any heed to their outbursts.

The Friends of India groups are formidable. Its members have regularly visited India, gone to Kashmir and met academics, people of various parties and taken part in seminars. The understanding of India and perception of important issues related to it amongst the British leaders has never been better. This was made possible due solely to the diplomatic initiative of Lalit Mansingh, when he was High Commissioner in London. He was ably supported by K.M. Singh, then minister coordination in-charge of community relations and visa section. His efforts to bring together MPs and make them take interest in Indian issues succeeded remarkably well. There could be no better contribution to India's cause by an ambassador.

The Diplomatic Coup

K.M. Singh described to me the preparations for the meeting which started almost a year before the Bournemouth dinner meeting in 1999. Soon after taking over as High Commissioner Mansingh expressed surprise that there was no India lobby like the Indian caucus in Washington where he was the deputy chief of mission. Singh was entrusted to get in touch with MPs and moot the idea. The plan was to form a group based on the pattern of the

The Friends of India groups are formidable. Its members have regularly visited India, gone to Kashmir and met academics, people of various parties and taken part in seminars. The understanding of India and perception of important issues related to it amongst the British leaders has never been better.

already existing Labour Friends of Israel, a powerful Jewish lobby in the British Parliament.

While the practice of inviting MPs in small groups regularly for lunch was initiated, K.M. Singh went to various cities meeting Indian-origin councillors. They too were invited for meetings in the High Commission or Mansingh went to places like Birmingham, Nottingham, Leicester and Slough where he met them. They were requested to persuade their constituency MPs to attend the meeting to be hosted by Mansingh in Bournemouth.

The councillors really worked hard, recalled Singh. "They were happy that the High Commission had recognized their value and entrusted them some responsibility." But both Mansingh and K.M. Singh said that their effort would not have succeeded as quickly as it did but for the excellent rapport L.M. Singhvi, Mansingh's predecessor, had established between the High Commission and the Indian community.

These councillors were also invited to the Bournemouth meet and in fact asked to see that their MPs came to the party. The result was that almost 50, including several prominent ministers, came and joined the Labour Friends of India at its launch in a hotel near the venue of the Labour's on-going conference.

I attended that meeting. The huge hall was teeming with Indian-origin Labour councillors. There was no way to know how many MPs busy with the conference would be able to come. But they started coming in trickles and then John Prescott, the Deputy Prime Minister, breezed in. He electrified the atmosphere. Until then 40 MPs had signed their consent to join the Labour Friends of India. It was much more than expected. But then suddenly Prescott said could we make it 41. In fact, it went up to 47. Six ministers including Margaret Beckett, Patricia Hewitt and Prescott himself had to wait for protocol clearance to join.

The bonhomie there was unique. Prescott in jovial mood while laughing at the criticism in the media for going in a Jaguar from his hotel to the conference venue—just a 10-minute walk—'my wife's hairstyle could have been ruined by the strong wind from the sea', remarked that the LFIN would bring new warmth to relations between Britain and India. 'You can feel it in the room.'

Tony McNulty, who asked other MPs who joined LFIN that evening to come on the dais for a group photograph, remarked 'hopefully the dais will not collapse'. The first chair of LFIN, Barry Gardiner called the meet as an occasion to 'celebrate 50 years of divorce'. He also declared that the group was firmly established and then outlined LFIN's objectives, to promote understanding between India and Pakistan (which was sorely missing) while maximizing Indians' support for Labour. He had set his priorities sensibly. Lalit Mansingh too was candid saying that India hoped that LFIN members would 'speak for us' in the Houses of Parliament.

I met Anand Sharma too. He came as a representative of the Congress Party to attend the Conference. It was nearly midnight when the party broke after dinner; I and Raj Loomba went back to London in the car of Keith Vaz, then a minister. On the way we discussed how so many MPs joined and in fact most seemed eager to try to improve relations with India. It was obvious that the Indian High Commission had to take the initiative to make MPs aware of the facts in Kashmir.

It was evident that evening itself that for the first time Indians had evolved a pressure group in the British Parliament. Until then P.S. Khabra, Southall MP, used to raise his lone voice against the pro-Pak pressure groups which had vitiated the political scene for India. In the House of Lords, Lord Navnit Dholakia was the lone 'sentinel' countering the onslaughts and anti-India diatribes of Pak-origin Peers.

End of anti-India Era

The sudden sea-change in the perception of MPs and the Government on the Kashmir issue since 1999 was purely due to the formation of this LFIN and such groups of Conservative and Liberal Democrats MPs, which followed soon after the Labour Friends of India (LFIN). Over 30 per cent of the MPs gradually joined these groups, the LFIN leading with almost 175 members that included Peers as well.

Moreover, with the India-origin councillors energized, their constituency MPs realized that it was not electorally prudent to antagonize the Indian

The sudden sea-change in the perception of MPs and the Government on the Kashmir issue since 1999 was purely due to the formation of this (LFIN) and such groups of Conservative and Liberal Democrats MPs...

voters. The Indians were almost double in number then as compared to the Pakistanis and also more resourceful and influential. They could swing outcomes in almost 30 to 45 constituencies, which could affect which party emerged with majority. The diplomatic initiative, the first of its kind, had succeeded in ensuring that MPs who were vociferous in supporting and encouraging anti-India lobbies would think twice before going on echoing false propaganda of such lobbies.

The importance of such groups could be gauged at the annual meetings of these Friends of India parliamentary groups. I attended several such meetings including the annual lunch hosted by the Labour Friends of India at Joginder Sanger-owned Washington Hotel on Curzon Street in London in 2008. Prime Minister Gordon Brown and other senior ministers and party leaders like Baron Neil Kinnock not only attended it but stayed for almost two hours. They all spoke about how valuable the ties with India were and predicted that it would be a super power. Kinnock had so much to say that he ran out of his time and was reminded to wind up his address. Gardiner, in his second stint as chair of LFIN, echoed the view of the members when he said, 'India is not only the world's largest democracy but also one of the world's most mature.'

The era of denunciation of India ended. Britain no longer views India from the Kashmir prism. Stephen Pound, a senior Labour MP and twice Chair of the Labour Friends of India, following his visit as part of a delegation of MPs in the group demanded that international pressure be brought on Pakistan to end cross-border terrorism in Jammu and Kashmir where 'mercenaries' are waging a 'proxy' war. He told me on return to London that a proxy war was being fought by mercenaries and terrorist groups that have agendas other than Kashmir. The delegation also rubbished the allegations that the Indian forces were behaving like army in occupation. Pound and other MPs said that the army was a disciplined force.

Gardiner, in his second stint as chair of LFIN, echoed the view of the members when he said, 'India is not only the world's largest democracy but also one of the World's most mature.'

More 'Friends' come on Board

Once the LFIN was formed and had started to gain prominence it was obvious that the other two parties would swiftly get into the act. They did not want to lose the Indian community's support or goodwill. Lord Dholakia recalled that 'since the election of Tony Blair in 1997, a number of MPs established links with the Indian High Commission. There were regular 'curry club' gatherings at India House and this was followed by political briefings from the High Commissioner'.

He added that the credit for setting up the Liberal Democrat Friends of India 'goes to Lalit Mansingh when he was High Commissioner here. He wanted a strong political caucus in Parliament. 'I remember having discussions with him following which we set up Liberal Democrat Friends of India. He then encouraged the Conservatives in a similar exercise.'

But, the Liberal-Democrats Friends of India Society, whose president then was Lord Dholakia, the first ever Indian to head a British political party, was actually launched at the party's annual political convention with a long line of lords, ladies and gentlemen in attendance during the time when Nareshwar Dayal was High Commissioner. I remember several Barons, Baronesses and members of the House of Commons mingling with the Indian media and senior Indian diplomats at the Carlton Hotel. It was declared that the group aimed to promote better ties with India. Some 73 party members, including 25 legislators, signed up as members. Their names were registered in a large leather-bound book.

In his address Lord Dholakia referred to his visit to India along with Lib-Dem leader Charles Kennedy. 'One of the things that opened our eyes was that we saw the world's largest democracy functioning, despite all the difficulties since independence. If you go anywhere in the world today and fail to see an Indian, you are lost. I want us to develop our ties with India. Our primary objective is to learn much more about this democracy.'

> 'One of the things that opened our eyes was that we saw the world's largest democracy functioning, despite all the difficulties since independence. If you go anywhere in the world today and fail to see an Indian, you are lost," Lord Dholkia after India visit.

Kennedy said: 'We hope that the Lib-Dem Friends of India goes from strength to strength. We want as many friends of India as possible and as many Lib-Dem friends of India. This party is a very fundamental and sincere friend of India.' Responding to the speeches, Dayal said, 'India faces many challenges of poverty, literacy and development. But we have developed resilience to the forces that challenge our progress. India today is one of the 10 fastest growing economies in the world.'

The Conservative Friends of India was formed when William Hague was the party leader. Like the other two groups this one also attracted a large number of MPs and Lords. Hague had visited India and knew first- hand the real facts about various issues including the Kashmir dispute.

So the process of building a 'caucus' initiated by Mansingh grew fast into a powerful lobby comprising of influential members in both the Houses. There is no likelihood of British politicians slipping back to the anti-India phase of the mid-90s. But I am not sure whether the spirit of camaraderie shown by the members of the LFIN would be kept up by the Conservatives if and when they came to power. Much would depend on how the Indian diplomats reacted to the change.

13

Lingering Memories

> *Life is real! Life is earnest!... Still achieving, still pursuing*
>
> —*Longfellow*

The Bus Foot

I had never heard of this 'illness'. I thought it was some affliction one caught by travelling in buses too often. But then it should have been in an epidemic form in India. I asked about it from an Indian-origin GP. After she stopped guffawing she explained that the Bus Foot was an affliction of newcomers to London — I was one then—and tourists. It meant a close brush with buses, or to be run over by it as the doctor aptly put it. Tourists try to cross busy streets like Oxford or Regent Streets even when 'No Sign' is on. Since they have only a few days for London, they try to save time. Others, especially

The lady GP was explicit. She said she advised her Indian patients to warn their relatives and friends on a visit to the city of the Bus Foot disease. Her cure was simple. Do not gape at women, for such 'diversions' cause accidents.

from the subcontinent, who come in large numbers during summers, cannot help ogling at 'scantily' dressed women. Often in that trance they forget all about the buses closing in on them.

The lady GP was explicit. She said she advised her Indian patients to warn their relatives and friends on a visit to the city of the Bus Foot disease. Her cure was simple. Do not gape at women, for such 'diversions' cause accidents. Instead of such bird-watching on the streets, her counsel was to go to galleries and book stores. There would be enough paintings and literature to satisfy the most discerning voyeurs.

Her diagnosis was quite correct. But in later years, possibly thanks to the Indian heroines who generally prefer to cover themselves less and less in movies, I think the bird watching on the streets went down sharply. We are now more liberated!

When Feminists Meowed

It was the Yuletide season of goodwill. But a war of the women— variously called as the lipstick war, feminist mud-wrestling and fur-flying--- broke out much to the delight of us journalists. The American dissident feminist Camille Pagalia, while lecturing on 'The Modern Battle of Sexes', judged British feminist Beatrix Campbell a "stupid little mediocrity". In response Campbell called Pagalia a crazed star. Their war, I learnt at a pub frequented by many tabloid journalists – dubbed Male Chauvinist Pigs by supporters of either combatant—stemmed from the basic difference between Barbara Bush feminism and crew-cut style traditionalism. All this was Greek to me.

An 'MCP' of my tribe gleefully opined that with such cat fights between feminists any hope of sisterhood among anti-male females was doomed.

The sparkling war battle between the well-known feminist Germaine Green and Suzanne Moore was more to my understanding. Greer had commented that the formation of Moore's hair was like a bird's nest and she described her contours as "three inches of fat cleavage". The worst insult was condemning Moore for wearing "f... me shoes". The excited male columnists went on about this Greer vs. Moore battle for months. But Greer, I was told, remained unapologetic. In fact, she said that her criticism had done a lot of good to Moore.

All this for me, then rather naïve, about wars between feminists, was part of my learning. An 'MCP' of my tribe gleefully opined that with such cat fights between feminists any hope of sisterhood among anti-male females was doomed.

Goodwill Gift from Italy

I was in Turin to cover G7 Summit when I experienced something so nice at the media centre that I am unable to forget it. Being rather new on a foreign posting, I had not taken the plug converter for my laptop. The city was around 10 miles from the Summit venue, a converted Fiat factory and I had to open the press release of the statement of the British Prime Minister John Major sent on email.

I must have looked very nonplussed and fidgety for a young and tall Italian from the Italian Telecom suddenly came to me. "Is there a problem?" he asked, "Can I help?" I told him my problem. He just went away without saying anything but then I saw him coming back with a laptop. It was his personal laptop. He said I could use it and said that he would buy a converter for me during lunch.

When he brought the converter I asked him how much did I owe him? "It's with my compliments. Whenever you might remember this incident, I would feel proud to have given you a goodwill gift from Italy." Well, I never forgot about him.

Helpful German Railways

There is another such instance that I never tire of relating. This was many years after my Italian goodwill gift. I had been asked by my editor to cover two meets one in Hamburg and the other two days later in Berlin. Pranab

Mukherjee, the then External Affairs Minister, was participating in both meets.

I had asked the hotel in Hamburg to book a train ticket for me to Berlin. I intended to leave immediately after the Minister's Press Conference and be ready for the meet in Berlin the following day.

When I reached the Hamburg station, I leant that the train was to leave from a platform quite a distance away. I had to climb up and down two flights of stairs. I had a slight cramp in my left foot and since there were no porters to be seen, I began to walk dragging my suitcase slowly, on one step at a time. Suddenly I then heard a voice saying "let me help, sir". I looked up and saw a teenager running towards me. He picked up the suitcase and asked me my coach number. He took me to the platform and told me that the train would come in about seven minutes and the coach would be where he asked me to stand.

I asked him if he was posted there by the railways. I learnt from the young boy that there was an organization which recruited volunteers like him—mostly students—to help the aged, disabled or pregnant women or those with kids at stations. He was studying computer technology. As the train steamed in I offered him 10 Euros. He refused saying he was a volunteer and would take no money. He then added that his organization in Berlin would be informed by him and they would send a volunteer to help me. As he said there was another teenager at the Berlin station standing near the door of my coach. He too refused to accept any money.

More than the organization, these young boys and girls deserve all the praise for their spirit to help without expecting anything in return.

'Sexist' MPs

I had enjoyed writing in my 'London Diary' about the grievances of Labour women MPs, who were elected in huge numbers (101) in 1997. Known

> Most alleged cases of crude gesturing and rude remarks about their anatomy. It was said that Tory MPs indulged in remarking about the face or legs of any lady MP who might be speaking.

as Blair babes, they accused a few Tory MPs of being sexists and harassing them. They said these MPs were playing public school antics to distract lady ministers and MPs from discharging their parliamentary obligations. The likes of Nicholas Soames, a friend of Prince Charles, countered the accusations with threats to report to the Speaker—Betty Boothroyd, now after retirement a Baroness—that Labour women MPs were resorting to 'werewolf sounds' during debates and distracting them.

But the babes were no walkovers. I met one of them, in her late thirties or early forties, and she seemed really het-up. Most alleged cases of crude gesturing and rude remarks about their anatomy. It was said that Tory MPs indulged in remarking about the face or legs of any lady MP who might be speaking. One woman MP, to the great glee of spicy news hungry journalists, said that the obese Soames allegedly used to wriggle in his seat and emphasized his chest in an unpleasant manner.

It was all rather hilarious. I don't think either side was serious enough to complain to the Speaker. A woman MP also remarked that during a debate on agriculture the moment she mentioned the word 'birds', the Tory MPs started laughing and falling about like schoolboys on an outing.

The Tories were also upset when the women MPs managed to oust a barber who used to trim the Tory hair for over 17 years from the premises and replace him with a unisex hair stylist. Women alleged that the Tory MPs were upset because they used to pick up juicy gossip at the saloon.

The wrangle finally died down. Men MPs, so accused, said that Labour women MPs must take the rough with the smooth and they must dress like women and should avoid trousers. Any way I think in that Parliament the Tories were in such small numbers they could not do much and possibly created diversions to be in the news.

Chicken for Tories, Bulldog for Labour

The 1997 General Election was historic for more than the shameful defeat of the Tories by the New Labour led by a youthful Tony Blair. Dogs and chickens, to their misfortune, were deployed for the first time to show up John Major or shame Tony Blair. It was hilarious.

After Blair refused a face-to-face TV debate with Major, Tories hired a chicken to tail Blair, message being Blair had chickened out. I was told that many young Tories avoided the Parry Central Office, fearing they might be asked to be 'minders' of the chicken.

Then *Daily Mirror*, which has been a solid backer of Labour, propped up another 'chicken' to chase the Tory chicken. No battle of chickens took place but both were extensively 'clicked' by the media photographers while the two were engaged in verbal crowing.

The chicken war over, a Bulldog called Fitz was brought into the fray. He was paraded in a Labour Party TV broadcast looking glum—the message, he was sad at the state of affairs under Major. But he perked up his ears as Blair started to outline his plans. Fitz was ecstatic when Blair ended his speech. He ran into a sunny horizon, seemingly happy that his Britain was safe in the hands of Blair.

It was rather lucky for Labour and misfortune of the Tories that the views of a psychologist, vet I am sure, came out much after the Fitz show. According to him, Bulldogs, although symbolic of patriotism, were the third stupidest among 133 different breeds of canines.

In Dublin, where Irish abhor everything British, Fitz was declared of weak virility. His manhood was suspected after his photograph from the rear was published. A tabloid's young lady correspondent, apparently a dog-lover, said in all seriousness that the owner of Fitz should inform the media whenever the 'poor' Fitz became a father. The stigma about his prowess had to be removed. I don't not know whether Fitz could prove his manhood but I am sure whenever the 1997 election is discussed Fitz would be remembered.

Holi in Warsaw

I do not think Lord Krishna ever went on a State visit to Poland. But it was interesting to discover that a form of Holi, with the sole intent to convey one's ardour to one's beloved or beloved-to be, is celebrated with great zeal in Poland. The occasion is akin to Krishna playing Holi with Radha and gopis. The Polish Holi is played on Easter Monday, when men traditionally drench their women of choice with water to declare their love.

The Indian Holi twist came when someone discovered the potency of the Indian *pichkaris*. Soon plastic toy guns were retailed which could spray the target four metres away. Those Romeos who were accepted were rewarded a bottle of wine and if there was intimacy, a glass of vodka to drink, under the loving eyes of their Juliet. Lord Krishna of Vrindavan, I am sure' must be *maha* pleased.

From Magnifico to Ludicrous

Dogs chain owners

I could not resist writing about some bizarre happenings and activities during my stay in London. They did appear amusing but I think they provided rare glimpses of the personality of different people. For instance, a young man in need of some additional income, offered through door-to-door contact, to walk dogs in the morning. His rates were reasonable, one pound for big dogs and 15 to 5p for small, and lap dogs. But as luck would have it, the dogs preferred their owners to walk them rather than being taken out by a hired walker. The initiative was commendable but the dogs barked down the young man's plan.

Cat in Wikipedia

Then there was the case of Humphrey, the Tom cat. I called it Lord Cat, for it lived at 10, Downing Street and was thus treated with respect. Having unrestricted prowling rights all over, including the Cabinet Office, he was witness to intrigues and politicking for years. And Humphrey had endeared himself to the media persons and senior civil servants. I was told he was on very friendly terms with a few of them and was always pleased to welcome them.

But then he suddenly went on AWOL. He just vanished overnight. Everyone at Downing Street was forlorn. It was believed that since he suffered from kidney ailment—although he definitely was not alcoholic—he had returned to his roots to spend his last days in communion with nature.

I am told when he appeared after a few months at his old domain, the then Prime Minister John Major was immediately informed and so was the Press. He was given a royal welcome. TV and print media persons rushed to record the historic return of the prodigal. He was photographed with a bowl of fish, sitting on red carpet with a bobby standing on his side.

It was discovered only later that Humphrey had been treacherous. When Major was in the midst of warding off dissidents in his party, Humphrey deserted him and went across the nearby Royal Marine Hospital. He liked the hospitality of the hospital staff and stayed there for months.

A veteran journalist told me that Humphrey was in fact an ungrateful cat. A few years earlier when he killed four robins in the back garden, he escaped being put down. Major intervened to declare that Humphrey was no serial killer.

The last I heard of him was that he was retired some time after Blairs replaced Major, and was given to an elderly couple living in a suburb of London. His exact whereabouts were kept secret, out of fear that he might be kidnapped. But Tories raised a storm in the Commons. Alan Clark, an animal lover MP, said he would presume that Humphrey had been killed until he heard from him or his picture shown. Ultimately, a few media persons, avowed to secrecy, were taken to photograph him. When he died in 2006, I came across a news flash from Reuters and all papers carried his obit. Anyone wishing to know more about him can refer to Wikipedia. Believe me he is there.

Social waiters

No one possibly remembers a news report long time ago about 'informed' waiters at a high class restaurant in Knightsbridge not far from the famous Harrods. I had written about this in my 'London Diary'. The waiters, according to reports, were given various tabloids to read juicy bits about High Society. The 'enlightened' waiters were expected to comment or converse with celeb guests on what was going on in their world.

An irreverent columnist gave a few instances--He alleged that a waiter serving one of the Gallagher brothers said, 'I expect it'll be Lager—all brothers love Lager'. Another time a writer reportedly said 'Lager louts for you, Mr. Gallagher.' The latter remark seemed rather lurid, I could not believe a waiter saying something like that. But obviously the columnist had his sources. According to him, a rather petty waiter said to Elizabeth Hurley—at that time she was unaware of Arun Nayar—'So I hear you don't wear a bra Ms Hurley.' There was no subsequent report about the waiter being hurled out or his face clawed beyond recognition. Ms Hurley took it sportingly, I suppose. Celebrities are used to all sorts of fans. The columnist did not write anything about the well-being of the indiscreet waiter.

But over the years I realized the strange, unbelievable and bizarre happenings in London had given the Shangri-la effect to the city. After all it attracts people from the world over.

Threats in a free society

The caller refused to divulge his name but threatened that he would have me declared *persona non grata* and thrown out of England. He added in hissing tones that I might be dragged to the Press Commission and the court for publishing a false story. The caller sounded like a Scot but I was not too sure, having been in London for only a short time.

The source of his anger was a report I sent to my paper of a meeting organized by Indian councillors for Robin Cook. Before his address several councillors expressed their views on the Kashmir issue and referred to the assembly election in Jammu and Kashmir. They also urged him to forget about plebiscite as Pakistan had not fully complied with the terms of the UN Resolution and that several state elections were evidence enough of democracy in Kashmir and wishes of the people.

Cook spoke at length and commended the fact that elections were being held, and democratic process had been initiated. Later I had gone backstage where Cook was talking with the then Indian High Commissioner Dr L.M. Singhvi. *The Times of India* special correspondent L.K. Sharma was standing close by. I requested Dr Singhvi to let me ask Cook two or three questions. I asked him why while he commended the elections in the state many MPs of his party were pressing for plebiscite, to which Cook replied that much time had passed since the UN Resolution and he did not see it was any longer relevant. Then I asked him if he agreed that Kashmir under India was part of the country to which he said for all substantive purposes it was. 'Then,' I repeated, 'it means Kashmir is an integral part of India.'

I sent the report and it was published on the first page with the heading that Cook said Kashmir was an integral part of India. The caller was angry that I had twisted Cook's words and said he would have me 'thrown' out from London. I told him if he or Cook thought the report was not correct, a letter to the editor could be written, which I would assure that it would be given as much prominence as the report. But the caller was not ready to listen and continued with his threats. I asked him if I could talk with Cook. The caller told me that Cook was in Scotland. So I told him that I would talk with him when he got back.

The caller informed me that the report had badly damaged Cook's credibility and there was a demonstration against him. I was losing my patience by then and I told him that before I came to England I believed there was freedom of expression and of the Press. "I have already suggested that you write a letter denying whatever I said in my report. But I stand by what I wrote. You can do whatever you like, but may I remind you that my country is not a Banana Republic and a push-over." The caller put down the phone. Later, a report by a journalist of Indian-origin was published saying that he had tape-recorded Cook's speech and he never said that Kashmir is an integral part of India.

He was right, although I wish he had checked with me. Cook did not say that in his address but had agreed during my conversation that for all substantive purposes it was. Cook never mentioned this or showed any reservation with me on several occasions I met him. In fact, at a function at Portman Hotel, while being photographed with a few Indians, Cook called me over and made me stand along with him.

I did mention this call to a senior Labour Party leader some months after at a reception at the Indian High Commission. He was quick to name a member who was sure to be the caller. 'He has to nurse his constituency, be sure he must have kept with him a few Kashmiri lobbyists near him while calling you. I am sorry about the whole thing.'

There was another threat that was more menacing. I had been told by two senior members of the Southall BJP that a meeting organized by some people belonging to a Hindu organization in the aftermath of Gujarat riots was not getting good response. They said that a secretary of the London-based Congress group sent some people to swell up the audience. I tried to get through to the organizers of the meet but they were unavailable. So I sent a report quoting reliable sources one of whom attended the meeting.

I received a call a couple of days later and without much ado the caller asked me to name the BJP person who told me that help was sought from the local Congress unit official. I replied that sources are never revealed and asked who I was speaking to. There was a near shout and the caller named one person who he said was surely my informant and if I did not tell the identity I would be dealt with severely. The caller was almost hysterical. He put down the phone.

I was told later that someone had called him from India and asked him to explain, and obviously the caller was nervous. I telephoned Ashok Tandon, who was then the press secretary of Atal Behari Vajpayee, then prime minister. I knew him when he was posted in London as PTI representative.

After that it was all quiet. Later, I came to know who the caller was. In fact, at a reception by the then High Commissioner Nareshwar Dayal at his

London Bus; beware of buses, stop ogling while crossing street

Prince Charles talking with Indian pilots for Hawk trainer fighters: full of praise for their talent

Kensington Palace Garden residence, the caller came over and told me, 'We are all for our country. Let there be no differences between us.' That was most welcome for me.

Some Unforgettable Personalities

An extraordinary bhadralok

I was fortunate to meet some very interesting personalities during my tenure, both in London and Europe. I have mentioned a couple of them.

I had heard and read about him while in India. But I met Nirad Babu, as Nirad Chaudhari was popularly called, for the first time at Nehru Centre. He was 98 and had been invited by the director of the Centre, Gopal Gandhi to speak on, amongst other things, on the historic differences between Netaji Subhas Chandra Bose and Mahatma Gandhi.

When I saw him, belying his age he was standing straight, wearing a velvet reddish jacket with tie, a bowler hat and sporting all the medals and medallions given to honour him by the British. I remembered what the writer Dr Jay Dubashi once jokingly commented, 'Every time Nirad Babu says something unflattering about India the British honour him'. Having said this he kept smiling. I soon realized that it was one of his usual witty remarks.

Nirad Babu started his address—which lasted almost an hour, and during which he remained standing— with his usual acerbic comments while tempering his analysis and comparison of the Mahatma's background with that of Netaji. He acknowledged that Gandhi was a man of the masses whereas Netaji was a typical Bengali 'bhadralok', a product of the social system which was not just based on caste but class consideration as well. The nationalism in Bengal, he said, was rooted in militarism, whereas Gandhi preached ahimsa. There could be no reconciling of ways to awaken nationalist movement between the two, he said.

Until then the very attentive audience was with him, but some squirmed when there was denigration of Gandhi's attitude and conduct in comparison to that of Subhash Chandra Bose. Nirad Babu said Gandhi lacked honesty in behaviour and he interpreted the British rule in India according to his experiences of the White Rule in South Africa. There was more!

Chaudhari said that Gandhi's approach to freedom movement and management of the Congress Party was thus based on the western outlook.

His averred that Gandhi's concept of ahimsa was not founded on Gita but the Bible—verse 39 chapter five in the Gospel of Mathew. Nirad Babu said that Gandhi had picked up the interpretation of ahimsa from Tolstoy. He added that Netaji's nationalism was primarily nurtured by the resurgence movement in Bengal in 1905 and later, cemented with the lessons from the English Civil War, American War of Independence, Italian Fascism and the Russian anarchism. He recited verses in Sanskrit and Bengali to illustrate his point. He cited many incidents in South Africa to assert that Netaji would have reacted to them differently than the way Gandhi did.

The other point that struck the audience was his assertion that Gandhi chose Jawaharlal Nehru to become prime minister because he wanted someone with western education and understanding of the western outlook, which was entirely different from the revolutionary background of the Bengali nationalism which had influenced Netaji.

It emerged that Nirad Babu had not got over the hurt and anger at the treatment of the Indian Government which he said kept him in penury for 12 years. His fault, he said, was his statement that unlike Nehru, he did not learn India's history from western books nor did he need to discover India.

Many of us did not agree with him on several points he made but I respected him for his convictions against which he did not brook any opposition. I had sent a report to my paper which was neither critical nor laudatory of him. But whenever I telephoned him at Oxford he was always nice and explained to me with great patience any issue I wanted him to comment about.

When I went to Oxford after his death, I realised how much he was admired by both the Dons and the people for his intellect and courage to speak his mind.

Meeting the Prince

Another very nice meeting I had was with Prince Charles and Camilla, Duchess of Cornwall, at Bhartiya Vidya Bhavan. When I asked the Duchess if she would like to go to India, Prince Charles responded before she could and said they loved India and would go 'anytime', but there was always the problem of dates. The Duchess told me that her brother loved the country.

I met Prince Charles again when he came especially to award a group of six Indian Air Force's fighter pilots their graduation medals at a ceremony at the Royal Air Force Valley, the RAF's advanced tactics and training unit located on a remote Welsh island, after they completed a year-long course in learning to fly the British-made Hawk Advanced Jet Trainer.

He was happy to meet them and I felt the Indian media, too, which was gathered there in full strength. "This is a very special day for Valley," said Prince Charles. When at the reception he spotted me he grinned and said he was planning to go to India. His remarkable memory was amazing. His admiration for India, about which I had only heard, was evident in both meetings with him.

At Wales he said, 'This unique training scheme has been a huge success and the Indian pilots should be justly proud of their achievements. They leave behind many friends'. He said the Indian pilots deserved to be congratulated for completing the course, which involved 'immense hard work'.

He lived memories of 1947

I can never forget the sense of history I felt when I met Alan Campbell Johnson, the powerful Press Adviser of Lord Mountbatten when he was Viceroy. I met him at his apartment on Ambrosden Avenue, near Westminster Cathedral in central London. Campbell was 83, but he seemed to have a sharp memory of every small detail during the transfer of power. He was also obviously privy to the delicate and often 'frustrating' negotiations during the '144 days that Lord Mountbatten was in India' for brokering an agreement on the pact that led to Partition.

It was enlightening talking with him. In the nearly two hours he brought alive those tumultuous days, bringing in flashes of momentous meetings of Nehru, Sardar Patel, Jinnah and, of course, Mahatma Gandhi. A close confidant of Mountbatten he acted as his emissary on a number of occasions to both thr Congress and Jinnah camps.

With some trepidation I asked him about the alleged affair between Nehru and Edwina Mountbatten. I also asked him about Pakistani academics alleging that Nehru's closeness with both Lady and Lord Mountbatten had made him favour India at the cost of Pakistan. Campbell-Johnson was clearly upset. He looked at me and then spoke in measured tones. What had Lady Mountbatten having an affair with Nehru got to do with Pakistan or Kashmir?

> 'A nation with great potentiality was born on August 15 midnight fifty years ago.'

He was sure that her relation with Nehru, in the sense that they were lovers, was an absolute myth. 'They admired each other. As John Kenneth Galbraith, the American Ambassador to India, once said, 'Can't people realise that men and women can be friends', Lady Mountbatten had nothing at all to do with Kashmir.'

I took him back to the weeks before 15 August. The gleam in his eyes as he reminisced bespoke of his emotion and excitement as he recalled those days. He seemed to be transported back to India on the eve of Independence. His final comment (this was the year 1997) as I got up to leave was prophetic. 'The miracle of it all is that India has emerged with the potential of becoming a world power' and then added emotionally, 'A nation with great potentiality was born on August 15 midnight fifty years ago.'

As I bade him goodbye I could see he loved India as if he was part of its creation as an independent free country. I never met him again. He died a few years later. But I was surprised that his wife recognized me when we happened to meet at a dinner few years after his death.

Sometime later I happened to meet Lady Pamela Mountbatten, the younger daughter of Lord Mountbatten, at a function at Nehru Centre. She warmed up the moment I started talking about the time she was in Delhi with her parents. Apparently, she regarded Nehru almost as a family friend. I decided to ask her about the alleged relations between Nehru and her mother. I still remember her laughing as we both were coming down the stairs.

She said everyone seem to ask the same question. They became very close. Nehru was lonely and understandably very tense those days. But she averred it was a platonic relationship, the times were too turbulent for anyone involved in tricky and often frustrating negotiations to think about physical intimacy. But to illustrate the informal relations of Nehru with her mother she related an incident. There was a slight tremor and her mother who was extremely nervous about earthquakes cowered under a table. Nehru who was there laughed and bent down to bring her out from under the table.

I regret that I never met her again although she did give me a phone number of some flat in Piccadilly. I believe that the entire Mountbatten ménage fell in love with India.

A journalist knows it all

I still smile when I remember the incident. It was before six in the morning that I got a call from my Delhi office. The Executive Editor asked me, 'You know about Diana'. Groggy eyed, half asleep, I did not have any idea of what he was talking about. What was I supposed to know about the Princess? But the journalist in me refused to acknowledge that I was completely ignorant about anything new about her. I replied, of course, and was asked to do a detailed story.

I rushed to the living room and switched on the T.V. A shock awaited me. Diana had died in a car crash in Paris. I was by then wide awake and thinking how to do a story which would continue to develop throughout the day. One had to depend on T.V., for papers would come out only by the following morning. Also one had to switch to different channels to get a fuller picture.

I called up Nabanita Sircar, a journalist and friend, who lived not too far and asked if she could come over so that we could jointly follow the news and send our respective reports. Being in a similar dilemma she agreed immediately. But there was one problem. Her laptop was not working. She had planned to go to an internet café. I told her I had an electric typewriter apart from my laptop and we could take turns on either of them. I must say that it helped. One could go and prepare tea or breakfast while the other jotted down notes.

My workload doubled as my editorial director later called and asked that I do an analysis if the paparazzi were to be blamed for Diana's fatal accident. Another call followed, the paper wanted at least one exclusive picture along with my reports.

I called *The Independent* photo syndication, with which we did have an arrangement. It took me over an hour to get through the lady in-charge. She was I must say, quite understanding. Though hard pressed she said she would surely try, but it would cost money. That was the least of all worries at that time. The young lady called soon to confirm that an exclusive picture would be sent. I happily informed my office about it.

By evening, around 10 pm in India, I got the call that they had not received the picture as yet. The lady was untraceable and I did not have her mobile number. There weren't many of them those days. I left messages for her every 10 minutes. Meanwhile, calls from my office were getting frantic, causing my tension levels to climb higher. The young lady ultimately rang up at seven my time and said she had sent the picture six hours ago. I asked her if she could send it again. She did and I asked my office if they had received the picture but the dreaded response was no. Her technical department told her that all lines must be jammed because of the unprecedented traffic that day.

I kept praying and was relieved when I got the call from Delhi at almost one o'clock their time to say that they had received the picture. My only thought thereafter was to rush to my local, Old Bush and Bull.

The London Biryani Club

The idea for biryani dinner by rotation was mooted during an evening at the Charles Dicken's favourite Old Bull and Bush pub near Golders Green. All of us, Ashok Pande, former senior bureaucrat, his wife Reena, a counsellor at the High Commission and P.C.Haldar, then Minister in the Indian High Commissioner who lived quite close to the Pub were there one Saturday evening. It was at the pub that we mooted the idea and agreed that each of us would host a biryani dinner once a month by rotation. Thus the first Biryani Club in London was set up and we three became charter members.

We had some informal get-togethers where while enjoying delicious biryani and curry we discussed many topical issues relating to the community. The concept was so attractive that many more joined in— Brajesh Prasad, hotelier and businessman and councillor and Nabanita Sircar, who was then Resident Editor *Asian Age*.

Amongst all of us members, I was the only one who lived alone. So every time my turn came the women would offer to ghost cook for me. Their offer was tempting but I decided to be independent. I used to get biryani and kebab from the famous Raavi Kebabs in Drummond Street.

The club closed when all the members, except Sircar and I, left London. Most of us are now in Delhi and hope to restart the club here. That would be, I am sure, the best way to meet regularly. And as Haldar put it to me, 'You have now enhanced power as your wife is with you. We have the old power'.

Some Nostalgic Moments

I have kept for the very end memories of two unforgettable people, who had a deep impact on my thinking and broadened my vision.

The late Madhavrao Scindia, whom I called Maharaj, although he told me several times to call him bhaiya, 'all persons who are close to me call me bhayia' used to be in London during summer. I first saw him in Lucknow in the mid-seventies where he had gone to attend the wedding of the Datia scion Krishan Singh's daughter, as far as I recall into Alwar's former ruling family. I was amused to see old, much older ex-princes get up, some with great difficulty, as soon as a very young Scindia came into the Hall of the Carlton Hotel.

But I came to know him quite closely after we met at his Tilak Marg residence when he was MP in the eighties.

Vijay Dhar— then a close adviser of Rajiv Gandhi, had asked me to go and see an interview Scindia had given to a Mumbai weekly. I found him very informal and we kept talking for over two hours.

That was the start of a long, I can say, friendship with him. He used to say he met me not because I was a journalist but as a friend. I enjoyed a special chicken dish with him a number times at his residence on Safdarjung Road in New Delhi.

I would invariably meet him whenever he came to London and stay at St. James Court apartments. The last time I met him was, I think, during his last visit to London. I knew he was in town but I did not call him, hoping he would whenever he would be free. He rang me up one day in the morning and said he was very busy as his son and family too were with him. But then he added 'I would give you the privilege of driving me and my grandson around London, come at 11.'

I went to the hotel at eleven and he came out with his grandson, who I guess was three-year-old or so. We drove for almost two hours, from Buckingham Palace to Piccadilly, to Regent Street, Regent Park and then past Harrods in Knightsbridge before returning to the hotel. See you soon, he said as he went. That soon never came. Those two hours are still etched in my memory. We talked so much, going over the years since he became an MP. I still wonder why he was in a nostalgic, emotional mood. I lost the most sincere well-wisher.

The other person, who I got the opportunity to meet a number of times, being posted in London, was my Chairman Dr K.K. Birla. Every meeting with him was a sort of learning for me. Despite being such a senior and eminent person, he was always considerate and affectionate. I never telephoned him or anyone else from the management even if I knew they were in London, leaving it to them to call if they needed me.

So it was the Chairman who used to telephone and 'ask' me if I was free to come and see him on a particular day. I could not say I was and had to be free anytime he wished to see me. He generally called me to come to Grosvenor

House around 11 am to have coffee. He would then ask me about politics and NRIs. Once he called me and asked if I could meet him on a certain day. I was to go to Paris to cover a UK-France Summit. I hesitatingly told him about it adding that if he wished I would cancel the trip. He immediately said no, work was first. He also told me that I should call him on my return to find out the time I could come and meet him.

After his death, it became very difficult for me to go to Grosvenor House where he usually stayed and met me. When I had to go there to meet the former Maharana of Mewar at the new restaurant, which the hotel management insisted must be opened by Dr Birla, I felt a bit of a vacuum. It seemed I could see him at that evening when he opened the place formally.

The Assistant Manager, who had seen me with Dr Birla a few times, came over and told me that Dr Birla was scheduled to come on such and date and his usual room was booked. Then I told him he was no more. The Assistant Manager suddenly bent down holding the arm of my chair, and with choked voice he said, 'Please do not say that. It means I won't see him again. He was so nice to us, even to waiters. The whole management respected and loved him.' He then rushed away. I did not see him in the evening after that. The Maharana was taken aback. He said it meant that he was truly of a generation which evoked regard for themselves in others without any effort. 'There are none left like them anymore.' He summed it well.

Summing Up

There are many more memories, many incidents, meetings (some turned out to be encounters) and occasions that remain etched into my mind. After all 15 years plus is a long time, there were phases of satisfaction, disappointments, frustrations, loneliness but there never was any regret at my being posted there. I knew I was missing mainstream journalism back in my country, but the experience I gained there was enough compensation.

I met people, went to countries, and attended conferences, an opportunity I could never have had if I had remained in Delhi. All the people I met, befriended, during the years and the events I covered, they all came back in flashback, seemingly almost in a rush, as I sat in front of the computer to write this book. It was difficult to concentrate and select what to write. I did not want it to be a diary of my stay in London. Ultimately it has turned out to be a kaleidoscope of impressions. Right or wrong, I have been sincere and honest in recording them in this book.

I must also mention the friendship of people like Jack Straw, Stephen Pound, Barry Gardiner and many Lords and Baronesses like Lord Dholakia, Lord Parekh, Baroness Usha Prashar, people in Southall like Krishan Bhatia, late P.S. Khabra and Virendra Sharma, and some in Leicester, Birmingham and Manchester, and British journalists. I was lucky to have extremely warm relations with the Indian journalist corps. They were most helpful and it was always fun to have a glass of wine with them. There is lot of nostalgia.

In conclusion I quote Seren Kierkegard, the Danish philosopher, 'Life must be lived forwards, but it can only be understood backwards.' How true!

Index